Richard Dee is a native of Brixham was in his teens and settled in Kent. Leaving school at 16 he briefly worked in a supermarket, then went to sea and travelled the world in the Merchant Navy, qualifying as a Master Mariner in 1986.

Coming ashore to be with his growing family, he used his sea-going knowledge in several jobs, working as a Marine Insurance Surveyor and as Dockmaster at Tilbury, before becoming a Port Control Officer in Sheerness and then at the Thames Barrier in Woolwich.

In 1994 he was head-hunted and offered a job as a Thames Estuary Pilot. In 1999 he transferred to the Thames River Pilots, where he regularly took vessels of all sizes through the Thames Barrier and upriver as far as HMS Belfast and through Tower Bridge. In all, he piloted over 3,500 vessels in a 22-year career with the Port of London Authority.

Richard is married with three adult children and three grandchildren.

His first science-fiction novel Freefall was published in 2013, followed by Ribbonworld in 2015. September 2016 saw the publication of his first Steampunk adventure The Rocks of Aserol and of Flash Fiction, a collection of short stories. Myra, the prequel to Freefall was published in 2017, along with Andorra Pett and the Oort Cloud Café, a murder mystery set in space and the start of a series featuring Andorra Pett, an amateur detective.

He contributed a story to the 1066 Turned Upside Down collection and is currently working on prequels, sequels, and new projects.

He can be found at https://richarddeescifi.co.uk
and contacted at richarddeescifi@gmail.com

Also by Richard Dee

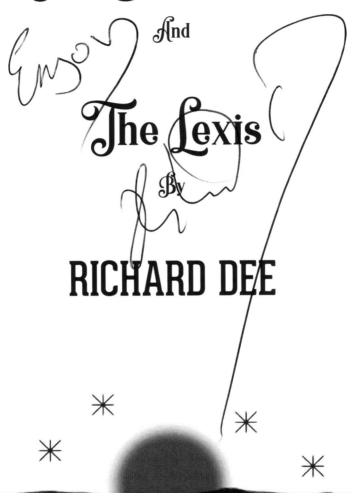

The Sensaurum

And

The Lexis

By

RICHARD DEE

4Star Scifi

A chance remark, overheard,

can lead you on an amazing journey.

Prologue

Despite the bright, low autumnal sunlight, the laboratorium was in semi-darkness. Gas lights flickered behind grime-stained windows as the room's single occupant worked, muttering to himself in a monotone. The room around him was littered with a forest of artificial limbs; arms and legs frozen in various attitudes. Some were complete, some mere shells of metal, their inner workings exposed. A collapsible bed sat in an alcove, off to one side of the room, with clothes and personal items scattered around it. A grubby velvet curtain, designed to give the sleeper some privacy, hung from a brass rail, its lower edge trailing in the rubbish on the floor.

In the main part of the room, glass-fronted cupboards held rows of hands, feet, fingers and assembled limbs. The room was clearly warm; the man was hatless, dressed in a shirt with an open collar, a once-white dustcoat over the top. The whole ensemble appeared to have been worn for many days and frequently slept in.

The workbench was cluttered with the paraphernalia of his trade; tools, wires and cogs as well as a strange contraption, consisting of a glass-sided box and a small wooden board. Looking inside the clear walls of the box, there were metal plates suspended in a liquid. Two shining wires projected through the top of this box, leading to the board where more wires were fixed in a circular arrangement. The wire was not complete; there was a gap in its circuit around the board. This gap had brass clips at each end, into which the man was placing cylindrical objects picked from a pile on the bench.

Situated to one side of the apparatus and unconnected to it, was some sort of measuring instrument with a graduated dial and a needle. The man was comparing the motion of the needle and writing notes as each object was placed between the clips.

The door opened and a tall man, dressed in fashionable clothes, entered.

The door slammed shut behind him, but the man at the bench was so intent on his work that he didn't notice. After being ignored for several moments the entrant coughed.

The worker never flinched from his task. "What is it? I'm extremely busy," he said impatiently.

"May I remind you, Professor, that you exist here to serve me? I rescued you from the gutter and could just as easily return you there." The tone was slightly mocking, it was plain who was the servant and who the master. And his use of the honorific was significant, if he was displeased with progress, he used the rank. If things were going well, first name terms indicated his pleasure.

At the words, the Professor looked up. He remembered his life before. After qualifying, he had been apprenticed to Professor Woolon at the Institute of Medical Statics, a branch of the military investigating the forces in man that enabled life. They had a ready supply of maimed servicemen and women to practise on, those who would obey orders and endure any amount of experimentation.

Under Woolon, artificial limbs, controlled by the body's own nervous system, had been developed and perfected. They were offered at first to the servicemen who had undergone the trials, with the intention that once the process had been perfected, with lower production costs they could be made more generally available.

Then he had gone too far, against Woolon's instructions he had tried to advance the work in ways that were considered unethical, inevitably they proved to be fatal to many of those chosen for testing.

As far as the Professor had been concerned, the few successes were sufficient proof that his ideas were sound, all that was needed was more time and subjects to perfect his methods. A few casualties were inevitable; it was all a necessary part of progress.

But his protestations had fallen on deaf ears.

He had been thrown out of the Institute, his qualifications cancelled, leaving him destitute and friendless. He had spent days lost in alcohol and introspection; seething at the injustice.

In his opinion, Woolon was a fool. He failed to understand or accept that progress demanded sacrifice. Putting an individual's life before the common good, that was not the way to advance science.

Which was when he had been found by his present employer and offered the chance to continue his work, in secret, for some unspecified purpose. Anything he had asked for had been provided; it was all of the finest quality. He knew not from where it came, had decided that it was probably better not to ask. The reason would be clear in time. He had the feeling that today's visit might give him a clue as to whether the time was nigh.

"Come, Professor," the man's tone changed, becoming friendlier. He even put his arm around the Professor's bony shoulders. "How are your works on the Sensaurum progressing?"

The question was unwanted, he had said, many times, that all progress would be reported. The Sensaurum was his project. People had laughed at the name, but what did they know?

"As promised, I have found a way of switching control remotely," he replied. "I need only to increase the range of the effect."

"And when shall we be ready for a demonstration?"

"For a test, I will need a subject, a live person I can work on, with a fully functioning artificial limb, preferably an arm."

"I will find one; I merely need to know when they will be required?"

"Give me three days to encase the parts and devise a way to modify the interior of the limb to accept them."

"Very well then, you have three days."

"And shut the door behind you," said the Professor, bending back to his task. It was the only power he possessed; he was determined to exercise it whilst he could.

He had come so much further than Woolon had or could. The man might have been feted as a genius, but he was his equal; no, he was his better. It was not true that Woolon's understanding of the human nervous system was second to none. He, not Woolon, had discerned its use of what was called statics energy to transmit messages from brain to muscle.

He had isolated the pathways along which the signals were passed and devised a way to connect them to the inanimate. Woolon, as the man in charge, had merely taken the credit.

There was so much more that he had found and Woolon had taken it as his own. Woolon had failed to accept that the same signals could be generated outside the body, and it now appeared that they could be transmitted remotely through the air. He had seen the clues in the work of others, discoveries in statics and applications in apparently unconnected fields. He alone could see how it all fitted together. To be used and then cast aside in that way was humiliating. As far as he was concerned, his rescue was only right. Thanks to his new benefactor, time would show who the greatest scientist was; he was sure that it would not be Woolon.

As to the legality of what he was doing, he had closed his mind to the concept as soon as Woolon had appropriated his findings. And it was obvious to him that the work he was now doing, what he was now capable of, had no lawful purpose. Nevertheless, he was convinced that history would absolve him.

What he had said was not strictly true; he might not be ready in three days. At least it had got rid of the interruption. Pleased to be alone again, he rummaged on the bench and found the next device he wanted to test. He was sure that it would work this time. If it failed in three days, he could always blame the subject.

Whistling a popular tune, he bent to his task.

Chapter 1

Jackson Thwaite was hungry. That was the trouble with the orphanage; there were just too many mouths and never enough in the serving dishes to fill them all. The staff were well-meaning, it was among the children that the trouble started.

The bullies and their gangs of sycophants generally did alright; it was the young and the weak that went hungry. Jackson was not young, as far as he could remember he was nearly one and twenty, but because he was polite and avoided picking on those smaller than him, he was seen as weak and ripe for exploitation.

In consequence, he was always hungry or bruised from his encounters with the bullies, who were the only well-fed ones among the inmates. This mealtime had been the same. As soon as their rations had been slopped into the bowls the bigger had descended and grabbed at the plates of the slowest. The staff were supposed to intervene but rarely did. Only when Mr Templestowe, the headmaster, was watching would they call for order or discipline a pupil.

Even so, life in the orphanage was better than a life on the streets. Metropol City was not the safest place to grow to adulthood; there were dangers on every corner; from the machines in the factories to the new-fangled things that moved along the roads. And the people who preyed on their fellows, press gangs, robbers, slave-masters and all sorts of felons. That was before the effects that the smoke and choking fumes from industry had on your body and mind. At least here you were fed something and only had to do light work, picking oakum or cutting cloth for the military.

Jackson did have an advantage though, unknown to the bullies he had been befriended by Mrs Grimble, the cook's assistant, she had seen him share what little he had and had developed a soft spot for the lad.

"My boy Edgar was like you," she would say as she smuggled him a treat. Sometimes it was a biscuit, rich with honey, on other occasions a fruited bun from Mr Templestowe's own table. "He went away with the army and never came back, my Edgar did. Lost in some foreign land he was, killed by savages and buried where he fell."

Jackson thought her simple in the head, for she said the same thing every time they met. But it would be foolish of him to mention it; the treats might well stop if he did. He may have been many things, but he was not stupid.

Instead, he merely pulled a sorrowful face and said, "How sad," being careful not to show too much emotion. To be honest, he was not really interested in the tale, people died, that was the way it was. Whether you were dead in Metropol City or dead in a foreign land it was all the same in the end.

Although he supposed, if you had to be dead, being dead in a foreign land had some attractions; at least you would have lived in bright sunshine and clean air for a while. And it was safe to assume that you were generally well fed in the army, or at least better fed than you were in the orphanage.

Jackson's stomach rumbled again, and he sneaked away from the din of the common room towards the kitchen. At this time of the day Mrs Grimble would be there alone and that meant more chance of a treat.

It was dark as he crossed the yard, flitting from pool to pool of gas-lit cobbles. A fine, misty rain fell, dragging the coal dust from the air, making the drops on his face feel coarse and gritty. His feet felt the wetness of the ground through the worn soles of his boots.

He looked up at a mechanical rumble, saw the lights on a flying machine as it passed over his head. It was unnatural, he thought, all those people in a box in the air, held up by goodness knew what, with two roaring gas fires pushing them forward.

He resolved never to go in one of them; as if it were ever a possibility. The walls shut off the sound as the machine passed by, allowing him to hear again the ever-present soft growl of life in the city outside.

It was another world out there; it had been six years since he was last outside the wall. He wondered what changes he would see, if he were ever to be allowed. The way things were in his life, seeing outside was about as likely as flying. If he were really one and twenty in a matter of days though, he would legally be an adult. That was more than old enough to marry, old enough to die for Norlandia. Many men of his age, and women too, would have five or six years of working under their belts. They might even be married, with children to care for. Perhaps he could request to see Mr Templestowe; he could petition him to be allowed out, to make his own way in the world.

When he got to the kitchen doorway and peered around it, Mrs Grimble was absent. She must have gone home already, Jackson thought. At least she had left the gas lamp burning, there was light to aid him in his search.

He ventured into the room; his hunger a real thing now, it felt like a worm writhing in his belly. Perhaps some comestibles had been left unattended. If he were lucky, he could maybe find a mouthful or two.

In the corner of the kitchen there was a large coal range, at least it was usually in the corner, now it seemed to be moved away from the wall into the middle of the room. Jackson could see that it was mounted on wheels, together with its tiled surround. He had never noticed that before, the flue had also been uncoupled and hung from the ceiling.

There was a dark hole in the wall behind its place. He crept towards it, expecting all the time to hear a shout, he was poised to run and dodge the blow from a master's swishing, stinging cane.

Reaching the hole, he saw the start of a flight of stone steps that led down. They were poorly lit by more flickering gas lamps. The plain brick walls had dark lines of condensation staining their faces. It smelt faintly musty, like the crypt at the church they were forced to attend most days.

There were voices below, faint and indistinct. As he tentatively moved toward the top step, he kicked a solid object, it made a scraping noise as his foot moved it across the flags.

The noise below stopped. Jackson bent down; there were a pair of boots on the ground, stout boots with hobnailed soles, better than his boots which were more hole than sole.

The tread had a strange pattern but Jackson assumed that it was to enable better grip on muddy paths.

He removed his own, battered boots and tried them on as, below him, the muttering resumed. The boots fitted him perfectly and when he laced them, he felt their robust construction holding his feet in unaccustomed comfort. Standing upright, they felt strange; perhaps it was due to the thickness of the soles. They were his now, he would soon get used to that.

There was an obstruction in each boot, a hard place by his big toe, like a stone. Apart from that, they were perfect. He had no qualms about taking them, just as long as no-one saw him do it.

He was more worried about how he could hide them from the attention of the other boys, especially from Alyious, who was the biggest and worst of the bullies. Perhaps if he dirtied them so they looked less like a new pair, they might remain his for a while.

His attention had been distracted by the boots; he had not noticed the soft tread of the person who approached. The hand on his shoulder was totally unexpected. He tried to duck and spin away but his new boots let him down. Sparks flew from their nails as they slipped on the flags and his feet skidded for purchase.

His balance lost, he fell. He bounced off each step on the way down, landing in a bruised, dazed heap at the foot of the stairs.

Fear took control of him, despite his bruising and dizziness he tried to get up and flee. No sooner was he on his feet than he found himself held from behind. His feet were lifted off the ground.

Unable to turn, he faced the stairs. He struggled but whoever was holding him was strong and pinned his arms to his sides with ease. He kicked back but his lunges encountered nothing but air.

"Be still," a gruff voice said in his ear. He saw the feet of a man coming down the stairs, then his waist and then, just as he was about to see the face, a cloth bag was thrown over his head.

"What shall we do with this one then?" said the voice.

"That's Jackson," answered Mrs Grimble, in a voice which was hers and yet not so. "He's the one that I told you about." Her tone was no longer that of a slightly bemused cook, she sounded like a refined and confident lady of class.

A third voice, also rich with the tones of the ruling classes, joined in the conversation. "He's all skin and bone, what good would he be?" it asked.

Jackson tried to speak through the folds of cloth. "I'm strong, let me go," he shouted, but if any of them heard him they did not show it.

"He seems to have found the boots," the first man said, "and they fit him."

"They ought," said Mrs Grimble. "Alyious stole his others to make a pattern."

What was going on? Jackson's boots had gone missing a week ago; he wondered who had taken them. He had looked at all the other boys expecting to see them on another's feet. He had had to walk barefoot for a day and a half, cutting his feet badly on the rough cobbles of the yard, then the boots had reappeared by the side of his bed and nobody could explain it.

How could Mrs Grimble, old, silly Mrs Grimble, be involved in plots and plans like this? And Alyious, he was Jackson's chief tormentor, what was his part?

"Let him go," ordered the voice in the distance.

"Yes, Mr Langdon," said the man holding him and the bag was removed, as were the arms.

Jackson turned around and blinked, he was in a richly decorated drawing room, lit by many gas lamps. The walls were panelled in dark wood, there was a fine carpet on the floor, framed paintings and highly polished mahogany furniture.

As well as Mrs Grimble, two men who he had never seen before were present. Alyious was beside him, had he been the one who had grabbed at him back in the kitchen?

Mrs Grimble stood before him. "Hello, Jackson," she said. "I see you've found us then; I expect you want to know what's going on. Let us give you a meal and then we'll tell you."

An hour later, Jackson was replete for the first time that he could remember. He had been given a plate of roasted bovine, with potatoes cooked in fat rendered from anserine, cabbage, carrots and thick gravy.

The gravy had been the best part, so rich and full of flavour that it would have made a better meal on its own than anything he usually ate. He could feel his belt tightening with each mouthful.

Apple pie and custard sauce, rich with cream, had followed. He had struggled to cram it all into his protesting stomach.

Mrs Grimble and the man referred to as Langdon watched in fascination as he ate. Alyious and the other man had departed, up the stairway. He had heard the range slide across the kitchen floor, closing that exit.

Jackson took a sip from the glass of lemonade that had been placed by his side. He had never tasted anything so refreshing. And he was warm; actually warm. In the dormitory, he often awoke to ice in the water jugs. Relaxed and feeling drowsy, he sat back.

"Is that better?" asked Mrs Grimble.

"Thank you, yes," said Jackson, remembering his manners. No doubt the reason behind the meal would shortly appear; there was sure to be a price to pay. He must stay alert for any trickery.

"We should explain," began the man, Langdon.

"Hadn't we better warn him first?" suggested Mrs Grimble. "Before we explain his new purpose?"

Jackson was suddenly alert; warn him? What was this about a new purpose? The thought occurred that he would be forced into something against his will. He looked around for another escape but could see none.

"Of course." Langdon showed no emotion. "Do you know what a patriot is, Jackson?"

"I do, sir; it's a man who loves his country."

"Correct, and a traitor?"

Jackson's face darkened. "That would be the opposite," he said.

"And which are you, Jackson?"

Jackson had the sense to realise that the rest of his life hung on his answer, not that he was in any doubt about which he was. It might be that he was not the richest person in the land, but he felt no anger over his status.

"A patriot, sir," he said defiantly.

"That's the correct answer," Mrs Grimble said kindly. "If you had been unsure, that brisket would have been your last meal. You would never have been seen again." The words were so at odds with her tone that it took Jackson a moment to comprehend what he had heard.

Jackson knew a little of the workings of the state, the overseer in the workroom often discussed the news of the day with them. So he was aware that the influence of Norlandia stretched way beyond its shores, and of the continual wars that engulfed foreign parts as all major countries vied for power.

It was said that enemy spies and agents were everywhere, battling to corrupt and terrorise innocent folk. Was this man such an agent, would his words be enough, or was his fealty to be further questioned, tested?

Langdon continued, "We represent a part of the government, a part that is interested in all sorts of things, all over the world."

"And in this country as well," added Mrs Grimble. "We are always looking for people to help us, to gather information, watch people and perform small tasks. We've been keeping an eye on you."

"Are you the Watchmen?" Jackson asked. The Watchmen were the law in Norlandia, they had absolute power, were uncorrupted and indefatigable. Get on their wrong side and they would never cease in their pursuit. 'Honest as the Watch' was a great compliment in life.

"Oh no," replied Langdon. "If the Watch knew of us, they would be most unhappy. Some of the things we do would not be to their liking. Officially, we do not exist."

That made it sound much more exciting, a secret part of society, with intrigues and plots of importance to the common good. "Is Alyious one of your... people?" asked Jackson. The two nodded.

"He is, that is why you never see him in the workroom. He lodges in the home but ventures out by day, sometimes by night, as required."

It made sense. Jackson had always thought that Alyious knew of some trick to avoid working, to find that he was allowed to go outside was a revelation; perhaps he could do the same. The bullying must be an act, if he worked for this man, on matters of importance; well, he could not be such a bad sort, could he? And he had a hand in Jackson's new boots. His mind raced, this might be the chance he was looking for, a way to get outside, to start a new life.

"We also test the inventions that our scientists produce," Mrs Grimble said. "Mechanical devices and the like. Things such as your new boots."

Jackson looked down at his feet. The part about working outside was interesting, getting away from the orphanage sounded like fun, even testing machinery, as long as you kept your hands and feet clear of the workings. But his boots. New and well made, to be sure; but still, they were just boots.

One of the wood panels on the far wall swung open. Alyious and the other man had returned. "Alyious you know," said Langdon. "His companion is Mr Fairview."

Alyious held out his hand. "No hard feelings, Jackson," he said.

Hardly knowing what to make of the last few hours, Jackson shook it.

"We're all prepared outside. Sir Mortimer, ma'am," Fairview spoke in the accent of a man from the wild, forbidding northern parts of the country.

"Good. Come on then, Jackson, you're about to find out what the boots can do. Did you feel the lump by your toe? It has a purpose."

Intrigued and excited, Jackson fell in with the rest as they moved outside. He prodded at the lump with his toe, but nothing happened.

They went through the door in the panelled wall and arrived in a small courtyard, between the back of the house and the wall that encircled the orphanage.

It was hidden by the shape of the building and Jackson had never guessed at its existence before now.

The wall was at least fifteen feet high, of red brick with a small door set in it. Gas lamps threw dark shadows. It had stopped raining and a pale moon added to the illumination.

Jackson gazed about. He thought that he saw movement; a figure came from the shadows and moved towards them. Jackson saw that it was a girl; in fact, it was one that he recognised.

Tall and pleasantly rounded, she had long dark hair piled on her head and secured with an ornate pin, looking like two entwined swans.

Jackson had often wondered how she had retained it from the lighter fingered among the females, now he was starting to understand a lot more of the hierarchy of the orphanage,

"Jessamine Batterlee," he said. "What are you doing here?"

She smiled. "I'm to be your accomplice, Jackson. I see you have the boots, like mine."

Jackson stole a glance at her feet. Peeping out from beneath her skirts were the toes of boots, highly polished like his. He had never noticed her wearing them before, and he had stolen more than a glance at her when he thought he was unnoticed. Now, she tugged at her waist and the skirts fell away.

Underneath, she was clad in trousers not unlike his, except they were tighter. Jackson felt embarrassment, he had never seen a woman dressed so, never guessed at the shape that was revealed.

The narrowness of her waist was emphasised by the wide black belt she wore, her hips full and shapely, the legs longer than he had supposed.

Jessamine was obviously unconcerned with her new appearance.
"Follow me, Jackson," she called, running toward the wall. Jackson was about to shout at her to be careful, it seemed that she could not stop before she dashed herself against the brick.
She jumped at the vertical face, swinging her feet up to kick at the wall.

Jackson fancied that he heard a click as she stuck fast, her feet three feet from the ground. Then she started to climb, moving up the wall as a babe crawls over the floor. It was as if the wall were horizontal. She swiftly reached the top and sat astride the bricks, her leg swinging.

"Well, Jackson?" said Mrs Grimble. "Your turn. What are you waiting for?"

Chapter 2

Jackson looked at Mrs Grimble. "How can I do that?" he asked.

"You climb with the boots on the brick, and you wear these on your hands." Mrs Grimble passed Jackson a pair of fingerless gloves. "Press the palms onto the brick," she said, "and kick the toe of your boots against the wall, you will stick."

Jackson reached up and placed the palm of the right glove against the wall. He tried to pull it away, it was firm. He lifted his left boot and kicked at the wall with the toe. There was a click and when he tried to pull it away, he found that it too, was stuck fast.

"How?" he asked.

"Does it matter?" came the swift reply from the new Mrs Grimble. "Just climb."

"No." Jackson shook his head, he was becoming uncomfortable, attached to the wall as he was, by one hand and one foot, but he wanted answers.

"Tell me how to move myself," he demanded. "My hand and foot are stuck."

"This one will be trouble," she said to no-one in particular. "I suppose it's to your credit that you're inquisitive. All will be explained, but now is not the time. You merely have to adjust your position so that you remove the weight, do that and your hands and feet will release."

Jackson tried it and found it to be true. He put his left hand on the wall, slightly higher and transferred all his weight on it. He lifted his right. It came away easily and he moved it higher and placed it against the wall again.

Swinging, the hand held his weight. He tried the same with his feet. Now he had the method, he began to climb easily.

He reached the top, slightly out of breath. Muscles unused to such exercise ached as he straddled the bricks, sitting facing Jessamine. She was grinning, her teeth white and even.

Now that he had a chance, he inspected the gloves. He found that they had a fine web of hook-like bristles all over the palm. In one direction the surface felt silk-like and smooth, in the other, he could feel many barbs digging into his flesh. He reached down and felt the tip of his boot, it was the same.

"It's the same principle as the arachnid," Jessamine explained. "It mimics their feet, 'tis how they climb walls."

Jackson was about to ask how she knew that; he felt swept up by events. His shoulders ached, his stomach felt like a heavy weight around his middle, there was so much that needed to be explained. Instead of asking, he simply gazed out over the city.

It was a place that he had not seen once the orphanage door had shut behind him, six years before. Even though it was dark, moonlight and the lights of the city itself revealed a bustling metropolis.

There seemed to be so much more of everything than he recalled, more lights in the houses, more factory and local chimneys belching smoke and sparks, more vehicles on the road.

There were several sets of lights in the sky from flying machines. He could even see people, taking a late evening walk. If they had looked up, what would they have thought?

Before he could speak again, Jessamine shouted. "Come on, Jackson. Race you down."

She swung a long leg over the wall and descended rapidly. Jackson followed and by dropping the last six feet, managed to arrive on the ground at the same time as her. He landed on bended knees, puffing from the exertion.

Jessamine seemed unbothered, breathing easily, her face was not even flushed. She went to her skirt and fixed it again around her waist.

"You need to get yourself fit, Jackson," remarked Langdon. Jackson was unable to reply as, hands on his knees, he forced air into his lungs.

"We'll have to feed him up a little," suggested Alyious. "And the training will harden him. Patching will see to that."

"We'll begin in the morning," Mrs Grimble said, "after fast-breaker. Now give me the gloves, Jackson."

Reluctantly Jackson handed them over. "In case you had decided to take a little excursion before we have trained you," she said, "let me explain. You will not go outside without our permission, or alone until you are trained and have made your oath. There are two reasons; you may be captured by our enemies, or you may decide that there is the chance for you to disappear. In either case, we would have to find you, silence you. We can scarce let you go and blab all our secrets, can we?"

She said it so seriously that Jackson realised his plan would not work without further study, he was freer than he had been but still entrapped.

"Come on then, Jackson." Alyious put an arm about his shoulders and led him to the shadows, a door that opened onto some steps and into the kitchen pantry. "Let's not spoil a good day with worrying about what might never be. We'd better get some sleep," he suggested, "before the night-watch notices that you are not in your cot."

Despite the change in Alyious's status, Jackson found it hard to adjust to the idea that he was now to be his friend. He was also slightly annoyed as he realised that he hadn't noticed Jessamine's departure. He had wanted to wish her goodnight.

The two boys crept into the dormitory block and parted ways. Alyious was in a different part of the building to Jackson, for which he had once been grateful. Now it seemed like a barrier between them.

"I will get you moved," Alyious said. "All of us who work for Langdon are together, it simplifies matters."

Jackson spent a sleepless night, he was part apprehensive about his new role, but at the same time excited to have a purpose. And surprised that someone had thought enough of him to offer him the chance. He clutched the boots to him, under the covers, in case they be taken.

His last thought before sleep was of the curve of Jessamine's legs in the tight trousers, the way her form changed shape as she moved.

Chapter 3

Next morning, he was stood in line for fast-breaker when he felt a tap on his shoulder. It was Skies, one of the wardens. He knew without looking; the other boys had whispered his name as he approached. He turned, ready to obey. Skies was a sadistic man, pinch-faced and small in stature. He was ever filled with the pleasure that certain folk took from the exercise of power, often choosing pupils for a job at mealtime, depriving them of food whilst they cleaned a blocked drain or performed some other task.

Today, however, Skies was smiling, or at least snarling in a less threatening way. "Come with me," he said and, grabbing his collar in one hand, he took Jackson to the head of the line. "In future, you're to get here half an hour before everyone else," he added.

"Yes, Mr Skies sir," Jackson said.

"This 'un needs feeding up for a job; he's one of Sir Mortimer's merry band," Skies announced to the servers and Jackson found his bowl replaced with a proper plate. Instead of the thin porridge and husk of old bread that was normal, he received fried eggs and rashers of porker, fresh buttered bread and a glass of milk.

"And every meal from now on, Mrs Grimble's orders," Skies added. The server nodded.

A few of the other children murmured angrily. "Why him, Mr Skies?" one asked.

Skies cuffed the nearest boy and grabbed his ear, pulling him away from the line, his bowl fell with a clatter. "Because," he answered, "he's got a job to do. So have you now, there's a latrine that needs cleaning and it has your name on it."

To laughter, the boy was taken away. Skies grabbed another. "Clean that mess up," he ordered, pointing at the spilled porridge.

Jackson ate his food quickly, half afraid that someone might take it from him. Such special treatment could mark him out as a target for retribution. The two who had missed breakfast would be after him, once they had finished the tasks set by Skies. As he wiped the plate with the last of his bread, Alyious was at his elbow.

"Good day, Jackson," he said. "Don't worry, I'll not be bullying you today, nor will any other. We have business to attend to. If you're replete, come with me."

The two of them left the hall and went through a door that Jackson had never passed before. As far as he had known, it led to Mr Templestowe's own quarters.

"Is this not the way to Templestowe's rooms?" Jackson asked.

Alyious laughed. "Templestowe, you have no need to fear him. He is naught but a figurehead. Langdon is the real power here."

Jackson followed on, eventually coming to a room where Jessamine was sat, along with several others. They passed a room where a few of the younger children were clustered in one corner.

"The young ones who show a bit of promise, as you did," explained Alyious. "The bulk of the children here are no more than a diversion for us to hide behind."

He recognised some of the people sat looking at him, others he only knew of by name. There were Leopold, Mularky, Hortense, Winifred, Capricia, Vyner and Milburn. Like Alyious, the boys were never seen at the day's work, the girls were kept away from any male contact.

The man Fairview was stood in front of a large green board. Another man, a soldier by his bearing, stood to one side. Fairview swiftly wrote three sentences on it with a chalk.

Jackson could read well enough, 'Know your enemy' the first one said. 'Trust no-one outside these walls' the second. The last one was the most poignant, 'Leave no friend behind you, we go and return together' it said.

"Gentlemen, ladies." Fairview had the ability to talk quietly yet command a room. "We welcome Jackson today; he will restore us to full complement, once he has been trained."

There was a round of "Welcome, Jackson," and "Good to see you," from the others. Jessamine smiled and gestured that he sit next to her. What did he mean, full complement? He was about to ask Jessamine when Fairview rapped on the board.

"Then we begin," said Fairview. He pointed to the board. "The others know this, Jackson, but for your benefit, these are the most important things about what we do."

"And what do we do?" asked Jackson. "I have heard many things but am none the wiser. You test inventions, I was told. It was hinted that I might go outside, but nothing more."

"Jackson, we are the watchers for Langdon, we see everything he needs to see in this city, yet we are not seen. And we perform tasks that aid in keeping Norlandia safe from its enemies."

All the words were a puzzle to Jackson. What did it all mean? He was about to ask when Jessamine whispered in his ear, "Worry not, just listen. I will take care to see that you have all the skill you need when the time comes. 'Tis all about hiding and watching, maybe a little light pilfering or disruption. We need to have no knowledge of what we see, merely the ability to report it to those who do."

"Thank you, Jessamine. Now, Jackson," said Fairview, "those of us that are not working meet in this room every morning after fast-breaker. We are given our tasks for the day. Yours for today is to start to get yourself fit enough to be useful. Later, we will teach you what you need to know. Follow Sergeant Patching, he will see to it that you are toughened up and made ready."

"Come along then, Jackson," said the man, marching off. Jackson followed as he went through a door and down a corridor. There were so many places in the orphanage that Jackson had never imagined existed, now they were in a room filled with strange objects.

It looked like the chamber of tortures that he had read of, in one of the books from the library.

"We will get you fit," said Patching, taking off his jacket to reveal a singlet, through which muscles bulged. "But first, let's see what we are starting from. Take off your shirt."

Jackson did so and Patching tutted in disappointment as he looked. He poked and prodded at Jackson with a short stick. "You have muscles," he grudgingly admitted, "but they need some work. Get on the belt."

He pointed to one of the machines. Jackson walked over; it was little more than a strip of black material on a metal frame, with handholds at one end.

"Climb on and hold the handles," instructed Patching. When Jackson did, Patching started a clockwork at the side of the frame. Jackson felt his feet move behind him as the material moved. He grasped the handle more firmly and started to walk, gaining his balance.

Patching increased the speed of the machine. Now Jackson understood why it was called a belt, it must be endless, like the belts that drove machinery. Except that this one was driven by a clockwork. He walked faster, breaking into a trot, then a run.

He started to pant, his chest heaving at the unexpected exertion. Patching left him and went to the other side of the room. Jackson reached over with one hand; he could not quite touch the switch.

He tried to bend down but the distraction made him stumble and he lost his balance. The belt deposited him on the floor in an untidy, breathless heap. Patching returned. "Lost your footing eh?" he inquired, holding out his hand.

"I was trying to make it go slower," gasped Jackson. He took the hand and felt the power in Patching's arm as he was hauled upright.

The soldier grinned. "It's situated there, just out of reach, so that you cannot," he said with a laugh. "Now, how is your breathing?"

Jackson gulped air. "Better," he said.

Patching nodded. "Good. Fitness is about recovery, not exertion. You are sound, you just need building up a little. The extra rations will help. You will spend some of your own time here every day. I believe the rest of your group come down after supper. One of them will turn the belt on and off for you."

He showed Jackson the other devices; each was designed to exercise a different part of his body, the arms, shoulders, stomach and legs. Jackson tried them all.

By the time he was familiar with them they had made him ache all over. He was glad of the extra food he had eaten at fast-breaker, even on a normal day the rations barely sustained him to luncheon.

"Now," said Patching, "we need to see how you can fight." He stood relaxed. "Attack me," he said. "Try and hurt me, in any way you wish."

Jackson was not a violent boy; he had no real idea of how to respond. Patching waited for a moment, then he leant forward with deceptive speed and slapped Jackson's face. "Come on," he shouted, "hit me."

Jackson balled his fist and swung at Patching's face. The man rocked back, avoiding the blow easily. Before Jackson knew it, Patching had returned it with one of his own. Once again Jackson found himself on the floor. "Try again," he suggested, helping him to his feet.

Three more times Jackson attempted to strike his opponent, with fists and a kick from his new boots, each time his blow was easily avoided and he was returned to the floor. He had the impression that Patching was holding power in reserve, the blows he received were enough to unbalance him but not too much as to render him incapable.

Jackson was growing angry with his failure to land a blow, but determined to carry on trying, the last thing he wanted was a return to his old life.

Once more, Patching held out his arm. "Again," he said wearily, as if he was tiring of this one-sided contest.

As he rose, Jackson had an idea, something he had seen one of the boys do. He held on to Patching's hand and used the momentum it gave him to his advantage. As his legs straightened, he pulled Patching toward him, ducked his head and butted the soldier's face as he moved forward, hitting him on his nose.

There was a crunch and the soldier reeled back, blood pouring from his nostrils.

"Very good, Jackson," he mumbled. "I wasn't expecting that one."

There was the sound of hand-clapping from the door. Jackson turned to see Langdon standing in the entrance. He suddenly felt guilty; how long had he been watching? Would he be in trouble?

"He told me to attack him, sir," he blurted.

Langdon stopped clapping. "I'm sure he did," he said. The words were warm but again, there was no emotion on the face. "You're getting old, Philias, or were you just over-confident?"

"He's a revelation, sir," Patching replied, his words distorted by the fact that he was gripping his nose to try and stop the blood. "He might not be strong yet, but he's game enough and can clearly think on his feet. I'd never have thought of doing that."

"Get yourself attended to, Mr Patching," said Langdon. "I wish to converse with Jackson for a moment." Langdon sat on one of the benches, up against a lattice of bars that covered one wall, Jackson took a seat on a green mat, facing him. He avoided the blood on the floor, sat cross-legged and leaned forward.

"What can I do, sir?" he asked.

"Do not worry, Jackson, your situation hasn't changed. I just need to know a bit more. Mrs Grimble has vouched for your character, I need more practical information."

"Whatever you wish," Jackson replied.

"Where did you live before you came here?"

"In Cobblebottom, sir," Jackson replied. "It's—"

"I know where it is," interrupted Langdon, in a voice that suggested the knowledge was sufficient. "And when did you see it last?"

"It must be six years, sir, since I was outside these walls."

Jackson remembered Cobblebottom very well; he could understand Langdon's meaning, it was not the sort of place for one like him to visit. If he did so after dark, he might not return. Even the Watch operated in pairs in Cobblebottom.

Langdon thought for a moment. "There has been much change in the world in six months, let alone six years. Very well, I expected as much. In addition to your training, we will have to get you familiar with the town as it is now, a few visits might be in order."

Jackson cheered up a little at that, this new game might yet provide the means of escape. "Now to your parents," continued Langdon. "Where did they work?"

"At the Prosthesium Company works," replied Jackson. "But they are both dead."

"I know," said Langdon, "and I'm sorry. Do you know the details?"

Jackson gulped; the memory was raw and undimmed by the years: his happiness as he arrived at the factory gate as usual and the sad face of the overseer. The looks of the factory girls had told him all he needed to know.

"I do, I used to go into the factory, the floor manager welcomed me at luncheon and after my lessons; he would let me sit with them as they worked. My mother was in charge of a moulding machine and my father inspected the quality of the pieces that she and her workmates made. One day the great drive shaft, spinning in the ceiling and driving all the machines in the room..." he paused, close to tears and Langdon waited for him to continue.

"Well, sir," Jackson continued, "it broke loose and with all the spinning leather drive belts cut through the room like a knife through butter. Every soul in the room, more than thirty people, were killed as it flailed about. The factory floor was destroyed, all the machinery wrecked. When everything was finally still and rescuers entered the place, it was impossible to tell what was man and what was mechanical, they were so mangled and entwined."

Telling the tale again had reduced Jackson to sobs, Langdon had listened without sympathy on his face, he made no move to comfort the boy. He knew that no sign of emotion was permissible in the times that lay ahead. Inside, he was relieved.

His information had been correct, this was the boy he needed. He had his confirmation in what the boy had said; he possessed the lever to control Jackson, it was just a case of pulling it at the right moment.

"Again, I'm sorry, Jackson," he said, rising to his feet. "Get yourself back to the classroom; there is much that you have to learn and little time to learn it."

When Jackson arrived back in the classroom, they had already broken for luncheon. There was a platter of bread, cheese and fresh tomatoes, the first of the red fruits that Jackson had seen in a long while. There were mugs of tea, with sweetened milk and lump sugar. And there was enough for everyone, with no need to fight for your share.

Jackson was ravenous from his exertions and he filled one of the plates and ate quickly, sitting alone. He noted that several of this morning's attendees were absent, only Vyner, Jessamine and Capricia remained. They were huddled in a corner in deep discussion. They seemed so close a group, and he an interloper, he felt unable to join in.

Then he was noticed, by Vyner. "Come on over and join us, Jackson," he shouted. "We are all one now, and we want to hear how you bested Philias." The group stood and moved chairs. Jackson went over and soon they were talking and laughing together as Jackson told of his morning in the exercise room, or Gymnazien as they referred to it.

They laughed as he described how he had fallen from the belt, nodded approvingly at his tale of breaking Philias' nose. "I have never got near his face with a blow," confided Vyner, "a tap on the shoulder occasionally."

"Nor I," added Jessamine. If Jackson was surprised to find that the women also trained in fighting, he had the sense not to say anything.

"I just got lucky," he mumbled, around a mouthful of cheese.

"I think you will be a wonderful addition to our group," gushed Capricia in a trilling voice that reminded Jackson of a small equine, lost and searching for its mother. "Enoch was boring... oh." She stopped talking as the realisation of her words silenced her.

"Enoch is in dire straits," said Vyner in a voice that told of his guilt.

"Oh Vyner," Capricia said, "I didn't mean... you did your best." She flapped her hands as she spoke.

Jackson knew of a boy called Enoch; before he could ask about his connection to the group, Fairview returned and lessons resumed. Fairview made a joke about Patching being unable to poke his nose into everyone else's business, then sent Jackson back to him.

Patching was sitting in the Gymnazien with black bruises on his face. The blood on the floor had been cleaned away; the room now smelt more of soap than sweat.

He stood and walked towards Jackson, who flinched. Then he saw that Patching was grinning and he relaxed. "Well done, Jackson," the soldier said, clasping him by the hand. "You won't catch me out like that again, I hope. Now let us progress; I will show you some methods for street-fighting, no rules and no quarter."

The afternoon was spent improvising defence against weapons; a book was used against a knife, a table made a shield. Then they turned to attack. Patching showed how even the most innocent of items, such as the wire from a speaker, could be turned into a strangler's rope and how many other innocuous objects could be made lethal.

"Always do what they will not expect," he was told. "When they think you should step back, step forward. View everything in sight and measure its potential. Watch your opponent's eyes; they never fail to give away the intended stroke."

They sparred for most of the afternoon, then Patching sent him away. "You should go and rest, do some book-learning, allow your muscles to recover. We will start again after fast-breaker."

On his return to the classroom, Jackson found that Alyious had returned and the others were absent. "They have gone to change for supper," he said. "I have this report to write on my day's work, for Langdon."

Jackson saw the pile of papers, covered with scrawling lines of handwriting. Alyious looked up. "You weren't expecting this eh?" he said. "Nobody does. 'Tis bad enough to go and do what we have to, then we must return and write it all down. Where we went, what we did, who we saw, what *they* said and did. Goodness knows what becomes of it all."

"I can't do all that," Jackson said. "Do you have to write it all out by hand, could you not do it by machine?"

"You mean, like the scriber?" said Alyious. "I cannot use that mechanical thing, hitting those keys for any length of time is no fun, and if you make a mistake, there is that awful smelling white ink and that ridiculous brush. These are just rough notes, ready to be processed. Oswald has a new device, not unlike the Fenesh that the islanders used to control Drogans, at least according to legend."

Jackson listened to Alyious's words, understanding perhaps one in every three. He had never heard of such things especially the last. "A machine to control Drogans?" he said. "Is that some sort of a jest?" He also had not heard of the name Oswald, he must be another of Langdon's retinue. One thing at a time.

"Perhaps control is the wrong word," said Alyious. "Of course, you would have been inside when it was all the news, with Horis Strongman and Christoph Leash. It was a way to understand the beast, reason with it, using sound and a pen. Oswald has adapted it to turn speech into text. Anyone merely has to read these notes into it; it writes the words as they do. He calls it the Lexiograph."

"I see." Jackson was not sure that Alyious was not playing a game, it all sounded so preposterous. But then, he had been out of touch for six years, who knew what might have occurred?

"Who is Oswald?"

Alyious smiled. "You will see, he is the genius behind much of what we have." He looked at his timepiece. "And that is suppertime." He gathered up the notes. "Time to eat, I can pass these to the secretaries, they will do the rest."

The two boys returned to the common spaces. "You were supposed to be moving to our dormitory after supper," said Alyious, "but Enoch's room has not yet been cleared."

Jackson already knew of Enoch, he had also been mentioned by Capricia at lunch. Was he another of Langdon's men then? He had been an irregular presence in the orphanage, the word was that he had escaped and been injured outside, two nights ago. 'And serve him right', Skies had told them gleefully.

"Is Enoch one of us? I thought him to be an escapee?"

Alyious shook his head. "He was on a job for Langdon but got a bit close for comfort. He was stabbed by foul anarchists; Vyner was his partner that evening and managed to get him back to us.

He lies now in the infirmary, more dead than alive. That story was concocted to quiet the rumours. As Fairview said, you are to be his replacement."

"I cannot stay in the dormitory tonight," Jackson protested. "Two boys were punished because of me this morning."

"They will probably have forgotten," Alyious assured him confidently.

They took their places in the line for supper, Alyious in front. Jackson had just collected his meal, a bowl of stew with a fine aroma, when he was pushed in the back.

He and his meal fell to the floor. As he landed he felt a kick in his ribs and was about to curl into a ball, when he saw a booted foot swinging toward his face. Remembering his unexpected victory over Patching, how he had not retreated, he decided to see if he had learned anything else from his encounters.

'Do the unexpected', Patching had said. Jackson brought his right arm across his face, the boot hit him just below the elbow, numbing his arm but protecting him from any more serious injury. Now he rolled, sliding through hot stew; bringing his other arm up, he grabbed at the foot that he could see in front of him and heaved.

There was a cry and Morgan, one of this morning's tormentors, was now on the floor next to him. He must have cracked his head on the edge of the servery as he fell; he lay still as death.

Jackson rolled back the other way and started to get to his feet as he took another kick, no doubt that was from the other boy.

The others in the dining hall were cheering and banging a rhythm on their metal bowls with their spoons.

"Fight! Fight!" they shouted, as Jackson gained his feet and faced his assailant. The boy, who he recognised as Erastus Crabb, had a dark-bladed knife in his hand and waved it in front of him.

"Come on then, Mr Clever, Skies' new friend," he said. "I missed my breakfast and spent half a day in the latrines because of you."

Jackson was momentarily unnerved by the sight of the blade; the boys backed away, Alyious included. He could expect no help there, which was fair, he had to learn to stand on his own and face this danger down. Again, it would be an unexpected thing for him to do. In any event, Jackson had nowhere to go, behind him he heard the other boy groan, he had to act quickly, before he was outnumbered.

He looked around desperately for something to use against the knife. There was a pile of serving trays by his arm, he picked one up and held it in front of him. It was made of thin wood, cheap and flimsy, but it would serve as a shield.

The crowd bayed. "Go, on Rastie, stick him," one called.

Jackson changed his grip on the tray, holding it flat and two handed, he lunged with it, trying to knock the blade from Erastus's grip. Erastus tried to swing outside the arc of the tray, but Jackson changed its direction and the blade stuck in the wood, half an inch of metal protruding through the board. He twisted the tray and Erastus cried out, letting go of his weapon as his wrist was bent back.

Jackson dropped the tray to his side and advanced. Erastus backed away, until he was stopped by the press of boys.

"I don't want to hurt you, Rastie," Jackson said, surprised at how calm he sounded. The tray swung by his side.

"Behind you," a female voice called, Jackson jumped to one side as the other boy rushed at him. He felt a sting in his side, heard a gasp.

"That's enough." Jessamine had come to stand by him; together they faced Erasmus and Morgan. Morgan waved his knife around threateningly. "I have no blade," said Erastus. "He has it, stuck in that tray."

"Need my help do ya, Rastie?" sneered Morgan. "Want me to stick 'im for ya?"

Jessamine pulled the knife from the tray. "Ohh," said Morgan. "Lady has a knife. Careful, love, you might cut yourself. Jackson your new squeeze, is he?"

Jessamine's cheeks coloured. It was almost as if she flickered, she moved forward and back so quickly. Morgan howled and grabbed at his trousers, dropping the blade. Jessamine had sliced his braces in one movement; left and right, without touching his shirt. They fell to the floor, exposing shirt tails and spindly legs.

"How?" he gasped, as gales of laughter erupted from the onlookers. Erastus had melted away, Morgan tried to depart and fell, legs tangled. Skies appeared, shouting, he grabbed at the boys closest him, who evaded his clutching fingers easily. Morgan tried to stand, Skies kicked his knife away from his reach.

Jessamine looked at Jackson's side, his shirt was cut and there was a thin trickle of blood. "He has cut you," she said.

Skies picked up the tray. "How did this happen?" he asked, looking at the hole. He saw the knife in Jessamine's hand. "A little difference of opinion, Mr Skies," she said. "I must take this one to the nurse." Skies saw the blood and nodded.

"Be quick," he suggested, "before he stains the flooring."

Jessamine grabbed a serving cloth and wadded it. "Hold this tight against the wound," she said, as she led him out of the room.

Instead of crossing the yard to the infirmary, Jessamine took him back through the door to the classrooms and up a flight of stairs.

"Where are we going?" asked Jackson.

"These are our rooms," she said, "and now yours too. The nurse will be full of cooking wine by now, more danger than Morgan or Erastus in her state. I will tend it myself."

"Alyious told me that I was to have Enoch's room, but not yet."

"I suppose that you could sleep in Enoch's room tonight; if you don't mind his possessions being there. You cannot return to the dormitory; you would be dead before sunrise."

On the landing, there was a row of doors, each with a name tag, housed in a brass frame on the door. Boys names were on one side, girls on the other. He saw Alyious, Vyner, Capricia and Jessamine.

They stopped at the one labelled Enoch. So this was to be his new home. The fact that he was training to replace Enoch suggested to him that Enoch would never recover fully enough to resume his role. Jessamine pushed the door open.

"In you go. Remove your shirt," she commanded, "and lie down on the bed." Jackson did so. "Look away," she said. He averted his eyes as once again Jessamine lifted her skirts. He thought it strange that he was permitted to see her legs when she was outside, but not in here. Perhaps she was not wearing the trousers?

"You may turn back," she said. She had removed her black belt. Jackson could see that it contained many pockets and she opened one and removed a packet. Inside it was a rectangle of what looked like thick parchment.

"What is that?" he asked, as she held it over the wound, which had almost stopped bleeding. The serving cloth was stained red, he must have lost a lot of blood, he felt no pain, a little sore but that was all.

"This is one of Oswald's inventions; it's a dressing for wounds, made from a tree resin. It's held between two pieces of parchment." She ripped the parchment in half and peeled away a layer of material covering one side.

Underneath was a green coloured paste. "When this touches skin, the moisture in your body causes a chemical reaction and it sets hard, sealing the wound and preventing infection. It also contains a chemical based on allium bulbs and honey, which promotes healing."

She pressed it to Jackson's side, her touch gentle. Then she removed the parchment, the green paste stayed, stuck to the skin.

Jackson looked up and their eyes met. There was a sudden tension. Close up, her lips were red and inviting, as bright and glossy as the tomato that he had enjoyed at lunchtime.

He felt an almost irresistible urge to touch them with his. As he leant forward, Jessamine pulled away. "No," she said, standing up. "Do not look at me in that way. I'm just helping you."

Jackson did not understand what had happened, at first, he had merely been smiling in gratitude. Then he had felt something, a sort of attraction between them. He was sure that her eyes had revealed the same feeling, just for a second.

To break the spell, he glanced down, his wound was covered with the green paste, as he watched it changed colour, becoming clear. He could feel it stiffening and pulling the cut edges of skin together.

Jessamine folded the remainder of the parchment and replaced it in her belt. "Thank you," he said. "I have already asked Alyious but he would not say. Who is Oswald?"

She laughed, "Oswald is, well, it would be easier if you saw him for yourself. He is just Oswald. Imagine a man who is probably the cleverest in the world, yet one who is also unable to live in that world."

She thought for a moment, still smiling as if at some secret joke. "No, that sounds harsh, he is a genius yet shy and unworldly, that describes him better. I think you will like him; we all do."

Her attitude was now business-like. "The wound is nothing, the cut will heal, the resin will protect it while you bathe, or exert yourself. It will fall off in a day or so. And don't fret at the sight of the serving cloth. Blood always looks more on the outside of the body. I must go now; there will be clean bedding and some sundries in the store at the end of the corridor. Put all of Enoch's possessions in the corner. Goodnight."

She swept out of the room, leaving Jackson alone to wonder at the emotions coursing through his head and the vagaries of the female mind. He was not overly experienced with women and their emotions; while he had engaged in fumbling encounters with two of the girls in the orphanage, they had been emotionless and instinctive, neither had developed into anything more.

In a daze and aching all over, he stripped the bed and fetched clean linen and towels from the store, together with a cake of cresylic soap and a brush for cleaning his teeth.

All of Enoch's clothes and possessions were taken from the drawers and cupboards and placed in a neat pile in front of the window, beside a heavy iron radiator that actually issued heat into the room.

He was careful not to stretch the resin on his cut, but it seemed to be firmly affixed. He looked forward to meeting this Oswald; if he could do such a thing with tree bark, perhaps the Lexiograph was real after all.

Jackson now explored his new home. The door could be locked from the inside; that meant his possessions would be secure, a novel experience for him. He bounced on the bed, it felt soft and comfortable. A window offered a view of the outer wall of the orphanage, at least six feet away. There were heavy curtains and he drew them, blotting out the view of the bricks. Now, he could almost pretend he was in some other world, one where he was the master of his own destiny. There was a cupboard and a wardrobe, but he had nothing to put in them save what he stood in.

He could return to the dormitory for his possessions, but that would mean facing Erastus and Morgan. In all likelihood, his things would by now have been divided up between the boys and nothing would remain. There was another door and he found a washroom behind it. Surely it could not be for his own use?

There was another radiator in there, as well as a white enamelled bath and all the things that he had been required to share previously.

There was a knock at the door. Jackson opened it; Mrs Grimble was stood outside, carrying two large bags.

"Here are your things from the dormitory," she said. "I had to persuade their new owners to relinquish them to me, I hope everything is there. Also, I have some of the tools of your new trade."

She eyed the pile of belongings by the window. "Help me get those bundled up. I can take them down to the infirmary and reunite them with their owner."

Jack exchanged the items in her bags, Enoch's for his own. "I heard about your altercation in the servery," she said. "Sir Mortimer is concerned; he will not have his agents put in danger in their own dwelling. From tomorrow, all agents will be fed separately, in the classroom."

Jackson was relieved to hear it, the last thing he wanted was to be injured before he had the chance to get outside. Mrs Grimble left with a cheery, 'Goodnight, Jackson, sleep well and be ready for the morrow.'

Jack was suddenly tired, he was interested in the 'tools of the trade', as she had described them, but too much had happened for him to take any more information this day.

He removed his boots, locked the door and enjoyed a deep, warm bath, washing his hair with liquid soap, drying himself with the thick towels that he had collected from the store. Then he donned a new flannel sleeping suit of blue and white stripes that he had also found. He laid out on the bed, within minutes, he was fast asleep.

In his dreams, he went again to his parents' house and his youth. He saw the rows of poorly constructed houses, built back to back, the smoke from the myriad chimneys settling in the natural hollow of ground that gave the place its name. And towering over it all, The Prosthesium Works, surrounded by its high walls.

It was the place where everyone local laboured, assembling artificial limbs for men and women ruined by war or industrial accident. Rudimentary they might have been, with fixed joints and fingers, a different one for each task, the more expensive ones had rotatable and lockable elbows, ankles and wrists, and fingers that could be bent.

They attached to the stumps with leather harnesses, taking hours and several people to fix properly. In every way, they were useful but no substitute for the original. His parents had both worked there, his mother moulding and assembling arms and his father, inspecting the finished pieces for quality.

He remembered the lessons he had been forced to endure, at the school attached to the works, when he would rather have been out in the world. Once he had learned to read and write and calculate, the rest of it had seemed pointless. It was the learning of things for the sake of it that frustrated him.

When would he ever need to speak in the tongue of the Western Isles, or have to talk of the lives of heroes of the past, men like Maloney and Horis Strongman? And who cared of Drogans? They too were a thing of the past, rarely seen in the city, keeping far away from man and his intolerance.

Then, after he had exhausted dreams of his past, he dreamed of his future, a future that now included Jessamine. In this life to come, they were both happy and away from the orphanage, sharing a life together in some sort of domestic idyll.

Jackson was awoken from this dream by a knocking on his door. "Wake up, sleepyhead," shouted a voice he knew, the tones harsher than in his reverie. "It's near time for fast-breaker, then your real work will start."

"I will be there," he replied, swinging his legs from the bed, the muscles protesting at the movement. What would happen today? he wondered as he washed and dressed. Would his tormenters return, did he even care?

Chapter 4

Over the next few weeks, Jackson's life became a blur of action, with all too brief periods of rest. Every time he awoke in his new room he found it a struggle to persuade his limbs to move. His muscles screamed for mercy from the exertions they were put through.

Mrs Grimble provided him with some sort of salts, for his daily hot bath. They helped relieve the aches, at least enough so that he could sleep. It was still a novelty to have a whole room to himself; once he had arranged his meagre possessions, he was proud of his quarters and even though he was tired, he still spent time in cleaning and tidying.

Every day, as he exercised more, his frame filled out. The good food he ate gave him strength; repetition of the exercises nightly gave him stamina. Gradually, as his fitness improved, the aches lessened, he noticed in the mirror that his shape had altered dramatically. There was a distinct broadening of his shoulders and shrinking of his waist. Outlines of muscle appeared on his abdomen.

When tested, he could climb the wall in the yard as fast as anyone, and not be out of breath at the top. Along with the others, he used the bathing pool and exercising machines daily. They all competed on the various machines, to be the fastest, last the longest, or do the most of any exercise.

His knife wound had healed practically overnight; when the resin fell away there was a small scar, little more than a ridge in the skin.

Jackson was amazed by their camaraderie, the sense that they were a family. There was no animosity, no boasting or ill-feeling if bested at any activity. Jackson began to feel a part of the group, although he had never participated in any real work.

Occasionally, one or more of them would be absent for a day; or longer, when they returned all they would say was, 'it went well,' or 'sadly we failed.' No details of what they did were ever discussed, but he saw lots of written notes passed through to the secretaries.

Not only did he exercise, he also sparred with all the others in turn, whoever was available. To his surprise, both Jessamine and Capricia, both his height but slighter of build, were his equal in strength. The other women, being shorter were only slightly less so, but that lack was made up with clever tricks they had learnt to reduce any disadvantage.

As time went on, he suffered less and less defeat at any hand, until one day Patching said, "I can teach you no more, you are as ready as you'll ever be."

His muscles were not the only casualty of this new regime, while he recovered his breath between bouts of physical exercise, his mind was assaulted; more and more information was imparted till his head ached with the strain of packing it all in.

The difference between this and the schooling he had hated was striking. There he had failed to see the reason for the knowledge; here the lessons were in things that he needed to know, interesting things that he could apply in his life. Because it was relevant, it stuck in his head.

He learned how to watch unnoticed, how to follow one man in a crowd and tricks of memory, how to remember faces and long lists of items. He also learned how enemies might try to turn his head with promises of money and how to resist interrogation by focusing on trivialities and talking in riddles.

He learnt codes and how to leave messages by marking symbols on walls, street corners and other special places. He was given a story to tell, about his past life and learned how to embellish it and weave a fiction around it. Some of the advice was so obvious and so simple, other parts showed deviousness on the part of Langdon and Fairview.

But the thing he loved the most was when they were taught practical tasks, by Patching and others who never gave their names. Things such as opening locks with a set of special tools, how engines worked and how to control or sabotage them.

Jessamine had become distant; although friendly, she no longer seemed to show Jackson as much attention as she had. He wondered what he had done to upset her, remembering the awkwardness in his room, had he been too forward in some way?

There were several days when she did not appear at all, on those she must have been working on some task for Langdon, perhaps it was distracting her.

The other women in the group paid him attention though, he was unused to it and slightly embarrassed by their worldly-wise attitudes and coarse humour. Jackson was far from an innocent, but quieter and more reserved than they. He was also aware of his status and feared to do anything that might jeopardise his chances of getting outside. Despite everything, he still had hopes of making his escape.

Somehow, Capricia and Winifred always seemed to be in the vicinity when he had removed his shirt or was clad only in a towel or bathing shorts. They chattered away behind their hands, obviously talking about him and giggling.

He wondered what they were saying, the attention made him squirm. It seemed that the redder and more flustered he got, the better they liked it.

Patching taught him far better ways of defence and attack, with his fists and boots, with knife and gas-gun and how to disable an opponent with the Watchmen's weapons. There was the innocent looking truncheon that extended into a stave, just by pushing a button and flicking the wrist. One was worn on each thigh, ready for instant action. When wielding both, they made a formidable weapon.

Then there was the hobble ball, a sphere that worked on the same principle. When thrown, it released two metal pins on contact with the ground, thrown between a runner's legs; it tripped him and sent him sprawling.

These items, and others, were secreted about his person by the same means as they were on the Watchmen. A leather belt with many pockets and clips, called a quip-belt, fitted around his waist.

He had already seen it worn by Jessamine, now he looked forward to getting his own. The special pockets were sewn into his trousers to hold the truncheons. The hobble balls were kept in his backpack. Once he had completed training, he would receive his own issue, until then, he had to return the training versions at the end of every day.

There were also lectures on the politics of the modern world. The principal country was Norlandia, its major adversary the Western Isles. However, things were never that simple. The Isles provided a lot of the produce that Norlandians took for granted, Café, Char leaves and fine fabrics, all that Norlandia could not produce. In return, they were sold manufactured goods. Trade was, as ever, the cause of many of the wars and skirmishes.

Also important were the Spice Islands, another nation at the furthest reaches of the world. This was the place where peppers and other exotic flavourings were grown. In addition, there existed many other nations and states, all vying to be the strongest on the globe.

Alliances were made and broken between all of them as governments changed; so that it was difficult to know with any certainty who was currently a friend and who an enemy.

War was cited as the greatest spur to technological development, yet wars and aggressive governance was becoming less common. At least on the part of Norlandia, largely due to the influence of a women's group, the Ladies who Lunch, which had started life in a Café house.

Appalled at the waste of life and the lack of compassion shown to those affected by war, they had set out to change the world, led by a senior minister's wife called Aphra Claringbold. They campaigned for the rights of those left behind, the peaceful settlement of disputes and dignity for all.

There had been initial resistance from men but using their femininity as a weapon, they found it to be just as effective as any gas-gun.

Jackson even found these lectures interesting, as they explained the purpose and reasoning behind the people he now worked for, after all, if foreigners wished to disrupt his way of life, a defence was essential.

At the end of each part of his training, there were all sorts of tests, of memory, of dexterity, of going around the orphanage and finding objects left or hidden. Of reading maps, secret writing and how to see if you were. To his surprise, he found them enjoyable and passed each one with ease.

In his mind, he was halfway outside already. The problem was that he had doubts about running away as soon as he was able. Over the weeks, he had come to know and respect all the other agents, as well as his instructors, from the nameless ones to Langdon himself.

He was beginning to feel guilty for wanting to leave. 'Perhaps I shall do a little work for them first,' he thought, 'spy out a proper escape route rather than just run.'

Then one day, Jessamine was present again when he arrived in the classroom. She was her old cheerful self. "Hello, Jackson," she greeted him. "I'm sorry I haven't seen you for a few days, I have been on a special job for Sir Mortimer, it required all my attention to prepare and carry out, hence my behaviour. I had to distance myself from all acquaintances and play a part. All is done now and I'm ready to be part of the group again." He noticed that she walked as though injured.

"Have you hurt your legs?" he asked. She shook her head.

"No, I'm just a little sore from my exertions. Worry not, I will be fit enough to spar, and beat you by tomorrow."

A man called Henderson was taking that morning's lesson; he was discussing new advances in the science of statics, a study of the forces produced by magnetic metals.

"Like the ship's compass?" asked Vyner. "We know all that."

"Yes, but do you know this?" Henderson replied. "Watch closely, I have a piece of magnetic metal here." He produced a lump of a dark substance and laid it on the table. "Now we all know that magnets attract some materials," he took a container from the desk, "these are filings of iron."

He placed the magnet under a sheet of glass and tipped the filings on top. They immediately formed a circular pattern on the glass. "You can see the direction of the forces," he said. "Now scientists have found that if a coil of copper wires is placed in this pattern and the magnet rotated, the force transfers to the wires."

"How, through thin air?" demanded Alyious.

Henderson lifted a small mechanism from under the desk. "This is a cylinder of magnetic iron on a shaft," he explained. "Around it, yet not touching, you can see the coiled wire." The two ends of the coil were bare and protruding from the ends of the coil.

"You," he indicated Jackson, "hold the wires tightly, one in each hand." He pointed at Vyner. "If you would like to crank the magnet when he has them held firm."

Jackson spent the next half hour massaging his hands. As soon as Vyner had cranked, he had received a tingling jolt that sent him staggering across the room.

Henderson grinned. "That is the power of statics," he said to laughter.

"How is it possible to gain so much energy from such a small mechanism?" asked Vyner.

"A good question and one that I cannot answer, what I can say is this. The latest thinking is that statics will revolutionise our lives, there are many applications, we can turn the magnet using steam, much as the engine of a flying machine works by a spinning fan in hot gas, or by water power, as a mill wheel. The real expert is not I but Mr Thorogood, who works in the room below."

At last, Jackson was to meet Mr Oswald Thorogood. Jessamine accompanied him down to the room he used, she called it his laboratorium. "I need to ask Oswald something," she had said. "I will take you down to meet him, and rescue you if he talks too much."

Jackson felt he knew Oswald already, from Jessamine's description and what he had heard the others say. It was plain that they all regarded him with affection, but more than that, they showed real concern over his shyness and tendency to babble or talk in a language they could not understand.

They were not mocking, as Jackson had expected, but sympathetic to his character.

And they appeared to be right about the man himself. As he entered the basement, Jackson could see that Oswald indeed lived a troglodyte's existence, next to the room where Jackson was recruited. In there were all manner of scientific apparatus, arranged in haphazard piles. The air smelt vaguely of burning sulphur and of Thorogood himself.

He was dressed in a worn suit, several sizes too voluminous, with small, blackened holes in the sleeves and trouser legs. His black tie bore stains, maybe of soup or some other substance.

He had two tufts of white hair, one located over each ear, glasses so thick that they might have been the bottoms of bottles, behind them the eyes were distorted in shape, bright and twinkling.

He shook Jackson's hand in a distracted manner, glancing nervously around.

"I'm honoured to meet you," said Jackson. "Are you the one who invented the gloves?"

"Ahh... not invented," Oswald replied. "Since I cannot really claim a theft from nature, shall we say borrowed? I merely deduced how the arachnid climbs and replicated it. Of course, we cannot turn it on and off, as the creature can, but it works in the same way."

The basement room was lit, not by gaslight but by a row of bright globes, suspended on chains from the ceiling. The light was blue-white, compared to the yellow of the gas flame.

"The illuminations, how do they work?" asked Jackson.

"They use what has become known as the Wasperton-Byler effect," replied the scientist. "A form of the new science known as statics. Steam from the house supply is used to spin a magnet, in a coil of metal wires. It somehow produces this effect. I don't understand the why of it, nobody does, but it works."

Jackson had never heard of such a thing before today, the jolt his arms had received testified to the power of this new force. If it could be made to light rooms, what else might it do?

"I can't believe you don't understand it," said Jessamine. Oswald blushed and turned his head away.

"Why the name?" asked Jackson.

"The Minister of Sciences who found it was called Millicent Wasperton. Legend has it that a man called Byler was her lover, not a stretch of the imagination, she had many, and all of them people of influence." He looked wistfully around as he spoke of lovers. "Between them, they produced the mechanism. Apart from the coil and the magnet we know nothing of its principles. As you can see, the case is sealed; they trust me to know its workings, but no other. They were a secretive pair and it's only just becoming well known, but I foresee a revolution, equal to the industrial one that steam power wrought, once it catches on."

"Alyious mentioned something called a Lexiograph," Jackson said. "It sounded improbable. How does it work?"

Oswald looked pleased. "I can explain it easily," he said. "It's all to do with the shape of sound waves in air. Each word has its own form; my machine merely traces it on a moving paper, in the first part of the transcribing operation." He paused for breath.

Before he could speak again Jessamine interrupted the conversation. "If I can ask; before you start Oswald running, I need some supplies." She handed him a list. "Can you send these up to my room please?"

Oswald looked and flushed. What could Jessamine want that would make him react so? Before he could ask, Oswald said, "Of course, I can get them now, excuse me a moment."

He turned and went through a small door, leaving them alone together.

"They are supplies of women's things," she said, "and sundries to refill my belt, like the healing patch I used on you. It is your own task to replenish the contents every time you use something."

Oswald returned with a small bag, which he handed over. "Here we are," he said. "Another three months' supply, and everything else you wanted."

"Thank you," she said, she bent to kiss his cheek, causing the flush again. "I will leave you to finish your explanation to Jackson, goodnight." She swept out.

"A fine woman," Oswald said, gazing at the doorway. "Now then, where was I?"

"The Lexiograph, you told me the first part, where the words move a pen and draw a shape."

"Ah yes, well after that the shape is translated into text, 'tis better if I show you."

Oswald took him into the room where the secretaries worked, where the notes were posted through the door. The room was filled with a huge device, looking like the steam organ Jackson knew from chapel and the fairground.

Except that this one was laid on its side and in place of a keyboard, had a row of small pins, under which a long belt passed. There were brass rods and pistons, a fine sheen of lubricant made all the metal parts gleam. The other end of the belt emerged from a box with a speaking trumpet on its side, with a seat for an operator.

"The Lexiograph," announced Oswald, "my own invention. Watch closely." He turned the steam on and the belt started to move.

"You speak into the trumpet and a groove is made on the belt by a pen," Oswald said. "The belt then passes into the second part of the Lexiograph, where this mark is read by the pins, which press onto the belt under pressure. Their movement corresponds to the shape of the groove, itself a representation of the word spoken. Hence links are moved, a printing system is activated, words are printed on the page. Finally, the groove on the belt is smoothed by rollers, the belt then passes back into the first part, ready to be marked again."

"May I?" Jackson asked. Oswald nodded.

Jackson bent to the trumpet. "What should I say?" he asked in a whisper. There was a muted clicking, a hiss of steam. Oswald went to the back of the machine. He returned with a sheet of parchment.

'What should I say' was inscribed on it in the finest copperplate.

Jackson was stunned; the script was more perfect than any he had seen from any mechanical writer.

"It needs a lot of work," said Oswald, "to make it smaller for one thing, and improve the recognition, it works best when tuned to one person's voice. And punctuation, spacing, all the nuances of speech. But I have made a start; the possibilities that can be developed from the principles are endless."

"It's amazing, truly, I thought it a silly idea, after all we have mechanical writers; now I have seen the product, well, this should be on show for everyone to wonder at."

"It will be," said Oswald, "just as soon as I have worked out how to get it from this room."

Chapter 5

One day, Fairview announced that the first part of his training was at an end. "Now you will be thoroughly tested, to see how much information you have retained," he said. Jackson was kept in the classroom while everyone else was dispersed to other tasks. They all shouted 'good luck' as they departed.

Fairview, Langdon and a man he had never seen before then sat in front of him. For the next three hours, he was questioned about everything he had been taught.

He found the experience both unnerving and pleasing, he had not anticipated such a concentrated grilling, had considered the regular testing to be all he would have to endure, so was unprepared for the barrage of questions.

They were relentless in their probing, teasing out his knowledge and making him apply it in a variety of situations. He began to sweat and had to force himself to concentrate.

Yet it was also pleasing; to his surprise and relief, he was able to answer most of what they asked, only faltering twice, once when asked about interrogation and again on his actions if taken to an alehouse by a man who was becoming suspicious of him. In the end, Langdon said, "We are finished, please wait outside."

He left the room, standing in the corridor. Jessamine came past; she took his hand. "Are you waiting to hear?"

"I am," he admitted, revelling in the contact. He had missed Jessamine, although the others had been attentive, too much so at times. He enjoyed her company best. He trusted her; perhaps he could ask why Capricia and Winnifred were always so close, why they teased him so.

"You will be fine, of that I'm sure," she said. "You can tell me all about it later."

"Come back in, Jackson," shouted Langdon.

She kissed his cheek. "Good luck."

Hoping that he was not blushing, he re-entered the room and sat. The three gazed at him. "We have considered," the quiet man said.

"No need to keep the lad in suspense for any longer, Quinby." Langdon smiled at Jackson. "Congratulations, Jackson, you have passed all your initial testing. We now require you to swear an oath of loyalty, before we proceed to the next part of your training."

Jackson was made to stand in front of the Norlandian flag and handed a card. "Read the words and mean them," Langdon said.

"I promise, on pain of death," Jackson swore, "to serve Norlandia, to honour its sovereign and legally appointed government, to the utmost of my strength, all my days. To never divulge secrets entrusted to me, to care for my companions and to uphold all that is right."

The three clapped. "Then you are one of us."

That night there was a small celebration in the Gymnazien. Food and drink had been laid on and as many of the group were there as Jackson had seen. They all congratulated him. Capricia presented him with a scarf she had made herself from knitted ovine wool, dyed in many colours.

Later that evening, as people were starting to drift away to bed, Fairview announced the news that Jackson had been waiting for. "Tomorrow, you will go outside," he said. "It's about time that you saw the world and got reacquainted with it. Someone will take you and start to show you what has changed since last you saw it."

Jackson could hardly contain his excitement, he wondered what he would see and who would accompany him. He hoped it would be Jessamine but if any of the others knew, they were not sharing the information.

Next morning, after fast-breaker, Jackson ventured outside, to his delight, he was indeed accompanied by Jessamine. It was a rainy morning when they slipped through the gates and stood together on the road. Jackson had forgotten what it was like to be outside the wall. He was happier than he had ever been.

Dressed in a new suit that had been waiting in his room when he had retired after the party, he felt a gentleman, so far removed from the youth he had been a few short months ago. He was confident that he could cope with all the city could throw at him. Jessamine was dressed in a fetching gown of bright red, with white trims. She carried a woven basket, covered with a cloth that matched her gown.

"What's in the basket?" he asked her, as they walked across the courtyard to the main gate.

"We have our luncheon," she said, lifting the corner of the cloth to show the presence of pies and bottles. "Capricia was to come with you, but she was called away for another errand."

Jackson was pleased; he found Capricia tiresome, with her braying laugh and exaggerated self-confidence. He had still to ask Jessamine about the behaviour of the other women, perhaps he would get the chance today.

They reached the gatehouse. "Good morning to you," said the uniformed man on duty. "Not the best day for a picnic." He pulled a lever and the gates swung open.

Chapter 6

Right up to that moment, Jackson had not thought this time would ever come. To start with, food and peace from bullying were his only hopes from this new life. The training had been useful information; he was stronger and less naive now, better able to survive. To be allowed outside was a bonus. Prior to his encounter with Langdon, he had almost put the idea from his mind.

Yet having sat on the top of the wall and seen the world, he had found a renewed longing. Then he had entertained the idea of escape, that had changed as he had learned more, he felt like his new friends were now the family he could barely remember. To leave them now, for an uncertain life alone, was not a sensible idea. Yet, he still yearned for freedom, he would see how the day progressed and decide later.

Taking Jessamine's hand, Jackson slipped nervously through the gate. For the first time in six years, he was in the outside world. It started to rain, Jessamine pulled a small cylinder from her basket.

"What is that?" Jackson asked as she flicked the end of it downwards. "'Tis an Umbell," she replied as it opened out into a large shield. She held it aloft. "Take my arm and walk close to me," she said.

Jackson did so, feeling comforted by the contact. He felt protected, in this strange world. There was ample room for them both to shelter beneath it. Jackson could hear the rain falling on its surface. "Oswald invented it; rather he copied it from the sunshade used in the Spice Islands. His version is a lot easier to carry and is also waterproof." They walked down the alleyway and around a corner.

He blinked, what were all these things? There seemed to be so much more of everything than he remembered.

Huge vehicles, belching steam and black smoke roared past him, filled with crates of goods, or seated people. There was a distinct lack of equines. The last time he had been in the city, they were still providing the majority of motive power. Equines had pulled trams and carts, driven machines by walking in circles attached to shafts. Now there were hardly any in sight, the ones that were visible had heavy blinkers and seemed to be protected from the bustle of modern life.

If they had not been, surely they would surely have been terrified by the racket and bolted. The smell of sweat and manure had been replaced by that of coal and combustion.

The machines had changed in the time he had been inside too, they had become less, he struggled for the word, amateurish. They were better finished, less obvious in their mechanics, even graceful, in a way.

There were Exo-men, the walking machines, oversized, faceless men, he remembered them well enough. They strode purposefully about, carrying huge loads or performing tasks, closely attended by their generators, the operators hung in their harness, limbs waggling furiously.

He saw groups of soldiers and sailors in uniforms, women in fine gowns and the usual assortment of beggars, street urchins and hawkers, shouting of their wares. Strange and enticing smells came from the stalls of street food sellers.

Behind the walls, there was naught but the distant hum of life, close-up it assaulted Jackson's unprepared senses, like a physical thing. He stopped still, aghast at the racket. Jessamine seemed not to notice; he felt his arm pulled by her.

"Come on," she shouted, "we need to see what we have come to see, 'twill not wait for us."

They jumped on to one of the cable-trams; at least they were familiar to him. Jessamine pushed at a button on the Umbell's handle and it collapsed into the small cylinder shape. How did it do that? he wondered.

There was a jolt as the tram's motion clamps engaged with the moving cable beneath the street and they set off. Jackson was thrown against Jessamine and together they tumbled into a seat. Jackson had thought that her body would be hard, from the muscle she so obviously possessed; he was surprised to find it pleasantly soft. Blushing, he pulled away and they sat side-by-side in silence.

"I remember these," he said, "from when I was... before."

"They are old now, and replaced by the aerialway, look up." They rounded a corner and Jackson saw the line of pillars marching away into the distance. Running between them, a long track extended across the sky. Jackson could see where the buildings had been altered to make way for its advance.

There were stations located in the sides of them, places where the line was doubled to allow passing and the sudden shadow as a carriage moved in front of the sun. It was beautiful, almost magical.

How does it work?" he asked.

"I don't really know; you'll have to ask Oswald. There is some sort of gear arrangement on the track; an engine in the carriage drives a cog that engages on the rail, like the cogs in a clockwork. We can ride on one later, if you wish."

Considering she claimed ignorance, Jackson could picture the workings perfectly from her description. He added a trip on the aerialway to the list of things he desired. What else could be better than a ride above the city, over the river? It would be like travelling in a flying machine.

"Anyway," Jessamine continued, "today is a day away from work, as far as possible. We must enjoy ourselves. Although we have a place to go, Langdon has told me that I should also show you around the city, so that you can see how it has changed. Then, we will have luncheon in the park and go to visit a most useful person, someone who will be a great help to you, if ever you're in need."

Jackson savoured the sights and sounds, the noise of conversation, the squeal of tram wheels as the thick wire cables dragged them along. As he got more used to his situation, he spotted a few equines still clopping on the cobbles. To his surprise, they seemed less bothered by all the noise than he was.

They disembarked near the main square, close to the river. The rain had ceased, the clouds thinned and parted, allowing sunshine to brighten up the dark buildings. Jessamine led him around the city, pointing out the landmarks, some of which he remembered from happier times, days out with this mother. Others were new to him, places they were intending to visit, before the accident that had changed everything.

He saw the great buildings of state, where decisions were taken that shaped the world. Victory Square, the wide-open space on the north of the River Norland, with the great promenade along the shore. The bridges of Stafford, Maloney and Giles, brick arches stood solid in the raging torrent. And all the while, Jessamine explained how everything fitted together in the scheme of Langdon's machinations.

"Langdon keeps a network of houses, all over the city," Jessamine said. "On a map in your belt, when you get it, will be a list. If you are in danger or outside and unable to return, you should be safe in any one of them."

She took him up First Avenue, where the rich and famous had their town houses, past the theatres and gaming rooms, then they were in the Aldondo, the home of the most exclusive shops and emporia. Jackson's mother had cherished the idea of one day browsing the fine clothes and jewellery, so far beyond her means. He felt his chest tighten at the memory of her, blinked back a tear.

"Now we have to get the most important job done," she said, as they stood outside the premises of Hardspill and Walker, tailors to gentlefolk.

"You are to be measured for suitable clothing. That is a part of today's purpose; you need to be outfitted to pass as a gentleman, or as a tradesman. Sir Mortimer keeps an account here."

"Is it Mortimer or Sir Mortimer?" asked Jackson. "You call him by both."

"He is Sir Mortimer, the last king but one honoured him, for what he will not say. In normal conversation, Mortimer; or even Langdon is sufficient. He always says that he is unconcerned about his honorific. That there are others more deserving. He is a modest man, and a patriot too." There was true affection in her tone.

Inside the shop, Jackson was treated was greeted with an array of waxen, faceless, model men; arranged in lifelike poses. They were clad in all manner of garments. An assistant provided a chair for Jessamine, a cup of Char and a journal to read, while Jackson was taken away and thoroughly measured. He was made to strip to his under things as two men with tapes gauged the size of his every part.

They called out a string of numbers to a third who recorded them all in a small book. The only words uttered were 'raise your arms,' and, 'lower them.'

Finally, he dressed and returned to Jessamine, who was in conversation with a female assistant. She had a book, with pages made of cloth and was pleased to see him.

"Jackson, what do you think of these patterns?" she asked. "You will need three suits, as well as shirts, hats and accoutrements. Oh, and clothes for walking the land and labouring."

Jackson didn't know what to say, he had one set of clothes, the idea that different ones were needed for different functions was beyond him. He was about to say so when he was saved by the assistant.

"Shall we make up the collection as we did for Sir Mortimer's last apprentice?" he asked.

"Yes, that would be the best plan," Jackson replied. He realised that he had learned another lesson. When in doubt, say as little as possible and wait for clues.

"The clothes will be made up and sent to the usual place," the assistant said, and they were free to leave.

In a daze, Jackson walked down the street. "That was a terrifying experience," he said. "To be measured like that, I felt as if I was being judged, like a prize bovine in some country fair. And what do I know of which clothes are for what function."

Jessamine laughed; Jackson was becoming used to that laugh. Unlike Capricia's bray, it was a pleasant sound. He liked the way her mouth turned as she laughed and now that he thought, he realised that he was trying to make it happen as much as he could.

"You did well, agreeing that they do what they had done before; it was clever not to show your ignorance. I think Cofé is in order; here is a favourite place of mine."

She led him across the busy road, dodging between the trams and mobiles. Ahead was a place calling itself the Excelsior Char Rooms, its long frontage one great sheet of clear glass. As they peered through it, Jackson could see inside that people were taking Char and Cofé, eating small cakes and talking. He vaguely remembered the name. "Isn't this a famous place?"

"You remembered," she said. "Yes, this is the very place frequented by Aphra Claringbold in the early days of the Ladies who Lunch. She is a hero of mine."

Jackson remembered the name from one of the lectures, it had been back at the start of his training and at first, he thought it of little interest or relevance to him. He recalled that when he had heard it, he had almost been asleep with boredom.

He decided that it would not be a good idea to reveal that he could remember little save the name. After all, he had changed his attitude toward absorbing knowledge soon after.

"Well then," he said, "we must go in and take a cup of Cofé."

"You're right, the rest of the day is ours, now that we have performed that duty. We have to meet Clarry this after, but that is a long time away."

Chapter 7

They went inside and a waitress found them a table. Jackson looked at the menu, then saw the prices. "How will we pay? I have no money," he said.

Jessamine laughed again. "It's alright, I have money."

"How? Did Sir Mortimer give it to you for today?"

A shadow crossed her face. "It's not polite to ask how a lady obtains her money," she said. "However, this time I will tell you. Some of the work I do for Sir Mortimer involves being paid for services rendered. If I did not take the money offered, it would throw suspicion on my true motives."

Jackson understood. "Forgive me, I did to mean to pry. I suppose you mean paid employment, in shops or offices, whilst obtaining information."

"You understand it completely," she said. "But remember, it's impolite to enquire." The waitress returned and Jessamine ordered Cofé and cakes for them both.

"You are one of us now," she said.

He nodded. "Thank you, it feels good to know that I am a part of something again. What of the future? Will I soon be off on some daring escapade?"

"I don't think of the future," she said, "none of us do. We are alive, we function in the moment. We all know that each day could be our last. There is no point in dreaming of a future, there are no old agents. It might be best if you did the same, enjoy every day, wring as much from it as there is, but never expect a tomorrow. When you wake, it will be a bonus."

Listening to her, she seemed old beyond her years, what things had she seen to make her think that way? Was it because Enoch was lying close to death, or was there more?

"I want to get away," said Jackson, giving voice to his dreams.

She grew agitated, grabbed his hand across the table. "You cannot," she hissed, causing others to look at them. "You have sworn an oath."

Just then, the waitress appeared with a trolley, on which sat an array of cups and pots. There was also a three-tiered glass and metal stand, filled with dainty cakes and morsels of refined cacao in paper cases. "Shall I pour?" the waitress asked.

"No, I can manage," replied Jessamine. The atmosphere crackled with tension; Jackson knew that he should not have said it but wondered at the ferocity of her response. Obviously annoyed, Jessamine poured them both Cofé and selected a cake.

He laughed, "What of it, oaths are made to be broken, the great and the good break them all the time."

"Jackson, let me tell you about Rufus Seymour. He was once one of us and he thought the same. He vanished one day, after he had been trained. He is the reason why you do not have your own quip-belt, he took his and all the other trappings when he went."

She took a sip of her Cofé. Jackson did too, it was delicious, it could have been another thing entirely to the drink they called Cofé in the orphanage.

"Langdon flew into a rage, I'd never seen him so angry, 'ungrateful wretch', he said, he got us all outside looking, even Patching and Clarry, the man you will be meeting later. We turned the city upside down. Eventually we found him, cornered him in a disused warehouse by the docks."

"What happened?" asked Jackson, although he half knew what she would say.

"It was awful. Patching did it, we were all made to watch. He was as casual as if he were killing a porker for our lunch. It must have been nothing to him. 'Let that be a lesson to you all', Langdon said when it was done, 'if you're not in; then this is the only way out'."

There was real anguish on her face. "Be warned, Jackson, I would be loath to see the same happen to you. But if we had to, we would find you and do it, without a second thought."

Jackson tried to rescue the situation, explain that he had changed his mind. "I said that I wanted to, not that I would. That was my initial thought; I saw all this as a way to gain my freedom, now I'm not so sure."

"That's wise; now eat your cakes, before I take yours as well as mine. They are delicious."

Jackson tried one of the cacao squares; he had not tasted the substance since before he had been in the orphanage. It was as he remembered it, melting slowly on his tongue, its sweetness filling his senses.

"If days like this are on offer, I would be mad to run," he said, taking another sip of his drink. "There is all this talk of work, but when? And what? Is it all spying and secret meetings?"

"Who knows?" she said. "All we can do is wait for the call. There is always some intrigue in progress, someone bent on disrupting the governance of the country, by money or secrets, men seek power and our life as a nation is ever under threat."

"What are the most interesting things you have done?"

"I wondered when you would want to know about my exciting life," she said. "Well, I have been on a ship through a fierce storm, jumped from Rail Rydes, been chased by canines and had many other adventures." It sounded exciting; in his mind, Jackson has glimpses of doing the same.

Then she went back to seriousness. "But there is one part of this work that I will not reveal, the part concerning my dealings with men. You will hear of things that might seem callous or beyond the bounds of respectable behaviour. I will only say this once; I've done things that you might not approve of. I'm not ashamed of any of it, I did it all in the name of Norlandia and I would do it again if I thought it would keep my country safe. More than that, I will not discuss."

As she finished he saw that her hand was shaking as she placed her cup down. The delicate material rattled against the saucer. He had never considered the toll that clandestine work might take on mind as well as body.

"I will not judge you," he said as kindly as he could, taking her hand, feeling the tremor subside. "Although this is a new world for me and I find it strange, the casual attitudes to life and death; to mind and body... well, they are not what I feel comfortable with at present. I will try to understand."

She looked at him across the table, he saw tears welling up. "If you stay with us, you will want for nothing," she muttered.

"Except freedom?"

"Freedom? Look around. Who is truly free? We all have responsibilities, things that tie us. You have to decide where you are contented."

"It sounds as if I have little choice in the matter. I have either to live and be content here or spend my life on the run, hunted by those who used to be friends."

"It's not a bad life, with all its faults. Once you accept that your time may be short, you take the maximum pleasure from each day, take every chance for enjoyment that is offered to you."

They finished their Café in silence, Jackson wanted to ask so much, but could not find the words. Jessamine paid at the desk and they left, catching a tram across the Stafford Bridge.

They strolled through the more genteel suburbs of the south side of the city. There were huge houses, behind stone walls, with wrought iron clockwork gates, manned by old soldiers. Then they came upon rows of well-kept terraced houses, with neat gardens and brightly painted doors. It was a world away from the bustle of the north side. The mood had changed between them, it was now more serious; he felt uncomfortable. If only he had not mentioned his thoughts of escape.

"I'm sorry, I was stupid," he said. "I should never have said it."

"Said what?" she asked.

"That I wanted to leave, it has spoiled the day."

"Don't be silly," she replied. "We all wanted to leave at some point. It's not that, just some memories stirred up by our conversation. I should not allow them to intrude. I will banish them to the back of my mind."

They reached the end of the houses, beyond them, a vast expanse of green, dotted with small buildings and groups of people. "This is the great park," she said, "a place of recreation and enjoyment, let's sit for a moment, we can have our luncheon."

They strolled among the trees, climbing a small hill, sitting finally against the bole of a huge querca. "There are so many of these glorious trees," Jessamine said, "of great age now that the navy no longer wants them for its ships."

Jackson felt the power in the tree; he relaxed for the first time since he could remember, here and now, there was no threat, no need for caution. He began to see what Jessamine had meant when she had said take every moment, and that even if he wasn't free, this would be as good a way as any to live.

"When was the last time that you went outside those walls?" Jessamine asked.

"I've been at the Orphanage for six years," he replied. "I had a normal life, till my parents died."

She gasped. "It must have been so awful, to have been with a family, then not."

Jackson nodded. "With my parents dead there was nobody, save an aunt, to take me in. She had no husband or children and quickly tired of caring for me. We argued all the time, then one day, I decided that I was leaving, to take my chances on my own. It happened that was the day she had sold me."

Jessamine looked surprised. "Sold you?"

"Yes, she had sold me to a man who supplied workers for the Rail Ryde company. People who dug tunnels and built brick bridges. They had paid her to take me off her hands. No doubt they were hoping to make the cost back by using me to build something."

"What happened?" Jessamine had heard of the forced labour gangs; men were desperately needed in the rapid expansion of the rails and the roads. To begin with, she had thought that only convicts were made to work in such conditions.

The men were worked like canines, till they dropped, then they were stripped of any valuables and buried where they fell.

Children were especially prized for their ability to get into small spaces and lay blasting charges in mines and rail tunnels. To have it confirmed that men were buying children to turn a profit didn't surprise her; after working for Langdon, little was left that could shock.

Jackson was still telling his tale. "They had me and several others in the back of a mobile, the driver was drunk, we were swerving all over the road. The Watch gave chase and we were all pleased, with luck it meant an end to our captivity. But the driver would not stop, he just laughed and drove faster. We saw nothing of his route, only our pursuers first gaining, then losing ground on us. In the end, we crashed into a wall and turned over, the back door opened. Before the Watch arrived, everyone else had run away, I had hit my head and was dazed. The Watch brought me to the orphanage."

"That's a terrible tale," she said, "and as much as any of my adventures. My childhood was boring, my mother died in childbirth, my father remarried, his new wife did not like me. She put me into the orphanage whilst he was away, serving in the army somewhere. To be honest, I was glad to be away from her. I miss my father terribly, I know not if he lived through the wars, I suspect not, as he has never returned to find me. It saddens me; the last I saw of him was when he marched off, in his uniform."

So they were both bruised by life. "But now we have a family," she said. "As good as any made of blood." She got up. "Come, let's gaze on the city."

She set off again, through the trees they came to a clearing, they had swung around and were now facing back towards the river. Jessamine sat Jackson down on the grass, it felt as soft as silk, the warm air was on his face and below him he could see the river and the city on the north shore. All the smoke from the multitude of chimneys was blown away, over the sea.

She spread the cloth on the ground and set out their luncheon. Jackson looked around, there were many other such scenes, this was the life he remembered. There was a pie and bread, some tomatoes and apples and a bottle of Mrs Grimble's lemonade.

They ate in silence for a while, Jackson gazing around at the city spread out below them, the sunshine on the river and in the distance, the sea.

They ate and chatted about trivialities; the talk of their childhoods had changed the mood again. Jackson now felt able to broach the subject that had been bothering him. "You became cold to me, partway through my training, before you went away," he said.

"I'm sorry if I was distant," she said. "I was preparing myself for a mission, but couldn't tell you about it. I suppose that, as it was all new to you, you must have wondered what you had done."

"I thought that I was too forward, that night in the room when you dressed my wound."

She laughed. "You are naive, Jackson, maybe you were but that's not always a bad thing. I wanted to kiss you but knew that I had to resist. Langdon frowns upon such activities between his agents. When you get to know everyone better, you will see the reasons. Then I got involved in an investigation and had to concentrate on that."

"Then we are still friends?"

"Of course we are." She took his hand. "The best of friends." Jackson was pleased, it was a start; friends could always become more.

"In fact," she said, "now that you will have a little more time, there are things that I can teach you, that may help your new life."

"And what are they?" he asked. "Some more clandestine subterfuges?"

She laughed. "Oh no, this is pure pleasure. It may be that you will need to blend in socially. I will teach you to dance, play cards, engage in small conversations."

Jackson was relieved; he had fretted about his lack of social skills. Seeing how the other agents acted together had made him nervous of joining in, concerned that he may have to do or say anything that would show up his lack of etiquette.

"That will be fun, I need to know how to behave in company," he said. "It's all very well learning how to spy on folk if you can't mingle with them."

She gently touched his shoulder. "You should not fret, you will soon grasp the elements. It will be something to look forward to."

"I still can't believe what has happened to me," Jackson said, as he ate his pie. Pastry crumbs dropped to the ground and small birds came nervously to peck at them.

"I would guess that Langdon has had his eye on you for some time," she said, taking his hand. "There are always things that are coming to a head, things that he needs to investigate, and no doubt you are the perfect one to do something for him."

What are they? Jackson could not think how he could be useful; he was nobody special, an orphan, his parents dead in a factory accident, six years in an orphanage. How could he help in matters of national security, the like of which would interest a man like Langdon?

"Has he asked you about your home?" she asked.

"Yes, in Cobblebottom, I told him all of it."

"And your parents, their lives and works?"

"Everything. They worked in the Prosthesium, making artificial limbs for the government to dispense to war veterans and the like."

"Until an accident at the works killed them both," she said.

"How did you know that?" Jackson had never told anyone in the orphanage about his parents' deaths; the subject was too raw. Except for one person. "Langdon," he muttered, "Langdon told you."

She nodded. "Langdon spoke to me before I brought you out today. He has something in motion, I know not what it is but you are clearly important to it."

"And what else did Langdon say about me?" Jackson demanded, his voice rising.

She changed the subject. "Nothing, no need for suspicion, Jackson, this is how it works. We are a small group and it's better if we all know everything. Then nobody can use knowledge, or secrets, against us."

Jackson had to accept that explanation; in any event he did to want to spoil his renewed friendship. "What do we do now? You mentioned a meeting of some sort."

"Now we have eaten, I am taking you to meet a man called Clarence, although everyone knows him as Clarry. He is one of Langdon's men, living as a labourer. It's a good disguise; it allows him to be in all sorts of places without suspicion. He will tell us what is occurring on the streets, any little snippets of information."

They finished their food and set off, plunging into the streets of the artisans, with their wide pavements and genteel inhabitants. Jackson soon lost track of his bearings and had to hold Jessamine's hand as they went into the areas where the manual workers lived; not that he minded that.

Here the streets were narrower and more crowded, there were small furnaces and other works, the hiss of steam was ever present, clouds of the stuff billowed, disorientating him.

The smell of hot metal gave the place a sinister air as workmen pushed past him, clutching barrels and sacks. "Avoid eye contact," Jessamine advised. "Stay close to me."

In a matter of moments, he was totally lost; if he should he let go of her hand he would have no clue of his whereabouts.

Jessamine suddenly stopped short. "Wait a moment," she said. "I've dropped my glove. Stay here." She let go of his hand and hurried away. Jackson was alone in a dark alley. He could feel the eyes on him, from inside the blank windows. People jostled him as they passed, carrying bundles, carcasses of porker and goodness knew what.

"Get out of the way," one growled. Where was Jessamine? He should have gone with her. Jackson shrank into a doorway, to his surprise it opened.

Chapter 8

"Come here, boy," growled a voice. Jackson ignored it and tried to move back into the press of people in the street. "Boy, I'm talking to you," it repeated. Jackson could not get away, a man now stood in front of him and there was the sound of a gas-gun being readied to fire.

Before he could even move, Jackson was bundled into the dwelling, the door shut out the daylight.

They were in a workman's house, the carpet poor and walls stained with soot from badly trimmed gas lamps. A large man faced him, his huge arms folded over an ale drinker's belly.

There were three other men in the room; a large table held the remnants of a meal, the smell of cooked fowl was overlaid with that of grease and ale. They all looked up as Jackson appeared. "What you got there, Herbert?" asked the largest.

"Found 'im outside," Jackson's abductor said. He was so close to Jackson that he could smell the ale on his breath, feel the heat from his torso. "Might have a bit of money on 'im I suppose," said another. "Could be the Watch, spying on us," suggested the third.

"Put 'im in the chair." Hands grabbed him; Jackson suddenly woke up to his situation and started to struggle. The men surrounded him and forced him into a large armchair, his wrists and ankles were secured with rope.

At the last moment he had remembered his training, to make his body an awkward shape as they tied him, so that he would have slack in the bonds later. He braced his shoulders and legs against the chair, made himself as large as he could while they secured him.

Jackson was starting to wonder; was he not a spy? He supposed that he might be, or at least an apprentice one, although not for the Watch. Would it make any difference if he said he was working on a matter of national security?

No, he might be trained but he had no proof, no truncheons or quip-belt. Fairview had told him that if he was ever captured, he should endeavour not to volunteer information, to be calm and wait for a question. Then tell nothing, talk meaningless rubbish. How he wished that he had gone with Jessamine to find her stupid glove.

"Now then." Another man had come into the room; how many people lived here? wondered Jackson. This new arrival looked more like a leader than a follower, he was neatly dressed in a striped shirt and braces, with heavy corduroyed trousers. "What have you got for us, Mr Herbert?" he asked.

"He was loitering in the doorway; reckon he's up to no good."

"Well, were you, boy, up to no good?"

"No, sir," said Jackson, he felt relieved, this was all a misunderstanding. He could explain, they would let him go.

"My friend was showing me around the city, she dropped her glove. I stood in your doorway to keep out of the way of the traffic while she retrieved it."

His story was dismissed by the man. "Oh yes, a likely tale; you, a well-dressed man, here with a lady, or so you claim. Where is she, what does she look like?"

"She's tall, with a red gown and bonnet, she has a basket, it had our luncheon in it. She will be here shortly and wonder where I am."

"Boys, outside and look for the lady, you heard what she looks like. I want a chat with our new friend."

"Right you are," they said and departed, grinning.

Jackson was now alone with the man. He stood in front of the chair. The silence stretched. Jackson was determined not to speak first, to let the other ask the first question. Even so, he began to wonder if that was the right thing.

His abductor seemed to be considering his choices. Jackson pulled his hands against the rope, they were tight, but he felt a little room to wriggle. Even if he untied himself, he would be no match for the man.

"Your story is all wrong," the man finally spoke. "Nobody comes to this part of the city sightseeing, you're up to no good, at least as far as we are concerned. And you found us, that means you knew where to look."

"You have it all backwards." Jackson had decided on a plan. "You should have let me go, accepted that this was all a coincidence. Now you have admitted that you are worthy of scrutiny."

The man roared, "Ha! Is that the best you can muster? We must be guilty, or we would pretend innocence?" He moved forward and slapped Jackson's face. The chair rocked, Jackson saw stars. "And do you think it matters, you will never see the daylight again to tell."

He drew a knife from his belt, a butcher's knife, long bladed and thin. "See this blade? I spend all day turning porkers into food with this. You will join them, unless you tell me all the plans against us."

Jackson knew fear at that point. If he had been free, he could at least have tried to defend himself, as it was, he would be killed where he sat and his body disposed of with the rest of the offal from this man's trade. Why had he chosen that doorway?

"Why tell me of your plans then?" Jackson asked, surprised at how calm he sounded. The comment made no sense, he had been told no plans but he had been told to talk in riddles, to delay and to never reveal any useful information. At least Jessamine was free, provided the three did not catch her.

The man picked up a piece of wood from the table and stood in front of Jackson. He held it in one hand and the knife in the other. He started to whittle; as the knife worked its magic shavings flew from the wood.

"You will tell me why you came to this house," he said, "or your bones will be carved in the same way."

Jackson's bowels were churning and it was an effort to maintain control of them; he was sure his end was nigh. He knew not what to say; there was a commotion in the room beyond, a female scream.

"Looks like my boys have her then. I'll see if the lady is more open about your purpose." He left the knife and the room, shutting the door behind him.

Jackson relaxed his posture. Fairview's advice had been good, there was a little room in his bonds. He tried to move the chair across the room. He had an idea. The knife was tantalisingly close. If he could just lean over a little.

The chair toppled over, the crash brought the man back into the room. "Where do you think you're off to then?" he said, picking Jackson and the chair back up with one hand. "I'm just talking to your friend; she tells it different, I fancy that she's not as strong as you. Perhaps I should make you watch as I fillet her; it might loosen your tongue."

Jackson was silent; ignore the words, Patching had said, they are merely threats, pay attention only to actions. It felt like his plan had worked, the chair felt unstable, he had weakened the joints, would it be enough?

The knife still lay where it was, now he needed quiet. Hard though it was, he needed to get the man out of the room, whatever it meant for Jessamine. He could not help her yet, but if he could get free and have the knife, all things were possible.

"Go then," he said, "do your worst with her, make me watch if you must, it will not make me talk, I have nothing to say."

"You will change your tune when you hear her wail, see her blood flow and know you could stop it all with a word." The man left, slamming the door.

Jackson knew he had to be quick. He twisted his body and felt the chair's right arm detach from the frame. Lifting his wrist, he bit at his bonds. He managed to untie his hand. From then, it was a matter of moments to release his other limbs. Standing quietly, he felt elated. He was free and ready to rescue Jessamine or die in the attempt.

He picked the knife up from the table, moved to the door. There may be four men on the other side but that was immaterial if they were hurting Jessamine. His anger flared as he grabbed the handle and pushed the door open.

Chapter 9

He was in a deserted kitchen.

Cautiously he crept through the space; finding himself in a long corridor. He could hear noise from a room at the end. That must be where they had her. Holding the knife as Patching had shown, blade on top, finger underneath, he crept forward.

The door was ajar, the noise not like any interrogation he had imagined.

"Come on in, Jackson," said Langdon. What was he doing here? Perplexed, Jackson entered a drawing room, thick with brocades and lace. A brisk coal fire burned in the corner.

Langdon was sat in a high sided armchair sipping Char from a cup, the saucer balanced on his knee. Jessamine was talking to another lady, nibbling at some sort of cake. And the large man was stood by a table, which was laden with food.

"Hello again, Jackson," he said, extending one large hand. "I'm pleased to see that you're holding the knife correctly, but you can give it to me now." Jackson reversed the blade and handed it over

"Sit," ordered Langdon and Jackson complied; choosing a chair filled with plump cushions. He sank into its embrace and could bear it no longer. "Can someone explain what is going on?"

"Certainly," said Langdon, "and then a cup of Char. As you've probably gathered, this is one of my houses, where you will be safe. Now, let me make the introductions." The large man moved forward, no longer threatening, now he seemed like a favourite uncle. "You've already met this man; his name is Clarence Riggs."

The man smiled. "Pleased to meet you, sir, my apologies for the slap, it will all become clear in due course."

Jackson shook the hand, his fingers lost to sight. "This is another strange day, no offence taken. Since I met Sir Mortimer, my life gets stranger and stranger."

Clarence laughed. "I reckon it has, and I would not be surprised if there were not more strangeness to come; your friend Jessamine is drinking Char with Mrs Riggs."

The other lady looked up at him and smiled, she had been turned away and he had not seen her face properly. "Hello again, Jackson," said Mrs Grimble.

"We wanted to see how you would respond to the threats against you and Jessamine," said Langdon, "see if our training was bearing fruit."

"And were you content, Sir Mortimer?" asked Mrs Grimble, or Riggs or whatever she was called.

"I was, Jackson is turning into a resourceful young man," he replied. "You have been working hard, with no end in sight. Jessamine and others tell me that you are learning quickly. It's time for you to have a little freedom and something to reward your efforts."

Jessamine spoke, "We are to go to the entertainments tonight. Clarence will get us tickets for entrance and Langdon has provided a little money for food and sundries."

Clarence smiled. "I know the man on the entrance gate; he receives treats from me and in return, knows when to look away."

"Thank you, sir," Jackson said, before today, he would have taken his chance to slip away and disappear forever. He had been ready to try for freedom, there were places he could go, they would never find him.

Now, after all that had happened, he had changed his mind. He considered Jessamine. He knew that there was something about her, life without her, on the run, would be unbearable. He had a sudden vision of Patching, stood over him, Jessamine watching.

Yet as he thought it, he had the feeling that Langdon knew his plan, could see inside his head. Perhaps this was also part of the test.

"What are these entertainments?" Jackson asked.

Clarence gave him a strange look. "Have you never heard of them?"

"I recall something, are they not a fair of some sort? Remember, I have been in the orphanage for six years, I know little about the modern world."

"No wonder then," Clarry replied. "Yes, they are a fair of sorts, but there is so much more. You did well today but the times coming need strong men, doers as well as thinkers, I hope you're a quick study."

"I will take care of him," Jessamine replied.

"I believe you will," Mrs Grimble said. "Then he is in safe hands."

"Jessamine," Clarry said in a worried tone, "changing the subject, I heard about Enoch. What happened?"

"He wasn't as careful as he could have been, Jackson is his replacement," Langdon said.

"Gawd help us all then," replied the man. "Now where's that Char?"

The three left Langdon and Mrs Grimble in discussion and shortly arrived at the great park, on the other side to the place where Jackson and Jessamine had lunched. Here was a permanent exhibition of the wonders of the world, chiefly a showcase of Norlandian talents and enterprise, but with exhibits from all countries.

The man on the gate gave them both pieces of card with the word 'Unlimited Admission' printed on them.

"These are today's, Clarry," he said, pocketing the small bottle. "They can get into most places with them, no questions asked."

Clarry handed them the tickets. "You have a good evening. It was a pleasure to meet you, Jackson." He shook his hand again. "Well done in your test, now enjoy your reward."

The entertainments were a sprawling area in the park, enclosed by a tall wire fence, dotted with gawping children. The place was packed with people, with lines of tents and mechanical contraptions.

As they had walked past the fence on their way to the entrance, Jackson had caught glimpses of what was on offer. There were huge steam powered carousels, thrill rides with blaring music from a contraption that sounded like nothing he had ever heard. Everywhere was the smell of fried foods and ale, he saw brightly dressed marching bands and exotic animals. There were fire-eaters, jugglers and magicians, stalls with games of skill and chance, even a Drogan, a sullen looking beast in a huge steel cage.

Now they were inside, they wandered up and down the rows. "Let's ride on that," Jessamine shouted, as they passed a thing that Jackson saw as a vision of some nightmare. A large wooden platform rotated at speed and upon it were what looked like half-barrels with seats. They also rotated, swung by a man who balanced on the boards and moved among them.

They showed their tickets and were placed in one of the barrels. The sensations it produced were violent, but Jessamine laughed and after a while he too found it exhilarating. The best part of it was the way they were pushed together by the forces. Jackson revelled in the contact, felt the heat from her body.

Then, as they staggered from that, she insisted on riding a thing like a miniature Rail Ryde. Carts were pulled to the top of a slope by a steam engine. There they were released to ride a track that looped and turned sharply. They were only kept from falling by a leather belt, gravity meant that they often left the seats and were held by it.

This was more exciting than the last one, especially when they held hands and shrieked at the acceleration down the slopes.

Next, Jackson tried his hand at a game where hard balls were thrown at targets. The rewards were toy animals made of felted cloth, the like of which he had never seen before. He imagined them to be a product of the stallholder's dreams.

In the event, he won a splendid looking Macquette, at least that was what the stallholder said as he handed it over. "It's a beast from the Spice Islands," he explained. "Never seen in real life by the people of this land." It was simian in form, orange in colour with exaggerated limbs and a fixed grin.

Jessamine held it to her chest. "Thank you, Jackson," she said and impulsively hugged him. Again, Jackson felt the softness of her against him and the smell of fresh flowers from her hair.

The smells of fresh foods, exotic and spicy, drew them towards an area filled with stalls, all selling different comestibles.

"Try this," Jessamine suggested, pulling Jackson to one manned by a tall, bearded fellow in the garb of the Spice Islands, all multicoloured robes, a bushy beard and gold rings on fingers and in his ears.

"Greetings," he said. "Would you have some of my Khorri?"

"What is that?" asked Jackson, all he could smell was overlaid spice and oil. "A meat and allium stew, heavily spiced and served in a rolled bread," the man explained.

Jackson tried it; there may have been flavour but the spice brought tears to his eyes.

Jessamine laughed at his discomfort. "'Tis an acquired taste?" she said, as his eyes watered and he felt himself flush.

"Water," he eventually managed to gasp. The stallholder smiled. "Water will make it worse, young sir," he said. "You need plain Char to counter the effects."

He passed Jackson a small glass of the liquid and Jackson gulped it down. It was true, he felt less affected and he took another bite. This one tasted different, more flavour than heat. "I'm starting to like this," he said, while the stallholder smiled.

As they strolled on through the seemingly endless stalls, darkness fell and they came to a huge glass and metal structure, rising above the trees and lit from within. "That's the Palais of Curiosities," Jessamine exclaimed. "I've been in here before. Come, Jackson, you must see it."

"What is it? Some sort of theatre?"

"It's an exhibition, of all the new inventions and discoveries from all nations, under one roof. There is a separate hall for statics; you will love it – as long as you can keep your hands from touching the wires."

"That was unfair, I was tricked," he replied.

"I know, we all have been on the receiving end of that trick at some time."

They showed their tickets and went through the entrance. Inside, the floor was covered in wooden boards, through which trees grew, as well as the metal pillars that supported the glass roof.

Everywhere was hung with gas lights; the whole effect was akin to being in an enchanted forest.

The crowds were less, Jackson recalled from one of the lectures that Fairview had said science frightened a lot of people, they saw it as magical and somehow not to be trusted.

"Will there be things that we could purchase?" he asked. She shook her head.

"Oh no, it's not that sort of display. Anyway, Oswald has all we need, he keeps his eye on the latest developments. Indeed he is responsible for many of them. The scientific community all share each other's ideas and we get all the latest equipment before the public knows of it. If you see something you find interesting, remember it and tell him when we return."

Chapter 10

If Jackson had been surprised at the land outside the orphanage, then the Palais was another revelation. Here were wonders from the very reaches of the globe. There were folk from foreign lands and things that were claimed to have never before been seen in Norlandia.

"The displays change every month," she explained, "as new wonders are discovered or invented. Oswald comes here for ideas and to show some of the devices he has made. Businesses buy his inventions, the money he makes helps pay for our operations. Did I mention that there's a whole part of the building dedicated to statics? Apparently they are the coming thing."

She was clearly excited by the Palais, she was repeating herself. Jackson could understand why. He found it hard to take it all in.

First, they saw the displays of machinery, devices of every type were on show, together with an army of men and women demonstrating them to onlookers.

There was a mechanical calculator, where numbers were manipulated by the turn of a crank. The hardest problems could be solved. Jackson spoke to the inventor, who declined to explain the workings. He promised that he was working on a more advanced version, driven by clockwork, that could do ever more complex calculations with speed and ease.

He also hoped to reduce the size, eventually producing a machine that might be carried in the palm of the hand and slipped into a pocket.

It sounded preposterous, but the man's enthusiasm made it feel possible. "With this machine to help us," he said, "we can build ever more complex machines, by testing the theories and proving the science more quickly. Think of what might be achieved."

They passed by stands showing machines to automate the business of farming, all manner of attachments for the farm-mobile, a version of the new conveyance but with a continuous belt of hinged metal along each side instead of wheels, designed for use on muddy or rough ground. Machines that could sow and plough, plant and harvest, even ones that took a live fowl at one end and produced a plucked and drawn carcass at the other. There seemed to be no limit to man's ingenuity.

Then he saw a thing that seemed almost too impossible, even for this place. It was called the Rotaplane, a strange looking version of a flying machine, more an elongated wingless bubble, with two giant propellers on top of the body, one at each end. The demonstrator was extolling its virtues.

"The Rotaplane needs no field," he said. "Indeed, it can depart from any flat surface vertically. Witness this model, at one twentieth actual size. It is exact in every detail, save that the model's engine is driven by clockwork, instead of burning gas."

He attached the model on a vertical wire and released the spring. Both propellers rotated quickly, almost before the man could move his hand, the model rose up the wire, yawing gently as it did.

"That was amazing," said Jackson. "Jessamine, did you see this contraption?"

"There is more control in the real thing," said the man as Jessamine came over to stand by them. "We cannot fit all the controls into the model, hence the wire."

"It's very impressive," Jessamine said. "I suppose the propellers spin in opposite directions to balance out the rotational forces?"

The man was stunned. "Hardly anybody notices that; you are correct, madam. Tell me, are you an engineer of some sort?"

"No," she replied, "just a student and observant."

"Well, if you ever want a more technical discussion, then please seek me out," he said and handed her a small card. "My address is on there," he added.

"Thank you," she replied. "I will consider it."

Jackson waited until they had moved away from the stall. "He was attracted to you," he said.

Jessamine laughed. "He was, and I fancy he would expect more than a discussion about rotational forces from me; if I were to accept his offer."

She tore the card in two and threw the pieces into a small receptacle by the path. "He was not my type," she said enigmatically. She took Jackson's arm. "Let us visit the statics display."

After the visible wonders of the mechanical, the room of statics was a different place. Lit by Wasperton-Byler globes it had the quiet, contemplative air of a library. Here was no grease or complex moving hunks of metal. Instead, white-coated men wrote long sentences of what looked like children's scribblings on large sheets of paper, then argued over them. There were fewer items on display, a lot more drawings and ideas.

But there was one thing that caught Jackson's eye. A torch worked by what the handbill described as a 'friction motor'. It was demonstrated and threw a beam of light that could be varied, from a pin-point to a wide arc. It was charged by compressing the handle. "The workings are secret," whispered the woman who was demonstrating the device. "I cannot tell you; the details are protected by government order."

"She doesn't know how it works," Jessamine declared behind her hand. "I will speak to Oswald, he will know, they would be a useful addition to our equipment."

Just then Jackson heard a clock strike ten bells of the evening. "Should we not be going back?" he asked.

"Only if you wish," she replied. "We are not bound by Skies and his curfew. There is another entrance, direct to our sleeping quarters. We have a special key."

That was a relief; Jackson had visions of arriving at a locked gate and having to climb the wall again. They spent another hour exploring, then caught the tram back to the orphanage, sharing it with groups of revellers returning from a night's entertainment.

There was high spirited talk, singing and camaraderie among them, helped in no small part by the ale and wine they had consumed. They had parcels of fried foods and opened bottles that they passed around between the passengers, continuing their revelries. They were rowdy but good-natured and insisted on Jessamine and Jackson partaking of their repast. Jackson was offered a small piece of the food. He found that it was a sort of piscine, cooked in spiced breadcrumbs. It was delicious. Jessamine declined, but in such a charming way that no offence could be taken.

When they arrived at the orphanage, they walked past the closed gates and sleeping watchman in his hut. Around the corner, Jackson saw a recess in the wall, with a stout black door.

To one side was a small silver box. "This is the lock," explained Jessamine, "one of Oswald's devices. You have to enter a number; it changes every day."

"How do we know it?"

"'Tis simple, when you are ready to work, you will be given a number, you use it, and the day's date, my number is seven and today is the fourteenth of the month, so I enter seven and then fourteen. The lock opens, I am recorded as entering.

Oswald keeps a record of who uses the door. That, and the man in the gatehouse, confirms where everyone is. We are not all together very often; many of us are out working, we don't all come home for tea at four."

"I suppose not." The door opened onto the small courtyard where Jackson had first met Jessamine, the night they had climbed the wall. Across it and up the steps and they were in the pantry.

Alyious was sat in the classroom, his head in his hands.

"Enoch is dead," he said. "He succumbed this morning, just after you left. There will be a meeting to decide what we must do to avenge him, Vyner is distraught. I'm sorry, Jackson, but this is a thing that does not concern you. Please leave us to grieve and discuss this in private."

Jackson was shocked; he mumbled, "Of course, I'm so sorry. Thank you for today," he said to Jessamine. Her face had disolved into a mask of tears and anguish, her shoulders shaking with sobs. Alyious moved to hug and console her.

Not really knowing what else to do, he returned to his room. There was a lot for him to think about, this day had given him much to mull over before he could sleep.

Jackson sat on his bed, his good mood forgotten. This was no longer a game, people died doing what he was learning to do. At least he had more training to undergo, and maybe a few more pleasant trips outside, before he got involved in anything dangerous.

That was all very well, he realised. Jessamine was correct in what she had said. She was involved, she could be in danger at any time. He could not leave her now.

Interlude

The Professor shook his head as he looked at the corpse on the operating table; there was no sympathy in his expression, only annoyance. Why did they keep dying?

He had proved that the modification to the prosthetic arm worked, after much trial and effort he had found an implant that worked perfectly. There had been many versions of his initial idea that had not, they would have to be retrieved and exchanged for the ones that had.

Fortunately, he had a plan and a method for doing just that. With the mechanical version now having an unblemished success rate, he had a large number of unsuspecting individuals, scattered across the city and beyond, who could be controlled, their limbs switched on and off, at the touch of a button on his Sensaurum.

With that knowledge, it should have been simple for him to transfer his process to humans, after all the physiology was identical, just flesh instead of metal.

It was only the same as the work involved in fitting a prosthetic limb, attaching wires to nerves. It was proven science, done a thousand times. Maybe more delicate, as it involved the brain itself but nothing that could not be done. In his mind, there was no reason why it did not work in every case.

He had bought time with his initial success, just as he had when he had worked with Professor Woolon. The process had been shown to work, even his present employer, a non-scientist, could see the logic and agree that the transition to implantation in humans was possible.

The crucial difference was that his present employer was more tolerant of his failures, less bothered about the human cost. True there were successes, but more than half of his subjects never regained consciousness or if they did, were unable to function. There was no logic or pattern to suggest which would live and which would not.

Thanks to some method that he would rather not know about, there was a steady stream of volunteers, so he could practise to his heart's content, keep copious notes and try to repeat the successes. He had asked; but had been told that a record of the failures was not required; they were removed, that was sufficient.

He heard the door open and the squeak of a badly oiled wheel. Why could they not oil the thing? It reminded him of his failures, the successes were taken to recover on the bed they had been operated on, the squeaking wheel indicated failure. And if he had heard it, his employer must have. How much more patience would he exhibit?

"Another one for the porkers, Prof?" asked the man pushing the trolley. His mate laughed. He said that every time and it irritated him. He would love to operate on that man, he thought, it would be nice to be able to stop him saying that, treating the dead with such little respect.

He nodded and they loaded the still warm body onto their trolley. It squeaked away and shortly after, the frenzied squeals told him that it was gone forever.

He pulled off his gloves and mask. After passing instructions to his assistants to clean everything and prepare for the next subject, he left the operating room by the other door. He went to the ward, where the latest of the survivors were resting and checked with the nurses that they were all well.

There were minor infections in some of the wounds, these he treated. In all other respects they were healing nicely, their mental functions undamaged. Then he crossed the corridor to his employer's office.

"Another failure," he said, after he had been admitted. "I was unable to attach to the spinal cord this time. Shock did the rest."

"No matter." The other man was in good spirits. "Have you any more subjects to experiment on?"

"No," replied the Professor. "That was the last. We had fewer failures with this last batch, less than four of every ten. That is better but still too high for my understanding. When last I spoke, your associate told me that he will shortly be on the way with another charabanc load. I'm having everything cleaned thoroughly; we can try again when he gets here."

The man nodded. "That is encouraging news; you are obviously solving the problem. However, there has been a change of plans, we return to the city in the morning. I have a legitimate business to run as well as all this; I have neglected it for too long."

That explained his employer's good humour, his lady and children were in the city, they had been away for several weeks. The Professor had no such female attachment, he found himself unable to cope with their emotions; hated being with many of them for more than his pleasure.

To his annoyance, so often the ones that he was attracted to failed to enjoy the same things that he did. Fortunately, his employer understood this and knew where to procure those who would not complain. A return to the city would suit him as well, at least in that respect.

He disliked the dark room at the top of the factory that served as his workroom in the city, it felt like a prison compared to this place, deep as it was in the countryside.

"I'm sorry about the failures," he said. "I can't see what to do differently. It's so frustrating."

"It's not a problem, I understand." His employer was definitely in a good mood. "You have already provided me with more than enough to start; my plans can be put in motion with what we already have. Once you have mastered the next step, we can advance until our final objective is in sight. And, looking on the bright side, nothing is wasted. We have fine porkers to sell at market."

There it was again, the lack of respect. Feeling powerless to complain, the Professor said nothing, save to excuse himself. With no new subjects to operate on, the Professor left the room and went first to his chief assistant. He told him that he would be in charge whilst he was gone and made sure that he understood the state of all the recovering patients.

Next, he went to his laboratorium. He spent an hour writing up his notes, then he packed everything he would need in the city. A lot of his equipment was duplicated there, but he had made modifications to his Sensaurum whilst here and needed to apply the changes to the ones in the factory. Apart from the surgery, the Sensaurum was the other, and in a way more demanding, part of the project.

It was a device designed to control the implanted objects by clever use of statics energy. He turned it on, watched the fine needle swing on its bearings as it detected the presence of implants in the people around him.

"Lexis," he said into the trumpet on top of the Sensaurum. Across the estate and in the ward next door, his surviving subjects stopped what they were doing and listened for his next command.

Chapter 11

There seemed to be something going on, the next day, at fast-breaker, there were only Jackson and Alyious present in the classroom. Fairview was also absent, the pair waited for a while but nobody appeared.

"Let's get down to the Gymnazien," suggested Alyious, "see if Patching is about, he might know what's occurring."

But the soldier was nowhere to be found.

"There's something big going on," Alyious said. "It's happened before, when one of us is killed, the order goes out to find the killers and mete out our own justice. Jessamine and the rest may have been called early, they will already be searching."

"Then why are you still here?" asked Jackson. "Myself I can understand, as I'm not trained yet, but you?"

"Someone has to be here, in case of a need and to assist you. I told Langdon yesterday, while you were out, that I would stand aside to let Vyner go. It's his right to avenge his friend. Winifred is upstairs, she is too upset to do much, her and Enoch were much more than friends. We will go to Mrs Grimble, she will know what to do."

But she was also absent. Alyious found a note by her desk. He read it in silence.

"Well, what's occurring?" asked Jackson as he read.

"As I thought, there is an effort underway to catch the people who murdered Enoch. Langdon is away on some new business, I'm to take you on a trip. You need to practise your fieldwork, we will play a game. We are going into the city. Go and get ready for adventure."

As Jackson prepared, he wondered at his luck, outside, two days running. And an adventure. He had completely forgotten about the idea of running away, this was the second time he had seen or heard of the retribution the group handed out. He was better off in, he had decided.

Alyious led Jackson onto the tram, this time they were heading in a different direction to his previous journey. He wondered where they would go. "Whilst we are outside, if you don't mind, I have a call to make," Alyious explained. "Then I will take you to see some places that you need to know and explain what I have planned. We will make you do what I had to." Before Jackson could enquire further, he changed the subject. "Where did you go with Jessamine?"

"We went to the park, then on to meet a man called Clarry," Jackson answered. "And I had the test, as Clarry liked to call it. Then to the entertainments for the evening."

Alyious laughed. "I remember the test, and I also heard that you passed yours with all flags flying. Well done for keeping your head."

"It was a close thing. When he said he would not hurt me, but hurt Jessamine, I nearly faltered."

Alyious nodded. "A fine man is Clarry, he knows how to put a man under pressure by threatening something dear to him. He can be a real help to you. I will show you some other useful things. Which part of town are you familiar with?"

"I grew up in Cobblebottom, my parents worked in the Prosthesium." Unlike Jessamine, Alyious seemed unaware of Jackson's tale, nor did he press for details.

"How about the river, or the south side, do you know them?"

"Not so well, I went across the river for the first time yesterday."

They disembarked at a place that Jackson did not know, an area of neat houses, neither poor nor as sumptuous as the big houses he had seen on the south side.

"Follow me," said Alyious as he led him through streets until they came to a memorial yard, with its rows of marble stones.

"My mother is remembered here," he said. "I know not where my father lies, or even if he lives, but my mother is here. I come to feel near to her when I can, to tell her what I'm doing and to remind her of my love. Give me a few moments alone, Jackson, then we shall carry on with our day."

He bent over one of the memorial stones; like the rest, it was clean and polished.

Jackson wandered off and inspected the stones. Some had one name, some remembered whole families, with ever smaller carved names as the space reduced. He knew that no bodies were buried here, just the stones to remember those who had gone before. After about twenty minutes Alyious called him over. "Thank you for your patience," he said, "and if you would, not a word to the others, it might spoil my reputation."

"I will keep it to myself." Jackson had changed his opinion. Alyious, who he had once hated, had shown a totally different personality over the last few months. "What are your plans for the rest of our day?"

"All will be revealed. We should take the aerialway to the river, down to the marketplace at Wharfside. As we ride, you'll get a fine view of the city and the area."

They walked for a mile or so, to a large building. Jackson could see the aerialway on its other side, the line leading away in each direction, pillars planted in the ground. As they drew closer, he saw that some of the supports were also attached to other buildings, leaving the street below clear.

When they rounded the final corner, he could see that the side of the building had been removed and altered to make a platform, not unlike a Rail-Ryde station, to facilitate boarding. They entered the building and rose in a continuous elevator to the correct floor.

This was another new thing, it moved slowly but there were no doors, you simply jumped on and off. The platform was quiet; Alyious purchased tickets for them both.

"I'm sorry, I have no money," Jackson said as Alyious handed him the ticket. "Jessamine paid for everything yesterday from her own funds. I must speak with someone and arrange to repay all that has been spent on me."

Alyious shrugged. "'Tis only money, we all have some of our own, from payments received, once you are working properly, you will see." Those were the same words that Jessamine had used; it must be so.

They stood behind the safety rail; there was a gate, manned by a uniformed employee of the Aerialway Express Company, according to the letters sewn onto his uniform jacket. Jackson took time to look at the track; it was as Jessamine had told him, a toothed rack sat on the side of the cast rail. Jackson wondered how the carriages passed; perhaps they only went in one direction?

Then he remembered he had seen a section of doubled rail. He peered along the line, there it was, doubled for the length between two of the tripod pillars that supported it.

The rail began to sing and vibrate; suddenly a carriage appeared from behind him and shuddered to a halt. A door opened and, as the attendant opened the gate, a gangway extended. People stepped off.

"Come on, Jackson." Alyious and Jackson boarded, along with four or five others. Inside the carriage were rows of wooden benches, a standing space at each end. They sat and there was a hiss and a clunk as the door closed. With a jolt, accompanied by a voice saying 'hold tight', they set off. There was a click as they passed the doubled rail; another carriage was now sitting in the loop.

"That is the one that travels in the opposite direction," Alyious explained. "The timing is kept such that carriages pass at every stop. Mechanical devices prevent collisions. We wait alternately."

The system was beautiful in its simplicity; Jackson gazed from the windows as more of the city was revealed. In the distance he could see the port, thick with the masts and funnels of many vessels.

Leading to it was the river, threading its way through the city. The great bridges, named after kings and famous men, were in sight, striding across the water. They arrived and departed at another station, then the rail turned slightly, they slowed and entered one of the loops.

As they sat still, another carriage passed them. The view was as good as the one from the hill yesterday, except that it changed as they progressed.

They disembarked as they grew closer to the river, and on reaching ground level, found that they were in a wide street with warehouses on one side. They were all built into the arches of the rail lines that led out of the terminus and down to the mighty brick bridge over the river.

"This is the bonded store," Alyious explained. "All manner of valuables are kept here, under the eye of the government, until taxes have been paid."

"And why are we here?" asked Jackson.

"I want to test your ability to follow the code we leave on the walls," Alyious said. "Shut your eyes, stay here, count to fifty and then follow me, if you can. There will be a reward at the end of it, providing you are successful."

Jackson shut his eyes, then he had a thought. "Where will I find the first sign?" he asked. There was no answer. Although he had not counted, he opened his eyes and looked around him. The road stretched out under the rails in both directions, then he spotted it, a cross, it looked freshly marked on the bricks on the other side.

He racked his brains; that meant left, he was sure.

He set off; coming to the roadway at the end of the arch he looked for his next clue. There was a fruit seller to his right, with boxes of fresh apples and plums.

"Juicy fruits from Ventis, this year's harvest," he sang out. One of the boxes had a bright circle drawn on it, the next mark. He should head towards the sun. He was tempted to grab an apple, the vendor's attention was elsewhere. No, that was wrong; he turned away and ran straight into a Watchman.

"Oi! What are you about?" said the man, resplendent in his black uniform, the leather and brass gleaming. Jackson tried to turn away but the Watchman held him easily. "Don't struggle, lad, just tell me your business."

"I've done nothing, let me go."

"Did you take an apple from this vendor?" the stern voice asked.

"No, sir, I did not." Jackson held out his empty hands. "I admit to temptation but then I remembered my family, they were sellers of produce and they suffered from thieves."

With practised ease the Watchman searched Jackson, patting his pockets and peering into his pack. At least he was not wearing his quip-belt, which was a relief, how would he have explained that? "Fair enough, lad. I see you tell me truly, mind you stay out of trouble, we are ever watching."

"I will, sir, thank you, sir," Jackson backed away. Alyious would be long gone and think him lost and useless. He moved on towards the sun, his eyes scanning the walls and window frames for his next clue.

And so the chase went on, there were more marks and Jackson struggled to remember the meaning of them. He took a wrong turning at one point and found himself face to face with an onrushing tram, issuing forth from a tunnel in a blank wall. He had to jump smartly to one side and landed in a stall selling scraps of lace and fine cloth from the Western Isles.

"Looking for something for your lady?" asked the merchant. Jackson blushed as he realised that the man was selling those garments that his mother used to describe as unmentionables, the ones that should always be worn clean, in case one were involved in an accident. He had never understood the logic.

"No, sir, I fell," he muttered, feeling his face turn red.

"No need for embarrassment, young sir," the man replied. "Here, take a sample for her. When she sees the quality, she will send you for more. I'm always here."

He pressed a scrap of fine cloth into Jackson's hands and bowed. Not knowing what to do, Jackson returned the bow, thanked him and moved back to the last mark he had seen. He had mistaken the lines added to the cross; he should have taken the second road, not the first.

He pushed the material into his pocket; he would give it to Jessamine – if he could find the courage.

He turned the corner and saw Alyious standing in front of an ale house. Its name was *The Chase*. There was a picture, of men mounted on equines and a pack of canines, all moving across the painted sign.

Alyious grinned. "Well done," he said, clapping Jackson on the back, "although tardy."

Jackson was about to explain what had happened when Alyious went to the door.

"Would you take an ale, Jackson?"

"I've never imbibed," he answered, then he remembered the sips his father had let him have, sat around the fireside, at home, in the good old days. It had tasted bitter and he had only drunk it to please.

"And a good thing too, it slows your mind and your body. Be warned, it can be a weapon, as evil as anything. If you have to, you should ask for workers ale, it appears the same as ale but has no alcohol. Then your mind will stay alert."

Alyious ordered two mugs of workers ale from the girl who was serving; she bent low to draw them. Jackson could not help but look down.

Alyious saw the glance and elbowed him. "Pay attention," he said. "Distraction, though pleasant, can mean death when we are working."

Was that intended to scare him? They were safe, surely? Jackson looked around, nobody was taking any notice of them.

"Here you are," said the girl, placing the mugs before them. "Will there be anything else?"

"Thank you, no." Alyious threw some coins onto the serving bar and they moved away, finding seats in an alcove, secluded and private.

"Your health," said Alyious and they touched mugs. Jackson took a sip, it was not unpleasant, less bitter than he remembered.

"Do you like Jessamine?" The question came from nowhere.

"Yes I do," Jackson answered, in truth he had been thinking more and more of her as the days had passed. Whether it was in her trousers or a pretty frock, she seemed just as beautiful.

"Be careful," Alyious said. "'Tis best not to get involved." Jackson was confused, was Alyious trying to tell him that Jessamine was his? And what of Winifred and Enoch? That had seemed common knowledge.

Alyious saw his look. "I do not mean with her in particular," he explained. "I warn you against involvement with any of the women in our group. There may come a time when a choice must be made, emotion or attachment should not cause you hesitation."

"I see," he said carefully. "She hinted as much, but then, her words and deeds often seem at odds. Her mood changes like the wind."

Alyious nodded. "That's the pleasure and the pain of women," he said. "My words are not meant in a cruel way, just from my experience. I had the same feelings, for one of the women in the group, when I first started. Patching warned me, as I warn you, that if I were forced to sacrifice her wellbeing for the greater good, I would hesitate if I were involved with her. And he was right, although I told him to mind his own business at the time. I found out, the hard way, the truth of his advice."

He looked so sad at the memory. Alyious shook his head and continued. "It's a cruel game, this one of subterfuge that we play, Jackson. You only know the half of it, females have to do much worse things than we menfolk can imagine."

Jackson understood; when Clarry had suggested harming Jessamine, the feeling of desperation was more than that which he might feel if Alyious, or Vyner, had been threatened. Which was strange, as he knew Jessamine could take care of herself as well as any.

"What do you mean?"

Alyious took a swallow of his ale. "A woman is a powerful weapon, she has wiles and things that men want. She can barter them for secrets, favours and the like. But it often leaves them in a bad place. And it can make them unattractive, once it's known what they have done."

"Does Jessamine...?" Jackson didn't feel able to say the words. He knew what men and women did in private; there was ribald and boastful talk in the orphanage and some of the girls who were known for offering themselves.

Jackson had been too shy to experiment much, largely as a result of the things he had heard his mother say, dire warnings of the results of such activities. Still, he knew of those who did, or at least claimed to.

They seemed to be hale and untroubled by the act. He hadn't considered the implications of being a woman in Langdon's world.

"If you knew what Jessamine has done," said Alyious, "will you think any the less of her?"

Jackson was stuck, it was all new to him, he had no right to control her behaviour; the fact that she was willing to do such things in the service of her country made her more of a special person to him. He said nothing. But he remembered what she had said to him, in the Cofé house.

"I have soured the mood, I'm sorry," said Alyious. "I think none of us actually realise the full import of what we do."

This was safer ground for Jackson. "I confess, I thought it a game, until I learned of Enoch," he said. "That was the first time that I thought about it as a serious matter."

"Enoch was the first for some time," Alyious replied. "And from what I hear, more bad luck than mischance. Vyner is distraught, he blames himself." He stopped for a moment. "No that's not right; it's more that he feels guilt for surviving."

"I understand that," said Jackson. "My parents died, not an hour before I would have been with them. I felt the same, that I should have been there." He paused, feeling himself about to sob. "That it was somehow wrong to have survived."

"It's a natural emotion, so I've been told," said Alyious, who also seemed affected by their conversation. "Which is why he wanted to be involved in the hunt. He will be given the time to recover, Patching will talk to him, he has experience from the wars, leading people into battle who have a much worse time of it than us."

At least there was the care, the responsibility of command, Jackson thought, it reinforced his decision to remain.

"Anyway," said Alyious, drinking again. "To other matters, I marked the walls, then doubled back and watched you as you followed. You did well. What did the Watchman want?"

"He thought I had taken an apple, but he was mistaken."

"Good, we are not thieves, though you will find that the opportunity often presents itself to have something with no risk of reprisal. Do not succumb."

"I will not." Jackson was about to ask him about his belt, but Alyious continued.

"And the frippery merchant, you took something from him?"

"No, he offered it to me. A sample, he called it."

Alyious smiled. "May I see?"

Jackson pulled the garment from his pocket and Alyious took it. He turned it over in his hands and whistled approvingly.

"Yes, a fine piece, it will look good on Jessamine, or any lady. When will you give it to her?"

Jackson could feel himself flush. "I don't know," he stammered.

"Jackson, you have been with a lady?"

Jackson shook his head. "Never."

"Well, there is another part of your education that is lacking then, we can remedy that deficiency today, should you wish." He glanced over at the serving girl, who waved back.

Jackson shook his head and returned the garment to his pocket. "Thank you but no, I will come to that in my own time."

"As you wish," said Alyious. "But take my advice, don't wait forever. When you do, you will wish you had earlier. In that case, we are finished here. Let's get back; drink your ale, Jackson."

"One more thing," Jackson asked the question that the Watchman's search had prompted. "I did wonder, what would you do if a Watchman searched you and found your quip-belt?"

Alyious thought for a moment, then he pulled his jacket aside and opened one of the pockets in his belt. He produced a card, which he showed to Jackson.

It carried a drawn likeness of fine quality, clearly produced by a clever artist. Underneath it stated that the bearer was an agent of Sir Mortimer Langdon and should be offered every assistance. If in doubt, it said, the reader should call the following number. "You will have one," Alyious said, "in your belt. The drawing has already been made by Capricia; she has been closely observing you. She has artistic talents."

Jackson pondered that on the journey. Had that been the reason for her attention?

When they went upstairs to their rooms, Jackson toyed with the idea of giving the garment to Jessamine, but he could hear conversation from behind her door, from the braying it sounded as if Capricia was inside, in full flow. He passed on.

To give her the garment required more of his courage than he had needed to face Clarry. How ridiculous was that?

Chapter 12

"I hear you did well, Jackson," said Fairview when they met the next morning, "in your test yesterday."

Jackson looked pleased to be mentioned. "Yes, sir, I think I did."

"Good, you are progressing well in your training; however, that has to stop for a while. There is a matter which requires your special knowledge. Go with Alyious and Jessamine to see Langdon and he will explain. He is with Oswald."

"We have a problem," Langdon said to the assembled group. "A situation has come to light and we need some people to investigate. Jackson, you have the honour of being included. Although you are not completely trained, Alyious and others say that you are ready and we are in need of your knowledge."

"Thank you," Jackson replied, although he was unsure what he could know that would help. "I'll do my best."

"What's amiss?" asked Alyious.

"I was contacted, a while ago," Langdon said, "by a technician, connected with artificial limbs. This man knows a little of my interest in mystery and has stumbled upon one. I have been researching it ever since, with some of your help."

He uncovered the object on the table. "Gather around," he invited. Everyone who was present stood and formed a group around the table.

The thing was an artificial arm. Seen apart from a body it was strange, it had parts of its case removed, inside were springs, levers and all sorts of mechanisms.

Jackson had seen artificial limbs before, but never one like this. When his parents had worked in the Prosthesium, the limbs they produced were rigid, the joints locked into place as required to perform each task.

This one appeared to be filled with clockworks, springs, rods and pulleys. "It is the same as a human limb," explained Oswald, who seemed uneasy at the presence of so many in his laboratorium. "Save that instead of a bone, the case provides the strength. The workings replicate muscle and sinew. Their motion is controlled by nerve impulses, the same as in a real arm."

"Thank you, Oswald," Langdon said. "Allow me to continue. Scientists at the Institute of Medical Statics have discovered, through research on injured soldiers, how the body works and have replicated it in metal. Professor Woolon has perfected the work in this version of the limb. Now, with advanced techniques, they are to be made available to all, not just the monied few. This limb was returned for repair, as it had stopped working. Oswald, can you tell us what you have discovered?"

"Gladly." Oswald took off his glasses and polished them furiously on his coat before taking up the story.

"Under examination, all that could be found amiss was a piece that should not be there. A filament of some strange material encased in a padded brass tube. Placed where it would not be seen by a casual inspection. Even then, one would have to be an expert, or very observant, to realise that it was not part of the original design. It appeared to control the whole thing. The filament was unbroken but once it had been removed, the limb functioned perfectly."

Oswald pointed to the offending item, a short bright metallic connector, not unlike the cartridge from a gas-gun. It joined two of the wires that made a web around the metallic workings of the arm.

"And what is the mystery?" asked Alyious.

"This filament is not part of the original design, according to experts we have spoken to. It has been added, probably when the limb received its last service and inspection. The fact that it was functioning and suddenly stopped, suggests that the filament has some part in that. We need to find out what that might be."

Jessamine and Alyious exchanged excited glances. "Another interesting affair," said Jessamine. Jackson suddenly understood why he was here; they needed his knowledge of the factory. But that was years ago, and never making something as complex as this. Langdon spoke again.

"The limbs are manufactured by a company in the city. Jackson,

I think you know where we are leading with this. We need to investigate; it would appear that the owner is a man who we now suspect of being involved in some unsavoury enterprises. He seems to have some associations that are dubious. In fact, we believe him to be a danger to the state."

"Can you not merely get the Watch to detain him?" asked Jessamine.

"And take away all the fun of the chase?" queried Alyious. Langdon shot him a cautioning look.

"While that is the logical solution," he said, "we know not how deep his dealings lead. If he has accomplices or is himself under a master. We need a lot more information. If there is a conspiracy here, we need to know about it before we act. The factory in question is the Prosthesium, in Cobblebottom. You have a connection, do you not, Jackson?"

"Yes, sir. I know where it is. We used to live close by, I played in the streets around the factory, my parents worked there, I attended the factory school and I know the insides of the buildings."

"That is why you will be perfect," he said. "The people we want to know about are a Mister Rodney Nethersole, the owner and manager and his associate, a Mr Winstanley."

Jackson gasped. "I remember that man, Nethersole. He was my father's manager, before the accident. He tried to save people, at his own risk, or so I heard. But he was not the manager. A Mr Clynes was in charge of the whole place. Winstanley I have never heard of."

"Clynes seems to have disappeared," said Langdon. "We know very little about the Prosthesium, it never gave us any cause to be interested. It worked for the government and seemed to be a normal company. Their products were licensed and useful. There was no scientist in the works, they merely manufactured and assembled the parts, under the direction of the Institute. This new discovery has changed things. We need to look into the whole operation. Nethersole has the ownership and all that goes with it. We think that Winstanley is little more than a hired thug. Our real interest is in their scientific capability. Do they have one and are they able to make such a device as this? If there is a scientist employed there, then we know nothing about them. It may be that he is kept prisoner and forced to work on this scheme against his will."

Jackson had never heard of a scientist at the works. "There were no scientists that I recall my father ever mentioning," he said. "They had no need, the limbs were crude and merely pieces of shaped wood and metal, fixed to the body by a harness of leather."

Langdon nodded. "I know, Jackson, that was then. Since you have been with us, things have moved on considerably. Those limbs did not need harnesses, they attach directly to the body by some means. You will not have heard of Professor Woolon at the Institute of Medical Statics, a government facility."

Jackson shook his head. "No, sir."

"Hardly surprising, many of the general population have not heard of him either. It's the place where the army doctors test the latest theories, building articulated limbs for wounded soldiers. Woolon has learned the body's own methods and made a mechanised copy." He gestured at the arm.

Oswald joined in. "Woolon found that a form of statics, not unlike the Wasperton-Byler effect, controls the muscles. He has replicated it in a system of gears and clockworks. By studying animals such as the Urodeles, the fabled giant Sal-y-mand from the Western Isles, who can grow new limbs in nature, he has perfected a method of attachment that requires no harness. The new limb becomes a part of the body. All that is required is a winding of the clockworks at intervals to provide the power to move the joints at the brain's command."

"Thank you, Oswald," said Langdon. "I have more details to review, hence I will brief you all in the morning, but this is my rough plan. I will set some of you to find out what you can about Mr Winstanley. We will go to all his haunts and find his every secret. Jackson, you and Jessamine will be visiting the factory. We will have to think of a suitable story for you. Jackson, did you ever meet Mr Nethersole?"

Jackson thought for a moment. "No, sir."

"That is good news; you would not be recognised then. To be sure, we will give you a different name, let me ponder it."

"There is one more thing we will need to know," Oswald said as they left the room. "If the filament can control the arm, how does the signal get to the filament?"

They returned to the classroom and Fairview presented Jackson with his own quip-belt and backpack. "Mark the contents well, Jackson," he said, "so you can find any of them in an instant. Someone will show you how to wear and use it."

"Do you remember the torch? The one we saw at the Palais?" Jessamine asked. "Oswald has prevailed on the manufacturers to supply us with them; you will find it with the other large pieces of equipment."

Jackson sat in his room that evening; he would be going on a real spying mission. He felt both excited and scared. The contents of the pack had been examined, as well as the torch and the hobble balls, there were several other things, a bi-ocular glass, a lodestone and a strange sort of hat. Made of wool, it pulled down to hide his face.

There was a knock at the door. "Come in," he called.

Capricia was outside; she entered and shut the door behind her. Jackson thought that he heard the lock click.

"Now, Jackson," she said. "I've come to show you how to wear your quip-belt." She picked it up from his desk, where he had left it, intending to inspect it after his bath.

Jackson took it from her and looked at it properly for the first time. Close up, it was two layers of leather, one fixed inside the other. The inner was secured with a fastening that Jackson recognised.

It was the same as his gloves on one side, and the opposite on the other. The top layer, the one with the pockets, was secured in the usual way, with a pin and a hasp.

"Take off your shirt," Capricia commanded. Thinking it a part of the preparation Jackson did so, remembering that he was not wearing a singlet.

Capricia licked her lips. She ran an appreciative eye over his new musculature, then she reached forward and traced the line of his stomach.

"What are you doing?" he asked, he was beginning to feel uncomfortable.

"Come, Jackson, we are all friends together, there is much we could enjoy."

"I thought you were helping me with my belt?"

"There will be time for that, you have passed your tests and are one of us, a celebration is in order, a reward for all your efforts."

Her meaning was made even clearer as she fiddled with her skirts. Jackson had a feeling that it wasn't just to show him how the belt was worn.

He was in a quandary; on the one hand, he remembered Alyious's words, on the other he felt little desire for Capricia but knew not how to say it without causing offence.

Perhaps he could imagine himself with Jessamine? No, that was perverse; he might call out the wrong name, and that would be mortifying.

Just as he was about to say that he was tired and needed sleep, the door rattled, "Jackson," called Jessamine.

Capricia stopped her fiddling and embraced him. "Ignore that," she whispered, biting at his ear and running her hands over his naked back.

He had been saved. "Come in," he replied before she could say anything.

The door rattled again. "I can't, it's locked." Jackson unwound himself from Capricia's embrace and triumphant look. He went to the door. "What is it?" he asked.

"Jackson, I need to talk to you, let me in for a moment," she insisted.

Hiding his half naked body behind the door, he unlocked it and opened it a fraction. "What do you want?" he asked.

Jessamine pushed past him and came into the room. "I've come to help you with your quip-belt... Oh!"

Jackson turned at the noise, he looked at the bed. Capricia was under the covers, her head and hands the only parts showing. Her skirts lay on the ground.

"Hello, Jessamine," she said. "You're too late, I'm already helping Jackson."

"So I can see," she replied acidly, she turned and looked at Jackson, who was at a loss for words. Capricia had been fully clothed and standing by the bed when he had gone to the door.

He knew not what to do, it seemed to him that Jessamine was trying not to cry, her hands hid her face. "I'll leave you to it then," she said as she left.

Jackson was mortified. He went to the bed and pulled the covers away. Capricia was revealed, fully clothed. She was wearing the same tight trousers as Jessamine had been. The skirts must also be the same then, designed to be removed quickly. It was the only way she could have done what she had.

Capricia started laughing, "Did you see her face," she gasped. "She thought that we were about to... and she was right." She could speak no more.

"We were not!" Any attraction for Capricia had long gone. To be sure she was pretty, but there was just no spark between them. If he were honest, he had thought her to be an irritating character from the outset and if she had soured his friendship with Jessamine, he would not be amused. And Fairview had reckoned them to be a harmonious group.

"Come, Jackson, it's only a bit of fun. We are all friends together, this is not like the life you had in the other part of the orphanage. Nobody here is trying to embarrass you or gain an advantage. I will speak to Jessamine and we will laugh at your discomfort. But never in a nasty way."

She swept up her skirts and left him. Jackson fiddled with the belt and managed to fix it to his waist with little effort. When he closed the fastening on the inner belt the outer slid over it like a tram on a track.

Now he saw the logic, in this way, all the pockets were easily accessible at any time, just by rotating the belt.

One by one, he opened the pockets; he was amazed at what he found.

Chapter 13

Next morning, Jessamine and Capricia were deep in conversation in the classroom. They were not scratching each other's eyes out, so Jackson assumed that normal relations had been resumed. He must have been the butt of some prank. When the others saw him enter, they stood and clapped him as he sat.

Vyner, a boy Jackson had had little to do with came over and sat beside him.

"I hear you resisted the advances of our fair Capricia," he said, his tone faintly mocking.

Jackson had decided that, if the whole thing were a tease, he would join in and play the game.

"I did," he admitted, "but only out of deference." He paused for a moment. "Only because I had heard that you were her true love."

Vyner went red and the others, Capricia included, laughed.

"He has you there," Capricia said between chuckles.

Vyner punched him gently on the shoulder. "Welcome to our world, Jackson," he said. "The naive orphan is growing worldly wise, it's good to see."

"Settle down, one and all," Fairview had come into the room. "Capricia, would you repair to Mrs Grimble, she has some matters for you to attend to." She got up and left, closing the door behind her.

"Three of you saw the arm yesterday. Langdon and I have spent the time since discussing a strategy, this is our plan. Vyner, you did not but I'm sure that the rest will tell you all, if they have not already. Sir Mortimer has spoken with the Institute; the mysterious part we found is not connected with Professor Woolon's work. The limb itself was manufactured in the Prosthesium, under licence from the Institute. The limb was last serviced at the Prosthesium works repair facility, attached to the factory. We assume that is where the piece was fitted, yet as far as we are aware, the people working there are not competent in much more than assembly under supervision, greasing and minor adjustments. This tends to confirm the presence of a scientist in the works. Woolon has given us a list of staff who might have the skills needed and who were employed by him in the past.

Alyious, you and Vyner need to investigate these names, find out what they are doing now and where they have been since leaving the institute. Mularky, you and Winifred will investigate Winstanley, Nethersole's assistant. Jackson, you and Jessamine will become the patrons of the Ladies who Lunch, a charity for wounded soldiers. You will gain access to the works and look around. Hopefully, you can find this mysterious man, interview Rodney and perhaps even work out what his ultimate aims are."

This was more like it, Jackson thought. He was involved in a real mystery and would soon be spying on a matter of importance. He could see the reason that he had been chosen, his knowledge of the Prosthesium would prove invaluable.

While the others jabbered, he cast his mind back to the factory. It was surrounded by a high wall, with two gates, the main one used by most of the traffic, wide enough for two mobiles to pass and secured by tall wrought iron gates. And there was a side entrance, used by workers sneaking to the ale house.

Both were guarded, as long as they were expected, they would be able to get in and out. But what if they were discovered? Then he remembered the way he could climb. As long as he had his quip-belt and boots, no wall could hold him in.

Fairview interrupted his reverie. "Jackson, if you can stop daydreaming about the pneumatic Capricia for a moment." There was laughter, did everyone know?

"We need to pick your brains about the layout of the factory. Come up to the board and draw us a plan of the place."

Fairview was grinning as he handed Jackson a lump of chalk.

Jackson quickly drew a large box shape. "This is the outer wall," he said. "It is fronted by Cobblebottom High Road and surrounded by streets of workers' houses on two other sides."

He resisted the urge to mark in his old family home. "To the rear is scrubland and the River Vulpine, named after the abundance of the creatures thereabouts. The factory owns this land, it's poorly fenced and used as a dump for wastes. Pipes lead into the river, supplying water for the steam plant; the pump is water-powered via a spiral screw wheel. We used to play there as children. Unless things have changed drastically, it provides a means of escape, as long as we can get over the wall. There is a Local; here. It produces all the power for the site."

Again, he drew on the board marking the Local and the main works inside the walls. "There are two gates." He rubbed portions of the box out to show the main gate on the High Road and the side gate.

"We can enter and exit through the main gate," Jessamine said, "as long as we have credentials and are expected."

"That is in hand," Fairview said. "The leader of the Ladies, Mrs Claringbold, is a friend of Sir Mortimer and will cooperate with proof of identity."

"Then do we need to know the other way out?" asked Alyious. "They will be legitimate visitors."

"Alyious," chided Vyner, "it's always best to have a backup plan, and you should know that no knowledge is ever wasted."

"Anyway," said Fairview, "the way in unnoticed is essential to our plan, as two people will be seen going in and coming out. That is only part of the story; for you will be staying in, Jackson."

"What do you mean?" Jackson was confused. "Surely, I will have to leave at some time."

"Well you will both go in legitimately, it's better than the clandestine approach, since we know not where to look. It's always best to hide in full view. Another will come in over the wall at the back and take your place when you are supposed to be leaving. Meaning that you can remain inside after hours. You can snoop to your heart's content, as nobody will be aware that you are inside. Then when you have collected all the intelligence, you can get out over the wall, we will be waiting for you."

Jackson saw the beauty of the plan. "And who is this third man?" he asked. "Since it appears that everyone else will be engaged."

"It will be someone who looks like you in stature. You will exchange jackets and hats inside the wall. If he is to be a credible you, it must be so. Either of these two overfed youths will never pass for you." There were more laughs at that. "Come in," called Fairview and a tall boy entered the room.

"This is Harrison," Fairview explained. The boy stood next to Jackson. He was the same height and build, the face was different, but with the same hat it would not be so easy to tell them apart.

"Harrison will meet you in the men's changing rooms; make an excuse to visit them when you have finished with Rodney, before you leave. He will be wearing a black jacket and cap. You will exchange hats and jackets, give him your pass and he will leave with Jessamine in your stead. Hide then, until the works are quiet, I'll leave the rest to you."

The boy shook Jackson's hand. "I'll be there, sir, never you fear."

"Thank you, Harrison. He's from another establishment," Fairview continued, as the boy nodded and left. "In case of capture, he knows nothing about what you are doing, save that he has to help you. If he is caught before you meet, he will not lead anyone to you. Now, Jackson, back to your description of the factory."

"The factory is on three levels, the main floor and two levels of offices above."

"So this is where a scientist might work?" asked Fairview.

"Yes, and we have to find a way of getting to them."

"Aphra, Mrs Claringbold, is arranging a meeting with Mr Nethersole, hopefully that will take place in one of those offices. I will leave it to you to come up with a plan to search the place. I suspect that you will have to think on your feet. I need to know what is going on at the Prosthesium."

"Yes, sir," said Jackson, his mind's eye full of the corridors and stairways of the Prosthesium.

"You may sit, Jackson," said Fairview. "Alyious and Vyner, away you go, you are expected at the Institute. Get a list of all ex-employees who may be able to construct this device. Track them down, where they are and what they are doing. Winifred, you and Mularky know what's to be done. Jackson, you and Jessamine away to Mrs Grimble, she will fit you up to be gentlefolk, suitable to represent the Ladies."

Jackson was now glad that he had paid attention, he knew that the Ladies who Lunch were some sort of force for good. They would undoubtedly take an interest in artificial limbs for injured men. They had started in a Cofé shop, that he knew, he had even visited the place.

Fairview might have called them a charity; at first he had taken it to mean that they dispensed soup to the homeless and sold badges, like the other charities he remembered from his youth. Always poking their noses in and dispensing aid with a sniff, as if the recipients did not deserve the largess of the donor. Now, he had a different opinion of their worth.

Mrs Grimble was in buoyant mood. "Good morning all," she said. "I've just finished outfitting Capricia for her next employment; we'll not be seeing her for a while."

"What will she be doing?" asked Jessamine.

"Well dear, you know I can't tell you that. Suffice to say that it involves becoming a tutor for a child, largely to test the fealty of a certain politician, who may be the target of bribery and blackmail."

"It sounds fascinating, and will she be gone long?"

Mrs Grimble sighed. "As long as it takes, poor girl, she may have to compromise herself to get what we need."

Jessamine put her hand on the older lady's shoulder. "I know, we all have to do what we dislike at times. I think of the greater good."

She nodded. "You are all fine people, made old before your time. Now, to business. You must be well attired and fashionable. Aphra insists on high standards."

"Am I suitable?" asked Jackson. "After all, they are called the Ladies, not the Gentlemen or the People."

"You will do," she said. "Aphra has many male adherents, once they came to see the justice in what she was setting out to achieve."

Jackson nodded, still trying to remember more details about her. Beside him Jessamine whispered, "I will tell you all about her later, as I said before, in the Excelsior Char Rooms, she is a hero of mine."

"And the good news, Jackson," Mrs Grimble continued, "is that your clothes have arrived from Hardspill and Walker, so that we can outfit you perfectly."

Jackson looked resplendent in his suit, with its long jacket in a vivid shade of red. Its cut hid his quip-belt and truncheon pockets, a tall matching hat and cane completed the look. The hat contained his backpack, with its extra equipment, folded in on itself. It made it heavy and awkward to wear, though it fitted snugly enough.

He would have to remember the extra height in doorways. Jessamine was dressed in a gown of palest blue, her bonnet tied under her chin with a silken scarf. She carried a rolled parasol, which would serve the same purpose as the cane. However, she had to leave her belt behind.

"I cannot wear it over the gown," she said. "And I cannot use it if underneath, the design of the gown will not allow for a split, nor trousers underneath."

"You need to be a demure lady," said Mrs Grimble. "A man can get away with a belt and some sort of weapon."

"Is that not what the Ladies who Lunch would call discrimination?"

Mrs Grimble smiled. "Perhaps, if you ever met Aphra, you could discuss it."

"I think we would have a lot to talk about," Jessamine replied wistfully.

"A mobile has been arranged, to complete the effect," continued Mrs Grimble. "'Tis but a short journey but your arrival will be noticed. Were you to arrive on foot, it might seem strange."

They took the costumes off and changed back into their normal attire. Mrs Grimble gave them wire hangers to take the clothes to their rooms.

"In the morning you will dress in them. We have received word that Rodney will see you. Remember, say nothing that might alert him as to your real purpose. You are Mr and Mrs Widge, Prosiah and Gertie."

"And how we will conduct ourselves in a meeting with Rodney?" Jackson asked. "I know nothing of business matters. How does one arrange a shipment of goods, price, payment and the like?"

"You are only there for propriety," Mrs Grimble said. Jackson had to remind himself that she was not the cook, but a talented woman in her own right, with knowledge of the world that eclipsed his. "In business, men are still expected to lead matters. The Ladies take men as chaperones, you can expect Rodney to direct all questions to you. Jessamine will take control of the situation, which may unsettle him. You will need to do nothing except look around and prepare yourself for your true purpose."

"I need to talk to you, about our visit," Jackson said as they left Mrs Grimble. "It will be my first mission and I want it to be a success."

She nodded. "Did you understand all that Fairview said, about the Ladies?"

"I think so, but it was early in my training and I may have missed something."

"Thinking of Capricia I expect," she said.

Jackson almost blurted out the truth, that he had been thinking of her. Instead he just looked away.

"Jackson, you are so easy to embarrass," she said. "I will tell you of the Ladies after supper, come to my room."

Jackson knocked on Jessamine's door, the lace garment still heavy in his pocket. Perhaps he could leave it where she would find it after he had gone? He considered, she would know who it had come from and he wanted her to know it was his gift.

She called for him to enter. "I'm in the bathroom," she said, "make yourself comfortable."

The room was a revelation, decorated in shades of pastel colours, it had plump cushions and an abundance of what Jackson's father used to term 'fripperies'. It was not at all what he had expected.

There was a strange chair, at least he assumed that was what it was, it was wide enough for three, with a cushioned arm at one end yet had a curved back that only stretched over half the width. He decided not to sit on it, instead he perched on the edge of the bed.

Jessamine emerged from the bathroom, she had let her hair down and it cascaded to her waist in dark chestnut waves. It had the effect of making her look so much more appealing.

She had also changed into some sort of silken gown, tied around her waist. Bare feet poked from the hem, the nails were coloured in dark crimson polish.

To Jackson she looked like some sort of ethereal vision. She sat on the chair, back against the arm and swung her legs up to lie longways.

"Do you like my humble room?" she asked.

He made the mistake of mentioning the fripperies. Immediately she seized on his remark, turning her head the hair flew around her face like a wave on the beach.

"What do you mean, Jackson?" she asked, anger in her voice.

"That I'm not as feminine as the room, or perhaps that I am not entitled to some comfort?"

Jackson squirmed, he seemed to have the knack of saying the wrong thing.

"I didn't mean that, you are, well, a lady," he started to babble, the words falling in a stream. "It's beautiful, I mean, it's not to my taste but all the same... yes beautiful, as you are, I like your hair, it suits your face, what is that seat called?"

Why, he wondered, had he said such things? And with such haste, the words all running together. Jessamine seemed to have some effect on him, he was acting like a silly child, his brain and his mouth seemed to be unconnected.

"It's called a sophir," she said, apparently unaware of his discomfort, "from the Western Isles, it's a lovers' seat; you know what that is?"

As she spoke, she bent one leg up, the gown fell away and Jackson was treated to a sight of the creamy white flesh of her thigh. Immediately he looked away.

"I'm sorry, Jackson," she said. "I forget sometimes that you are quite the innocent. I am decent again."

Jackson looked back, she had covered her thigh and sat demurely. That had been his chance, he could have given her the lace, told her its provenance. Instead he had hesitated; as Patching was fond of saying, 'he who hesitates, is often no more.'

"Alyious said that I should not get attached, yet I can't help myself," he muttered. "I only came to talk to you about the Ladies, I should have listened in class."

"Alyious is quite right," she said. "We should concentrate on the task at hand. The Ladies was the result of one woman's annoyance with the system that guaranteed men superiority. She saw that women had power but were unaware of it and she showed them how they might use it to make a better world."

"Is that it?"

"To begin with, Aphra Claringbold merely intended to persuade men that war was not the answer to everything, neither was the automation of the workplace if it meant people suffered. Her mission turned into a crusade. She fought for dignity for everyone, for the rights of people who had served and been injured, to try and ensure that nobody was hungry because of injuries sustained in war. It was her who forced the government to set up the Institute, found men like Professor Woolon to work in it. Single-handedly, she advanced the science of false limbs."

To Jackson, it seemed like a huge leap, from campaigning to setting up a whole Institute. "What could have prompted her to start such a crusade?"

"She was annoyed that she seemed to be insufficient for her husband. She did everything that was expected of her, yet still he strayed, with the maid, with other women. And the system allowed it, even encouraged it. At first, she railed against it, then in discussion with her peers did as they did and took a lover of her own."

"Then she was no better than he was."

"You might say that, initially she says that she did it to prove to herself that she was not unattractive. Then she saw the unfairness;

his behaviour was condoned, hers would not have been. It was made her determined that things must change. All else grew from that sense of injustice."

"Thank you, I will try and pay more attention. And you're not right, when you say I'm innocent. I know a lot more than an innocent man, just not as much as some of those in the group. This world of yours is all so new to me. I'm used to keeping quiet, to avoiding attention. I feel like I'm acting a part that I'm not capable of and frightened that I won't be accepted as part of your group. I seem to get attention from women and wonder why, as I consider myself to be nothing special."

Jessamine swung her legs and stood up; the gown fell open again as she walked across to Jackson. To his surprise, he could see that she was wearing the twin of the garment that was in his pocket, except this one was coloured in palest pink. She pulled him upright and held him. He could feel her heat through the thin material.

His arms hung by his sides, he felt unable to move. "I'm not a tease," she whispered. "I'm your good friend. No-one here will turn on you, you're quite safe to be you."

Jackson moved his arms and she let him enfold her. They hugged for a moment then she pulled away. "Go," she said. 'Before I change my mind,' she thought.

She found him so attractive, even more because he genuinely did not realise the effect that his good looks had on people. But she must resist, at least for a little longer.

It would make it all the more delicious in the end.

Chapter 14

The next morning, Jackson and Jessamine arrived for fast-break dressed to visit the factory. After their meal, Fairview escorted them to the gates, where a steam-mobile waited. He handed them a letter.

"This is from Mrs Claringbold," he said. "It identifies you as employees charged with arranging the supply and delivery of mechanical limbs for her charity. You are to view the factory and speak with Nethersole. Be careful and meet up with Harrison as we arranged. Remember, he will be waiting in the gentlemen's changing facilities from mid-afternoon."

He then took the controls and drove them efficiently through the traffic, to the place that Jackson remembered so well. The mobile was luxurious with soft leather seats; Jackson could get used to this sort of life. He realised that Jessamine was right; for as long as he survived, life would be good.

There was a tree Jackson remembered, by the wall that surrounded the works. "We children simply called it the big tree, when I was a lad," he said. "We used to play around it, used it as our meeting place and were ever climbing it to see inside the factory."

"Then we will meet there, tonight when you are done," said Fairview. "I will be waiting, in this mobile."

They stopped outside the gate, the factory seemed to be much busier than he remembered, there were coal lorries queued up to enter; no doubt supplying the Local, while a lorry with the words Prosthesium Company on the side was in the process of leaving.

The man on the gate gave them both yellow waistcoats with the word 'Visitor' printed on them. "You are expected," he said, making a note in his ledger. "Wear these at all times and return them when you leave. Please follow the roadway to the brown door, you will be met."

Feeling confident, the pair set off into the factory. They were met at the door by an assistant, dressed all in white. He introduced himself as the head of information and directed all his attention to Jackson, blatantly ignoring Jessamine. It was clear that he was no fan of the Ladies. He took them inside the doors.

"Before I show you and your companion our process," he said, again directing his words to Jackson, "I must ask you to change from your street clothes."

This was new. In the past Jackson had come straight from his lessons and through this door, pausing only to wipe the mud from his boots, if he remembered.

"The inside of the factory is kept scrupulously clean," the man continued. "Our products are comprised of delicate parts and there is always the risk of contamination with dust and dirt. Please take off your boots and leave them in a locker. Put on the white oversuits and footwear provided, there are several sizes for you to choose from."

They entered the room and saw the suits hanging in a line. "I will have to remove my gown to get into one of those suits," Jessamine said and did so, in front of Jackson.

"I think it's another way to show women who is in charge," she added as her bare shoulders and undershirt were revealed. Jackson meanwhile had removed his boots and stepped into the oversuit.

He found that it was secured not by buttons but by a continuous fastener of small links, activated by pulling on a metal device that somehow joined them together.

"Have you seen one of these?" he asked.

"Yes, it's called a Continuous Clasper; or simply a Clasper," she said, pulling hers upward in one movement. The garment was slightly too small for her and revealed her shape. "I sometimes forget that you have been away from science for so long," she said. "They make clothes so much easier to remove."

They re-joined their guide, who made no effort to hide the look he gave Jessamine's legs, revealed as they were by the tight oversuit.

His condescending attitude and obvious thinking was starting to grate with Jackson, however he kept his temper in check as they entered the machine room.

This was the room Jackson remembered from happier days. He had never seen it as a charnel house, so although he knew it as the place where his parents met their end, it provoked no more than a wave of sadness in him.

He saw the rotating shaft, no doubt a replacement, this one was heavily guarded and supported by strong frames set into the building's skeleton. The room was busier than he remembered and smelt of hot grease, overlaid with a faint odour of something that was vaguely familiar.

It was his mother's scent, it must have been a memory of her presence in this place waiting his return. He could see her face clearly in his mind. There were the rows of machines that he remembered, although these were newer, painted in light green and almost silent.

Jessamine must have noticed his blank gaze, felt his sadness. She nudged him in the ribs. Their guide was talking, he had to pay attention.

"Of course, the exact details are not for public consumption," he was saying, "experts have found a way to mimic the body's own systems. The instructions which the brain sends to our muscles have been identified and the means of transmission found. Scientists have discovered how we may capture these signals at the point where the real limb ends and transfer them to the prosthetic. Thus, the brain itself controls the workings of the limb. There is no other requirement than the thought. All that is needed is a daily winding of the springs that provide the motive power and a regular application of grease. We also offer a service facility for heavily used limbs. They can be returned to us for maintenance and repairs, at no extra cost, in our well-appointed workshops."

"Do you have your own scientists here?" asked Jessamine innocently.

The guide shook his head, and directed his response to Jackson, as if she had somehow spoken through him. "Oh no, sir, we work under contract to the Institute of Medical Statics, they supply the specifications and materials, we are merely manufacturers. The completed parts go to their hospital facilities for final tuning and fitting. Their staff, not ours, man the repair facility."

Lines of men and women sat and fixed small pieces of metal together. Overhead a series of metal rods spun, driven by the main shaft through elaborate gearing. Belts led down to each bench, where they drove a variety of small tools, lathes and drills.

Nobody spoke, or even noticed their presence, all were bent and oblivious, intent on their tasks. Small boys pushed wheeled bins, passing raw materials and collecting finished products.

Starting at one end of the room, with two pieces of bent metal, by the time the process had come to the far end, the results of the labours were completed arms and legs, ready for the next part of the manufacturing process.

The arms were identical to the one they had seen in the orphanage, except that the workings were hidden.

They passed through a set of doors into another room, this one had a lot more of a serious air. There were fewer machines, instead a line of women were bent over benches, peering through thick magnifying lenses at the objects before them. They appeared to resemble cups, made of some thick black fabric.

On one side were a series of brass dots, like the heads of pins. On the other, fine wires that were hanging loose.

"In this room, the other part of the limb is being assembled," their guide told Jackson, "the piece that fits over the stump of the limb. This is the part that connects the man to the machine and passes all the information. Hence the magnifying lens and delicate work."

"Why are all the workers in this room women?" asked Jessamine.

She received the look again. "We find that women are most suited to this part of the process."

"So, there is something that we are good at?" asked Jessamine.

She received a blank stare. "Men and women both have their forte," he said. "The knack is using it," he paused, "and in being content with one's place in the scheme of things."

"How does this part function?" asked Jackson, it was plain that any question Jessamine asked would be answered to him, so he saved her the bother of asking.

"The sheath fits over the stump, on the other side of it, the fine wires extended. They carry the nerve impulses and are fitted into the patient's own nerves, in surgery designed by our medicians."

"Where are these limbs fitted to the patients? Does that happen here?"

"No, the parts are collected and taken to the Institute, where they are tested and tuned, before being fitted at their own hospital, attached to the Institute."

"But surely you must test them," Jessamine said, "before they leave. Is that in the same place as the repairs, servicing and maintenance are done?"

The man looked suspicious. "For a woman, you have an unsettling demeanour, you ask many questions. There are places that I cannot show you, where these processes are carried out."

He waved his arm at the far wall, where there were two doors. "Over there are those areas. Mr Nethersole may choose to let you view them, I am not permitted."

"Pardon my forthright approach," said Jessamine. "I ask because the Ladies will be investing heavily in this place, should I, not my husband, decide it. I need to know everything so that I can report to our committee, before we can commit our funds," she paused for a second, "and our patronage."

The man looked at Jackson, as if to say, curb your woman's tongue and stop her imagining that she has power. But Jackson merely smiled. "My wife and the Ladies make the decisions," he said. "She has a sharp brain, as they all do, and I willingly defer to her."

The man looked uncomfortable, unsure of how to reply. He consulted his timepiece. "Now you are to meet our manager, Mr Nethersole." They were taken back to the room where they had started, once again passing the assembly room. The workers never looked up, so engrossed were they in their tasks. They divested themselves of the oversuits and shoes; dressed again in their street clothes and the yellow waistcoats, they were taken up the stairs.

The man handed them over to a female secretary, who welcomed them. The man was unable to get away quickly enough, he left without so much as a 'goodbye' shouted over his shoulder as he scuttled for the stairs.

"Mr Nethersole is engaged for a moment," the secretary said. "To be honest, we expected your tour to take longer. I will get you Char while you wait."

"Thank you," said Jessamine. "I think your guide was uncomfortable dealing with a woman as an equal."

She sighed. "I know, we all suspect that he treats his poor wife abominably."

"Then she should assume her power and educate him," Jessamine replied fiercely.

The other woman nodded. "I agree, we supposedly live in enlightened times, thanks in no small part to your founder. It's a very patriarchal place here; we are permitted to assemble the delicate parts, given tremendous responsibility for their correct function. Despite that, we are expected to know our place, have no say. I admire the achievements of your principal and her group. Were he my husband, I would indeed educate him so."

She turned to Jackson. "And you, sir, to be as comfortable as you are with your wife's authority, it speaks well of you. How long have you been wed?"

"A few short months," he replied. "Although we have moved in the same circles for several years, it's only been recently that I came to appreciate what a woman she was."

"Ahh, true love," said the secretary. "How wonderful for you."

After a short wait, the door opened and a tall, bewhiskered man in a fine suit came to them. He shook their hands.

"Delighted to make your acquaintance," he said as they introduced themselves. "I'm Rodney Nethersole, please step into my office."

He called for more Char and they talked of the weather, of the Palais and the state of the world while they drank. Jackson left Jessamine to do most of the talking, he merely added a word here and there. Rodney seemed at ease taking of worldly matters with a female, which clearly endeared him to Jessamine, her conversation grew more animated and he more voluble.

"So, to business," said Rodney, leaning back in his chair. "Mrs Claringbold is known to me, to our organisation, I'm honoured to be the subject of her scrutiny."

"Thank you, sir, it's nice to be spoken to as an equal, so many people will only talk to me through my husband," said Jessamine, leaning forward and fixing her gaze on his face. He looked down then guiltily looked back up, his face reddening.

Jessamine pretended that she had not noticed his gaze. "We at the Ladies have funds to help the lives of those damaged by their duty to society." She continued, "Not just servicemen but workers injured in factories or mines. We wish to purchase limbs and already have medical premises and staff promised to us for fitting." Her hands fiddled with the knob on her parasol and again his gaze shifted. He was sweating now, pulling a kerchief from his pocket to mop his brow.

"Ah but do you have experts, men trained to affix and tune the appendages?" he asked. "We can offer you the services of skilled men to oversee your programme, at very reasonable cost to your organisation."

"And can these men perform the operations to join the parts together?" she asked, smiling sweetly, her hands still busy with the parasol. She licked her lips.

He shook his head and mopped his crimson brow again. "Not at present, but we are in discussion with the Institute as we speak, to widen the scope of what we can do here."

"I see. Then we may need people from the Institute as well, it would seem redundant to employ yours as well as theirs, would it not?"

Her hand moved; the parasol dropped to the floor. The sound was sudden, it made Rodney jerk as if struck. Jackson bent and retrieved it for her. As he passed it, unseen by Rodney, she winked. "Your pardon," she said, "please continue."

"By the time you need them, I will be in a position to provide you with men to fulfil all your needs," Rodney persisted. "Fitting, testing and maintenance."

Jackson was fascinated by the interplay, the cut and thrust of argument. It seemed almost that Jessamine was playing with Rodney's emotions, using what Alyious had described as her wiles to distract and unsettle him.

He saw that she was leading his conversation, teasing out his real intentions. Her words and actions were making him uncomfortable, yet he could see the art in her performance.

"We can find them ourselves, thank you, and not necessarily men, women can do this work."

Nethersole was about to insist again, Jackson sensed sudden tension, the last thing they needed was to be ejected before they had begun. And it was interesting how desperately he wished to retain some control over the prosthetics once they had left his factory.

If they hadn't known of the extra pieces in the arm, it might have seemed sensible, as it were it smacked of hiding the truth, or retaining control over the process.

"Your workers here," said Jackson, seeing a chance to enter the conversation, "they seem very skilled and dedicated. Perhaps we could employ some of them at our new facility, with your agreement, they could work for us?"

"They are, although not in the workings of the things they make, they are dexterous in assembly of the fine parts, but there is no-one here who understands how the limbs function. As for loaning some, that might well be possible, if terms could be agreed."

The eagerness proved what Jackson was thinking, Nethersole wanted no-one who was not trusted by him seeing the workings of the limbs.

"What of testing, before dispatch?"

"We have a machine that does that, we merely plug the limb into it and check the workings for correct assembly. I cannot take you to it; my apologies, but it is on loan from the Institute and they have instructed me that it is so secret that I cannot show it."

"No matter," Jessamine said, "we will take your word. This is all a new venture for the Ladies, we are more usually acting as the introductor."

"If I may, the most important part for us is the number of units you would require. As you might have noticed, we are running at near capacity making limbs, how many pieces are you thinking of ordering?"

"That would depend on the price, due to the funds we have. It would not be a large number to begin with. Initially, we would like a sample piece, say an arm or a lower leg, to inspect and practise on."

"Then that is perfect, I'm considering increasing production by starting a night shift."

More valuable information.

The door flew open and a badly dressed man entered. "Rodney," he gasped, "I need to speak with you, there is a problem with the Sens—"

Rodney went pale and stood. "Do not barge in here, I have important visitors, now get back to your bench, I will attend to your concerns later."

The man left and Rodney relaxed. "Pardon him, he manages the final assembly and gets excited about every little mishap. If you will excuse me." He stood. "The Prosthesium Company will be delighted to work with the Ladies," he said. "I hope today has been edifying, please let us know your requirements and we will be happy to help you, we can arrange for samples to be supplied. My secretary will show you out."

It seemed a hurried dismissal but Jackson and Jessamine had no time to discuss it. The woman from the desk led them to the stairs. "I will take you to the gate," she said.

"Who was that man, the one who burst in? He seemed to unsettle Mr Nethersole."

"We call him the Professor," she said with a giggle. "He's a strange man. He works in the corner room; on the top floor, doing

125

goodness knows what, his project is known as the Sensaurum, as if that word means anything. We seldom see hide nor hair of him for days, he comes and goes down the back stairs."

They reached the yard. "I must use the facilities," said Jackson.

The woman nodded. "Can I leave you to make your way out? Hand in your passes at the gate." She left them.

"There is a lot to tell Fairview already," Jackson said. "The top floor corner room, that gives me four to search. I have a way up," he pointed the fire escape, "now I will go and meet Harrison, safe journey and I'll see you later, by the tree."

Jessamine pecked him on the cheek. "Good luck, husband," she said. "Now away with you. Get in there before someone notices us loitering."

Jackson went to the room, which was deserted. He looked around. Where was he?

"Harrison," he called. A man swung down from the rafters, dressed all in black. He pulled his cap off.

"Hello, Jackson," he said. "I was hidden aloft, there is a space."

Jackson pulled off his hat and extracted his pack. His jacket followed. Harrison did the same and they exchanged. The jacket he received was snug but cut so that he could reach his belt. Jackson handed Harrison the hat, he put the yellow waistcoat on. Now he was a replica of Jackson, enough to pass casual inspection. "Jessamine is outside, she has your pass."

"Good hunting," said Harrison and left. Jackson jumped up into the rafters and found the alcove that Harrison had described. He settled down to wait till evening, he had lots to plan. He had spotted the side door to the assembly rooms that he used to use, it would be easier and quieter to get in that way, he would avoid the main entrance.

And he could check the rooms at the side, where Rodney had said that repairs and testing took place. He had a clue as well; anything he could find about this mysterious Sensaurum would be useful.

Chapter 15

Jackson must have fallen into a doze; he awoke to the sounds of men coming into the changing rooms. There was banter and the sound of running water, then, after several minutes, silence. The shift had ended, the factory would now be quiet.

Jackson carefully dropped down to the floor and locked himself in a cubicle. He pulled on the hat from his pack and unrolled it, covering his face, leaving a small slit for his eyes. The climbing gloves went onto his fingers. He put his pack on his back, checked his truncheons were accessible and bent down to peer under the door of the cubicle. Seeing no feet, he cautiously opened the door.

The room was deserted. Jackson crept from the building. Outside, the yard was in semi-darkness, lit by gas floodlights which created dark shadows. Jackson kept to the darkness as much as he could until he had reached the side entrance to the factory.

The lock proved no barrier to his tools and once inside he locked the door again and set off, weaving through the machines, idle now, although the drive shaft still spun. He tried the first of the doors, unlocked. Jackson found himself in the repair workshop, several arms and legs were laid out on the benches, where they were being worked on.

Jackson peered inside each, using his new torch, set to a dim beam. A squeeze of the handle gave enough illumination to see if the extra piece had been fitted. In all cases it was either present or a place had been made for it. He saw a rack of the metal cartridges at the end of one bench. He grabbed two of them and placed them in a pocket. They might prove useful to Oswald.

He looked around for any notes or drawings that might give a clue as to the workings of the cartridge but could find none. Conscious of the need for haste, he went to the second room. This was dominated by a huge contraption of brass and steel, featuring four protuberances, shaped like a stump of arm or leg.

They must be for attaching limbs for testing, thought Jackson. On the other side of the machine were gauges and dials, presumably showing the results of the tests. Again, Jackson searched for papers, there were drawers in a desk but on opening them, nothing except pencils and stationery was inside.

He had to move quickly, lest he be spotted. He left the rooms and headed for the stairs. The corner room the secretary had said; he ignored the floor with Rodney's office and went straight to the top floor.

As he arrived he heard a sound, someone was coming along the passageway, in a second or two they would meet. Jackson was by a door, to his relief it opened and he quickly went inside. The room was lit by a single gas lamp hanging from the ceiling.

He was in some sort of archive, there were papers relating to the Prosthesium, going back years. Jackson wondered if there was anything about his parents. He started to take more notice of the labels on the cabinets, looking for the records from the time of the accident.

He found the drawer relating to the year and hunted. Then he realised, time was passing and he had not achieved his real purpose. He was about to shut the drawer when he spotted a folder that was newer than the rest. He pulled it out; it was headed Sensaurum and Lexis.

He opened it; the words were in some sort of code, a meaningless jumble of letters and numbers. He pushed it into the large pocket on the inside of his jacket and, as he was about to shut the cabinet, he saw another, dislodged by his searching. It was old and thinner, it was the report of the investigation into the fatal accident that had killed his parents and so many others.

That folder followed the first. He considered leaving the room by the corridor but he had heard the footsteps several times while he had been searching, maybe there was a regular patrol. He would be best using the window.

He opened the window as quietly as he could, checked his gloves and clicked his boots. The wall was in darkness, with his black attire he would be hard to spot, nobody would be watching for a man clinging to the walls. To his left was the fire escape, a framework ladder with handrails connecting all the floors. He made for it, clambered over the railings and rested for a moment on the platform. He was surprised to find his breathing was not laboured, he had become so much fitter in the last few months. He did not feel fear, only elation, his mind was working quickly and automatically to analyse all he could see and hear.

Leaving the platform and attaching himself to the wall again, he started to move sideways towards the windows. The first two rooms were in darkness and he moved on to the third. At least that was lit.

The window glass of this room was smeared with soot and grime, he could see at least two figures, but it was impossible to make out who they were. One voice he recognised as Rodney's, who he was talking to was uncertain.

"Well, do you have more of them finished?" Rodney asked. The reply was a muffled "Yes" "And the control for these? Is it the same?" was asked.

He was prevented from hearing the reply by the sound of a large vehicle coming into the yard. He tensed as the light from its passing washed over him, but there were no shouts to indicate that he had been discovered.

When he returned from the shadows to peer again through the grimy window, Jackson found a clear corner in one of the panes. Through it, he could see a lone figure, bent over a white bench. In contrast to the window, the inside of the room gleamed with cleanliness, the white surfaces screamed of sterility.

The man stood upright, it was he who had burst in, the one the secretary called the Professor. Jackson saw that he was working on a thin white object, looking like a small length of rope. It was held in the jaws of a clamp at each end, sagging slightly in the middle. Behind him, hung on the wall, was a row of wooden boxes, festooned with wires and switches. They appeared to have things like speaker trumpets fixed to them, could they be a communication system? wondered Jackson.

The man straightened up and crossed the room toward him; Jackson moved his head away from the window, lest he be spotted. When he risked a look back, the man's face was mere inches from his. He saw his expression change to one of surprise and his mouth opened. "Alarm!" he heard him shout.

Jackson shrank away, into the shadows. Now he had been discovered he had to move quickly to get outside the main gate before he was captured. He turned around and moved to one side of the window frame as behind him, he heard the window open. "There he is!" the shout went up as he climbed quickly to the gutter, over it and onto the flat roof. He stood and picked his way between the chimney pots. Some were hot to the touch; he almost lost his balance as he threaded his way between them.

Lights pierced the gloom. He could hear his pursuers and risked a glance over his shoulder. It nearly cost him, he blundered into a chimney stack, hot from the fumes it carried. He recoiled and teetered on the edge of a steep drop, windmilling his arms. He regained balance and set off again.

They were closer now and he heard the sharp hiss of a gas-gun, felt the wind of a projectile and heard the smack as it chipped fragments from the brick by his ear.

Then he was at the edge. He skidded to a halt. The next building was twenty feet away, too far to jump. "Got him now," a rough voice called. "Rodney will want to ask him a few things."

Jackson turned to face his attackers; he tapped his boots, heel on toe, and heard them click. His gloves were on. He smiled.

"Hands above your head and walk towards us," the leader said. Now they had come into the light, Jackson could see that there were four of them, all out of breath, brandishing gas-pistols.

What would they think? he wondered as he took a deep breath and stepped backwards.

As he fell, he heard shouts. He pushed his hands out and the gloves gripped the bricks, arresting his fall. He kicked and took the weight on his legs, his arms felt like they had been wrenched out of their sockets, but his fall had stopped.

He was in shadow, fifteen feet above him there was consternation.

"He jumped," said one. "No chance he'll be alive after that," another called. "Stay here, Nathen, the rest of you, back to the yard, let's make sure he's dead."

Jackson moved sideways, away from where they would be peering over the edge and started to descend, making as little noise as possible.

He reached solid ground and stood for a moment, flexing his shoulders, glad of the training, and the extra food. Now all he had to do was get over the outside wall and to the tree. The bigger problem would be in explaining to Langdon what had gone wrong. Perhaps what he had would be enough?

He hid in the shadows as the men arrived and watched as their lamps lit up the place where his body should be.

"Is this the place?" the leader said. "I can see no body."

"It is," replied another. "Look." He pointed and following his hand, Jackson could see the man on the roof, peering over the edge.

"Then where is he? There's no body, no blood and no marks. He can't have flown away. Look around." Two of them walked off, in opposite directions, fortunately not towards Jackson, leaving one man scratching his head. As he watched him, the man from the laboratorium came out of the door.

"Winstanley," he said, "have you found him?"

"No, sir," replied the searcher. "We're looking but I don't understand why he is not spread all over the ground here." So that was Winstanley, he looked a giant of a man, although most of his bulk was around his middle.

Still, if he got close enough, he could do you harm. Jack pulled the truncheons from his pockets, held them ready to snap open in an instant, should he be discovered.

"He must have some device to climb the walls, 'less he jumped down onto some ledge."

Just then the main gas lamps came on, the whole yard was bathed in blueish light. It was plain that the wall was devoid of any such place.

In the hubbub, Nethersole appeared. "Well, Winstanley," he said, "don't just stand here, get away with the others, keep looking, I wish to speak to the Professor for a moment."

Jackson stayed where he was, perhaps he could salvage something from the night. If he could get information from this conversation, maybe a name for the Professor, it would be something more to report. Langdon had been right, there was a scientist working here.

To his delight, Rodney and the Professor moved closer to his hiding place. Rodney placed his arm around the Professor's shoulder and leaned close to him.

"Did the man see what you were doing?"

"I don't know, Rodney," the Professor admitted, as Jackson crept closer.

"I can't afford to take this risk, he might be a competitor of mine, of yours, a government agent. He could be anybody, who knows his skills? Tell me, Aldithley, did he see the Sensaurum?"

There was the word again, together with the name Aldithley and the folder he had found, it could prove to be worth today's escapades. He had to get out to share the information. As he watched, Rodney grabbed the Professor. It was plain that they were not equals in their relationship.

"He may have," said the man now shaking with fear as Rodney gripped him tighter, "but how would he know what it was, or what it could do?"

"We had better hope, for your sake, that he did not. If the wrong person hears the words, who knows what might befall us all."

Still talking, they moved away. It was impossible for Jackson to follow unseen. He had good intelligence for Langdon, it was best to get away with it. Keeping to the shadows, he headed away from the searchers.

His target was the boundary wall by the big tree and safety. Fairview should be waiting outside. As he sat on top of the wall; he breathed a sigh of relief. The mobile was parked, exactly where promised. Fairview stood outside, leaning on a cane. He could see Jessamine sitting inside the mobile, she was safe.

"I heard shouts," he said as Jackson joined him on the ground. "Were there any problems?"

"I was spotted," admitted Jackson, "but not recognised. I have the information that we need."

"What does it mean?" wondered Langdon. "If only you had heard the rest."

They were sat in the underground room. Langdon had been waiting for their return. Jackson was anointing his scraped knees with a salve from Mrs Grimble's cupboard and longing for a soak in hot water.

Jessamine was also there, she had been waiting for him under the tree, together with Fairview and the mobile, when he had climbed the wall. To his surprise, she had driven it back to the orphanage herself, was there no end to her talents?

Under questioning, Jackson revealed what had transpired once Jessamine had left.

"You have done well, leave it with me, Jackson," Langdon said. "After their meeting, Alyious and Vyner have spent the day searching out those who had once worked with Woolon. They have one unaccounted for, Aldithley, who left under a cloud, thinking himself wronged. It would appear we have our man, the name of the project he is working on. Now I have an easy task. Tomorrow I will get my answers from Woolon. For now, you must rest; you are excused work in the morning, sleep till luncheon and recover."

Jackson remembered his haul. "I have these too," he said, pulling the objects and the papers from his pocket, all except the report on the accident. That was for his viewing alone. "The report seems to be in some sort of code."

Langdon took them. "Well done," he said. "Codes mean secrets. I will pass them to Oswald, see what he makes of them."

Jackson hid the folder under his clothes in the chest. He would look at it when he felt more able to concentrate, now he needed to sleep.

Chapter 16

When Jackson awoke, it was near luncheon. He had slept well and felt refreshed. After washing and dressing, he made his way to the classroom, to find everyone else assembled. "We have everyone here now," said Fairview. "Are you rested, Jackson?"

"I am," he replied, sitting next to Jessamine. "Was I late?"

"No, we have only just convened, we are about to hear of Mr Winstanley's foibles from Mularky and Winifred." Winstanley, that was the man Jackson had almost met on the roof, and later in the yard.

"Winstanley is a brute of a man," said Winifred, a slight girl with short fair hair and a piercing stare. "A criminal with no qualifications, he is unlikely to be associated with the likes of Nethersole in any way save the illegal."

"He frequents the roughest ale houses and consorts with criminals," added Mularky. Unlike Winifred, he was huge, with an adult's body. "He also appears to be engaged in the trafficking of pressed workers. Every week, a charabanc full of the people he has pressed leaves the city. Bound for Hammerham and the Nethersole estate."

Jackson gasped, perhaps Winstanley had been the one he had been sold to, all those years ago. If he now were instrumental in bringing him down, it would be ironic, to say the least.

"You know a little about Winstanley's type, don't you, Jackson?" asked Fairview.

"I once escaped from their clutches, if that's what you mean," he replied.

"We think that maybe there is more going on than merely controlling mechanical limbs. That may be just the tip of this riddle. Along with what has been found about your friend Aldithley and the papers you acquired, Oswald, Langdon and I have examined all the evidence and consider there is the basis for a plan to take control of the country."

That could not have been more shocking news. Everyone tried to speak at once. Langdon held up his hand for silence. "It all fits together," he said. "Oswald has suggested, and I agree, that the gadget in the limbs is little more than a test, a proof that the technology developed by Professor Aldithley works. Added to which, it sounds from what we have just heard that Winstanley could well be recruiting an army, if he's scouring the slums and taking people away by the charabanc load, what is their purpose, where are they housed?"

"What does the thing I found, the thing in the limbs, do?" asked Jackson.

"Oswald says it uses a particular function of what he calls the statics field. It's a switch, sensitive to statics vibration. A nearby statics field will alternately turn it on and off."

"Then we need to know how the statics field is generated and passed to the device."

"I have found a few things out about the Professor you saw. He is more than capable of creating mechanisms like this. He was once a part of Professor Woolon's team at the Institute of Medical Statics, until he was asked to leave."

"Why?"

"Because he got ideas above his ability, he wasn't content to work as the Professor instructed. Building arms and legs that worked was not enough. He wanted to control people by use of statics. Woolon was minded to proceed as they were, slowly and steadily, advancing the knowledge of the body and using it to control the limbs. Aldithley was in a rush to be famous; he wanted to take a huge leap, based not on science but on his own theories, which he would not share. He tried a new technique in secret and against orders. Men died and of course it was all found out." He paused. "And the most significant thing, his project was known as Sensaurum."

"So must we assume that this thing you call a filament is part of his plan? His project continues. Has Nethersole given him the chance to do what he couldn't when he was with Woolon?"

"It certainly seems to be capable of basic control remotely. The arm proves that. I would say that it's more than a test. Consider the consequences. Never mind the personal inconvenience of having your arm or leg stop working, think of the devastation he could cause if it were implanted in some piece of machinery, or the controls of a process. As for control of people, his original aim, we must hope that is still beyond him. This is enough to deal with."

"But where do all the people fit in?"

"We have to assume that they are his new test subjects, without the rigour of officialdom controlling him. He has been stopped by Woolon, now he is continuing, with a cadre of folk who none care about."

"The Ladies would care about them," said Jessamine. "Perhaps they might put pressure on Rodney?"

"Yes, I know they would care, and they would help. But we cannot involve them, any more than we can fix all society's ills in one fell swoop. For their own safety, the knowledge we have must remain between us. They must deal with their own affairs, whilst we thwart Rodney's plans. His behaviour warrants further investigation. We know that when Nethersole goes to his country estate, he takes the Professor with him. Winstanley is taking the people he collects there as well. You must go and see what is occurring there. Search his property and see if you can find out his plans."

"Someone will have to go back to the Prosthesium," said Fairview, "and find the rest from the factory."

"I will not send another after Jackson was seen," Langdon replied. "Rodney may well start to wonder, one break-in could be opportunistic, another would be more than a coincidence. We must think of another way."

"Very well, Sir Mortimer." Fairview's tone indicated that he was not in full agreement with his superior. "Meantime, I have tasked Oswald with deciphering the report Jackson found for us, as quickly as possible, it may give more answers."

Mrs Grimble came to the door. "Sir," she said, her eyes red. "I have just heard some awful news."

Chapter 17

All eyes turned to her, she was not known for displays of histrionics, something terrible must have occurred to make her so distraught. "What is it, Mrs Grimble?" asked Langdon.

"Sir," she sniffed, pulling a large cloth from her pocket and wiping her eyes. "Two cars from the aerialway have collided, in the centre of town, by the Fussels Building. The safety system failed to stop one at a passing place, they were both on the same rail, moving in opposite directions. There are many dead, the wreckage is spread over a wide area, falling as it did. Many more were killed on the ground. Fires have started, a section of track is destroyed."

Langdon once again showed no flicker of sadness, just his habitual blank face. "Thank you, Mrs Grimble, I'm not sure that this tragedy is within our remit, but in case it is, can you fetch Oswald. I would value his opinion."

"I can, sir." She left and a moment later Oswald appeared, hitching his trousers up and straightening his glasses.

"Do you know of the collision on the aerialway?" Langdon asked.

Oswald shook his head. "A collision? It's not possible, sir," he began. "Unless..."

Langdon suddenly became alert. "Unless what, Oswald? What do you know of the system, could this just be an act of sabotage, an accident or the result of human error?"

"Well," the man replied, polishing his glasses with a rag pulled from his pocket. "It occurs to me, that is, I think," he paused.

"Oswald, it's a simple question, could the accident be connected to what we know about the Sensaurum?"

"Oh yes," Oswald said. "We have seen that this filament can control an arm, turn it on and off. It could certainly control a carriage on the aerialway. Easily, if someone had access, they could insert one in a control box. They could then activate it, disabling the safety systems that prevent such an occurrence."

"Could it not just be an unfortunate accident, Oswald?"

"An accident is unlikely, although possible. We should remember that in four years there has never been so much as a hint of a problem."

He thought for a moment. "No, it has to be sabotage," he said. "The system itself prevents collisions by mechanical interlocks, operated by the passage of the carriage. There is no manual intervention. The driver merely stops and starts the traction and operates the doors. The carriage cannot move unless the control box is activated, when it is a metal bar is engaged on the track, it operates the points via linkages, as it passes. There is no possibility of failure unless the box is disconnected once the carriage is in motion. If the rod is withdrawn, then the linkage will not work. As far as the system, or any other carriage is concerned, the track is clear."

He paused for a moment more, blinking rapidly as he assembled his thoughts.

"Sealed in his cabin, the driver would not hear the link withdrawn, he would know of no problem until he saw the other carriage fail to enter the loop. By then, with their combined speeds, neither would be able to stop the carriages in time with the brakes, try as they might."

Jackson could see in his mind the two hurtling towards each other, each driver trying in vain to stop, knowing what was about to happen and yet being unable to prevent it. What a final moment. He shuddered at the vision his imagination had created.

The others were also silent, no doubt entertaining the same thought.

"Then, it must be that the control box in one carriage was fitted with a cartridge. If so, how was it operated?"

"Could it be activated by a person in a station, or by a driver, intent on euthanasia?" Alyious broke the sombre silence.

"Either scenario is possible. If the control was turned off once the carriage had left the station. The bar activates the points for an approaching carriage on departure. As for euthanasia, it's something to consider, but why now, just when we know of this other method?"

"Presumably the person intending to take his life would need knowledge of the workings of a control box?" muttered Langdon. "They would have to be well versed in the mechanics."

Oswald nodded. "That is so, to alter the box so that it did not fail-safe; that is to say stop all motion, would require skill. Would it not be easier to kill oneself in a myriad of other ways?"

"I think," said Langdon, "that this is the next part of our mystery."

"The only way to be sure," said Oswald, "will be to examine the control boxes and the tracks."

"Then we should go to the site and look for any evidence, the Watch will not know any of this. We must hope to find a cartridge in one of the control boxes, it's doubtful that either driver will have survived."

"Who should we take?" asked Jessamine. Swiftly Langdon set them to work.

"Winifred, you and Mularky get to the Prosthesium and see where the two players are. The rest of you, and you too, Oswald, come with me."

"Very well," said Oswald. "That will be a relief. I'm getting nowhere with my attempts to unravel the code in that report, a change of scene may well do me good."

It was difficult to get to the site of the accident; the Watch had set up barriers and were only allowing residents through. Langdon had a pass, in a leather case, that he showed to the Captain and the band were waved on.

There was devastation over a wide area. Wounded people wandered in a daze and several small fires still raged. There was a line of corpses, laid out under the canvas sheeting that Jackson recognised from his time cutting and sewing in the orphanage. They had never been told the purpose of their endeavours, now he could see his work in action.

Langdon dispatched Alyious and Vyner to gather accounts from any who had witnessed the events. Taking Oswald, Jackson and

Jessamine, he found the Aerialway Express Company investigator and asked him what he knew.

"And who might you be?" he demanded. "On whose authority do you ask?"

Langdon again showed the card in its case. "I am attached to the government, investigating possible acts of anarchy by foreign powers," Langdon replied. "These are my assistants."

The man's eyes gaped wide. "Foreign powers, anarchy? Surely this was an accident?"

"That is what we are all here to ascertain. Now, firstly describe the sequence of events, as you understand them."

"Very well," said the man. "The westbound had just left the station at the Fussels Building and would have been switched to use the main track. An eastbound should have gone into the loop but came on; there was either a failure at the points or in the carriage's control box, from where the signal to the points is sent mechanically."

"And has this ever happened before?"

The man shook his head. "Never, if I could not see that it had, I would have said it was impossible. To me, the system is foolproof, once activated. The only way for there to be two carriages on the same piece of track is if the interlock is switched off in one of them, after the carriage is in motion and has passed the activator."

"Then how can you explain it?"

"I cannot," the man said, somewhat angry now at the questioning. "From a position on the ground with no access to the wreckage. I need to see the control boxes from both carriages."

Langdon ignored the tone. "I take it they are still searching for them; I would like to see them too. My assistant," he indicated Oswald, who bowed, "would like to examine them. We are in possession of information that might be pertinent."

"Very well, Sir Mortimer. I will arrange it." The man made a note in his pocketbook. "And now, if you'll excuse me, I have a lot of work to do, not least of which will be explaining to the Minister how this system had failed so spectacularly."

There was nothing more they could do. "I don't envy you that job, sir," said Langdon. He turned to Jackson and Jessamine. "We need to go to the station and view the track, if it is not destroyed. Then if we still cannot determine anything, we need to speak to any witnesses that Alyious and Vyner have found."

They entered the Fussels Building and rode the deserted elevator to the station. At the gate was a Watchman, resplendent in his uniform.

"You cannot pass, this is a dangerous place," he said. Langdon again showed his pass and they gained access. The rail was ten feet above them, still held in place but looking towards the crash scene, two pillars away it ended suddenly.

"It's a good job the pillars stood," said Oswald, "else the toll might have been so much worse."

"Can you see aught?"

"I will have to climb up." At the end of the platform, outside the safety rail was a ladder, reaching up the side to the building it connected with the framework that supported the rail.

Oswald climbed up and along, coming to rest on the support. The rail was now in touching distance. He peered over, his glasses wobbled, and he grabbed at them. The motion unbalanced him and for a second it seemed that he must fall. Jessamine gasped; he righted himself.

"I need a strap for my glasses," Oswald muttered, "if I'm to wander the city, looking at twisted wreckage. I will have to devise one when I get back to solid ground."

"Never mind trying to fly," shouted Langdon, "what can you see?"

Oswald peered again. "The interlock is untouched," he said, "the bar on this carriage never engaged with it. There is part of your answer."

"Get yourself back to safety then."

Oswald needed no order, shortly he was back inside the barrier.

"Your conclusions, now that you are back on safe ground?"

"It appears that the carriage that left this place had no control," said Oswald. "The box would have to have been switched off once the carriage was in motion, before it reached the interlock, in such a way that power was still applied. The driver, if he had not orchestrated things, would know nothing. I need to see the box, once it has been recovered, to be sure."

"The Watch will have them," Jessamine said. "But what could they tell? They will know nothing of switches and interlocks."

Langdon nodded. "True, not forgetting that I'm not too popular with the senior men of the Watch. Perhaps it will be best to wait for the official investigation. But I have a horrible feeling that this is just the start, there will be worse to come unless we can disrupt this man's plans. Let us collect the others and return to the orphanage. Oswald, you can get back to making sense of the works of Aldithley, while we decide what to do next."

They repaired to the ground, where they found Alyious and Vyner. "Your reports?" Langdon said.

"Nobody has much to say," replied Vyner. "All are so used to seeing the aerialway now that they take no notice. We found one person whose son had said, 'look, both carriages are about to collide, neither has stopped,' but that was all. The first anyone noticed was the noise and the falling of the wreckage."

"That's the problem," agreed Oswald, "after the initial wonder, science becomes mundane, nobody sees it, until it fails."

Chapter 18

That evening, Jackson had his first look at the folder he had acquired from the Prosthesium. He opened it with trembling hands, more than once he had pulled it from its hiding place under his clothes and almost opened it. Then he had put it away again, as if he didn't want to know any more details. Now, he was determined to read it.

The first pages of the report were given over to the bald details of the factory, its age, construction and maintenance. There were plans of the floor showing the positions of the machines and details of the persons involved. Jackson saw that listed were Rodney Nethersole, Philton Clynes and his father, Emory Thwaite, as the main players in the drama that unfolded.

The known facts of the events leading up to the disaster were repeated. Jackson had thought that he knew enough about it, but he realised that he had only half the story, and that a lot of what he thought he knew was wrong. The report chronicled the times of the events.

At six am the boiler was brought back from its overnight state to full capacity.

At seven, when the pressure was raised, the beam and all its associated bearings were inspected before the drive was engaged to set the shaft spinning.

Here was the first point of contention in the account. According to Nethersole's evidence, Jackson's father had been the one to inspect the beam, shaft and all the belts. On his word, the drive was engaged. Jackson was surprised to find that his father had been the one to inspect the state of the bearings, the ones that had eventually failed.

According to the report, it was Nethersole's responsibility and that he normally did the work, but on that day, Jackson's father had done it in his stead, so as not to delay the start of the day's work. Nethersole made it seem as if he was giving Jackson's father more responsibility. He claimed to have trained him under his supervision and Nethersole stated on oath that he was content with his ability.

That seemed strange, his father had never remarked about performing inspections, or being given extra tasks. His job was to test completed prosthetics, what did he know about the condition of power systems? It was no good wondering about that now, his father was in no position to explain himself. But for the life of him, he couldn't understand how his father had missed any signs of impending doom, if he had been properly trained.

He had always been fastidious in the house, checking the range before lighting it, observing every recommendation for any household appliance that was in use.

Then there was the accident, at just after ten in the morning, just as production was in full swing and the room was full of workers. Nethersole said that he had just left the room, closing the door behind him. He was praised in the report for doing so; the damage had been contained by the doors. There was evidence stating that they were often left open to improve ventilation in the room.

There was a knock at his door, interrupting his reading. "Are you coming to the Gymnazien?" called Capricia.

"No not tonight, I have things to study," he replied. He heard her walk away and turned back to read on.

The next section listed the dead, with graphic descriptions of their injuries. Jackson skipped this part. They were dead, they were mostly known to him. He didn't want to learn how many pieces they had been cut into by flying steel and leather.

Then he came to the conclusions.

The findings were that the inspection regime was lax. Nethersole escaped severe censure by claiming that Jackson's father had been trained by him and had assured him that he was able to inspect the shaft. Even so, it had been suggested that such important work should be better supervised in future.

Clynes had accepted full responsibility for the failures and had resigned. To Jackson, it seemed that Nethersole had come out of it the best, indeed had he not taken over the company?

Jackson was shaking when he turned the final page, much had

been explained in the stark language of officialdom, but he could not accept that his father had been solely at fault. He was convinced that Nethersole had used him as a means to avoid disciplinary action for his own neglect.

Then he had a terrible thought. What if Nethersole had engineered the whole thing? He had much to gain, he had got control of the factory by it. Perhaps, and this was the worst thing, he had made the problem and shut the door on it, knowing he had the perfect alibi.

Even thinking that was too much. He had not liked Rodney Nethersole when they had met. He had become annoyed by Jessamine's flirting; the thought of his interest in her repulsed him. Knowing, or suspecting what he might have done made him feel very angry. He had to work off his anger somehow.

Despite his earlier excuses, he headed for the Gymnazien. He felt the urge to hit something, hard and repeatedly. If the others noticed his anger, they left him to assuage it.

Instead, their talk was all about the seriousness of the situation. "This is so much more than we normally deal with," opined Alyious. "A madman bent on world domination, and we are the ones to stop him. The tales of the carriages falling from the sky were horrific, to think that any person could do such a thing, to his own countrymen."

Vyner punched him. "Don't be so dramatic, Alyious," he said. "'Tis just another one of the regular scares, we are always stopping madmen bent on world domination."

"Speak for yourself, gangs of pickpockets bent on world domination maybe," said Mularky. "That's about as exciting as my life ever gets."

"Only because that's all you can cope with," suggested Winifred. "Does the time we spend together not excite you then?"

At that point Mularky looked embarrassed and everyone else started laughing. "I must admit to enjoying stalking Winstanley," she added. "It made a fine change from snaring errant husbands with a head full of secrets and weak wills."

"Why then is Langdon so involved?" asked Jessamine. "When else has he taken control of things from Fairview? We normally only see him when it's time to take the credit."

"Or give out the blame," added someone and there was more laughter.

"We must go," said Alyious as he heard the clock strike nine. "Clarry and his boys have been watching the players for us; we need to find what they have been about."

Everyone departed leaving Jackson alone with Capricia. She had that look in her eye, the one that made him nervous. Pleading tiredness, he left her for his bed.

Chapter 19

Next morning, Langdon was again present when everyone made their reports. And it was clear from his demeanour that he was not a happy man.

"I have been in early meetings with ministers of the crown," he said. "They have accepted my view that this Rodney Nethersole might present a serious threat to the security of the nation. Even if all he can do is stop a few limbs working or derail an aerialway car, panic will spread if it becomes known that he is orchestrating mayhem. Action must be taken before he can reveal himself to the populace or do anything worse. I have been told that, should he be allowed to continue, then heads will roll, mine being first." He looked at the group. "Let me hear your news."

Alyious spoke first. "We left here at nine to take over from Clarry. Nethersole left the factory as usual, with Winstanley and the Professor in tow. Winstanley left them in town, so we split up, Vyner and I followed Nethersole and the others followed Winstanley."

"We will get to Winstanley later, what of the main players?"

"Rodney and the Professor went to a club, the Gavan, in town, where we assume they dined. Later in the company of two women, who they must have met inside, they went to Rodney's house in the suburbs. We were prepared to wait overnight and follow him back this morning. However, at around an hour before the middle of the night, a mobile pulled up and they all left in it, together with luggage."

"What did you do then?"

"I followed at a distance, via a mobile, whilst Vyner stayed to see if they would return. In the end, they went to the rail and took the overnight service to Stynehouse, driving their mobile on to the flat car."

"We must assume that they were then to proceed to Hammerham, to the Nethersole estate," said Langdon. "Are you sure they departed?"

Alyious nodded. "I watched them onto the Ryde and waited until it left, then I returned to pick up Vyner."

"Well done," said Langdon. "I think it safe to assume they have gone to the country. What of Winstanley?"

"He had several ales with associates," said Mularky, "then went to the place where he keeps his charabanc. It was full of people, collected by his henchmen. There were women and children, a full load of fifty or more. He too set out from the city."

"It seems as if everyone of importance has gone to his country estate, this may be a regular occurrence, it may be that we have disturbed his plans, we can't be sure. In any event, we must follow him to see what he is doing, away from the city where there are fewer prying eyes."

"Now that Nethersole and Winstanley are away, would that not be the best time to return to the factory, to search without fear of hindrance?" asked Fairview.

"That is part of my plan," Langdon said, "and what I have proposed to the government. However, I do not trust them with all my intentions, for I know that there are some whose sympathies are, shall we say, questionable. What I have not told them, is that as well as searching the Prosthesium, I will be sending some of my agents to spy on the Nethersole estate."

There was a rustle of excitement. "You," he indicated Jackson and Jessamine, "are to go to Rodney's estate in the country, see what you can find there."

There were groans and mutterings of, "Why them."

"They have been seen in the factory," Langdon said. "The others of you have not. There will be someone left in charge. If they are recognised, they might be placed in danger." He stood. "I must leave you now, I have business to attend. Mr Fairview will continue."

Fairview had brought a rolled canvas map, which he now spread out on the desks. "Gather round," he said. "This is all the latest information we have."

The map showed the town of Hammerham and its surroundings. In the west of the country, the town was not connected to the Rail, the nearest station being at Stynehouse. It was at least a day's travel away; even by mobile. The map showed the roads as unsealed and difficult to pass. The Nethersole estate was located a mile or so outside the town, near the waterfalls of Los, apparently a popular spot for trippers.

"This is the reason for your visit," Fairview explained, "you will be newly-wedded, on a working holiday."

"Again?" said Winifred. "How is it Mularky and I are never newly-wedded? Why not marry them properly and have done with it?"

"We have no need for pretence with you two," suggested Alyious. "You argue like you have been wed for years."

Winifred persisted, "And why do they go? Nethersole knows who they are."

"They are not to meet him, but they will know him, and the Professor, if they see them," Fairview explained. "You would not."

"I still don't think it's right," she pouted.

Mularky nudged her. "Hush now, your point is made, you hate the countryside in any event."

"If I may continue," said Fairview acidly. "Thank you. As I was saying, you are newly-wedded. Jessamine, your father is a rich man, he is paying for your trip, but you have to do some work for him whilst you are away."

"What is that?" asked Jessamine.

"Oh, nothing too onerous, but a good reason for you to stick your nose into corners and be inquisitive. You are seeking new markets for his journals, periodical publications that carry what are becoming known as inducements.

All the details are in these notes, which you will have to memorise as quickly as you can." He passed the pair some sheets of parchment.

Jackson quickly glanced at the papers; the story was believable and seemed easy enough to learn.

"Now attend to the map."

They had a brief examination of the plans of the Nethersole estate as marked on the map. There was little information on the interior of their target, save that there was at least one large building behind the wall that encircled the estate.

"As you can see, the whole is surrounded by a high wall," said Fairview, "and with the urgency of things we have not been able to get details of what might lie inside. You will have to discover as you go."

"There is little to help us then," said Jessamine, "no knowledge of guards or any hazards?"

Fairview admitted it was a hasty plan. "I'm sorry but no. Nor is there time for you to rehearse your identities. Normally, we would have a lot longer to get you both ready, but this thing is in danger of escalating beyond any control. Langdon thinks you are ready, Jackson, and Jessamine is an able companion for you. Remember your training and you will be alright. Your flight takes place just before fast-break tomorrow, you will be called early."

"Did you say flight?" asked Jessamine. "Does that mean what I think?"

"Yes," said Fairview. "Even though the expense is vast, you will go by flying machine. Tickets have been arranged and can be collected when you arrive at the Aero-field."

This was exciting news, Jackson had seen the machines and longed to travel in one, now his dreams would become a reality. "Why fly?" asked Jessamine. "We normally go by rail and mobile."

"Time is of the essence, in this case. Sir Mortimer is keen to get you to Hammerham as near to Rodney's arrival as possible. We need to know what he does behind that wall, if that means spending money on flying machines, then it is a small price to pay, in the scheme of things."

"Even so," said Jackson, "flying is such a new thing, is it safe?"

Jessamine had an answer for that. "The rail is more dangerous, brigands still infest the lands, why do you suppose the Ryde has soldiers atop its carriages? At least in the air, we cannot be attacked, not even by Drogans anymore."

"Six years ago," Fairview said, "there were no such things as flying machines, the only flyers were balloonists, defending the land against the Drogans that still ruled the skies, the idea of controlled flight was still in the future. Now the Drogans have gone and it was man who had taken their place as masters of the air. We would be remiss not to utilise their gift to us."

"So why have the Drogans disappeared?" asked Jackson. "When I was outside last, they were a force, we were in danger and the skies were patrolled by balloons and watch towers."

"Now there is a tale, it is beyond the scope of this meeting, but since you ask, I will give you a summary. Jessamine can no doubt tell you more, it will pass the time on your way to Hammerham." He cleared his throat. "No doubt you won't have heard of Horis Strongman or indeed of Christoph Leash?"

"No, neither of them."

"Well, Horis was a great man, he was the first for some time to learn the ways of the Fenesh, the means by which Drogan and human conversed. Folk in the countryside had a rudimentary way of communicating with the beasts but not the formality of the Fenesh, Anyway, Christoph, who was a criminal by the way, also learned the finer points of the Fenesh and found a band of renegade Drogans to command."

Jackson remembered that someone had mentioned the Fenesh, was it not the basis of Oswald's Lexiograph?

"How did he do that?" he asked. "As I remember, Drogans were contemptuous of humans?"

"He took their minds over, using the fact that he was the only one who could converse to tell them only what he wanted them to hear. They were angry at man's arrogance and the destruction of their habitat. So they retaliated by defending themselves. Christoph offered them a more organised way of disrupting man's life, which coincided with his dreams of wealth and power. It suited his purpose to have an army behind him, he had no interest in the plight of the beasts, just in his own advancement.

Horis got involved in the argument, through his Drogan, the one that lived with him and helped him. The leaders of the government petitioned him to speak on the country's behalf, to reach a deal with the Drogans. Through Horis, the false promises of Christoph were exposed to the Drogans he was controlling. They initially refused to believe that he was misleading them. After a lot of adventures, they came to see his falsehood and dealt with him. Then a treaty was agreed. It ceded them a group of islands off the coast. They are theirs to have as their own kingdom and guaranteed its safety forever. In return the Drogans, who only ever wanted peace and the ability to live as they wished, were to be left alone. Our navy patrol the seas around the island, keeping all away."

"And what do the Drogans think of our flying machines?"

"Nobody knows, we have had no contact since the last ones left. That was the arrangement and we have kept our part."

Jackson was interested in the story, he resolved to search in the library as soon as he had the chance; the idea of talking to any beast fascinated him.

That was all of it, the group dispersed. Jackson and Jessamine went to his room to learn of the people they would become. They spent the next two hours discussing the story and Jackson learned again of the reach of Langdon.

There was a genuine background to all of it, and a man who would vouch for them if asked. They were Mr and Mrs Draftman, the real name of Langdon's associate, a cursory check would be unlikely to require more than that, at least that was the hope. As Fairview had said, it was a rushed plan, but plausible.

They practised talking of their imagined lives and the reasons for their visit to Hammerham until they had a way of bouncing the conversation between them that felt natural.

"Enough," said Jessamine at last. "It's almost time for sleep. You will need your wits in the morn. It's best if you check you have everything ready before you retire. Take sufficient of everything for four or five days' stay. Not the high fashion city clothes we wore to the factory, one good suit to travel in, the rest clean but practical this time. You recall, you need to wear your belt and keep your pack with you, the bulk of our supplies go into the hold of the flying machine, separate from us, should we need anything on the trip."

"I know nothing of flying machines," Jackson said. "To be sure I have seen them going over the orphanage, but when I lived outside, they were unknown, there seem to be so many requirements before travelling on one. And what of our gear might we need?"

"Who knows," she said. "We must be ever ready for threat. As for flying machines, they truly have been a sudden thing. From nothing to what they are today is a miracle to some, but of course, ether is much more to the story than that. Long before anyone was aware, flight was taking shape and being perfected by Ralf and his colleagues.

"Where? How was it kept secret?" asked Jackson, once again made aware that the general population was ignorant of the things that went on in secret in their own land.

"People in general never knew of the events at Northcastle," she replied. "Of the tract of land owned by the government and fenced to keep folk away. Of the brave flyers who tamed the first craft, which were little more than flying gas tanks. Of the innovators like Ralf, whose ideas are even now leading the way."

Jackson realised that she said the name with a raptured tone, as if he were some sort of deity.

"Ralf was the first to fly a plane from Northcastle to Metropol City, first to land a machine on a ship of the navy and so much more. What we will travel in today only exists because of him. Largely because so much was done behind the scenes, the science was proved before anyone was aware. Hence, we have a new thing appearing fully formed and few know the history."

"I've never heard of this man Ralf. Does everyone else know all this?"

"And more," she said. "Once the existence was admitted, the history came to be known. You have a lot of catching up to do, Jackson. Now I must leave you, I have my own packing to attend to, goodnight."

Jackson packed his case and made sure that he had everything he needed. He lay down to sleep, although he could not. Six months ago, he had looked into the sky, on the night where everything had changed and had seen a flying machine.

At that moment, if someone had told him he would soon be travelling in one, he would have laughed. But then, if he had been told that he could climb walls, or have a room to himself, they would have received the same response.

He fell asleep reading and reciting the details of his life of pretence. 'Jessamine and Jackson Draftman, newly wedded,' like 'Josiah and Gertie Wedge,' it had a good sound to it.

Chapter 20

They were called early. After a hurried mug of Char they travelled by tram to the flying field, which was located in the city at the place where Ralf had first landed on his maiden flight from Northcastle.

The sign at the gate said 'Metropol City Aero-port'. Jessamine was not as excited as Jackson clearly was. "I have flown in an Aero before," she said. "Stay close to me, I will keep you safe."

"Tell me, why do you call it by different names, an Aero, a plane, a flying machine. Which is it?"

"They are so new that no name has been settled on, people use all of them."

"And this Ralf, has he no other name?"

"I'm sure he does but it is never needed. He is just Ralf, everyone knows who is meant if you say Ralf or Ralf the flyer."

That is fame, thought Jackson, even the King had two names, yet this man had only the need of one.

Using a card that she had in her bag, Jessamine collected their tickets for the flight to Hammerham, the nearest town to Nethersole's estate. "There is no rail nearby," she said, "as we saw on the map yesterday. We would have to travel by road from the nearest station, a bone-shaking journey of at least a day, even without any complications, this is much better."

At least you were safe on the road, thought Jackson, despite what Fairview had said. Apart from the brigands, your bones might be shaken but calamity in an Aero and they would be worse affected. He wondered if whatever had happened to the aerialway could strike a plane in flight.

Their cases were put on a clockwork cart and taken away; they both kept their backpacks with them, as they contained all their secret equipment and devices. "We have an hour before we may board," Jessamine said. She pointed to a small stand, containing news-sheets and periodicals. "We should buy one of Draftman's journals, it would look strange if I knew nothing of my 'father's' work. This whole expedition is so hastily arranged that the finer details have not been considered."

They purchased the journal 'About Town', and Jackson also took a copy of 'An Illustrated Guide to Flight for the new Traveller'.

Sitting, they read avidly. Jackson was desperate to learn all he could about flight before he had to face the event, he learned the names of the parts of a flying machine, but he was continually interrupted by Jessamine, who insisted on showing him examples of the inducements that the pages of her publication appeared to be full of.

"Never mind flying," she said. "I can explain all that to you when we are aloft, you need to know what we are supposed to be expert in first. The job in hand takes precedence."

Looking at what she showed him, it seemed to him that anything could be purchased from the pages, without the need to ever enter a shop, there were drawings of the articles, everything from devices to sweep your floor, powered by steam or clockwork to the latest fashion, gowns, coats and all manner of other things. All that was required was to send a written request, and payment, the goods would arrive by delivery wagon within a few days.

"This is a work of genius," he said. "But you are wrong about my publication." He showed her the pages, they too contained inducements, these for flying equipment, medications for flying-sickness, stylish clothing for the flyer and the like.

"We will soon be a nation of people who hardly need to leave their dwellings" he said. "We may already work from home, via the mails, now we can shop there as well."

"It's not progress, according to some," she replied. "There are people who cannot bear to have the pages cluttered up with inducements, shops will go out of business over this if they cannot compete on price."

"Surely there will always be people who prefer the personal service from meeting a shopkeeper?" he countered.

"That is true, but as time passes, they will be replaced by folk who know no other way, then we might have problems to deal with, as people lose jobs in shops."

That was an interesting subject; Jackson considered the implications of something as apparently innocuous as an inducement in a journal. He was coming to realise that society was a web of threads, all dependant on each other for the strength of the whole. He had never even considered it when his whole world was a single space behind a wall.

"There is so much to discuss, everything in life that I have missed out on learning. Sometimes it feels like an impossible task."

"I will help you all I can," she replied.

A voice boomed through the room. "All passengers for the service to Hammerham, please assemble at the gate, we are boarding shortly."

"That's us," said Jessamine. "Come along, this will be fun."

Jackson passed through the barrier, and through the door into the sunshine. Ahead of him sat the flying machine, looking much bigger than he had imagined. It was painted in a light blue and had the words Norlandair Services in a bold typeface on the sides of the cabin. There was a drawing of a Drogan in flight on the tail.

The wings were underneath, with an engine attached to each, from which a large wheel protruded. He saw the cart, with his case, bouncing across the grass, heading for the rear of the plane, where a hatch was open and people waited. There was a smell of gas in the air; under each wing was a small mobile, with a huge gas tank on its bed. The tank was connected to the wings by pulsing hoses.

Jackson assumed they were filling some sort of fuel tank. He wanted to ask so many questions, Jessamine seemed to be totally familiar with their situation and he felt out of his depth.

"How many can it carry?" he asked. He had not got to that part in his reading.

"Ten or twelve passengers, two or three crew," answered Jessamine, "with their luggage."

A uniformed woman approached them, her light blue blouse decorated with a silver broach of a plane identical to the one before them.

She stood between Jackson and Jessamine and spoke to him. "Good morning, sir," she trilled. "I'm Francine, but you may call me Fanny. I will be looking after you this morning. Have you travelled by plane before?"

Jessamine moved. "I can take care of my man, thank you," she said sweetly. "We are seasoned travellers."

Francine backed away, still smiling. "Of course, madam, I hope I can satisfy any need either of you might have whilst we are aloft." She bowed slightly, then walked away to talk to some other passengers.

"Watch yourself, Jackson," she said. "These flying women have a reputation, it's said that they will devour anything in trousers, apparently there is a club for their kind who have... well you know, whilst aloft."

The thought occupied Jackson the rest of the way to the flying machine. They were headed towards the front, where there was a hatch with a ladder. As Jackson climbed up, he looked to his left and saw through a window a man in shirtsleeves was peering at a row of dials and making notes on a paper.

He was so engrossed that he forgot to duck his head and winced as it collided with the rim of the hatch. Muttering curses, and ignoring Jessamine's giggle, he entered the cabin of the flying machine. Inside it was set out like a gentlemen's club, with armchairs and small tables. There was a cabinet containing bottles and glasses, a uniformed waiter stood nearby, directing people to seats, collecting coats and stowing baggage.

Jackson and Jessamine chose a pair of seats opposite a low table and sat. Jackson was closest to a window and gazed in fascination at the wing of the machine, with its underslung engine.

"Why did you say that we were seasoned travellers?" he asked.

"To keep her from hovering over you," she replied. "Remember, trust no-one. If you have any questions, I can tell you the answers." Jackson failed to see how the woman could be one of Rodney's agents; perhaps Jessamine was harbouring some other emotion, a more proprietorial one?

The woman came on board, following the last of the passengers. Jackson noticed that she was flirting with another man. This one appeared to be unaccompanied and she made a great show of seating him and stowing his bag. The door closed with a click and Jackson felt the seat quiver as the engines were started. Where to begin? He wanted to know everything. Before he had time to speak, the woman addressed them.

"Good morning, ladies and gentlemen," she began, smoothing down imaginary creases in her gown, which was cut in a modern style, and more fitted than currently fashionable. In its way, it was as revealing of her form as Jessamine's trousered legs had been.

"We will shortly be departing for Hammerham; the journey will take us around two hours. Can I ask you to remain seated whilst we leave the ground, then to only stand if necessary, as the balance of the plane will be affected if everyone moves to the same side at once. I will shortly be serving a small meal and complimentary drinks. Thank you." She sat facing them in a seat which folded from the cabin's wall, or should that be bulkhead? he wondered. Gazing at Jackson, she made a show of crossing her legs, exposing her knees.

Beside him Jessamine nudged his ribs. "Pay no attention," she said. "She is doing it again."

Jackson drew his gaze away and focused on what was happening.

"How do the engines work?" he asked.

"That is an easy one. The first engines were little more than a naked flame, which heated and expanded air and forced it out of the rear, pushing the plane forwards. Then Ralf had an idea, gas is still burned but now the hot air produced turns a fan which sucks in and compresses more air. More air means more combustion, thus more hot air is ejected. Instead of the hot air merely pushing the plane forward, the suction caused by the fan also pulls it. The rest of the plane then follows the engine."

She had explained it so simply, yet once again, Jackson could understand perfectly. As she spoke, the machine began to roll forwards, the wheels rumbling on the hard surface, then it slowed, swung around and stopped.

But how does it fly? As he wondered, Jackson heard the whine of the engine's note increase, looking out again he was sure that he could see the wings shake; there was a haze from the back of the engine. Jessamine gripped his hand. "Fear not, they increase the power against the brakes. It's more efficient than a standing start. Once a certain speed is achieved, it is impossible for the machine to remain on the ground."

That sounded so improbable, no matter how fast any machine moved, it remained on the ground, what was so special about this one?

"It's to do with the way air flows over the wing," she said, as if reading his mind. At that moment, they began to move forwards, faster and faster, until suddenly, the rumble from the wheels ceased. Jackson looked out of the window, they were airborne.

By craning his neck, he could see the houses and the city reduce in size, then they turned, the wing dropped and Jackson had a perfect view of the river, the distant ocean and the streets of the suburbs.

Chapter 21

The cabin suddenly darkened, Jackson looked out of the window in panic, he realised that they must be flying in a cloud. Nobody else seemed to have noticed, lights came on, recessed in the panelling overhead, bright globes of blue, the same as the ones in Oswald's room. He remembered the spinning magnet, perhaps their forward motion was used to create the same effect?

"They must be the Wasperton-Byler lights," he said to Jessamine. A man sitting close turned at the words. "What do you know of that?" he asked.

"I have heard of it," he replied.

"We saw the effect demonstrated at the Palais this last week," Jessamine broke in. "It was a fascinating evening."

The stranger relaxed. "My pardon," he said. "I'm a Watchman, currently off duty, returning from a training week in the city to my patrol in Hammerham. I heard you talk of sensitive information; my training took over."

Jackson smiled. "Are you from Hammerham?" he asked.

"I am," the man replied. "It's a small place but very friendly, with the patronage of Mr Nethersole it has prospered. I'm proud to serve the people I have known all my life as their Watchman."

"Is that Rodney Nethersole?" asked Jessamine. "The manufacturer of prosthetics in the city?"

"The same, I see that his fame has spread, he is so well regarded locally, there are none who would not defend him. He even takes in the waifs and strays from the city, a charabanc load at a time. He houses them at his own expense in his estate and puts them to useful labour on his farms."

It was interesting to see this man's view of Nethersole's actions, how it differed from their suspicions.

"He has farms? I knew not. Is it not enough that he gives hope to our disabled veterans?"

"He has a manager, a Mr Winstanley, a great authority on farming matters; they produce porkers and vegetables, for local consumption. There is talk of extending the rail to Hammerham, at his expense, to allow him to better send produce to the city." He sat back. "You'll find nobody thereabouts who will say a bad word about him."

Jackson was pleased, he had put his lessons into practice and obtained useful information, he was about to try and get more when the woman, Fanny, appeared, pushing a trolley.

To his relief, she spoke first to the Watchman. Leaning forward over him, she offered him a metal tray on which were a selection of what looked like leftover morsels of food. "Some refreshment, sir?" she inquired, placing the tray in his lap with a flourish.

Jessamine grabbed his arm again. "Look, Jackson," she exclaimed, pointing out of the window. "There is the Leopold Bridge, as its builders never saw it."

Jackson followed her finger, looking away from the woman. He saw the thirty-nine brick arches, in a gentle curve that carried the rail south across the River Norland, which bisected the country and gave it its name. A Ryde was halfway across, the smoke puffing from its chimney drifted in a line of equally spaced dots, at this distance the soldiers in the roof passage showed clearly as they waved. It was modern, yet old fashioned at the same time.

The rail and its steam engine had been the end of the equine; would the flying machine have the same effect on the rails?

"Some food, sir." The woman was bent over him with another tray. "No thank you," he said, lifting his hand. Somehow, he managed to hit the tray, depositing the contents all over him. At least there was no hot soup, just a selection of neatly cut sandwiches and small cakes. Jackson noted that it was larger than the amount offered to the Watchman.

"Oh, I'm so sorry," she said dropping to her knees in front of him she started picking the items from his lap.

"I can manage," he said, pushing her away. He brushed the detritus onto the floor.

"She is so obvious," Jessamine remarked as she departed. "She moved the tray so you would hit it. It gave her an excuse to rummage in your clothes." Jackson was shocked, he squirmed in his seat, what was the matter with some women?

"They call it the five thousand club," the Watchman remarked. "The women, or attendants as they wish to be known, vie with each other to join it. They do say, and I could not comment, that the act in the air has a different quality, though I cannot imagine what."

The woman returned with a brush and swept the remains of the meal into a small bag. "May I have some food?" asked Jessamine.

"Of course, madam," she said frostily. She found another tray and handed it over. "And a drink of Char?" She poured it, splashing a little and stalked off, as far as she could in the cabin. Jackson had been forgotten, could it be because he had spurned her advances? He would have to ask.

"She likes you," remarked the Watchman. "I never enquired, what is your business in Hammerham?"

That was a tricky question, before Jackson had chance to answer, Jessamine broke in, "We are newly wedded and on a tour of the country, while we decide where to set up home together. My father has kindly paid for this trip, as a nuptial gift."

"That's extraordinarily kind," he said.

"I suspect my father's motives," Jessamine replied. "I fancy he is sending us to survey for expansion of his empire. He is involved in news and periodical publications, always searching for new markets. 'Get me copies of any local journals you might find', he said as he bade us farewell."

"And see if there is opportunity for my latest venture," added Jackson.

The man laughed. "No doubt he will be successful, if he sees opportunity in his daughter's holidays. And you, sir, what's your function?"

Jackson was on the spot. "Me, sir? Oh I am nothing much, I used to work in my parents' company, supplies for the navy, cloth and the like. Since their demise, I have tried many things, never finding one to excite me. Now my lady is teaching me the science of making and selling the inducements which are printed in her father's publications." If the man thought it strange that an adult male could be taught by a female, unlike some, he never showed it.

"Inducements," he said. "Yes, I have seen them in the news-sheets, they are a new and novel idea. I never imagined that a whole science could be involved in their design and placement. Can you tell me more?"

Jackson elaborated on the story that they had practised, glad to have seen some of them so recently. Outside the mountains passed by, so close they could almost be touched but they were ignored.

"Certainly, imagine you are reading an article about... Char." The man nodded. "Well, if an inducement were placed in the page, by a Char merchant, recommending his blend of leaves, you might remember it when next you purchased and ask for that particular one. The merchant would be happy; he has paid a small sum to tell many of his wares, he will make more sales as the result of his expenditure, sold Char he might not have. The journal makes money from selling the merchant a place on the page for the inducement."

Jessamine joined in. "As well as from purchase of the journal itself."

"And I get a good cup of Char," finished the man. "That's very clever; I can see that there is a gap in the market. There must be so many enterprises that I have not heard of, so much that I might be persuaded to sample. And I can learn of them, simply by reading an article that interests me. Your new father-in-law is a very clever man."

"Indeed, as well as gaining my lovely wife, I can see a purpose in my life at last. I'm sure there will be merchants and journals in Hammerham that we can pester with our ideas, between sampling the delights of the area."

"You must not work every day," said the man, "you are supposed to be on your holidays."

"I will not let him spend all his time on that," Jessamine replied with a laugh. "While there are none as passionate as the converted, I have inducements of my own for him."

They had hoped to discuss their plan of action; the presence of this man had made that impossible. They would have to decide what to do when they were alone. At least they had saved a day or more and would be able to start their covert operations that very night.

If flying was nothing much to be excited about, Jackson realised as they started to descend, landing might be another matter.

The speed reduced and Jackson could feel the plane start to lift from level into an attitude with the front higher. He wondered if that was normal, he wished that he had had more time to study the guide. Looking across he could see that Jessamine was unconcerned, as were the other passengers. They carried on their conversations and sipped at their drinks. He was thirsty, thanks to the clumsy actions of the attendant, he had never received one.

"We are about to land," the uniformed woman passed along the cabin. "Please finish your drinks and put the glasses in the holders on the deck," she said to each in turn. She bent over in front of Jackson to retrieve an object on the floor, her uniform gown stretching tight inches from his face. Jackson heard Jessamine mutter something under her breath.

When she was vertical again, Jackson asked her the question that was uppermost. "Excuse me, why do we now fly with our head higher?"

"Well," she smiled, altering her pose slightly, pushing one hip out towards him so that she showed off her body. "I do like a man who takes an interest. It's to increase the efficiency of the wing at lower speed. We land into the wind as well, meaning that we stop quicker." She turned and walked to her seat.

Jackson had been intent on her answer, now he saw that they were level with the treetops. The engine noise suddenly ceased and with a bounce, they were on the ground. Jackson let out a breath, it was alright, he had survived. Then the engine noise increased to a howl, surely that was abnormal. Jessamine saw his face. "The engines have been reversed," she said, "to stop us."

As they left, the woman was there again. "If you need any more questions answering, here is my address." She handed him a small card. Jessamine took it from her.

"He is with me, thank you so much," she snarled, tearing it to pieces and dropping it on the ground. They exited the plane in silence. Halfway to the building, Jackson could take it no longer.

"Why do women act so with me? I can tell that you are angry, so am I. They seem obsessed with innuendo and flirting, yet I do nothing to encourage them."

She laughed. "You poor boy, I'm not angry with you but with her. The trouble is, you do not realise how handsome you look, women of a certain sort are never content with what they have and will try and attract a male such as you, it's in their nature."

Jackson then thought of Capricia, had it really been a game, as she had suggested? He considered for a moment then decided it might be best not to raise the matter.

"You do not," he said. "Their behaviour makes me feel uncomfortable."

Jessamine had no answer for that; she looked away so that he could not see her expression. Jessamine was silent as they took an omnibus into the centre of the town; fortunately there was space for them to sit apart from their new friend. On the way, they passed by a tall wall, that seemed to go on for ever.

"That is the wall of Nethersole's estate," Jessamine whispered as huge gates in an arch with a building over it came into view. "We will not be going in that way."

"That was an interesting journey," said Jackson. "Apart from the novelty of flight, I soon forgot that I was in a metal box in the air. Between us though, we managed to get a lot of intelligence from the Watchman. And I managed to justify poking my nose into local matters, asking questions."

"We will have no friends in Hammerham, nowhere to be safe and nobody to trust," she replied. "Rodney has cleverly ingratiated himself and made all allies."

"Then we will have to rely on each other. And that talk of Winstanley, being a farmer. If Winifred says he's a thug, I'll take her opinion over anyone's."

The omnibus stopped by an inn, called the Nethersole Arms. The shops and businesses all reflected his presence, there was a

Nethersole Trading Company, Nethersole's general supplies and Winstanley's butchers all clustered around the square.

"Rooms may be had here," said the driver as they alighted and took their bags from the rack.

"I bid you good day," said the Watchman, "and hope your stay is pleasant and fruitful." He shook their hands. "If you need aught, mention that you are friends of Silas Mountmain, people know me and will aid you."

"This place is too obvious," said Jessamine. "We will lodge at another, quieter establishment, where we can come and go without being noticed. Perhaps one closer to the wall."

"I agree," said Jackson. "We would be best finding an inn that was not so much in thrall to him. There must be some in the town who do not like him, we just have to find them and bend them to our purpose."

"While never trusting them?"

"Exactly."

Chapter 22

Taking their cases, they left the market square and plunged into the backstreets. After wandering for a while, they found a small ale house, rejoicing in the name of the Lost Quarry. The sign had a vulpine tail disappearing into a burrow and two canines with annoyed faces.

"A room?" said the barman. "In my place? What's wrong with the Nethersole Arms?"

"We want seclusion," said Jessamine and the man smiled.

He turned to Jackson. "Lucky man," he said. "I have a room in the eaves, quiet and secluded, you will hear no raucous singing from the bar of an evening, likewise you may make as much noise as you wish and we will not notice."

They were shown up to the room and once the door was closed, Jessamine dissolved in laughter. "The innkeeper thinks we are on a tryst," she said. "We will get no disturbance."

The room was sparsely furnished but had a tiny washroom attached, a small window led out to a sloping roof of baked tiles. "Perfect, we can come and go with the door locked. No-one will be the wiser; they will not expect to see us anyway, though I would not be surprised if they do not listen at the door."

They laid out their possessions. "We will need dark clothes to blend in," said Jessamine taking her case and heading for the bathroom.

Jackson changed into what he thought of as his exploring clothes, the ones he had worn at the factory. Jessamine reappeared dressed in the tight trousers and a fitted blouse. "Now we wait," she said, "we may as well get some rest."

"But there is only the one bed." Jackson eyed it nervously; it was certainly big enough for two.

Jessamine laughed. "You're safe enough with me, safer than you would be with that woman from the Aero. If you are that worried for your honour, roll the counterpane and lay it between us."

Jackson was too embarrassed to comply, instead he lay down as close to the edge and opposite side to Jessamine as he could. He closed his eyes and tried to sleep, his mind was buzzing with all the new sensations he had experienced, even on this day. The next thing he knew he was dreaming.

He was with his mother and she was holding him close.

He woke, he was laid on his side, Jessamine was snuggled into his back, her form fitting against his, one arm draped over his chest. As she breathed, her hot breath blew hairs against his ear, tickling him. He moved and she woke.

She pulled away quickly. "Pardon me," she said. "I was sleeping and knew not what I was doing."

"It's nothing," said Jackson, then he realised how it sounded. "I don't mean it like that," he hastily added. "I was dreaming of my mother holding me, I hadn't thought of her for a long time."

"We must be professional," she added, she had also gone red. "It's getting dark, we should prepare to go and explore."

"Should we not eat?" Jackson was by now famished; his stomach was protesting the lack of sustenance provided by his mouth.

"Of course, I remember that your meal ended up on the floor. We don't want to appear in the inn though, it may be that we are seen by someone who should not know of us. Maybe there will be a place to get some food on our way to the estate."

They secured the door by moving the cupboard against it and exited via the window, crossing the tiles one by one and descending down the rain pipe.

On the ground, Jessamine turned around, while she got her bearings. "The main road is over there," she said. "We can run parallel to it until we reach the edge of town, then continue on our way once we are clear of habitation."

"Never mind that," Jackson said, pointing the opposite way. "I can smell food, in that direction."

"Very well then, a quick diversion to satisfy your stomach. We have much to do, we will eat as we walk."

They followed his nose and came upon a stand selling sandwiches of thick bread and cooked cuts of porker, with golden butter and a sauce of tomato, onion and pepper. They were beautiful to see and very reasonably priced. Jessamine purchased them, with money taken from her quip-belt. Jackson felt for his, to pay his share. It was not around his waist.

With a start, he realised that it was still in the room. They would have to go back for it. Jessamine should be told, although it meant admitting his mistake. The prospect of her ire frightened him, especially as time was short to achieve their aim.

In the event, he decided to keep quiet, at least his pack was on his back, gloves in his pocket. That would have to be sufficient. He was still unsure about what was in all the pockets of the belt, events having moved so fast that there hadn't been the opportunity to explore it properly. It was on the bed, or in his case. It would await his return, as long as none of its supplies were needed.

There was a group around the stand, drinking and eating. They were civil but engrossed in their own conversations, after greetings, they went back to their discussions of farming and ale. No questions came their way about their purpose. The food purchased, they retraced their steps and set out once more for the estate, eating as they went.

The town was quiet; even so, they kept to the shadows as they walked to the estate. The night was clear and warm, with a few clouds and a low moon. There was no traffic along the road, apart from the few people that were at the food stand the streets were deserted; although every inn that they passed appeared to be full. Once they were clear of the last buildings, they were alone.

They did not even see any Watchmen on their rounds. After a short while, they came to the point where the wall, cutting across country, formed a corner as it turned to run alongside the road. There was a sign that said, 'To the Falls', with a track leading through woods.

"Which way shall we go?" whispered Jackson. "The gate will be well guarded, it might be better to mount the wall from down there."

Jessamine thought for a moment, remembering the arched gates and the glimpse of the road leading deeper into the estate. "If the falls are as popular as suggested," she said, "there may be revellers returning, we should go past the gate where it might be less travelled. Our point of entry should be away from any road and the gatehouse, we have no information on the layout of the estate, we need to be close to the roadway once inside."

They ignored the wall and path leading away in the darkness and instead continued onwards, eventually they could hear the sounds of merriment carried on the still night air from the building at the gates. Lights burned bright around the entrance, throwing shadows across the road. They crept closer, the windows on each side of the huge gates were dark, all the noise was coming from those on the top of the arch.

There was singing and a badly played harmonium, hunting songs by the sound of it. Behind the gates, the road stretched away, white against the ground.

"They relax, thinking themselves secure, that we cannot get in," laughed Jessamine as they passed the lodge and came to the place where the wall started to curve away from the road again. A further fifty yards and they came upon a shadowed spot where trees grew close to the wall.

"Here will do," Jessamine said. "We are sheltered from the road; it sounds like the people in the lodge are past caring."

It was the work of a moment for them both to don their gloves, climb the wall and drop to the ground inside the estate. There was an expanse of treeless manicured grass, bisected by a road which led from the gate to what appeared to be another wall. Beside it, the upper works of a building loomed in the darkness. The grounds were in darkness, it was impossible to see the main house that they knew the estate contained.

"Let's get across the open ground as quickly as we can," said Jessamine as she set off. Remembering his training, Jackson counted to ten and followed her.

They crossed the grass without incident or detection towards the first of the shadowy shapes. It proved to be a long low building, windowless and with a door secured by a heavy padlock. The wall they had seen was at its rear, further away than they had realised.

Looking back, they could see the lights in the gatehouse. There was a faint odour in the air, Jackson could not place it, it was so unlike any city smell. They moved along the long side of the building, away from the door.

"Can you smell that?" he asked.

"It's the smell of the farmyard," said Jessamine. "Maybe it's the porkers that Silas mentioned."

"Inside the estate? I would have expected them to be in a separate place."

At the rear of the building was a wooden fence, with churned earth beyond. The fence ended at the side of the building, where there was another entrance, this one was open. The place must be connected to the husbandry. The smell was stronger here.

They heard voices and shrank back. There was the squeak of a badly oiled wheel. Two men were talking, just out of view inside the building.

"Here's another poor wretch," said one, "on their last journey."

"Come and get it, boys," called the other.

A herd of porkers, rough beasts of the forest, unlike the domestic porker in every way, suddenly rushed out of the darkness and clustered around.

"Another one gone. Was this during the cutting or after? Will the Professor ever get it right?" wondered the first voice.

"He gets more to live than die than he used to," said the second. "Although some still seem unable to cope with that thing what he puts in them. They go raving mad. That's the worst bit, seeing them recover and still having to kill them. Anyways, if this herd had no food from us, what would they do?"

Jackson peered around the corner and saw the edge of a trolley, it tipped and a bundle fell into the waiting porkers, who fought over its contents.

Jackson felt sick. He turned away, desperately trying to control his stomach.

The porkers had finished and must have caught the scent of them, as a pack they turned and made for where they hid. "Where are they off to?" said one of the men.

"Must be a vulpine or some other scavenger, caught the smell of fresh blood."

"They're too late." There was laughter as they wheeled the squeaking trolley back inside and closed the doors.

Jackson and Jessamine retreated and returned to the shadow of the wall. "That must be the medical building," said Jessamine. "Aldithley is carrying on his experiments here, on people supplied by Winstanley. His mistakes are fodder for the porkers."

"We have to get away, tell Langdon. This is a matter past us now, the Watch needs to get involved."

"Do you think that we can we go to that Silas?"

"I think not, after his glowing words of support for this man?"

"But surely, the Watch are incorruptible."

"Jackson, you have so much to learn, maybe in the city they are; out in the countryside, they move with the mood of the inhabitants. A man like Rodney will not make a fuss in his own nest; his behaviour hereabouts will appear to be impeccable."

"There must be more to see. If we are to make a case to Sir Mortimer, we need more. Come on."

They kept to the wall and soon the porkers were behind them. To the left was a gap, with the dark shape of a large house. To the right another wall.

"There is a choice here, which should we investigate first?"

"I think the house; we need to see no more porkers eating the corpses of the unfortunate."

There was a sudden burst of light; the bulk of the front of the house was extravagantly lit by floodlights. If they had been closer they would have been visible to any who were looking.

"We cannot get past the floodlights. Why is it lit so much? Rodney must use a prodigious amount of gas."

"There is no supply here. He might get it from the porkers; they produce a flammable gas in their wastes. We should get into the shadows; I suspect the lights have been put on for a reason."

They moved around to the side of the building, it was only lit from the front, as to show to anyone approaching from the main gate.

There was a noise, a fleet of mobiles were passing under the arch and coming down the road towards them. In front was a charabanc, behind it a luxurious mobile and then two open-topped lorries. The charabanc turned off and stopped in front of a door in the second wall, followed by the lorries, while the mobile continued on, stopping outside the house.

They saw Rodney disembark from it and walk up the steps accompanied by a female, the others disgorged men in drab grey uniforms, who escorted the people from the charabanc in to a door in the wall. The Professor was behind the marching group, carrying a box on his chest.

"There are too many people around for our safety." Jessamine made a decision. "I think we should get back to the inn and call Langdon by speaker in the morning. Tell him what we have seen and get his instructions. Perhaps we can return and look inside that other wall tonight."

They turned and made their way back to the outer wall, they were now on the other side of the estate, closer to town. It was the work of moments to climb over. Once over the wall they found themselves on a path and followed it back to the road.

On the way they discussed what they had seen. "There must be a connection," said Jackson, "between the events in the city and this place."

"I suppose so," Jessamine was sceptical. "We should be wary of jumping to conclusions. We only report the facts; it's up to others to unravel them."

Jackson was having none of it. "Don't you see, the Professor must be Aldithley, we saw him arrive. He is carrying on his work, which Woolon tried to stop. He might have mastered the art of controlling mechanical devices, such as limbs, now it seems that he is trying to do the same to humans."

"But how?"

"That is what we still need to know; we should return and see beyond the other wall."

Chapter 23

At that point they ended their discussion; they had arrived back on the edge of town. It appeared to be quiet and they made their way back to the inn without seeing anyone. Once onto the roof and across the tiles they were back in their room. It was in darkness and after taking off their boots and using the bathroom, they both collapsed exhausted onto the bed.

Jackson had used the time when Jessamine was abluting to search for his quip-belt. He could not find it anywhere, neither on the bed where he was sure he had left it nor in his possessions or even in his empty case. He must have left it back in the city; although he was sure he had not. There was no sign that the room had been searched, the cupboard was still across the door. What was he to do? In the end, he fell asleep, next to Jessamine.

In the morning the inn came to life, although they slept on. When they had not appeared for fast-breaker, the innkeeper's wife sent the maid upstairs. They were woken by her knock on the door.

"Fast-break and Char awaits you downstairs," she called. Jackson woke and stretched, he looked across towards the window, remembering the night's escapades. Jessamine was laid on her back, covers pulled up to her neck, a small smile on her face. The sunlight streamed in through the window and he could hear, not the low rumble of the city, but birdsong.

"Wake up, Jessamine," he called. "Fast-break and Char."

"I will sleep on, then take a bath," Jessamine muttered. "You go and eat, if you must, bring me some Char when you return."

Jackson went down the stairs. The bar was deserted save for a large lady who was bustling, as they all seemed to do. "Good morn," she greeted him. "Where is your lady, is she not hungry?"

"She is enjoying her sleep, and a leisurely bath," Jackson replied. She winked in the way of someone sharing a conspiracy.

"Bless her; you can take your food up to her if you wish. Eggs, bread fried in porker grease and fresh local sausage, along with fresh Char. Will that suffice?"

"That will be capital for me. Char will suffice for my lady, I will take it to her, thank you," said Jackson, then he thought of the porkers and their meal, his stomach churned. But he had to eat.

The woman bustled for a while. "You were on the flying machine yesterday," she said. "Silas was here last night drinking his weight in ale as usual and mentioned you."

Did everyone in this town know about them? Jessamine needed to know this, before they called Langdon. And Silas, had he followed them here?

"I would have thought he would be at the Nethersole Arms," he said. "Yesterday he was singing the man's praises for the duration of the flight."

"Oh, he is Nethersole's man, irrespective of the Watchman's code. He keeps an eye on all the goings on hereabouts, and keeps order, in his own way."

She had ignored him and produced food for them both while she had been talking, now she served two plates, after covering them with metal lids she stacked them on a tray. She added mugs of Char. "Here you are then," she said. "Can you manage on the stair?"

Jackson thanked her and took the tray up. He knocked on the door. "Jessamine, are you decent?"

"Come in," Jessamine said, and he heard the sound of the key turning in the lock. Balancing the tray, he pushed the door open. Jessamine was stood wrapped in a towel, her hair wet and hanging down her back.

"What have you there, Jackson?" she said.

"You asked for Char but I have more," he replied. "There is food, and I have some useful information."

"Now I'm awake and clean, I've realised that I'm starving," she said. Pulling the cover from one of the plates, she sat and attacked the food.

"Do you not think of the porkers we saw last night?" Jackson said, although he too ate. The food was delicious, the porker delicately flavoured with herbs.

"This is not the meat of a wild beast," she said, mumbling with a mouthful of fried bread. "Their flesh is more grained, these beasts were not foragers. Anyway, what is your news?"

"I think we should be cautious in calling Langdon," he said. "The woman who cooked this told me that Silas, the Watchman, was in the inn last night, drinking and telling everyone of us."

"He is clever," she replied, "making all in the town aware of strangers, we will have to change our plans for the day, do a little of what we profess to do."

After eating, they dressed for the town. "We must leave the room as innocent as we can," Jessamine said, "that means we secure our packs from a casual search."

Jackson looked around, there was no place to hide them. "Where?" He thought of his hat, surely it would not be forced to carry it in there again, but that did not serve Jessamine's needs, she had no hat.

"In your case," she said, "there is a false bottom; the pack will lay flat inside." Jackson opened his case. "There are four clips." Jessamine showed him where they appeared as part of the pattern of the lining, when pressed the base swung up. "Lay the pack in and close the flap," she instructed. "Then a few clothes on top and under the bed with it."

They completed preparations and went downstairs, Jackson carrying the now empty tray.

"Are you off sightseeing?" asked the lady who had cooked. As she spoke, she was joined by the innkeeper.

"Good morn," he said. "I did not expect to see you, after your exertions last night."

Jackson felt himself blush, but not for the reason the innkeeper surmised. "Why, sir, I do not know what you can mean," Jessamine asked him, wide-eyed. "We are respectable, married folk."

Now it was his turn to blush. "Excuse me," he replied, under the fierce gaze of the lady. "At one point, it sounded for all the world that the furniture was being moved."

There was an awkward silence, broken by Jackson, keeping to the story they had agreed. "Can you tell us, is there a local journal in this town?"

"Yes," replied the woman, "and take no notice of my husband, he has a wicked imagination and an offensive humour that takes getting used to. There is the Hammerham Notice, a weekly publication; its offices are in the town, next to the Trading Company building."

They left the building and were surprised to find Silas walking past the entrance. "Well hello," he said. "'Tis a fine morning for a stroll. Fancy me being here to greet you."

"If I didn't know better," said Jessamine, "I'd think that you were following us."

The Watchman laughed. "I'm just doing my job, patrolling and being visible should any need me. You are new in this town and it would be remiss of me not to keep my eye on you. What are your plans? No doubt you will see the Notice as well as take the air and see the sights?"

"That is our intent; we have heard tell of a big estate here and a model farm, they must have wares to sell. And to show that we are not at work all the time, we intend to visit various pretty places. I believe there are woods and waterfalls nearby, a favourite of mine when I can get away from the city."

Silas nodded. "There are indeed such places. There is a track near the Nethersole estate, we passed it yesterday. It runs alongside the boundary wall, if you venture along it for a mile or so, you will come upon the falls of the River Hamm, at a place the locals call Los. You will see the sign."

"A strange name, what is the meaning?"

"It's a local word for porker, due to the abundance of wild species in the land. They can be dangerous but rarely seen in the day. The word is the call of the hunter; it resembles the sound they make to each other."

Jackson resisted the sudden urge to say that they had passed the sign the night before, whilst investigating. Instead he merely said, "Thank you, you're most helpful."

The Watchman smiled. "'Tis part of my job," he said, "as well as keeping the land safe and free from anarchists and spies. I must away; no doubt we shall see each other again."

"That was interesting," Jackson remarked after he was out of sight. "Do you think he is aware of our purpose?"

She shook her head. "I do not see how, he has no information of our names, any enquiries will lead him to Fairview, who will back us up. I suspect he is just warning us that he has suspicions, as we are not known and Nethersole is important. Anyway, we have an excuse to be seen in walking gear, we can go to these falls later and wait until dark to continue our examination of the estate. We will already be halfway there."

Chapter 24

They crossed the market square and found the offices of the Notice with no trouble. It was closed, a sign indicated that it would be open, yet it was not. "Country folk have a different grasp of time," said Jessamine. "There is little rush when you leave the city." The town was not bustling. Jackson could understand the logic, if there was little to do, then why rush to do it.

There were enterprises open for business and a few carts with equines pulling them in view. Whilst waiting, they wandered over to the Trading Company and went inside.

There were shelves and bins containing all that a person would need to live comfortably, grains, fresh fruits and vegetables and a supply of the new types of food, ready-made portions of soups and stews, preserved in metal and glass containers with gaudy labels.

"I would not have thought to see these here," said Jessamine.

"Indeed not," replied an old woman, dressed in faded black. "Where is the skill passed down from mother to daughter in opening one of them? What has happened to the world? People flit about in stinking machines and lead unnatural lives, ever rushing here and there." She paused. "You are not local folk?" she said suspiciously.

"We are on a visit," Jackson replied. "Part business and part pleasure."

"And you've chosen our humble town," she said. "Welcome, I am Marie and I have lived here for eighty-five years. Everyone knows me and I know everything. Where do you intend to visit?"

"We have business at the office of the Notice," Jessamine replied. "Then after luncheon, we will visit the falls of Los."

Her face darkened. "Keep well away from the Nethersole estate if you do," she said. "They are not fond of strangers there. Many things go on that I do not like. There are arrivals and no departures, if you get my meaning."

"I thought that everyone loved Mr Nethersole," Jessamine said innocently. "Does he not do a lot for the town?"

She spat out the words, "Rodney Nethersole has this town in an iron grip. He has bought the law, and turned everyone's eyes away from his evil, by bribing them with money and promises. They cannot see it but Marie can."

She stopped talking and looked past them. She had seen someone enter the shop. "Here's his chief lackey now," she muttered. "Don't drop your guard; be aware of each word he hears you utter, for it will end up in every ear."

They left her and went back to the office, ignoring Silas, who was in conversation with the shopkeeper.

The office was now open. A girl was sitting behind a desk, her face long and thin, with the style of her hair she resembled an equine in a frock. "Good day," she brayed, reinforcing the illusion.

"May we see your proprietor?" asked Jessamine. "We are from the city and may have business with him."

"I know," she replied. "Your father has sent you to gather intelligence about our humble publication. I have a sample copy here for you." She handed it over. "Silas was telling us about your inducements, I believe he called them. Our Mr Chickering is available." She rose. "I will tell him you're here and fetch you Char."

When she had departed, Jackson turned to Jessamine. "Everyone knows."

"It's a small town, a fiefdom, Silas suspects us but we have the advantage."

"How so?"

"We know that he knows. It's like a game, one where everyone can see all the pieces in play. The skill lies in doing what is not expected, making it look like something else. We are secure, our story is robust enough, if Silas is as good as he appears, he will have called the city already."

Chickering came out, another fat man, like many they had seen in the town, his appearance shouted good living. "Come into my sanctum," he said. "I have heard of you and have been talking to friends in the city by speaker about you, in anticipation of this visit." Jessamine gave Jackson an 'I told you they would check on us', look.

The girl brought Char and they drank. "I know of inducements and I must admit that I have no time for them. In my opinion, they distract and annoy the reader."

"Perhaps," said Jackson, "it is because the local reader knows of local wares already. Surely it would be better to induce those who may not have heard of Hammerham's finest produce, say in the city. In exchange merchants in the city could tell of their products in the Notice."

"A good point, well made," said Chickering. He thought for a moment. "I have an idea. As you may have noticed, there is a local merchant, Rodney Nethersole, I'm sure that he would be interested in your ideas. He produces for local consumption, porkers and vegetables."

"We have seen his signs," said Jackson. "All folk speak highly of him; he seems to be a local force."

"He keeps involved in the town, you'll not find one who dislikes him, except maybe Marie, but she dislikes everyone. I could introduce you, over luncheon maybe, if he is in residence."

"That might be possible," said Jessamine, aghast at the idea of coming face to face with Rodney. Perhaps Winifred had been right, they should not have come. "We have also heard that he plans to get the rail extended to Hammerham, that it would fit in with expanding his business. With our and your help, he might induce people in the city with fresh produce, if he could guarantee delivery. And the man who sold him inducements might become wealthy."

Chickering's face let slip his love of money, as plain as his body showed his love of food.

"True," he muttered, "and no doubt, some sort of commission would be payable."

Jessamine inclined her head. "Why naturally, it's the nature of business, all benefit and profit is shared, as is any risk."

"Mr Nethersole is a philanthropic man; he will bear the full cost of extending the rail, from his own pocket. Although it is true that the rail will mostly benefit him and his business, he is willing to offer the service to everyone in Hammerham. He wishes to get to the capital more easily; he spends time in both places and wastes a lot of his days in travelling. Moving his goods and allowing others to travel will be a bonus for us in the town."

The speaker on his desk rang, interrupting his praises.

"Excuse me," he said, "that will be a call from one of my reporters. I will see if Mr Nethersole is able to meet you and send word, I understand that you are lodging at the Lost Quarry?"

"We are," said Jessamine, unsurprised that he knew. "Thank you for your time."

They left the building. "We need to discuss things; we must get to somewhere quiet," she said.

"Surely we cannot meet Rodney." Jackson was disturbed. "The game would be up; he would know us to be here under false pretences."

"I know," she said. "It will not be a problem. We will be away long before that is a possibility. Let us get a cup of Cofé while we decide our next move. I spied a house on the other side of the square when we arrived."

They sat in the Cofé house. "We have a lot to tell Langdon," said Jackson, once the waitress had departed. "About the town and Rodney, his estate and what goes on there. I think that it all fits together. If you are not willing to agree with my assumptions, we must decide how much to tell him."

"Just give him the facts," she cautioned him. "Save your opinions until we have seen beyond the wall."

"Very well," Jackson said. "Do you think Silas will have someone listening for our call? Can we risk the speakers?"

"They will go through an exchange in town; there is always the chance of eavesdropping."

"I have an idea," suggested Jackson. "I read in my journal that the flying machine carries the mails, as well as passengers. We can send a letter, the return flight to the one we arrived on will take it securely and the delivery boy will hand it to Langdon tomorrow."

"We should do both," she said. "If they are watching the speakers, then they will realise that I am not talking to my father.

I can write several letters, addressed to various people and include the important one. You can call Fairview in my stead, pretending that he is your uncle or some other relative and pass information cryptically. You have practised that, have you not?"

"I have, and I have the number memorised." Jackson was pleased to be of use.

"You go to the speaker office then," she instructed. "I will seek out writing materials, stay here, drink more Café and write my missives."

Jackson entered the speaker office. "Hello," said the girl, her hair tied back severely, a black pencil lodged behind one ear. "And what can I do for you?"

"I would like to place a call to my uncle in Metropol City," said Jackson.

She removed the pencil, licked the end and held it over a piece of parchment. "Of course, sir, the person and number in the city, please?"

"It is a Mr Fairview at the Makewright Orphanage, Metropol 27 – 1048," he said, the pencil scratched.

"Very well, please wait in booth one and I will make the connection."

Jackson sat in the booth and picked up the instrument. He could hear the girl talking to the exchange, asking for a line and getting connected to the city. As with flying, he found it hard to believe that he could talk to the city from his location.

"Your call is made," she said and there was a click as she disconnected her apparatus. "Fairview here," said the voice in his ear.

"Uncle, it's Jackson, we are in Hammerham," he said. "I'm calling to tell you that all is well, we have had an interesting time."

"Have you visited the places you had in mind?" asked Fairview, as clear as if he were stood next to Jackson.

"Some of them. We had an excellent view of the area on arrival, from the flying machine. It shows things you would never have imagined. There is a lot to view in the area. We are to visit the falls of Los this after, perhaps we will visit a farm as well, they have an excellent selection of porkers, nourished on all sorts of herbs and many other substances. In turn, we fed on them at fast-breaker."

"And are the people friendly?"

"They are, Uncle. The Watchman, one Silas Mountmain, has been most attentive to us. Many of the locals have nothing but praise for Mr Nethersole, one of the local landowners. He has plans for the future of this place. He employs a large number on his estate; we were told that his farm manager, a Mr Winstanley, takes folk from the city to work the land."

"That is interesting, and how is your good lady?"

"She is well, thank you. She will be talking to her father shortly. I believe tomorrow."

"I will speak to him then and get all her news, what are your plans?"

"We will see what happens on our visit today, it may be that we stay a little longer, or we may return."

"I will leave that to you, thank you for calling and safe exploring."

Jackson left the booth, as he did the girl replaced her instrument in its cradle. She saw him and looked nervous. "I was just getting the charges, from the exchange," she said, almost too quickly. "That will be five sol."

Jackson paid her, realising that he had little money left, the bulk of it was in his quip-belt, which of course he didn't have. He needed to overcome his fear of Jessamine's wrath and tell her, the longer that passed, the harder it would be.

He walked back to the Cofé house, where Jessamine was completing her writing.

"I've written the same thing four times," she said, "in letters to four different persons, to Langdon, to Clarry and to another two of the safe houses. I will have to hope that one arrives. We can walk to the office of the flying machine company and deposit them. How did your conversation with Uncle go?"

"Uncle Fairview was interested, he told me to use my discretion and report when I could. He is aware of your imminent message."

"Then we should deposit them and repair to our inn for luncheon, to prepare for our expedition."

Chapter 25

After another excellent repast, this time of porker leg, stuffed with apples and grains before roasting. "And where are you off to?" enquired the innkeeper.

"We have been recommended the falls of Los," Jackson answered. "It sounds like the kind of place we never see in the city."

"Then let me make you some refreshments," he offered. "It's a long walk and that porker will not keep you going forever. Prepare yourselves and I will hand it to you before you leave."

They changed again into their walking clothes and taking the parcel of food with them, set off, this time without subterfuge, for the falls. Jackson again set off without his belt, still afraid to mention it.

They reached the wall quickly and turned down the path, walking beside the wall. The falls were further away than they had expected. "It's strange that nobody mentioned it to us," mused Jessamine, "that we were starting late in the day to visit and return before dark."

Eventually, they arrived and discovered that they were there alone. There was an enchanting waterfall, a glade of fine trees and a few benches arranged around a fire pit. It was beautiful and yet the air was filled with a strange, heavy feeling. There was an absence of birdsong. In the distance, they could hear the porkers behind Nethersole's wall grunting as they fed. On what? wondered Jackson.

He thought of the people in the charabanc they had seen the night before. Were they lured by the prospect of a better life? Were they even now being cut by the Professor, in the hope that his foul scheme would give him and his master some sort of power?

"This must be a popular place in high summer," said Jackson, "for outdoor events and such. I don't suppose there is much else for entertainment."

"At least we are alone, we can slip away to the wall, and as we will be coming at it from the other direction, we are closer to that small, inner wall. We also don't have to get past the gatehouse, or the porkers."

Shadows started to lengthen; it seemed unlikely that anyone would arrive now. Jessamine pulled the package of food from her pack. "It will shortly be time to go, let us eat the meal that we have been provided," she said.

Jack took the water bottles from his pack. "I expect it's porker again. I'm getting weary of porker, despite the flavour," he said.

Jessamine unwrapped the package and sniffed at the pie which had been revealed. "It is, minced and cooked in a pie this time," she sounded happy as she passed him a piece and took a bite.

Jackson did the same, there were chunks of apple and onion mixed in with the minced meat, all bound up in a thick pastry. Despite himself, he had to admit that it was splendid.

They ate quickly, the pie fortifying them ready for the night's exertions, after eating their fill, drinking and refilling their bottles with cool water from the stream, they put the remnants in their packs and headed off towards the wall.

The outer wall was easy, and it was but a short distance to the second. This part of the estate was secluded and dark. They were tempted to use their torches but the moons gave enough light to see and they were soon scaling the second wall. Jessamine was first.

As her head came level with the top, she stopped and, using her left hand, waved urgently at Jackson. He understood her meaning and halted. She slowly climbed on to the top of the wall and lay flat, motioning him to continue.

Once Jackson had done the same and was stretched out, head to head with Jessamine, he understood her caution. It was important that they had lain down before they were seen by any of the multitude inside.

The wall enclosed an area not unlike the barracks that dotted the capital. A row of gas lamps on tall posts illuminated lines of low huts along one side of the wall, which formed a rectangular shape. With a bare earth square near them they were perfectly positioned to see the large group of people milling around. Of all ages, men and women, they appeared to be poor folk, dressed in tattered, dirt stained working clothes and boots.

"This is where they have been brought," Jessamine said, "the waifs and homeless from the city. As Silas said, they look like they have been working on the farms of Nethersole."

"I reckon that these are the ones that have survived the place where the porkers are."

"We have seen Winstanley bringing them here; we suspect his real purpose is not to supply farmworkers but to provide test subjects for the Professor, for him to practise something on."

"What can the Professor be doing? I will concede that it's connected to his experiments but how?"

"You heard the people last night; it's something that involves cutting them?"

"Could it be to implant the thing that we found in the arm?"

"Or maybe what it contains," he suggested. "We know they can attach wires to the nerves, it's done all the time when the limbs are fitted. Why not go one step further?"

A figure came into view. "That's the Professor, Aldithley," said Jackson.

The Professor carried a large box on a leather strap around his neck. It had dials and levers on the face and a long, spring-like wire extending into the air that waved as he walked.

"Who is that with him?" There were two other men present. Jessamine had taken a pair of naval lenses from her pack, now she put them to her eyes, she fiddled with the focus.

"Well, well," she muttered. "Our friend the Watchman is present, a part of the evening's proceedings. The other must be Winstanley." Jackson had no lenses but could see both men; the Watchman's companion was a tall florid faced individual, large of belly. It certainly looked like the fellow he had seen in the Prosthesium.

There was some sort of speaking trumpet, like the mouthpiece of a speaker near the Professor's face. Jackson realised that he had seen this thing before.

"There were a line of those boxes on the wall when I spied inside the workshop," he said.

"They must be the device that controls the filament, perhaps one of them was used in the aerialway sabotage?"

"Yes, but would you need that much apparatus to send a simple signal? If the Professor is putting things in the neck of people, it will not be simply to turn them on and off. We have gone beyond that."

"You mean, Fairview said that the Professor was working on controlling minds, the filament was only the first phase."

Before he could answer, Rodney came into view and stood next to the Professor.

"Are we ready?" he asked, his voice carrying to the watchers in the shadow.

"Yes, Rodney."

"Say it, Professor, show our friends what you have achieved."

"Lexis," the Professor said into the trumpet.

Instantly all the people stopped their milling and stood still. Their faces blank they all adopted the same posture, as if held up by invisible wires.

"Listen to me," said Rodney. Every face turned to him. "Form up in lines."

To the amazement of Jessamine and Jackson, the crowd moved into a military formation, shuffling their feet till they were equally spaced. A grey clad man appeared and stood before them. "This is your leader, you will obey him and only him," said the Professor.

"By the left, forward march," called the grey-clad man. As one the group obeyed.

"Remarkable," Silas said to Rodney. "If I hadn't seen it, I would not have believed it, so they are now under your control?"

"They are susceptible to my suggestions," he said. "The Professor could explain the intricacies."

"This is amazing." Jessamine showed shock on her face. "We must get this information to Langdon; it seems that Rodney has progressed from the control of artificial limbs to control of people."

The Professor was fiddling with the controls on top of his box. He suddenly tensed, swung the apparatus towards their hiding place and shouted, "Rodney, they are here." He pointed at them. "There!" he screamed.

"Sound the alarm, we must stop them leaving," Rodney shouted. A siren began to wail, the marching formation continued tramping, ignoring the hubbub. More of the grey uniformed men came from the huts and ran for the entrances. Faces turned to look up at the top of the wall.

"We are discovered. Come on, Jackson." Jessamine rolled away from the shout and dropped to the ground, without bothering to climb down. It was only six feet and she landed like a feline, bending her knees and immediately running for the second wall. Lights flickered as men approached from both directions.

Jackson had followed Jessamine; however, his landing was not so smooth, he felt a shooting pain in his ankle. Hobbling, he set off across the grass.

It was only a short distance but, halfway across, a shout went up behind them. "We are seen," said Jackson, and they increased their pace. Bright lights came on and crossed the air, painting bright circles on the wall. Then they caught them and focused as they attempted to dodge.

"Keep going," said Jessamine as they heard the flutter and whine of shots from a gas-gun. The range was still too great, the guns inaccurate in the hands of the running men. They climbed the outer wall as shots chipped the brickwork. They could hear the baying of hounds.

On the other side of the wall they stopped to catch their breath.

"We are safe for a moment, till they get around," panted Jessamine. "We need to get back to the inn and hide."

They could hear the shouts of the men on the other side of the wall. "Get a ladder," "How did they climb?" "Did we hit any?"

"Silence!" called a strong voice. It was Nethersole. "Who were they?" he asked.

"I suspect that they were the two strangers, from the city," replied the voice of Silas. "I have been following them. We need not search; all their possessions are left at the Lost Quarry. We can apprehend them when they return, as they surely must if they want to get back to the city."

Dismay fell over Jackson, like a black cloak. Of course, Silas would know where they were staying. How could they return and retrieve their possessions? The tickets for the Aero were there, together with all their clothes. And his belt.

He had a sinking feeling; he had failed to protect his belt. If he ever got back to Langdon, he would have to admit to losing it. Before that, how could he hide the fact from Jessamine?

"Come on," said Jessamine, breaking into his despair. "We must go the other way then." She pulled an object from her belt and glanced at it. "This way." She set off into the trees.

Chapter 26

Jackson followed her, deeper into the woods. He understood that they could not return to the town, but where were they heading and how could they get the message to Langdon? How could they find safety? They were heading in the wrong direction, following whatever it was she held in her hand.

They plunged through the night, through fields and over streams, blundering in the dark as clouds hid the moons. Jessamine never faltered, changing her direction at intervals. Jackson, feeling the pain from his ankle found it hard to keep up and fell behind. "Stop," he said after an hour or so, while they were sheltered by a thick hedge. "My ankle is hurt."

Jessamine came back to him. "We will rest here a while then, let me see." She felt for the joint. Jackson tried to take his boot off, impatiently, she stopped him. "No, keep it laced, if you remove it, your ankle will swell and you'll never replace it."

She relaxed a little. "We have put several miles between us and Rodney's men; they may have not expected us to come this way. My guess is that they would have followed Silas's suggestions and gone to the inn. We can sleep here till dawn and then assess our options. You rest first, Jackson, I will keep watch."

Jackson crawled into a thick patch of bracken, pulled off his pack for a pillow and despite his fear and alertness, slept. He was woken by a hand on his shoulder. It was still dark. He moved his leg, his ankle hurt, but no more than it had.

"I will sleep now," Jessamine said. "Keep a good watch." She wriggled into the bracken and made herself comfortable.

Jackson peered into the lightening gloom, day was coming and they were alone. He realised that he needed Jessamine now, more than ever. She seemed to have a plan; he would have to be as useful as he could, even though he had no clues on how to live in the wild.

He thought himself very much a child of the City and felt out of place. Close by, Strigine hooted and he jumped. Then, a large

Elaphine passed him by, his antlered head swinging around as he searched for scent. Jackson kept still and the beast moved away. He saw nor heard any human pursuit. Perhaps they would be safe after all.

Jessamine awoke as the sun rose between the trees. She stretched and smiled. "'Tis day and we live, we will be safe from pursuit, once they find we are not at the inn, they will not know which way to search for us. They cannot look in all directions." She stood, looking again at the small object.

"What is that, in your hand?" Jackson asked.

"It's a lode-arrow," she said. "The same as a ship on the sea has. It shows me the pole and the direction of sunrise, you have one in your belt."

She passed it to him, a red needle swung as he held the case. He realised that the needle was still, it was the case that moved.

"We head west," she said, "away from the sunrise, away from the town." She took the lode-arrow and placed it back in her belt.

His belt; Jackson had still not told her that he had mislaid his belt. That had been a perfect opportunity. He could have lied and said that it had come off in the pursuit. When could he tell her?

The longer he left it, the worse it would be. To deflect her mind from the belt, he mentioned another thing that had been bothering him. "What I don't understand," he said, "is how they knew we were inside the wall?"

"Someone must have seen us," she replied, "either coming over the wall or when we hid."

"That is not possible," he persisted. "We had no inkling of followers while we walked or ate. Once over the wall, we were in shadow."

"Does it matter now?" she asked. "Perhaps Silas followed us to Los and saw us go over. We were found and that was that."

She pulled a small parcel from her pack. "Here's the rest of the food from the inn. We should eat it all, it may be a while until we can eat again." They fell on the remnants of the pie and devoured the crumbs.

"How do you know where we are, and how to get us back to Metropol City, now that we cannot use the Aero?"

She opened one of the compartments in her belt and took out a folded piece of cloth. As she unfolded it, Jackson could see that it was covered with fine markings. She held it up. Fully two feet across and made of a fabric so thin that it was almost transparent, he recognised it as a map of the southern half of the country, with rail and roads marked. There were blocks of tiny script by the towns and other points of interest.

"Look," she pointed with her nose, "this is Rodney's estate and we are headed west, away from the rising sun. There is the Aero-field, and here, this line is the rail."

Jackson wondered what else might be in the belt, and why he had been so stupid as to leave his at the inn. He would have to tell her. But before that, he had seen a clear mistake in her route.

"But," he said, "it's east, not west, to get to the city, we are heading in the wrong direction."

"We walk this way," she said with a sigh, "precisely because it is the wrong thing to do. Rodney, or his minions, will have searched our room at the inn by now, and found our travel plans for our return to the capital. He will be searching for us at the Aero-field and the nearest rail halt to Hammerham. His mobiles and charabanc will be driving along every road around. So we walk across country, away from our destination, to foil his plans. He will not search for us in this direction; he will expect us to take the fastest way home."

"Then what do we do to return?"

"We head to the next large town, which is on the coast," her nose indicated a place called Port Lucas, "and there we take passage on a steamer to Queinton, where we alight and take the rail to the city. We can call Langdon by speaker from Port Lucas, pass our intelligence without eavesdropping Watchmen and get any instructions he may have, before we set sail."

"How will we pay for all this?"

She opened another pocket in the accursed belt. "Here is money, enough for passage and food. You have the same in your belt. All we need to do is get to Port Lucas, it's about two days and a night's good march."

She put everything back in the belt. "Come on," she said, "we are rested, we can make some time before the sun rises too far. According to my map, there is a village ahead, perchance we can get food there."

They set off down the road, which was laid to gravel and easy to walk along. There was no traffic; if any vehicle had approached they would have heard it clearly. After several hours, Jessamine called a halt.

"How much further to this village?" asked Jackson, his ankle was behaving itself, now the pain had become a dull ache.

"We will get there soon," she said. "Do you want to rest a while?"

"I think I do," he said.

Jessamine pulled Jackson into the ditch and behind a thin hedge. "Very well, we rest here," she said. "Try and get some sleep, we will carry on when afternoon turns to evening and the skies darken. By my reckoning, we will arrive in the village in the early morning."

Jackson lay down but he could not sleep, hunger gnawed at his stomach. He looked around, Jessamine was already sleeping, then he saw that there were some plump red berries on a tree in the hedge; were they safe to eat? As a City boy, he knew not. He would have to wake Jessamine to ask her.

He was just about to do so, when he heard the sound of equines coming up the road, iron shoes crunching on the gravel. There were three of them, moving fast, one on each side scanned the hedge for signs whilst the other, in the centre, looked down for footmarks. Their hiding place in the ditch meant that Jackson's eyes were level with the equines' legs, he noted that one had a distinctive blaze of white and ginger on a foreleg. Jessamine had awoken; her eyes wide with fear, she held Jackson tightly and they lay still until they had passed and the sound of hooves had faded into the distance.

They stood and brushed leaves from their hair and clothes.

"They have cast a wider net than I expected," Jessamine said. "I suppose that now they have not found us at the inn, they will be desperate to silence us before we can report what we saw. Rodney must have sent riders in all directions, my guess is that they will go ahead to the village and ask after us. Perhaps it will not be safe to stop there and seek assistance."

More days without food. Jackson's stomach rumbled in protest.

"Oh look, Jackson," said Jessamine, "cloud berries." She reached up and picked a few, eating them quickly, red juice running down her chin. Jackson was relieved, he did not have to show his ignorance. He too grabbed at the berries and ate. They were sweet and delicious, bursting in his mouth to release their flavour. Together they gorged on the berries, stripping the branches bare.

"It's in my pack," she said at last. "I can bear it no longer."

"What is?"

"Your quip-belt, you left it in the room at the inn, yesterday. I put it in my pack."

Relief flooded over Jackson. "Why did you not tell me before?"

"I wanted to see how long you took to admit forgetting it." She put her hand on his arm. "It's alright, Jackson. We all make mistakes, but if we are to work together, we must be totally honest with each other." She rummaged in her bag and passed him the belt. Gratefully, he clasped it around his waist and attached the safety chain to his braces.

The riders never returned, they must have passed on and returned via another path to the estate. They trudged on through the night, resting briefly in turn.

The village loomed into view early the next morning. Now that Jackson had his belt he had been able to study the map. It was more of a hamlet, nestled between hills with a small river running through the centre. There was no Local so no steam power, all their needs would be met by the force of the water, turning shafts to drive clockwork winders or machines like those in the factory.

It was unlikely that they even possessed a speaker. Certainly he could see no line of wooden poles, with the cables strung between them.

It was a simpler life here in the countryside, probably unchanged for many years. After his recent experiences, Jackson could see the attraction. In all likelihood, they would know little of the city, they might not even know of Nethersole or flying machines.

He could see three sets of farm buildings, flocks of grazing ovines and fields of grains, almost ready for harvest. There were also a handful of workers' cottages shown on the map. By turning it, he aligned it with his view. The legend, finely printed, said the place was called Hopewell, as well as the message, 'ale and rooms may be had'.

Chapter 27

Before going into the collection of dwellings, they hid in trees and watched. Men came out of the houses and went to the farms; they would be workers on the land and with the beasts.

From one of the cottages, a woman appeared and started to hang out washing, bed-sheets and gowns, on a line strung between two trees.

"Let me go and talk to her," said Jessamine, pulling her skirts from her pack and wrapping them around her waist. "I will tell her we are on a walking tour and ask to buy food. Wait here for me, if I sense danger I will try to signal to you. If I don't return, you must keep going and get to Port Lucas, find a speaker and warn Langdon."

Jackson watched as she made her way to the cottage. She had a brief conversation with the woman, then they both disappeared into the house. As Jackson waited, he took the chance to examine the contents of his belt in more detail. He found that he was the possessor of more money than he had ever seen in one place before.

There were bandages, some capsules whose function he had no idea of, the map, lucifers for lighting fires and many other tools and strange objects.

He was startled by the return of Jessamine, she was smiling.

"We are in luck," she said. "The three riders passed here yesterday. They were asking all about a pair from the city. I have told her that we hail from Stynehouse, that we are in government service and walking to Port Lucas, as training for some unspecified purpose. You have hurt your ankle and we lost some of our equipment when an ursine attacked our camp. She will give us food, her man is taking a load of fodder to the barracks at Port Lucas on the morrow, we can lodge the night and ride with him if we wish."

Jackson knew that Stynehouse was miles away from Hammerham; perhaps it would be good enough to allay suspicion.

They entered the cottage; a coal range was warming the room. "Sit and be comfortable," said the woman. The woman served them Char and introduced herself as Laurinda Boodel, wife of Osmon. She bustled about in the kitchen, returning with a bowl of hot water, from which fragrant steam issued, together with a towel and bandages.

"Take off your boot, sir," she instructed Jackson. Sitting in front of him she bathed the swollen, bruised ankle with the water, her hands gentle.

"The herbs and the warmth will aid recovery," she said.

"Thank you," replied Jackson, his ankle was feeling better already, whether from the bathing or the suggestion of healing he could not tell. He put his sock back on and tied the boot tightly.

"Now you must be hungry," she said. "My man will return for his luncheon shortly, I will introduce you over a bowl of stewed meats and roots; all will be well."

Osman Boodle had to stoop to enter his cottage; he was the largest man Jackson had ever seen, dwarfing the freaks in the entertainments. He seemed to be one solid muscle, his beard thick and grown long, the tip near to his navel. Black eyes gazed at the pair. "Woman," he said, in a voice that echoed, "who are these two?"

"They are on an expedition," she said. "The man has injured his leg, attacked by an ursine they were, between here and Stynehouse."

He looked suspicious for a moment. "Stynehouse eh? And just when we have been told to watch for strangers on the road from Hammerham."

"We have seen nobody on our travels," said Jackson, "save the ursine, which was not as large as you by the way. Just big enough and angry enough to disrupt our plans."

"And what exactly were those?"

"We are training for the military," said Jessamine. "We have to get from Stynehouse camp to Port Lucas as fast as possible."

He looked suspicious. "Is this for the Watch?"

"Not exactly, we are employed by a government department that works on all sorts of things."

"Hmmm," said the man, suspiciously. "Do you know aught about journals?"

They both shook their heads.

They dined in silence on a rich stew and, when Osman had returned to the fields, spent the afternoon in conversation with Laurinda, or at least Jessamine did. Jackson sat in the chair and rested his ankle. He could hear the two chattering like a pair of corvines, about the Ladies who Lunch and many other matters that he would have thought Laurinda to be ignorant of.

He must have dozed off; he was awoken by Jessamine with a steaming mug of Char.

"We are to stop in the guest room," she said. "The bed is made up, a meal is provided and hot baths are waiting. I think we would be best to retire soon after." There was something about her expression that told Jackson this was not a suggestion.

He stood. "Come then, wife, let us say our goodnights."

Once safe inside the room, Jessamine whispered, "The lady is no problem, it is her man and his friends who may be. I want to keep out of the way until the morn, once we are on the road we will see how the land lies."

They bathed and sat in the room, talking about the best way to describe what they had seen to Langdon in a call by speaker. From that, their thoughts turned to events in the city, had there been any more acts of sabotage? It was even possible that the information they carried had become common knowledge, whilst they were stuck at the other end of the country.

Much later, they heard Osman come back, it sounded by his clanking and booming that he had been imbibing ale. "Where are the strangers?" he shouted, then, "Don't hush me in my own house, woman, help me with my boots."

They could not hear Laurinda, just her husband's comments. "They spun you a story and I suspect you fell for it. We were talking in the ale house; they appear two days after Rodney's estate has had an intruder, when there is a hunt on. Never mind what they say, Stynehouse or Port Lucas, it's all a yarn."

There were a few moments of quiet, then he began again. "No, I don't think they are the folk Winstanley is seeking. They seem to be incapable of much in the way of espionage. And that story about training, well that's a likely tale. As far as I know, neither the Watch nor any service has female agents, at least not out in the country. 'Tis not women's work. Mark my words, they are runaways from an angry father, maybe she is with his child."

Jackson and Jessamine exchanged relieved glances, their story might not be believed, but at least he did not outwardly say he suspected them of being at Hammerham.

In the bed, Jessamine seethed. "Not capable," she muttered. "I suppose he thinks me only able to carry your child, no doubt he assumes you tricked me into that as well?"

Jackson wisely decided against replying, shortly after that the shouting stopped. Osman must have fallen asleep.

Laurinda woke them in the darkness. "Osman is ready to depart, he bids you join him on the cart." They dressed and collected all their gear, this time, Jackson made sure to wear his belt. Downstairs in the yard, two huge equines were stood in the traces of a cart filled with hay bales.

Osman sat on the seat, there was no room for another. "I have moved some bales," he said, jerking his finger over his shoulder at the stow. "There is a hollow for you to lie in. Jump up now."

They did so and before they were settled, Osman whipped the equines off and they lurched onto the road. Osman set a ferocious pace, as if the beasts were made of metal and tireless, they were too far away to talk to him and indeed could not see anything from their perch. It was more than an hour before the sun even arose.

Once the day was lit, Jackson stood for a better view. Immediately, the breeze whipped straws which stung his face and he quickly sat again.

"Look to the side," suggested Jessamine and she stood to show her meaning. She had her head turned to the left and seemed able to withstand the buffeting. Jackson stood next to her and looked to the right, it was bearable. By closing his left eye he could make out their progress. The road led on over low hills and through woods. The space was so restricted that they were pressed together and they held each other for balance. After a while Jackson felt Jessamine leaning into him more and more. He was quite enjoying the warmth of the contact when, with a jolt, Osman stopped the cart.

By now it was mid-afternoon, the last distance post they had spied reckoned that Port Lucas was but three miles away. At the top of the hills, with their extra height they had already seen the sea and the chimneys of the town.

As they looked down, Osman fed the beasts, using a bag of grains that he hung over their necks.

"Come down," he called. "I will not hurt you and I'm brewing Char.

They climbed down and drank. He had a package of sandwiches, cold ovine and onion slices, together with apples. They shared it in companionable silence for a while.

"What is the truth of your tale then?" Osman asked. Jackson tensed, his hands felt for the truncheons on his leg. Would he have to fight to save them? Could he best this mountain of a man?

"It's alright," Osman said gently. "I mean you no harm. I'm not sure if you are the ones at Hammerham. And then again, I have no time for your training yarn, although you may have convinced Laurinda. You are either runaways or you are spies. Believe me or not, I happen to hate Rodney Nethersole, though my workmates all think him a wonder. I can judge a little about him through his use of Winstanley and that alone tells me he is not what he wants folk to think he is. You do not deserve to be caught by that man, even if you have done him ill. That is why you are hidden in the gods. We are safe enough to eat for a short while."

"What of what we heard last night?" Jessamine asked him calmly. "You seem to have changed your tune."

Jackson could see that her hand had crept under her gown; he imagined her pulling the needle pointed knife half from its sheath on her thigh. Osman would struggle if they both attacked him at the same time. He readied himself for her signal.

"Laurinda is Nethersole's niece," he said. "It would not do to show my true feelings, for apart from her fealty to him, her only fault by the way, I love her dearly. She will doubtless be telling her uncle's riders of your visit by now, once she has, they will be after us. Now, if you have finished your food, get yourselves out of sight, Port Lucas is but an hour away. We need to get you there and disappeared before we are caught."

They arrived in Port Lucas almost exactly an hour later. "I should hand you over to the Watch," Osman had said, as he helped them down. "For my conscience and your own safety, let them decide the right of it all. But the Watch in Port Lucas is no better than that in Hammerham, so I will drop you here at the dockside hotel. Your fate will then be in your own hands."

They thanked him and he left, heading towards the port office with his load.

They stood in the street, in front of the hotel, relieved to be safe.

They had reached Port Lucas, the first part of their escape was over.

"We need to use a speaker," Jackson said. "It has been four days since we reported in, who knows what might be happening in the city, or indeed the country? The information we have could be crucial."

"Let us get into the hotel; they may have one of the new direct lines to the exchange in the capital." They brushed most of the straw from their hair and entered the hotel.

The concierge was a little perturbed at their appearance and request for a room. "You wish to stay?" he eventually spluttered. Jessamine produced a bank note; folded it small and pressed it into his pocket. Instantly, he changed his demeanour.

"Of course we have a room," he said, washing his hands with invisible soap.

"I also wish to book a call, to Metropol City," she said.

He looked at her, as if she could not possibly know anyone in Metropol City. "A private call," she repeated, whilst another note joined the first.

"Ah," he sucked air in through his teeth, "perhaps madam wishes to use the direct dialling facility, freshly connected from the city. I'll see what can be done, please wait." He departed, still washing his hands.

Jackson was mystified, everyone knew that the speakers were powered by sound itself, thus they had a short range. Hence the exchanges along the way to receive, amplify and retransmit the signal.

"What is a direct call?" he asked.

"Oswald told us of it," she explained, "remember the Wasperton-Byler effect?"

He nodded. "Well, another property of the field produced is that it can amplify a sound wave. He calls it modulation or something. Now the exchanges can be linked in a network, switched without human intervention and the signal amplified over the whole distance."

The concierge returned. "If you will come with me," he said, "I will take you to the booth and you may make your call."

The booth was familiar; the difference was in the instrument.

Instead of a plain box with a speaking tube, and a receiver to hold to your head, the box now featured a set of buttons, with the numbers written upon them. Jackson was instantly reminded of the boxes he had seen on the wall in the Prosthesium, and the one worn by Aldithley.

"Do you understand how to use the instrument?" asked the concierge, when Jessamine nodded he bowed. "I will leave you in privacy," he said, closing the door behind him.

"This is it," said Jackson, "it's been in my head and now I understand."

"What are you talking about?" asked Jessamine, pushing the buttons in sequence.

"It's about the scene inside the wall," he said. "I will tell Langdon, else I will have to explain it twice."

Jessamine finished entering the numbers. Within no time at all, they heard the sound that told them the instrument in the orphanage was ringing.

"Makewright Orphanage, Mrs Grimble speaking." It was as clear as if she had been stood with them, so different from the crackle of the old system.

"Mrs Grimble, it's Jessamine." Jackson heard the squeal of pleasure. "Oh Jessamine, you are safe, we have been so worried, and is Jackson with you?"

"I am here," he shouted into the horn.

"Wait a moment, here is Sir Mortimer." There was a rustling.

"Hello both," Sir Mortimer's deep tones echoed around the booth. "What news?"

Quickly, Jessamine told him of what had transpired in Hammerham. "I never received your letters," he said. "They must have been intercepted. Fairview had a call from Jackson with some cryptic message that made a little sense. Are we to believe that Nethersole is feeding the homeless people that he takes to his porkers?"

"Only the ones his experiments fail on, sir," said Jackson, "and apparently, he is getting better at whatever he is doing. He is putting something into the persons he takes from the city. It is activated by some sort of control box; they are as if in a trance and obey his every command."

"Jackson is right. We have seen what he is doing," Jessamine broke in. "He appears to have a way of controlling people."

"So he has progressed past turning machines off, there have been developments in the city, more of the accidents and the government is becoming concerned. I am under pressure to remedy the situation. People are dying; we are no closer to finding a way to stop it."

The line went dead for a few seconds. "Hello," said Jessamine. "Are you still there?"

Langdon's voice returned. "This new system, it seems unreliable. Quickly, give me anything more that I can use to placate the Minister. We still know not how the filament might be activated."

"I have an idea about that," Jackson said. "There is a box, not unlike this speaker box. The Professor wore one and spoke into it to control the people. At the Prosthesium I saw a line of these boxes in the Professor's laboratorium. But there was no connection between the box and the people. It seemed as though the signal went through the very air into their bodies."

"I will tell Oswald, a box with no connection you say, then how did it control the men?"

"And we know the word that he spoke to—" There was a high-pitched whine on the line, then it went dead.

They waited to see if the connection would be restored. After a few moments, it became apparent that it would not. They returned to the desk. "Your speaker has stopped working," Jackson told the man.

"Again?" he said in surprise. "That is the third time this week, my apologies; I will ensure that the cost does not go on your bill."

"We need to find a ship to take us to Queinton, the next part of our journey."

"Then the Acme agency is your place, Mr Billinghurst the agent." He looked at the timepiece hanging on the wall. "But it will be closed for the day."

"Then a bath, a meal and a decent sleep is our best plan, it has been a long day," Jessamine said. "We bid you good night, sir."

Chapter 28

They went to their room; Jessamine was more relaxed than she had been. "Langdon has new information," she said, "now he knows what we have learned he is forewarned."

After eating, bovine this time, which Jackson found a relief, they went to their room, a news-sheet was laid on the desk. Jackson scanned it.

"There is a report on the aerialway accident, yet nothing about any other trouble in the city," he said.

"I expect Langdon will be keeping it quiet," Jessamine replied. "The government has suppressed bad news before, you know." She took the sheet from his hand. "In any event, it's three days old. I'm first for the bath."

She ran into the room before Jackson could stop her, the door clicked shut and he heard the sound of running water. Left to himself, he considered the place. Port Lucas was clearly prosperous, the hotel was well appointed and the prices high. The people he had seen looked contented.

Yet they knew not what happened in the capital, for three days after the event. Surely the country was ripe for better communication? With nothing else to do, he took the map from his belt and studied their intended route to the capital.

Next morning, after another chaste night spent together in the room's large bed, they took fast-breaker, then set out to search for the shipping agency that had been suggested to them.

"But first, I need to purchase some new clothes," said Jessamine. "These are little more than rags."

"Leave enough money for passage, and the fare to the capital," said Jackson.

"I have money of my own," she replied, "saved from other work I have done, and anyway, why should I not look my best. I am supposed to be on my nuptials after all."

She seemed in some sort of mood, she was short and snappy. Jackson was unused to that, but then, he was unused to most female behaviour. Jessamine was no exception, she might act like an honorary boy, be able to climb and live rough in the woods but she was still a female and as such, a mystery to him.

Jackson wandered around the town while Jessamine was off buying her clothes. He happened upon an inn in the backstreets, with livery attached.

Boys were walking the equines and Jackson thought he recognised one such, the ginger and white pattern on its foreleg was all too familiar to him.

Surely it could not be the same as the one searching for them on the road? That would be too much of a chance. He had better find Jessamine and get her opinion. He found her outside the general store, dressed in a new gown, burdened with bags.

"I had to have these," she said, seemingly more cheerful. "Now let's find that agent."

"Jessamine," he said. "I've seen the equine, one of those that was searching for us. I recognise the mark on its leg."

Immediately her face changed. "I had hoped you had not," she said. "It has been in evidence twice since that night, once in a yard at the hamlet and again I spied it when we arrived here."

"Why did you not say? Then all our efforts have been in vain and we have not lost our pursuers."

"No, so we need to think of another plan. We are not going to Queinton."

He was surprised. "Are we not?"

"No, we go to Omnipa, it will be the call after Queinton, we can see who awaits us on the wharf."

Jackson spotted the flaw in her plan. "But surely, if we do not disembark at one, it will be obvious that we are headed for the next? I imagine our foe will have people at all ports by now."

"True," she said, "and your point is well made. However, once we are aboard ship we are safe. We will just have to think of another way to disembark without being noticed."

"Anyhow," said Jackson, "I have been looking at my map and there is no rail at Omnipa. After Queinton, we must go to Aserol or to the new rail in Ventis."

Before Jessamine could reply, they entered the Speedwell shipping agency, and sought an interview with the manager, a Mr Billinghurst.

"We are looking for passage to Ventis," Jackson said to the agent. "My wife and I have been spending our honeymoon on a tour of the country. We have used mobiles, a flying machine, our feet and a hay cart. Now we wish to travel by sea, visiting the towns on the coast, finishing by rail from Ventis to the capital."

The agent shook his head. Young people today, they had no idea of the hardships his generation had endured to allow their frivolity. A spell in the army, facing hostile tribesman would do them all the world of good. Then he had an idea. He smiled.

"There is a vessel, I think it would suit your purpose, she is loading for Queinton, Omnipa, Aserol and Ventis, sailing with the tide in two days."

"Is there none sooner?" asked Jessamine. "We have urgent work to attend in the capital."

The agent shook his head. "Not in Port Lucas, and none so fine as the *Esperance*. Captain Bludmonger is a character, a fine man to spend time with, you will enjoy his company."

And let a few days with the Captain be a lesson to you, he thought as he mentally calculated the value of his commission.

"And when may we board?" Jessamine was keen to get through the dock gates, there they would be safe from attack. Everyone knew that once you were on a ship, you were under the protection of the Captain.

"I can take you down to the vessel later today, if the Captain will have you. I have some stores and victuals to arrange. Once they are ready, I will go and ask him. I will be back after luncheon, at which time, if the Captain is in agreement, you can ride with me in the mobile. I will write you a passengers' pass for the gate."

"We have the time to return to the hotel, have some luncheon, pay our bill and return then," Jessamine remarked, relieved to be getting closer to safety, if only in small steps. "We will be back later."

In haste they returned to the hotel and collected their meagre belongings. Truly, things were progressing as well as they could.

They were almost safe. They descended to the dining room and partook of luncheon.

Once again the produce was local, again porker featured little on the menu. Apparently the area around Port Lucas was famed for its seafood.

They dined on bivalves, crustaceans and a whole medley of piscine, fried in oil, steamed and grilled. Accompanied with fresh vegetables and followed by a medley of local fruit and thick cream, it was as delicious as anything that they had tasted. After the last few days it was welcomed.

As they walked from the hotel back to the agency, Jackson noticed the equine again, this time it was tied up outside the port office. He was sure from the blaze on its leg that it was the same as the one he had seen from the ditch, and again at the livery yard. The rider must be following them, they had to get away as soon as they could.

"Jess," he said as they got to the agent's door, "the equine."

"I know," she replied, "let's get inside."

Two hours later, Billinghurst returned from what had clearly been a good luncheon. There was soup on his jacket and his eyes revealed that more than a drop of wine had accompanied the meal.

"Ah, it's you," he said, his voice slurred. "Captain Bludmonger bids you to come aboard. He will accept your cash on safe delivery to Ventis. As for the agency, we will require our commission now." He mentioned an amount that Jackson thought excessive, the agency had only made an introduction, but Jessamine agreed immediately.

"Pay the man, husband," she said and Jackson took a moment to realise she meant him. That surprise was replaced by a warm feeling. He could get used to being her husband. He handed the notes over and Billinghurst put them not in his desk but in his pocket.

"I will take you now," he said. "Where is your luggage?"

"We have only this," Jessamine replied, indicating their packs and her purchases. "We are ready."

They sat in the mobile of the agency, with its name written on the side and Billinghurst started the engine. As they drove through the town, three riders were approaching the agency building. Jessamine leaned over and whispered to Jackson, "We are in the very nick of time." If Billinghurst heard, he said nothing.

At the gate he showed his pass and produced one for them. "They are taking passage on the *Esperance*," he explained to the official.

The man rolled his eyes. "And the best of Norlandian luck to them, sailing on that," he said.

"What do you mean?" asked Jackson, suddenly concerned.

The customs man never answered but waved them through the barrier. Billinghurst accelerated away. "Well? Mr Billinghurst, what does he mean? Answer me," said Jackson.

"Oh, nothing much, Captain Bludmonger has a reputation as a scoundrel, but then, with the three riders who appear to be after you, he is your only option for a quick departure."

Jackson and Jessamine exchanged nervous glances, were they merely replacing one peril with another? Billinghurst had them in a trap, he might even be acquainted with their pursuers. They had already paid him; change their minds and they may well be in deeper trouble. They had to continue. Jessamine took Jackson's hand, "Do not react, there is little we can do. All will be well," she whispered in his ear.

The mobile was parked beside the warehouses and they walked around the corner, catching their first sight of the *Esperance*.

Chapter 29

The term rusty scarce did it justice. The hull was encrusted with great scabs of decay, the hull might originally have been painted in a light green colour, but what remained of that was chipped and hidden under red and brown rivulets of decay. The bow showed evidence of contact with many a harbour wall, on the main and after decks, cargo operations were in full swing. Pairs of derricks lifted goods from the hatch and swung them over-side on singing rigging, where they were seized by waiting stevedores and taken into the warehouses by clockwork trucks.

The band wove between the workers until they came to a gangway. Standing at the top was a sailor, dressed in faded green overalls and a cap that matched the original colour of the hull. He brandished a wooden stick, then when he saw Billinghurst he relaxed it. "Mr B," he said, "back for another glass of luncheon are we? Who might these two be then?"

"Hello again, Meriwether, I have your passengers here. Captain's expecting them."

"Better go on up then," he said. "Pleased to meet you, sir, madam." He touched his cap. Jackson was at the tail of the group and he noticed Meriwether's gaze linger on Jessamine's rear as she climbed the stair. It angered him, but only a little, it was a nice view and he knew she could take care of herself if needs be.

"Captain Bludmonger," said Billinghurst, as they entered the sanctum of the vessel's master. "I have the last of your stores in my mobile, and I also have the two passengers I told you of; a bit of new conversation and entertainment for your voyage."

Bludmonger rose from behind his desk and came to greet them. He was enormous, heavily bearded and walked as if his ship were storm tossed whilst still alongside.

"Hail, fellow," he said, slapping Jackson between the shoulders. "Do you drink ale, lad? Your wife is very pretty." He made a grab for Jessamine, but she evaded him. "Spirited as well, never mind, we have time at sea and a small ship with few hiding places." He roared with laughter.

Jackson had a sinking feeling. They were stuck with this man, on the ship he was the law and his crew would do his bidding without hesitation. Yet they must go with him, their lives and those of many others depended upon it.

"You are welcome; my Bosun will show you to your cabin, we eat at sundown." He waddled to the door, in a way that suggested the vessel was rolling heavily. "Bosun!" he bellowed down the alleyway. Almost instantly, a small wizened man appeared and touched his forelock.

"Cap'n," he muttered.

"Take these passengers to the guest suite," Bludmonger said. "Settle them in."

"Yes, Cap'n." The man scuttled away.

"There you are, follow him," Bludmonger said. "I will see you again when we eat."

In a daze they complied. Jessamine kept well away from the Captain as she left the cabin. The Bosun led them up a deck and outside. Behind the wheelhouse was a door, the words 'Certified for two Passengers' was inscribed over it.

Inside was a finely furnished bedroom, with seating and a desk. To one side was a washroom. Jackson tried the hot tap, the water was almost boiling. The Bosun had disappeared. Jackson sat on the bed, or should it be bunk? At least it wasn't a hammock.

"Will this do?" he asked Jessamine, who was arranging the contents of her pack on the desk.

"It will be only for a few days," she said. "The Captain's a strange one; it's as if everyone but us knows that we shouldn't be here. And the agent knows more than he says. He took our cash quickly enough; I think he has sold us a bad deal here."

"It feels like we must be on guard," he agreed. "What did you want to tell me?"

"Only that we should be safe now we are on-board. If we have the Captain's blessing, nobody would try to argue. Our followers will know we are aboard, but they cannot get to us, even if they bribe the customs men at the gate."

"Unless they do as we did and get a passenger's pass from an agent."

"They still have to get aboard, past the crewman with the stick."

"That's a good point; everyone quotes it but is it a myth? I'm going to ask the sailor at the gangway what the official position is."

Jackson went down to the vessel's gangway; there was a different crewman on duty. "Good day," he said, the man answered with a grunt. "Tell me," he asked, "do you let anyone on board who asks?"

The man looked at him. "Only those I know, like the agent, nobody else. If the agent vouches for them I will permit them, otherwise Captain's orders and they stay on land. Meriwether tells me you and your lady are on passage to Ventis."

Jackson did not know how much trust to place in this man. "We are, and if men came looking for me, for example, would you allow them on board."

"No," the man said definitely. "You are now part of the ship's company and without the Captain's permission you are inviolate."

Just then Jessamine called to him from inside the deckhouse. "Dinner is served," she said.

"That your lady?" asked the sailor.

"Yes, she is," Jackson proudly replied.

"Worth everything, a good woman," said the man wistfully. "I haven't seen my Ginny for near a year now. I do miss her, and the boys. You look after her, nobody will get you here."

After dinner, which was a jolly affair with wine and ale, and food enough for twice the number sat around the table, Bludmonger introduced them to the other officers. The Mate and his Second were quiet, or perhaps just not as boisterous as the Captain. The engineers reminded them both of Oswald, men used to the dark recesses suddenly caught in the light and unprepared. They all made a good bunch and by the time Jackson and Jessamine got to their cabin they were more the worse for wear. They bolted the door and collapsed onto the bed. Jackson was more used to sharing a bed with Jessamine now and took little notice of her. They had perfected an arrangement, to keep themselves separate she slept under the sheet, while he was on top of it; with both of them under the counterpane.

"We should stay out of sight until we leave," Jessamine suggested when they woke. "Send my apologies and say that I am unwell."

Jackson ventured down for fast-break, the salon was deserted save for a steward, who sympathised with Jessamine's plight and sent Char and food to the cabin for her.

They spent the next day in the cabin, listening to the noises of the cargo gear. They talked of what they had seen and its possible meaning.

"If Aldithley can send a signal from this box of his to a device in a man's head, then whatever else might he do?" wondered Jessamine. "How I wish that Oswald was here to shed some light on things."

"We will see him very soon," said Jackson. "I daresay he can explain it all to us, certainly disrupting the aerialway would not be difficult after what we have witnessed. Sir Mortimer says there have been more events, it may be that what we know is already old news."

Cargo finished in the afternoon, the derricks were stowed, hatches shut. Jessamine deemed it safe to leave for dinner. "Bludmonger will be suspicious if he does not see us," she decided. "Besides, the wharf is deserted, none can watch unnoticed."

"Beware of his attention," said Jackson, "he seems to be the worst sort where pretty women are concerned."

To his surprise Jessamine hugged him. "Do you think me pretty?" she said, striking a pose. "I've dealt with worse than him; they all have the same weakness."

Jackson said no more. She was pretty; it was silly to deny it. It was yet another thing about women that he didn't understand.

In the evening, they dined with the officers. "We have missed you today," said Bludmonger as they ate, "I was hoping to talk to you about your lives and purpose."

"Apologies, Captain," said Jessamine. "I think I ate a rogue bivalve yesterday. I have been indisposed."

"And your dutiful husband at your side," the Captain said, "only leaving to fetch Char. Well, we will depart in the morn, I hope you have recovered, the weather is set fair, we shall test your sea legs."

Jessamine ate sparingly and drank no wine. They excused themselves and left, just one more night and they would be safe, from pursuers on land at least.

Next day, in the early half-light, the tide was full and it was time to depart. Jackson woke as the ship's engine started and went to the deck behind the wheelhouse. His head ached, even though he had drunk little and only with the meal. Perhaps the strain of avoiding capture was playing on his mind.

As he watched, Bludmonger shouted orders at the crew, seemingly unaffected by the amount of wine he had consumed. Under his control, the mooring lines were let go and the *Esperance* departed its berth. As Jackson saw the wharf disappear behind them, the three men they had been fearing had got through the barrier, only to find that they had departed.

Shouting and waving arms, they stood at the dockside and cursed the vessel. "We'll get you!" one shouted. "You'll never evade us."

Bludmonger had heard the exchange from his position on the bridge wing. He looked thoughtfully at Jackson. I fancy there's a story to be told, he mused.

He looked again at the lad. He was tall and well-muscled. Bludmonger noticed something else. He had the Watchman's truncheon pockets in his trousers. That was normal, a lot of boys wore facsimiles of them, they considered it a badge. However, this lad's were the genuine article; he could see the tops of the weapons. And he wore a quip-belt as well.

A possible Watchman, with a lady in tow, chased by three dubious characters. He had intended to have a little fun with them on the voyage, as was his wont, perhaps he should instead get the story, before he found himself in more trouble than his rank could absolve.

He spoke to his Bosun, the man who ran the crew with a fist of iron. "These passengers we have, they are to be left alone."

The man looked upset, he had seen the lady, a little fun was in order. But his Captain had spoken, he would obey. "Aye, Cap'n," the man said, a disappointed look on his face.

"I think he's more than he says he is," explained the Captain. "I will find out the truth and decide what to do."

At fast-break, Bludmonger spoke to Jackson, who was on his second cup of Cofé. "Is this your first sea voyage?"

"It is." Jackson stuck to their story. "We are on our honeymoon and exploring the country. My wife is sleeping. I will take her a drink, with your permission."

"Of course," replied Bludmonger. "When she is awake and presentable, I need you to come to my cabin, both of you. There are papers to be signed and fees to be paid."

Jackson nodded, he was unsure of the reaction he would get. The Captain had seen their pursuers, he seemed to have an inkling that they were running, what could he do?

After the meal, Jackson took a mug of Char to the cabin, Jessamine was awake and dressed. "Here is some Char," he said. "The Captain wants to see us; he says that there are formalities."

"We will have to see what transpires," she said. "Perhaps he can aid us, but we must be cautious."

They repaired to the Captain's cabin and sat in comfortable chairs. "Now then," said Bludmonger, "I can see from your appearance that you are not what you claim." He held up his giant hand to silence their protests. "Oh, I don't want to judge but I will not be lied to on my vessel. So, tell me true, or I might consider returning you to the care of your three friends in Port Lucas."

Jackson looked him in the eye. "And what do you think we are about?"

"Well, I see that you are a Watchman, or at least an officer of the law, in plain clothes. And as your lady appears not to be, I surmise that you are escorting her for some reason. Maybe to rescue her or protect her. Perhaps she is a witness to some awful deed?"

That was so wide of the mark, Jackson and Jessamine looked at each other. "We should tell him," she said.

"Only if he promises that it goes no further."

Bludmonger was not impressed. "I'll not be told what to do on my own command."

"Then do your worst. We have a mission of utmost importance; the security of the nation is in doubt. If you are not with us, then you will be added to the list of those against."

"Very well, tell me and I will decide."

They related an edited version of the tale, leaving out the name Nethersole and some of the more fantastical elements they had witnessed. The Captain's eyes grew wider. "This man, you say that he is planning to overthrow the government. I distrust politicians from habit, but he sounds worse, keeping order with fear and violence, never. You shall have my aid and that of my crew. You say you plan to disembark at Ventis, well that is out of the question. He is sure to have men waiting for you at the port; you will be captured before you have passed the gates."

"We mentioned Ventis as a ruse. We must get off before then, preferably at Queinton; we need a port with a rail to the city."

"All ports will be watched if this man is as powerful as you say. But I have an idea. Now go and enjoy the day, you will be safe on my vessel." They left and he called for his Bosun, the man would be annoyed to be deprived of his fun, but bigger things were at stake.

Chapter 30

Jackson and Jessamine spent the rest of the day standing and watching the sea from the deck of the *Esperance*. They were more relaxed than they had been, it seemed any threat they had felt from the Captain or his crew had retreated. They crew they saw were civil and friendly, interrupting their labours to talk and joke.

Jessamine knew that her feelings for Jackson were deepening and she had been resisting them since that first evening back at the orphanage, when she had climbed the wall and seen him coming towards her. Somehow, even then, she had known that they were fated for each other. As he had trained alongside her and the rest, she had come to know him better; her feelings had grown, even though he seemed oblivious to her in any more than a brotherly way.

Capricia in his bed had been her idea, after being hurt so many times in the past, she wanted to see if Jackson would be swayed by availability. He had passed that test and his indifference to the other women he had met had reinforced her opinion of him.

Now they had been away from the orphanage for so long, forced to share life together, and sleep chaste side by side for many nights, she knew that the time was right for matters to progress. Many times since they had left the city, she had resisted the urge to ravish him, she had forced herself to remember the objectives of their mission.

Now they appeared to be safe, with a dubious character who had become an ally, she felt safe for the first time. It would not last, as soon as they arrived in port the game would start again. There was only tonight. It would have been nice to let him make the first move. If he would not progress, then she would have to take the lead.

Distasteful as it was, her training at the hands of the woman she had been sent to would have to be employed. She had been taught to seduce, as part of her work for Langdon, she had done things that she was not proud of. They would become lovers, she had decided. And here, on the ocean, was the perfect place. All her preparations were in place, tonight was the night.

She had pled tiredness and gone to the cabin, leaving him drinking ale with the officers. Now as she tidied up and prepared for bed, she noticed a cloth in his jacket pocket. Investigating further, she found a white lace undergarment, similar to the ones she wore. He must be saving it for a special night, she thought, perhaps his mind was working in the same way as hers after all.

Now she undressed completely, bathed and dried herself. She applied some of the perfume that she kept in her quip-belt, and thought about putting the scrap of lace on. She decided against it, that would be forward, it was up to him to give it, not hers to take. She got into the bed naked. 'I hope he's not long,' she thought, as she turned the light out.

Jackson opened the cabin door as quietly as he could, he tried not to disturb her, the light was off, she must be sleeping. Poor Jessamine, he thought, having to deal with him and his mistakes on his first mission, as well as the dangers posed by Rodney and his henchmen. It was a wonder she wasn't beset by headaches every day and night.

He could hear her regular breathing as he undressed and washed. He was about to climb into the bed when he found that she was on his side. He made his way around and gently lay down and turned away from her. As he went to pull the counterpane over, he realised that instead of being on top of the sheet, he was underneath it. About to move, he was stopped by a hand that came out of the darkness.

"No," said Jessamine. "I want you next to me, skin on skin." There was a rustle of covers and then she was lying beside him, pressed into his back, as she had been at the inn. He could feel the heat from her. With a start he realised that she was naked. "Turn to face me," she said in a voice so soft and compelling that Jackson did so without thinking.

Their lips met and they kissed, a long drawn out joining that took his breath away. He had never imagined that her lips could be so soft, her tongue so insistent.

When they broke apart, she spoke again. "Remove your clothes," she said, "and love me, like nature intended."

Without hesitation he divested himself of his clothes and then, as the *Esperance* chugged through the night, they became lovers.

When they finally broke apart, Jackson was not only exhausted, he was aware that he had found his love, for as long as this life lasted.

"I am yours forever," he whispered.

"And I am yours till my heart beats its last," she replied.

They both lay for a moment, at peace, then Jackson remembered a thing he had been told in the orphanage. Even though he knew that it was not the most romantic thing to say, he had to know. "Will you have a child?" he asked, placing a hand on her stomach, feeling the trembling muscle under the soft skin. At that moment, if she had said yes, he would not have been happier.

Instead she laughed, and pulled him even closer, her grip like iron. "You have a knack of saying the wrong thing, Jackson. The answer is no, thanks to Oswald. He invents other things than gloves and torches you know, things which have a much more enjoyable function. The act is safe from that result."

"Then if it's safe, can we do it again?" he asked.

Chapter 31

Next morning, Jackson woke to the ship's slow, steady motion. Beside him, Jessamine lay sleeping. He looked across at her relaxed form and realised two things. He was more joyful than he had ever been, not only that, he could see now that Alyious had been right about attachment clouding his judgement.

He would now do anything for Jessamine. If he had been tested by Clarry today, he would have failed miserably, telling all to try to spare her pain. And that meant the same would happen in reality.

He moved and realised that he ached all over, at least as much as he had from his first days training, which all seemed so long ago. He and Jessamine had done things he would never have dreamed of. In a moment's respite he had held her and whispered that; she replied in a matter-of-fact voice, "I have been taught to do these things; it seems a shame not to use them for my own pleasure."

Jackson had a sudden thought, had this been part of her job, to seduce him for some purpose yet to be revealed? No, surely not. She must have noticed that he was a novice, she had instructed him and he had done his best, even so, he could not believe that her pleasure was all feigned.

"I understand, Alyious has told me of the things you women have to do." For a moment she looked sad.

"I don't really want to talk about it, Jackson," she said. "But I will say this. What we did last night was not the same as what I do for Langdon. That is mechanical, during it I think of other things. With you, it was different, I don't mean that we should wed immediately, or anything like that, but it was a pleasure, not a duty. Take the night's pleasure, and the many others that I hope will follow, enjoy what is freely given, remember to never ask for more knowledge of what I have to do."

There was a knock at the door. "Luncheon in twenty minutes," was the call.

"Is that the time?" asked Jackson. "We have slept all night and half the day."

She giggled, holding him close. "I would scarce call that sleeping."

They washed and dressed, then went in search of food.

Captain Bludmonger watched them enter the dining saloon; there was a change about them, the way they reacted to each other. He smiled; 'sea air,' he thought, 'now I can complete their happiness.'

"You slept well?" he asked.

"Thank you, yes," Jessamine replied. "To be safe for even a day is a relief and for that we must thank you."

"Well, I have been pondering your dilemma. After discussion with the Bosun we think we have a solution. Find him when you have eaten, he will explain."

They enjoyed a fine meal and then repaired on the deck, where they found the Bosun waiting for them. Looking out to sea, the coast was close, tall cliffs and no sign of habitation.

"Where are we?" asked Jackson.

"On time," was all the man said. He then explained that their passage had been timed so that they arrived in Queinton at daybreak the next day. There was a Ryde to the city at lunchtime, with luck they would be on it.

"Come with me, to the hold," he said. "Captain and I have fixed a way for you to escape."

He led them down a ladder into the hold, lit by the miners' lamps they carried. The space was filled with a layer of crates and packages.

"They are all secured to wooden pallets, for ease of handling," said the Bosun. "Each stack is ready to lift. What we have done is simple." He pointed to one stack, which had a hollow centre. "You will get in there," he said, "it will be the first to be discharged. You will be lifted ashore by the cranes. The watchers will not be able to see you, as you sail over their heads."

It was an excellent plan and surely a trick that would not be expected. Jessamine saw the beauty of it. "With luck, they will assume we remain on board and pursue us to your next port, while we slip way."

The Bosun smiled. "Exactly, it's a ploy we have used in the past, in various foreign places, though never in Norlandia."

Now there was hope that once again they could escape their pursuit, Jackson and Jessamine spent the afternoon watching the coast and the other vessels they passed. A mixture of sailing ships, with full canvas in the light winds they whispered past gracefully, there were fishing boats, followed by gulls and once a grey navy ship of war, bristling with guns and moving at impossible speed, white foam at bow and stern.

After another meal, it was time for bed. They excused themselves and made for the cabin. Once the door was shut, there was a moment of awkwardness.

Jessamine went to the bathroom, leaving Jackson unsure of what to do. He turned the bed down and was hanging his jacket when he found the lace in his pocket. He had forgotten all about it. Surely, it would be an ideal gift for Jessamine; he could give it to her when she emerged.

The door opened, she stood there, a towel wrapped around her. "Jessamine, I have something for you," he said, holding out the garment in his hand.

She stepped forward and let the towel drop as she took it from his hand. "Oh thank you," she said, feigning surprise. She held it in the place it was to fit. "It's beautiful. Would you like me to wear it for you?"

"For me?" Jackson savoured the words, for him; that meant she was his. "I would like that very much," he managed to say.

"Then get you bathed," she said, "and I shall await your pleasure."

Jackson bathed himself in record time, when he came out, she was still stood in the light, this time the lace adorned her. If anything, it made the sight of her more exciting than her nakedness.

That night was better than the first, there was less haste and deeper satisfaction; for both of them. And between times, they talked of a future together, the present situation was forgotten for a moment, all that was important was the love that was growing. Too soon it seemed, they felt the engine note change as the *Esperance* slowed and they knew that their sojourn was almost over.

Chapter 32

Dressing, they made all their possessions ready for a swift departure to the hold. Then they stood on the deck, hidden behind the steam winches of the cargo derricks and watched as Bludmonger took the vessel between the breakwaters and into the port.

Compared to Port Lucas, Queinton was a bustling place with a vast expanse of docks and warehouses. The berth that they were destined for was at a place near the entrance. As they made their final approach and the first mooring lines were passed ashore, in the distance, they could see the terminus of the rail and their route home.

The air was thick with smoke from Local and factory, they were leaving the country behind, getting back to the city, that much was plain by the lack of greenery. As they finished securing to the wharf, they saw a group of people lounging by the warehouse, pretending not to watch while the gangway was lowered.

"They could well be our foe," said Jessamine. "Let us hope the plan works."

They went inside to say goodbye to the Captain, and to thank him for his aid. He brushed aside their words. "Make sure you stop this madman," he said, "that will be thanks enough. It seems the world is full of madmen these days. Now, get you to the hold and hide in the place Bosun has shown you. When the load is on the dock it will be taken by a cart to the warehouse. Wait in place until you hear the Char hooter; depart through the gate to freedom."

He embraced them both. "Farewell," his last word as they departed.

Keeping inside and out of sight, they took their things and went to the hold. There was no need for lamps, the hatch lid was opened and light enough to see clearly as they climbed into the space between the boxes. They held each other and as they looked up to daylight there was the hook of the crane descending.

228

"Hold tight," said the Bosun, as he attached it to the ropes that had been passed under the stack. "Safe journey," he shouted.

Then, "Haul away."

With a rush they were airborne, holding each other tight as they rose through the air. The next thing they knew, they landed with a thump on the dock, the hook was released and the stack was lifted again by a steam cart's forks.

This part of the journey was a bouncing, juddering ride from the sunlight to the shadows inside the warehouse. They were unceremoniously dumped against a wall and left in peace.

Hopefully, the first part of the plan had gone without a hitch. The swoop of the flight had been exhilarating, though they could see none of the reaction of their hunters. With luck they were still watching for them at the gangway.

As they waited, other loads of crates were brought in and stacked around them, it would be impossible for them to be found now, just as long as they remained hidden.

When the hooter sounded, they heard the stevedores depart and waited five minutes. Then they exited their hiding place, clambering over the stacks of goods. The warehouse was deserted, they could see through the door the watchers, still intent on the gangway.

Grinning, they left through the back of the warehouse and strolled through the dock gate; showing their disembarkation passes to the customs man, who wished them good day.

"I think we will be safe," said Jessamine. "Let us head for the Ryde, you obtain our tickets and I will make the call to Langdon. We will meet again in the refreshment rooms."

Jackson was on his second cup of Char when Jessamine finally returned from the speaker booths. He was starting to be concerned, even though they had avoided the watchers, they had always been found somehow, as if they had some sort of notice on them that they could not see.

She sat and he poured her a cup. She drank deeply.

"Well," she said, "that was an interesting call. There have been

229

many developments since we spoke last, even though it had only been a few days."

"Did Langdon tell you all of it? I was worried as to your whereabouts. I was beginning to wonder if you had been taken prisoner, if we had been spotted after all."

"I have seen nobody suspicious and I'm sorry if you were alarmed." She placed her hand on his. "It will all be well. I actually had little conversation with Langdon; he said he would brief us when we returned. Most of my time was spent waiting in line. There are sailors everywhere; some navy ship must have arrived after months at sea. Crews will be changing. Everyone must wish to talk to their families. The throng will help to hide us."

"We will arrive in the city before supper," he said. "With nothing to do, I looked at the timetable."

"Langdon knows that we keep attracting attention. I told him that every time we think we are clear, someone finds us. He said that it's either bad luck or we have been followed. I can't see how we could have been followed; in any event, we are being met at the terminus."

The news was a comfort, presumably there would be a squad of soldiers or similar to meet them on their arrival in Metropol City. Once under their protection, they would finally be safe from Rodney.

Jessamine looked up at the station timepiece, she drained her cup. "Come on, Jackson, we have only a few moments, we mustn't miss the Ryde."

As they hurried across the concourse towards the ticket barrier, Jessamine looked at every individual. Most of them seemed to be in the navy uniform of dark green. There were families, wives, parents and children. "They can't all be conspirators," Jackson reminded her, "and besides, they are looking for us at the ship. Even if Rodney had mobilised an army, he can scarce watch everywhere, all of the time."

"You are right," she said. "Most of our followers can be explained. There is no mystery, just a fanatical organisation."

"One which we will destroy," he added.

They showed their tickets to the attendant and were permitted onto the platform. They had to push their way through a throng of sailors and their wives, all goodbyes and damp eyes. Small children clutched at their fathers' legs, as if that could prevent them leaving.

Then there were the greetings, rushing together and shouts of joy at reunion. Jackson could feel the emotion in the place, happy and sad all mixed together. He had a sudden thought, what if the device he had seen was turned on here? Would all emotion drain away, as it had in the ranks of folk he had seen at the farm? How would the place feel then, to the unaffected?

The crowds made it quite impossible for anyone to get close to them. They boarded the carriage in a wave of humanity and were forced to stand; every seat was instantly taken.

On time to the second, the Ryde jerked into motion and set off. There was one stop scheduled, at the naval barracks of Whitehouse, no doubt after that they would be able to sit.

"I will go and see if there are any seats further along," suggested Jackson.

"Let us go together," Jessamine said, since their night of passion, she had become closer to him and was unwilling to leave his side. Jackson viewed this as a good thing, for one he was hoping that what had happened on the *Esperance* would be repeated at regular intervals, for another, it made him feel good to know that she wanted to be close to him.

Her admission of her past actions had done nothing to change his mind about how he felt; she said that it was business and he accepted that.

They walked the whole length of the Ryde, every seat was full, and they had to push past many people all engaged on the same search. In the end they gave up and stood in the corridor at the end of a carriage to wait for the exodus at Whitehouse.

The line followed the coast and the views were spectacular. To one side the sun-sparkled ocean, to the other the hills and fertile valleys of Norlandia. Harvest was approaching, the fields were heavy with grains, the trees full of fruits. They saw the steam-powered machines that Norlandia had pioneered; strung out ready to reap and thresh, together with the men preparing to capture the land's bounty before winter's grip.

Then the Ryde turned inland, the rail ran alongside the roadway and after an hour or so they passed through a small town, without stopping. "That was Lakesedge," Jessamine said.

"I saw it on the map when we purchased our tickets," agreed Jackson. "That means Whitehouse is nigh."

At Whitehouse the throng descended, the Ryde was now empty, save for a handful of civilians. A few more folk boarded, nodding greetings.

"There appears to be nobody interested in us," Jessamine remarked as they finally took seats and set off again. Yet they could not relax and watched the doors for anyone coming into their carriage. After they had crossed the Leopold Bridge, which they had seen from the air only a few short days ago, the fields and orchards were replaced by the signs of mechanisation.

The towns became closer together and the air started to darken from all the coal-smoke that modern civilisation produced.

Shortly after, they reached the outskirts of the city and slowed to negotiate the points as more and more lines converged on the terminus. Eventually, a platform appeared beside them, the great arched roof of glass and metal loomed over their heads, blocking out the late afternoon sunlight and they wheezed to a halt.

No sooner had the Ryde stopped than they rose to disembark. As they reached the platform, Jackson saw something that made his blood run cold.

Chapter 33

"Look, there," he said, grabbing Jessamine's arm. "That is one of the boxes that I saw on the wall. That man must be one of Rodney's henchmen."

Jessamine looked and could see a man dressed in a topcoat and hat, with the wooden box around his neck on a strap. He was looking at them and appeared to be talking into the trumpet on the top of the box.

Langdon appeared by their sides. "Welcome back," he said embracing Jessamine. He shook Jackson's hand and saw his expression. "What's amiss?" he asked.

"We are followed," said Jessamine, "although how I cannot say. Over there is a man with the box we see everywhere that there is mischief."

"Is that the box you were talking about in your speaker message from Port Lucas, before we were cut off?"

"The same, there is a lot to explain, we can tell you what it does, maybe Oswald can explain the how, and if he can stop the owner from using it."

"Once we can shake off your tail."

"Which had proved impossible so far."

Jackson was about to explain the apparent function of the box when Langdon saw it for himself. There was the sound of stamping feet. A phalanx of people had formed up, all blank faced, just as the ones at the estate had been.

They stared at the three, then as one, they started towards them.

"Come on," said Langdon, his face initially shocked, then his usual calm demeanour took control. "This is what I was feared of," he said. "An escalation. Your message was not a complete surprise. It is fortunate that I have a plan in place. Come with me and stay close."

At a fast walk they went through the barrier and out of the terminus. Jackson looked over his shoulder; the followers were twenty yards behind, coming as a group. They shoved people out of the way, children and women screamed. The ticket guard tried to stop them, he was overwhelmed. Still they came; a Watchman's whistle blew, the signal for all Watchmen who heard it to assist. "Down here, there is a reception committee," gasped Langdon as he led them through the lanes. They turned a corner, a blank wall stood in front of them.

"Have we gone wrong?" asked Jessamine.

"No," Langdon's voice was reassurance itself. "To the end. Wait and see." They went to the wall and stood with their backs to it. The group came around the corner. "Take out your truncheons," said Langdon; there was a volley of clicks.

"Now, if you please, Mr Fairview," shouted Langdon as the last of their pursuers was caught in the dead end. Behind them a mass of men with Fairview and Clarry at its head closed off the entrance.

The leaders were now in range of the truncheons and they rose and fell; whilst behind, the stragglers were attacked by Fairview's men.

The attackers put up little resistance, merely pushed and shoved, blows rained down on them but whatever had been done to make them attack had also rendered them insensitive to pain. Most frighteningly, there was complete silence, broken only by the sounds of breathing and of truncheon on flesh.

Finally, all were beaten to the ground and rendered unconscious.

"Did you see the man with the box around his neck?" Langdon asked Clarry.

"We did, he scuttled away as soon as he saw our intention," replied Clarry. "We have given chase and hope to catch him. Hello, Jackson and Jessamine, you have had some adventures by all accounts, it's good to see you again."

Fairview and Langdon inspected the bodies; they found one who was more than merely unconscious. An old man, his face was gaunt and relaxed in death. "This poor wretch has expired," said Fairview.

"There is no time for sentiment," replied Langdon. "We must get the corpse back to Oswald. We need to find how he is being controlled." He turned to Jackson. "Is this the same thing as you saw at the estate?"

Jackson nodded. "It is, we watched as the Professor used the box on his chest, the one I told you about. Just as the man on the platform was wearing. Aldithley spoke the word Lexis into it and the people obeyed him."

"This is another pieced of the puzzle then, there have been developments while you have been on your holidays, but now you must get back to work. Let us return to the orphanage, we will have a meeting with all parties, information can be shared, a plan agreed."

Leaving Fairview and Clary to search for the man with the box, the rest set off for the orphanage.

Chapter 34

Later that evening, they were all seated in the cellar room at the orphanage. Langdon brought them up to date on the events since they had departed for Hammerham. Char and pie had been served and eaten.

Oswald was preparing to examine the corpse, which had shared their journey in the luggage space of Langdon's mobile. The journey was taken in stunned silence, the presence of the corpse and the shock at the attack were still raw.

"Oswald has been busy, whilst you were away," Langdon informed them. "He has found that the crash of the aerialway was caused by at least one of the control boxes being switched off. We have only recovered one from the wreckage and under examination it revealed a cartridge in the workings. Oswald opened it and found that it contained one of your filaments, just like the ones we have already seen. And there have been other incidents," he added. "A boiler in a Local exploded. The blast was contained but a good part of the city was without steam for two days. An Exo went berserk and attacked a crowd, before being toppled. Again, cartridges were found in the wreckage, in places where they could disable the safety mechanisms."

"We saw a news-sheet in Port Lucas, the news of the accident to the aerialway has reached the provinces," said Jessamine. "But there was no suggestion of malign influences," added Jackson.

"Neither will there be, for the time," Langdon said. "The government does not want to start a panic, it's one of the few things everyone in the corridors of power agrees on, as you will learn. Privately, they are getting concerned. I've been agitating the ministers to round up Nethersole and all his henchmen. There has been resistance in the city, more of that later; in the country, we have had some success. The army have visited Nethersole's estate in Hammerham, they sent a message to the local Watch to warn of their arrival but when they deployed, they found that the whole estate was deserted."

"The Watchman, Silas somebody; he was Nethersole's man," said Jessamine. "We saw him in the place when we found Aldithley controlling his private army."

Langdon shook his head. "I advised the commander not to advertise his arrival to the local watch. It's unlikely that this Silas warned Nethersole, I will explain why in due course. A pity we never captured him, we may have learnt much."

"Did you find the place where they were working on those poor people? Or the tent lines and the parade ground?" asked Jessamine.

"The building where you say the medical work was carried out had been utterly destroyed by a fierce fire. There was evidence of human remains found in the field used by the porkers – that had been released, we assume into the forests. The tents were there yet contained little save a few personal effects. As for Rodney, or anyone from the estate, we know not of their location."

"Then what now?" Jackson blurted out. "We have not told you of our adventures since being discovered."

Langdon was dismissive. "That can wait till the morning. Your journeying across land and sea, fascinating though it may be are not as important as finding Nethersole and Aldithley. We have watchers everywhere; he is not at the factory, which is working as normal. Nor is he at his house in the city. Somehow, he has an army hidden away, we know not where, or anything about how he will strike next. The best thing you can do is rest and we will resume again in the morning."

Jackson and Jessamine went up to their rooms, Jessamine opened her door and Jackson went to follow her inside. To his surprise, she put her hand on his chest and stopped him at the door.

"We have to be circumspect," she said, "and cautious in our shows of affection. Langdon will not hesitate to discipline us for fraternisation; all that is going on will not distract him."

It was painful for both of them to spend time apart; sleep did not come easy for either of them, knowing that a few thin walls separated them.

Chapter 35

When they convened again in the morning, Oswald was also present. He looked more crumpled and bemused than usual. "Oswald has been working through the night," said Langdon, "while some were sleeping." He seemed tetchy, perhaps he had been up all night too?

"You would not believe the fuss since you've been gone," the scientist said. "We have searched through the records and inspected as many of the limbs that have been fitted or serviced as we could. We have found that all of them have had filaments installed in them during routine inspections at the Prosthesium. This has been going on for several months. Some have experienced problems, some not. Cartridges have been recovered; they were found to contain differing types of filament. This is enough evidence that testing was taking place."

"And now we have this new menace," added Langdon. "A box and its control of many people at once, if I had not seen it with my own eyes, I would have scarce believed it. It would appear that Aldithley has graduated from a simple switch to a more sophisticated system."

"This is what we were trying to tell you from Port Lucas," said Jessamine. "To forewarn you so you could work on the problem before we returned."

"I know and I thank you," said Langdon. "I apologise for my remarks last night, I wish to know all your adventures but I'm rather preoccupied. You did your best in trying circumstances and it is to your credit that you made it back. I'm confused as to how you were followed during all your wanderings, still, that is a problem that we may solve later. As it is, things are coming to a head; the problem is that you do not know all, as I do. I will tell you the other matter, which at first I thought unconnected, now I see that the issues are inseparable."

"May I go?" asked Oswald. "I will return but I need to see if my men have finished their tasks, I suspect that this part of the narrative does not concern me."

"You may," nodded Langdon. "Please return once you have completed what you have to do, we have questions for you."

"Thank you," replied Oswald. "I hope to have answers." He scuttled away, back to the safety of his basement.

"What other matter?" asked Jessamine.

"You remember Capricia? How she was sent on a mission?"

"I do," she replied.

"She was to be a children's nanny, for a lady," said Mrs Grimble.

"It was the day we had been fitted for clothes to visit the Prosthesium," said Jackson.

"Correct," said Langdon. "Normally I would not share information on what my agents are about; in this case, you need to know. Her mission was to ascertain the fealty of the Chief of the Watchmen in the city. His wife, who is a prominent member of the Ladies who Lunch, asked me to intervene as she was becoming aware of changes in his behaviour, mysterious meetings, a few extra funds in their accounts. She had suspected that he was either in the pay or under the control of someone; it now appears that person was Rodney Nethersole."

Before the visit to Hammerham, that news would have been a shock to Jackson; no more, after seeing Silas he was under no more illusion about the Watch and their supposed impartiality.

"And there are more implicated," Langdon was still talking. "Capricia has to be careful. Clearly, she is in danger. This means that I have a problem. I cannot investigate Rodney as I'm being blocked by Honorstan, the Watchman in question. He is preventing me from action; now Capricia reports that he is engaged in clandestine conversations and meetings with persons unknown. I fear that he is in league with Rodney, yet if I pursue the matter, I risk alerting him and losing sight of what Rodney is about. I might also endanger Capricia as well, which I also want to avoid if at all possible."

"Can we not infiltrate the factory again?" asked Alyious, who had come in unnoticed and was sitting at the back of the room. "We know that there are the boxes, Jackson has told us. Why can we not just go in and take one?"

Langdon shook his head, the others were waiting for him to dismiss Alyious, tell him he should not be here. Instead he answered, "If it were only that simple, Alyious. We know not what the situation is inside the factory. It might be filled with armed men, all under Rodney's control. Not only that, Rodney will have noticed our investigations, I'm sure that by now he has put the pieces together and knows that someone is aware of his machinations."

He paused for a moment. "I should not tell you this; I have been warned from investigating Rodney by senior ministers. If anyone connected with me is found in his works, I fear that my tenure of this organisation will be terminated. I cannot take the risk; we are the only thing that stands between this man and his despicable plans. I will not move until such time as there is no other option. Everything we now do must be done in secrecy. It is a fierce quandary and no mistake."

Fairview came in at that point. Langdon saw him and raised a rare smile. "Please give me something to work with," he said. "Have you caught the man we saw at the terminus, the one controlling the mob who followed us?"

Fairview also had the air of one who had been awake all night. "We have lost the man, I'm sorry to tell," he said. "He led us through the crowds around the terminus, where we could not apprehend him easily. He must have dodged into some doorway under their cover. We found his hat and coat lying on the ground."

"Very well, that is a setback. Now we must wait for Oswald, in the hope that he will have something to add to our store of knowledge."

Ten minutes later, one of his assistants came to the room. "Begging your pardon, sirs, ma'am," he said, touching his cap. "Would you come to the laboratorium? Mr Oswald has something to show you."

The group followed the man back to the cellar, where Oswald stood, in front of his bench, with a triumphant grin. Alyious joined them, as he had not been dismissed. Mrs Grimble was also present, dressed in bloodied green linen.

"What do you have for us?" asked Langdon.

"Well, sir, as you know, we have spent the night examining the remains of the poor wretch you brought back from your adventures."

"And what can you tell us?"

"Based on the events you described, we concluded that there must be some sign of that which controls, as well as the physical presence of the thing that exercises that control."

"Can you speak more clearly?" asked Langdon. "It seems that the more simplicity we require, the more technical you wish to be."

"Of course," Oswald replied. "I apologise. To put it plain, we first examined the body. However, the head and neck were badly bruised and we could see nothing obvious. Mrs Grimble then dissected the stomach, to see if any foreign object had been ingested. When that failed, she looked again."

Mrs Grimble smiled. "I found it, in the back of the neck. A small scar, just below the base of the skull bone. It concealed a filament, not unlike the one we already knew about, except this was composed of more than one strand, wound together and of course was not in a brass container. It had been implanted at the base of the brain and delicately connected to the nerves of the spinal column, and the brain itself. It's a really clever feat of surgery, and so precisely done. Our thought is that it can turn certain functions of the brain on and off, as the original one did with the arm, just in a more complex way."

"Then does that mean the box we saw is the controller? How is the signal sent through the air?"

"That, Sir Mortimer, is another work of brilliance," said Oswald.

"Give him no credit," said Langdon. "He is no more than a criminal and a murderer."

"Your pardon, I was referring to the application of science by Aldithley. Not its use. As you know I have decoded and read the notes that Jackson managed to obtain."

This was news to Jackson, things had moved on during their absence, in more ways than one.

"Aldithley has married all sorts of diverse scientific advancements," Oswald continued. "They all appear to be unconnected, yet he has joined them together. The man is clearly a genius. The box uses a novel form of statics as a power source; a combination of lead plates in an acid solution produces the force. As far as I can tell this force is sent as a wave – a signal through the very air, probably through the wire spring that protrudes from the box. This signal is somehow understood by the filament. I can think of no better way of describing it. The power and frequency are designed to activate some clever design in the filament. It appears to be connected directly to the base of the brain, to the part which we always thought controlled sleep. The filament must act like a mesmeriser, one you might see in some cheap entertainment. The filament works by putting the subject into a trance and making them susceptible to commands. It is why I called you to the laboratorium; there is something I wish to try, with your permission of course."

"Explain further, and sing no more praises, as far as I'm concerned, the man is a rogue and a criminal, even if a genius."

"Yes, sir. If I'm correct, then the filament is being controlled by some sort of statics wave. If you recall the pattern made by the magnet? Naturally I will need to make a box of my own to determine all the details. In the meantime, I have a high power Wasperton-Byler field creator here; I would like to see if the filament that Jackson obtained from the Prosthesium is sensitive to one."

Langdon nodded and Oswald turned the machine on. Steam coursed through it as it started to spin. Instead of an unwitting victim's hands, the two wires were connected to the ends of the filament.

This filament, now in a brass container was held in a vice. It instantly started to shudder and glow white. The vice it was held in also started to glow; the grease on it began to smoulder. Then it exploded with a sharp noise. The vice was blown apart by the force, fragments whizzed around the room, smashing equipment but missing everyone.

There was the smell of burning. Jackson felt a jolt in his foot, which became hot and he yelped and struggled to remove his boot. Jessamine was also hopping, trying to do the same. To their relief, they managed to get the boots from their feet, by which time the soles were smouldering and giving off an acrid smoke.

Oswald opened the windows and they threw the boots outside; the air was becoming quite tainted with the smell of burning rubber.

Chapter 36

"That's a shocker and no mistake," said Mrs Grimble. "More new boots required."

"That explains it," said Oswald, "how you were followed at every turn. Not only is there a mechanism to transmit to the filaments, there must also be a detector, to see when one is near. A person could follow you, far enough away to remain unseen."

"But how did our boots acquire a filament?" wondered Jackson.

Jessamine punched his shoulder. "At the factory, when we had to change before our inspection. They must have been tampered with, when we left them in the locker."

"A clever ruse, and one which we could not have predicted," said Langdon. "Oswald, what could be the strength of the signal?"

"The coded drawings indicate a range of up to a mile for the transmitting device," said Oswald. "There must have been a person following them, with a box like this one, except that it merely detects the presence of a filament. As it is unconnected to anything, it cannot be controlled. In that, I would expect its range to be somewhat less."

"Is that possible?" Langdon was dubious.

"According to the theories on the pages, yes," replied Oswald. "It's really quite exciting, all this new science. In the right hands, who knows what would not be possible."

Jackson thought of the horseman, after they had passed so close that first time, they must have been the followers, keeping their distance, all the way to Port Lucas. It would then have been easy to warn folk at Queinton, they had not kept their destination a secret from the shipping agent.

"If we had had a Wasperton-Byler machine at the terminus, could we have stopped the mob yesterday?" asked Fairview.

"Oh yes," nodded Oswald. "The filaments would have exploded, in the... Oh." The enormity of it sank in.

"Well done, Oswald, Mrs Grimble." Langdon was impressed with the results. "There is one thing though," he lifted his fingers as he made each point, "thanks to Jackson and Jessamine, we know the word that will activate the throng, but what of the one to stop them?"

Jackson was confused. "If we have the Sensaurum, can we not just call them to stop?"

"I'm sorry, I was not clear enough, I meant the word to release them from control. If we just stopped them, the man in control could just restart them."

Jackson thought for a moment. He was about to say that surely, the man could then just regain control anyway, but he stopped before he said another foolish thing. In any event, Langdon was still talking.

"We know not Rodney's plans. Nor of how many he has under his control. We need one of those Sensaurum boxes. It's good that we can stop a marching throng, but only by killing them all. It's crude but I suppose that it will be effective as a last resort. I would much rather have a way to disable the signal, or the filament, without wholesale slaughter. After all, these poor folks are innocent."

"They could be everywhere," Jessamine said. "Just as we encountered some on the Ryde, they might be walking the streets, unaware of their function, till called by the signal from the box."

"That is a frightening thought, and no mistake," Oswald added. "I have examined all the papers that you brought from the Prosthesium, once I managed to decipher them. There is a lot of information on how the signal is generated and transmitted. The principles are fascinating and will be the foundation of much in the world; it's just unfortunate that Aldithley has decided to use his skill for such evil ends. But I think, no I'm sure that I can create one of these control boxes from his drawings, given time and materials. Possibly even a means to block the statics signal from one. If only I wasn't continually distracted."

"Ignore everything else, you shall have whatever you need and as quickly as possible," said Langdon.

"Do you think Aldithley has been manipulated by Nethersole or vice versa?" asked Jessamine.

"I would say more that their ambitions matched. Nethersole was intent on taking over the factory; I suspect that initially it was for no more than the power and wealth. Then when he learnt of Woolon's achievements he consolidated his business with the work. After Aldithley's departure, there must have been a meeting of minds, a mutual pact for yet more power. Aldithley was aggrieved, he found a willing patron in the man who wanted control and was able to finance it."

"There was another disturbing discovery in the papers," added Oswald. "It appears that there are others, as well as implanting the filament in the strays taken to Nethersole's estate, we have found plans for a network of doctors who have been readied to implant these things in people, using some sort of simple technique to place them into the flesh of the neck. It's all hidden under the guise of a secret trial by the Institute, there are no names and we have no way of knowing if it has begun. I know not all the details, but it may be that large numbers of the population are potentially under Rodney's control."

"I have to go and meet again with the ministers and the Watch. I will plead for Rodney's factory to be searched and one of these boxes recovered. Oswald, proceed in your attempts to manufacture your own device."

"I will, sir, but it takes time, time we may not have."

Langdon nodded. "Do your best," he said as he left them.

Later that evening, Jackson, Jessamine and Alyious discussed the problem over Char and food.

"If Langdon has his hands tied, then perhaps it might be better to take a little unofficial action," suggested Alyious.

"What do you mean?"

"Well, clearly we cannot act with Langdon's blessing. He has been warned off by the powers that be, but if one of us, say one who is on the periphery of things, should accidentally stray into the factory, and if he should accidentally return with one of the boxes, would that not be a fortuitous thing?"

"Do you mean one of us? I know where they are," said Jackson.

"No not you, you are too close to Langdon, you would be

missed. I meant myself. Tell me where they might be found. I may take a little trip, without any of you knowing and see if one does not fall into my hands."

Jackson sat down with Alyious and told him everything he knew about the layout of the factory, the way in over the rough ground, the hiding place in the washroom, position of the stairs and the room with the boxes.

"I think it's a foolhardy idea," said Jessamine, "and I think you should consider carefully before you embark on it."

"Langdon saved my life," said Alyious simply. "He pulled me from the gutter; I would have been a dead man if he had not. I owe him more than life. I have had a new start. If this might help him, I think I must do it." Alyious stood. "I'm off to prepare," he said. "Forget this conversation. If anyone asks, I have gone out for a walk; tell them that I might be some time."

Chapter 37

Next morning, at fast-break, Alyious was absent. Jackson and Jessamine exchanged glances, nobody else had noticed. They repaired to the classroom, where they were addressed by Langdon.

"There are reports of a disturbance in the city in the middle of the night, a crowd suddenly formed, marched on a bank and attempted to rob it. When the Watch arrived, the crowd broke and dispersed. It sounds very much like they were under control, when the Watch arrived, that control was removed. The Watch treated it as a random crime, the people they detained all claimed to have no knowledge of why they were in the vicinity, or what they had been doing. The Watch had no choice but to let most of them go, they had insufficient cells to hold them all, and on what charges? Of course, they knew nothing about our investigation; we are fortunate that one of them was belligerent and assaulted a Watchman. He has been kept overnight. When I learned of these events, I went to the Watch station, where I was able to examine the fellow. I found that he had a scar on his neck, which he said was the result of a recent visit to his doctor."

He paused for breath while they digested this, then delivered the rest of his news.

"Not only that, last night I found that there has been a message received, it has been passed to the government in secret, they have now sent it on to me. It warns that the events on the aerialway and in the Locals are just the start. More and worse will happen unless certain demands are met. The events at the bank were not mentioned but it's obvious to me that the same man is involved, I have suggested that this is a continuation of the pattern that we have been tracking."

"It must be the work of Rodney," said Jackson. "Did he have the arrogance to sign the message?"

"He did not," said Langdon. "The sender simply refers to himself as the Master of Automata."

"But it must be him," added Jessamine. "This name is chosen to make him feel important, to create an aura and confer status on his evil plan."

"I agree; he is the most likely, on what I have seen. It's frustrating but I have been instructed again that I cannot move against him or his factory. As I said before, I'm sure that he has friends in the upper reaches, they bleat to me about requiring more evidence. In any event, the government are not minded to pay such a ransom, it would set a dangerous precedent. At the moment, they are asking him for more time, we know not if their response has been received."

"Then what can we do?"

"Our priority is to find the second word, the one that will stop the people being controlled. We also need to know what this Master's final plan is; I'm guessing the overthrow of the government in his favour will be only the start. Meanwhile Oswald has started building his own device and determining how it is activated. He says that it will take him some considerable time, to build and test, but he has everything he needs."

The rest of the morning was spent in devising a plan to search the city for anyone carrying one of the boxes. Jackson was about to depart for Clarry's with new instructions when Langdon received a message. Jackson was stopped at the gate and instructed to return.

"There has been a change of plan," he was told. "There are reports of a mob attacking a bank in the city; I want you both to attend, along with Fairview. Take Oswald and his device. If needs be; if you cannot find and stop the instigator, you may have to use it."

Oswald held the box tightly as they raced down the road in the mobile, Jessamine at the wheel. She swerved expertly through the traffic, avoiding trams and pedestrians without slowing, sliding the large vehicle around sharp corners.

"Have a care," cried Oswald from the rear seat, "my detonator is a piece of delicate scientific equipment."

"Why do you call it that?" asked Jackson, glad to have a reason to turn his head from their progress, which must surely end in disaster.

"I named it so, for the effect it had on your boots," said Fairview. "Like the blast of a gas-shell, detonating over our enemies."

"And which it may soon have on some poor innocent's head," added the flustered scientist. "I have not been outside for months, now I've hung from the aerialway and been flung around in a mobile, all in a few weeks."

"Ah but you love the excitement, don't you?" said Jessamine, as they slid by the side of a flailing Exo-man and entered a side street. "We're here," she muttered as the mobile screeched to a halt and they composed themselves.

They finished their journey on foot, arriving at a position opposite the bank, which was situated in a quiet square. They could see a throng of at least fifty had surrounded the building.

A group were at the doors, which were shut, the mob were pounding on them, the rest were attempting to climb in the windows and throwing stones at the panes, which were shattering.

There were about ten Watchmen standing in a group, without a senior man present they seemed unsure of how to proceed.

"What can we do?" asked Oswald. "Why are the Watch not taking control?" He gripped the box tightly, Jackson realised that there was something different about it. "How is it driven, without its steam supply?" he wondered.

"Well," said Oswald, "I have replaced that with a hand crank." He unfolded a handle from a recess in the side of the box. "This will now spin the magnet directly."

Before they could do anything else, a large group of Watchmen led by two officers entered the square. The men already present jumped to attention as Fairview and the others shrank into the alley. Orders were given.

The Watchmen surrounded the mob and instead of trying to stop them, let them continue their vandalism. They ripped at the fabric of the building with little effect, stones shattered a few more windows but the door held firm. Strangely, the Watchmen were ignored, the people never once looking behind them.

"We must find the man who is controlling the mob," whispered Fairview and as a group, they left the alley and searched around the periphery for anyone who was sporting a box. Arriving back at their starting point, they had failed to locate them.

"It may be that the range of the box is large enough to keep the operator safe," opined Fairview, "but it stands to reason that he will have been close enough to see what is going on and modify the orders he sends." Try as they might, they could not find him.

"He must be in one of the buildings, watching from a window or on a roof," said Jessamine.

As the people were oblivious to the Watchmen, so they in turn were unaware of the band behind them. "There must be an outer cordon of Watchmen," suggested Fairview, "as no-one else has ventured into the square, we are caught between the two rings. I propose that you set off your device and see the effect. It's cruel but it will send this Master a message, that we know his plans and have a way to stop him."

"If you are sure," said Oswald. With reluctance he moved a switch on the box and cranked the handle. There was no noise from the contraption. By the reaction of the people attacking the building, a statics charge must have been detonated. Without a sound, save a series of sharp cracks, accompanied by spurts of blood, the crowd fell to the ground as one. The Watchmen all jumped back in alarm, then they turned and looked at Fairview and the others.

"Who might you be?" asked one of the officers, his abundant moustache moving like two small rodents as he spoke. "Was that your doing?"

"I'm Special Investigator Fairview, from the Ministry." Fairview offered him a small card. The officer studied it for a moment.

"Very well," he said, "and are these your men?" He glanced at Jessamine. "Beg pardon, your agents?"

"They are," Fairview agreed. "And we had an inkling that we could stop the mob, using our new device."

"Have you seen?" prompted Jackson, with inappropriate enthusiasm. "Three Watchmen are also lying dead."

They regarded the scene; the Watchmen were sprawled on the ground, surrounded by a spreading pool of their life's blood, just as the folk around the bank's doors and windows. Beside them, one of the surviving Watchmen was being noisily sick in the gutter.

"How do you explain that?" the officer asked. "Why are some of my men and my superior afflicted, why indeed is anyone harmed by that box you carry?"

"I'm sorry," said Fairview, "but I cannot tell you, the information is secret and privileged. Suffice it to say, it is a matter of national importance."

"Very well then," replied the officer, his face anguished. "But those men were friends of mine, one of them my superior. What do I tell their families?"

"Form your men up," ordered Fairview. "Leave the outer cordon in place. I will address you all," said Fairview.

Once the men were assembled he addressed them, "A mob of anarchists was defeated today. And some of you died in the attempt. You will not, under pain of treason, mention anything about a box, or how they died. Do you understand?"

The men muttered but nodded.

"Very well," added Fairview, "remember your promise today. Now, sir," he turned to the officer, "you will keep the outer cordon in place until we have disposed of the bodies. Jessamine, go to Clarry and get him to bring a large mobile, these dead are coming back with us."

"That's not all," said Oswald. "I heard an explosion from a window, up there." His hand shaking, he pointed. There was a broken pane on a second floor of one of the buildings overlooking the square; a man's body was half out of the opening, a smoking object hung from his neck, swinging gently.

As they looked the body fell, hitting the ground with a thud. The box smashed into pieces. Oswald hurried to it, bending to examine the mess of flesh and metal.

"It's one of the control boxes," he said. "The fall alone did not break it; its workings had already been burnt beyond repair by the detonator."

"After the concussion had finished off its operator," said Fairview. "It seems as if the detonator not only disrupts the filaments, it must also set up a vibration in the generator and overload that as well. It's a pity it is so comprehensively destroyed, we need a box that we can examine."

"The threat is over then," said the Watch officer. "Now this device and its operator are no more."

"Only for a short time," said Fairview. "I expect the news of what happened here will travel, which is why I want to remove all evidence. Unfortunately, we still have no lead to the whereabouts of the person in control of things."

Chapter 38

They spent the rest of the day transporting all the bodies to the orphanage. It was a grisly job, requiring Clarry and a fleet of covered carts, each allowed through the growing crowds around the Watchmen's cordon.

By the time they had finished it was evening and they were dismissed, leaving Oswald the unpleasant task of examining them through the night.

Alyious had still not returned. Jessamine had looked in his room, but everything was untouched. "Langdon will be sure to notice his absence soon," she said to Jackson as they collected their food.

Sure enough, as soon as Langdon saw them, he asked straight away. "Where is Alyious?"

The pair kept quiet about the conversation they had had, instead repeating the words of the boy himself.

"The last we saw of him, he said that he was going for a walk."

Langdon looked suspicious. "Come on; you all whisper plans together, that was over a day ago, have you not seen him since?"

"We have been kept busy carrying Oswald's grisly acquisitions to the basement," she said innocently. Langdon was about to say more, a call from Oswald tore him away.

The next morning passed swiftly, Oswald reported privately to Langdon, what he said was unknown but soon the corpses were loaded back onto the mobile, save those of the Watchmen. A little while after it departed, a Watch-wagon arrived and took them away separately.

Langdon called Jackson and Jessamine to the basement, when they arrived Fairview was also present.

"Oswald tells me the men all died from injuries to the neck," he said, "consistent with the destruction of the filament. That is no surprise, what troubles me more is the presence of the device in Watchmen."

"We have investigated that," said Fairview. "According to records at the Watch-house, all three had recently attended a doctor in the city, all with symptoms of neuralgia. They were invited to take part in a trial of a new treatment."

"And you think that this doctor was connected to the information that we recovered from the Prosthesium?"

"We are still investigating that. It will take time to consult with the families and make connections. I cannot just go down to his consulting rooms and accuse him of working for Rodney."

Just before luncheon, Oswald was disturbed by a buzzing from an apparatus on his desk. He had returned to the less grisly task of making a Sensaurum box, using the plans Jackson had recovered.

He wanted to create a statics field, like the controlling one, that would make the filament immune to commands. The work was going well, he had all the parts needed, everything except time and a means to test it once completed.

'Someone is using the keypad to gain access', he noted, 'although I know of none that are abroad.' He watched as the code was entered. 'It's Alyious, there is his code.' But the entry stopped before the final digit of the date was entered. He waited for a moment, but there was no more action. 'It must have been children playing,' he thought and turned back to his task.

Five minutes later, there had been no further action at the gate. He had a memory, Alyious had been absent, Langdon had remarked on it. He hurried to tell someone.

On his way, he saw Jessamine. "Alyious is at the gate," he told her, out of breath from the exertion of the stairs. "The keypad on the door was activated minutes ago, with his code. At first I assumed it was children playing; before the numbers could be completed, they stopped. There has been nothing more. I remembered Alyious was missing and I'm concerned."

"I will come with you," she said, calling for Fairview. They went to investigate. Outside the gate, they found Alyious. He was slumped to the ground, a trail of blood led from the keypad to the floor, as if he had been typing the number with his last efforts. He was curled into a ball and quite dead.

"His body is not yet cold," said Fairview when he arrived. "He can only have expired a few short minutes ago. We must take him inside."

When Fairview lifted the body, he found scrawled in blood, the letters *r-e-v* in a shaky hand, drawn on the ground. It must have been daubed with Alyious's last actions in this life. There was also part of a leather harness under the corpse.

There was shock at the news, replaced by an anger that it had happened. "Alyious must have had a Sensaurum and was bringing it to us when he was caught," said Fairview. "It has been ripped from him and he has been savagely stabbed, several times."

"Could it have been common criminals, or must we again point the finger at Rodney?"

"It seems likely that he was followed, to see where he had come from, perhaps they thought him a Watchman or other official. Once they had the place, he was killed."

"Then will Rodney or his lackeys now know where we are based?"

"Quite possibly. What he was writing, it's clearly important, can 'rev' be the word to release control?"

"There is only one way to find out, we must await the next attack and rush to it, find the Professor or whoever is operating the equipment and take him alive. We can then persuade him to tell us."

Langdon paced the room, once he had been informed. "That is a setback, he should not have disobeyed me," he said, as if Alyious was somehow at fault. "Where did the idea come from?" he asked. "Does anyone know?"

Sometimes the cold nature of Langdon startled Jackson. Alyious had given his life to try and help yet Langdon blamed him for disobeying orders.

However, it seemed that Langdon's wrath had been tempered. "There is no time for criticism, another message has been received. 'Since you will not pay, or even acknowledge my messages I will show you more of my powers, fear me. The Master of Automata'."

"Does he not know that we can stop his men now, by use of the Detonator?"

"I've been considering." Langdon had clearly come to a decision, yet by his demeanour, all could tell that it was not one he relished. "Alyious has shown the way, through his insubordination. I have decided to go against the government, because I feel that they are wrong."

"What do you mean, move against the Prosthesium?"

He nodded. "We need the box. Oswald is going as fast as he can on his countermeasures; the problem is, we know not how much time we have. You two will have to do it; I have no time to spend getting others familiar with the layout of the factory. You will have to go and take a box. If the professor is present, Jessamine, you will have to distract him, seduce him if you must. While they are engaged, Jackson, you must make off with a box. Together you will return and give it to Oswald. It will help him in his search for a solution."

Jackson felt ill inside as he heard Langdon's orders. It was as if Alyious was speaking to him from beyond the grave, 'I warned you,' he heard him say in his head.

"Jackson," Langdon repeated. "Pay attention. What can you remember about the shape of the room?"

Jackson cast his mind back; his memory sharpened by the methods taught him by Fairview.

"Inside the room," Jackson said, "there is an alcove, hidden from the door. A bed is within and a velvet curtain draws across, for privacy."

"Then that is perfect. Jessamine, you can draw the curtain so that Jackson may work undisturbed. Now away and prepare. Let Fairview know when you are ready, he will transport you."

Once they were alone, Jackson gave voice to his thoughts. "I might not see what is occurring, but I will know. Alyious, rest him in peace, told me this would happen, if we got involved."

She put her arm around him. "You have to accept it's part of my job, it means nothing. I've had to before, you knew that, and I expect that I will have to again. It's not the same as what we do."

"Even so, I cannot stand nearby and listen to you cavorting with that old fool, or anyone else for that matter."

"Then I don't want you to be involved at all. Jackson, I care about you deeply, we will discuss this when the matter is resolved and we are all safe."

Jackson noticed that the word love was not included in either of their words, even though he realised that it was how he felt.

"Get us gone then," said Fairview, when they reported to him. "And good hunting. I will take you by mobile to the rear of the place and you can hop over the wall. I will wait for your return."

As they drove past the entrance, the gate was shut tight, a light burned in the gatehouse. "So Rodney has not started his night shift," remarked Jackson. "Why has the place not been overrun by soldiers, or the Watch come to that?"

"A long and terrible tale," said Fairview. "As Sir Mortimer has said, Nethersole has powerful friends; we are not sure if they are his allies or whether he holds sensitive information about them, but they support his freedom and hamper the investigations. We cannot move against him until we have such overwhelming evidence that nobody could argue against."

"Then how much more has to happen before he can be stopped?"

"If we can provide absolute proof of his wrongdoing, perhaps his friends will see the light and melt away. That is why we need a box. Together with the papers you have already found, that should be enough."

They came in over the waste ground and past the washroom where Jackson had hidden; it seemed so long ago now. The walls were no obstacle to them, they had sat on the tops and watched for a few moments before descending, to their surprise the place seemed deserted.

Jackson had expected the Prosthesium to be better guarded, perhaps Rodney has realised that his lair was known and was in the process of moving out. Or maybe he felt secure with his backing from on high. From their vantage point they could see a light in the corner room, the Professor was in residence. Jackson had been hoping that he was not, his stomach fluttered and he felt bile rise in his throat.

Whatever the reason for the deserted yard, they had to move. Quickly they descended to ground level. The yard was deserted; they crossed to the side door. It opened to their tools; silently they passed through the machine filled room, where the shaft still spun and up the stairs to the corner room.

The two crept along the corridor; the laboratorium was ahead of them. This was the moment when Jackson's loyalties were to be put to the ultimate test. Jessamine had come to mean so much to him, he could hardly bear to watch her go inside, knowing what would happen.

"Good luck," he whispered. "I hate what you have to do but love you for doing it." She smiled and pecked him on the cheek.

"Whilst I do this, my mind will be blank; I will take no pleasure, that only comes from being with you. Give me a few minutes, then follow me in when you hear the noise of the curtain."

Jackson nodded. "Once I have the box, I will wait for you in the washroom, whistle when you are nigh."

Jessamine nodded and opened the door. "Who's there?" said the Professor. "Leave me in peace or I will call for help."

"Hush," said Jessamine, in a soft whisper, "I have been sent to amuse you." The door was pushed shut but did not completely close. Jackson could hardly hear her talking to the Professor, it sounded like she was enticing him towards his bed. Jackson listened for the sound of the curtain being pulled. When he heard it swish across, he stole into the room, trying to block his ears to the sounds coming from behind the thick velvet curtain. He quietly took one of the boxes from its hook and using the leather harness he hoisted it onto his back. Carefully, he made his way out of the door. Now he had to wait for Jessamine and they both had to get out of the place unnoticed. He went down the stairs and made his way back to the washroom. There he waited, poised to climb to the hiding place he had used before; should anyone come in.

After what seemed like an age, but was only twenty minutes or so, he heard Jessamine whistle and went outside. She was flushed, her hair dishevelled. "Come on then," she said, "let's get out of here."

They retraced their steps, with nobody to challenge them they returned to Fairview in short time.

"Ah good, you have it," Fairview said when he saw the box. "Oswald will be most pleased." There was no mention of what Jessamine had been required to do to obtain it. The result had better be worth the effort, and the emotions it has produced in me, thought Jackson as the mobile sped through the streets.

Jessamine never uttered a word all the way back to the orphanage, Jackson sensed that it would be wrong of him to say much so he kept silent. Fairview was also quiet, the trip passed in strained silence.

"I'm away to bathe," Jessamine said, as soon as they were inside the gates. "I will need to scrub for an hour to remove the memory of that brief encounter."

Jackson followed her up the stairs, at her door she turned. "Please keep away from me tonight, Jackson," she said, and there was a tear in her eye. "I will see you again in the morning."

Jackson and Fairview went to see Langdon with the box. They found him with Oswald, deep in discussion. "We have it," Fairview exclaimed. Oswald practically fainted with excitement.

"Let me see." He grabbed the box and scuttled away.

Jackson was left with Langdon, who paced up and down like one of the fabled felines from the jungles of the Spice Islands. He gazed at Jackson, who was sure he could see all his secrets, even the truth of him and Jessamine. To change the subject, he asked the first question he could think of.

"Where did you find Oswald?" asked Jackson.

"I found him at the Palais," Langdon answered, without breaking stride. "He had invented a few things that seemed useful, built from rubbish and leavings. I offered him a chance to come and work for me, with everything he needed. I gather, from the fact that you have returned with a Sensaurum, that your mission went well."

"It was as smooth as anything," replied Jackson, neglecting to mention his upset. "We thought it strange that the place was unguarded."

"I expect you have been told; the man has powerful friends."

There was a sudden anguished cry from somewhere in the building. Jackson's first thought was that Jessamine had been overcome by some sort of grief, then it was repeated, this time they made out the word 'Useless!'

"That was Oswald," said Langdon.

Oswald entered, his face a mask of pain. "The box is empty," he said. "The workings have been removed."

"Then we are no further forward," said Langdon. "He has played us for fools; he must have reasoned that after Alyious's failure, we would be back for another attempt. No wonder it was easy, you were allowed to get to the Professor. He was alone in there. Rodney was waiting to see what we would do."

Jackson felt as if his world had turned upside down. Jessamine's actions had been in vain. It made the whole distasteful episode even more unpalatable. He would have to tell her in the morning, goodness alone knew how she would react.

"We still must rely on you, Oswald," said Langdon. You must give me the means to stop Rodney without killing everyone."

"I will do my best for you," replied the scientist.

Chapter 39

Jessamine was absent at fast-break, as was Fairview and the other agents, no doubt Langdon had them scouring the city for signs of Rodney and Winstanley. Jackson took a tray with food and Char up to Jessamine's room. He knocked. "Jessamine, it's me, with food and Char." He called.

The door opened. "Come in" she said. She was dressed in a long gown, buttoned from neck to knee. Her eyes were red from crying. Jackson set the tray down and took her in his arms. Unprotestingly she clung to him. "Can you bear to hold me?" she whispered.

Jackson kissed her face, her lips. "Of course I can," he said. He felt her shiver. "Come and eat," he said. She went to the desk and attacked the food.

"What news of the box?" she asked. Jackson knew no better way than to tell it straight, get the bad news over with, then reassure her.

"I'm sorry, it was worthless, the mechanics had been removed," he told her.

She laid down her cutlery. "It was all in vain." She shook her head. "Then I... for nothing."

"I'm sorry." He went to her and took her hands, kissing the palms.

"You were right to tell me straight," she said. "Does Langdon know?"

"He was with me when Oswald told him."

"Then his anger will be terrible, he thinks of us all as his children, despite his cold demeanour. What hurts us hurts him. I hope he does not get the Professor alone. We need some good fortune; it seems as if nothing is going well for us."

Later that day, they were seated in the classroom when Clarry arrived. "Well good after, everyone," he said. "Jessamine, can you fetch Oswald and Sir Mortimer? I have a gift."

While they were called he disappeared. Two minutes later, when they had both arrived, he was back and with a flourish, he presented Oswald with a box. The wire spring jutting from the top was a little bent but otherwise, it looked to be in perfect condition.

"How did you get one of these?" asked the scientist.

"My pride was hurt; I was ashamed that I had lost sight of the man at the terminus," Clarry replied. "I sent my men out to look for nothing else but a man with a box around his neck, looking like a speaker instrument with a large spring sticking from the top. Not an object that you would expect to see, I'm sure you'd agree. Anyhow, one of my boys spotted a man, lurking near to a bank. He was dressed in a heavy coat, with this device hanging and swinging, large as life. The boy sent his runner to find me and we managed to nab the man. I was as gentle with him and the box as I could be. When we grabbed him, he was trying to push this lever on the side. I have him in the mobile, well trussed, if you'd like a word?"

"Well done, Clarry," said Langdon. He slapped him on the back. "Bring him inside. Perhaps we should talk to him."

Within minutes, the man was bought in and tied to a chair in the Gymnazien, guarded by Patching. He looked unremarkable, yet defiant. Someone had clearly been involved in preparing him for questioning. He was bruised and bloodied around the face. Oswald went to him and spoke to Patching. The soldier moved the man's head so that Oswald could look for the tell-tale scar.

"Is there a mark on his neck, Oswald?" asked Langdon.

"No, sir," answered the scientist.

"Now then," said Langdon, "tell me all you know about this device and its uses."

"Never," replied the man, shaking his head. His expression was firm. "Kill me now and have done with it."

"You are loyal and I admire that, but your master is misguided, tell us all and we can help you."

Again, the man shook his head. "I will say nothing, you can beat me again if you wish. It will not be as bad anything that

Winstanley will deal out. He will find me if I talk, then enjoy throwing me to the porkers. If I'm lucky, I will be dead when they start to feed."

"Very well," said Langdon. "I will waste no more time on you. You are free to go. Untie him, Patching, let him loose. You can tell Winstanley that you said nothing."

"What?" the man looked distressed. "Are you insane? If I return without the box and Winstanley finds out I have been a captive, the result will be the same."

"But you can tell him that you said nothing. I'm sure he is like me, an honourable man who will take your word."

The man was quaking. "He'll never believe me."

"Then you have a dilemma, the only way you live is if you tell us everything you know. We will not kill you; we can keep you safe here till all this is resolved. We will return. Think on it."

Within an hour, Oswald announced he had a report to make. "It's a good job Clarry restrained the man from pulling the lever," he said. "It releases a control which destroys the contents, by creating an imbalance in the statics field. I found that there is a switch on the top, which turns the machine on and off. It's a marvel of design." He demonstrated the operation of the switch; then, removing the cover, how to disconnect the power supply.

"That's very good; we can stop a captured man destroying the evidence. More importantly, can you decipher its workings?"

"Oh certainly," he replied. "I think that I have found the method used to generate the signal, though not the complexity of it, at least not enough to explain how it controls the subject. I suspect that the filament is encoded with a representation of the Professor's voice. As I said, it works on the brain as a mesmeriser would."

"Enough, Oswald, can you produce your own version of the apparatus?"

He smiled triumphantly. "I believe that I can produce a tone which will cancel the signal from this apparatus, without killing the person."

Langdon slapped Oswald on the back. "Well done," he said. "Carry on with your endeavours. I will take this information to the few ministers that I feel I can trust." He thought for a moment. "Jackson, you and Jessamine come with me, you can explain all that you have seen on your travels. We can show them the boxes we have, explain their purpose. Perhaps we can persuade them to let me act."

Chapter 40

The journey would only take a few moments. Jackson was looking forward to entering the halls of government; he had seen them from a distance looming over the city. As with flying, he never imagined that he would be meeting ministers.

They stopped in traffic; a large lorry was ahead of them. Another came up behind and stopped. They were stuck, unable to move. Then there was a knock on the window.

A man stood, brandishing a gas-gun, pointed at Langdon's head. "Open the door," he said. "Make no attempt to stop me."

Another man opened the rear door on the other side, he too was armed. "Follow the lorry in front," he said to Langdon, "if you want to live. My master wishes a few words."

Both men squeezed into the mobile. The lorry ahead moved off and there was a jolt as the one behind them nudged them forward. "Keep up," said the man. Langdon had the look of anger as he complied.

They drove in silence, the gas-guns never wavering, for several minutes. There was no chance for Langdon to turn off and what was the use? Eventually, they turned from the road and down a lane.

"Stop here," said the man. "Get out." As they emerged, they were surrounded by a crowd of blank-faced automata, who parted to let them through. There, facing them, was Winstanley, Professor Aldithley and a masked man, who had the bearing and suiting of Rodney Nethersole.

"Welcome all," said the masked man. "I'm the Master of Automata, thank you for coming to see me. I wish to talk to you."

"Not that we had much choice," remarked Langdon. "And why the theatricals, when we all know who you are, Rodney Nethersole."

The Master inclined his masked face. "You are correct; however the mask does more than just hide my face and lend a, dare I say it, air of menace. No, the Professor had made me this, it includes a device that amplifies my voice. I can use it to control my automata, watch."

He turned to the blank-faced men around him, his voice boomed, its volume raised by the workings of the mask. "Guards, march forward two steps," he said. As one they did so.

"You see," he said, in a tone which had reverted to normal, "it is both stylish and practical. As you know who I am, let me guess, you are Mortimer Langdon, and these two," he indicated Jackson and Jessamine, "I have seen before. They came to me under false pretences. I assume it was they who broke into my offices and stole my papers. I recall you claimed to be representing the Ladies who Lunch."

"Hello, lass," said the Professor to Jessamine, an evil grin on his face. "I remember fondly our last meeting."

Jessamine glared at him, Jackson made a move and the guns pointed. "Not so fast," said Winstanley. "It does you credit but your lover would not wish to see your blood pouring onto the ground." Jackson stayed still but, in his head, he vowed to gain revenge.

"Winstanley," said the Master, "search the mobile, see if they have anything interesting inside."

He then looked straight at Jackson. "Am I right, was it you who stole the papers on the Sensaurum?"

Jackson nodded. "Yes, that was I."

The Master smiled. "Very clever, or very lucky. I suppose your knowledge of the place came in handy. By the way, I knew who you are, who your parents were. I imagine that is why you also took the report on the event that started my rise to power?"

Jessamine and Langdon looked blankly at Jackson. The Master saw their confusion and laughed.

"He has not told you? He found the report on the accident that killed his parents; they used to work in the Prosthesium you know. Tell me, lad, was it curiosity or some morbid fascination?"

"Yes, I took it," replied Jackson. "I wanted the answers that I never got when I was a lad. Except, of course, that it was no accident. You lied about it, created the problem, then closed the door and walked away, shifting the blame onto a dead man. I know not the reason for it yet, wealth and power I would imagine. I will not rest until I find out all the truth."

"Well that's an interesting idea, you'll never know for sure, will you?" said the Master. "But if it helps you to believe that—" Before he had chance to say more, Winstanley placed the boxes before him.

"Found these in the mobile," he grinned. "Reckon the Professor might want to take a look."

"Thank you, Winstanley." The Master looked at the two boxes. "Ah so kind, you have returned my transmitting box. I presume that means you have my agent safe; we will attend to him later. And what is this one? Some sort of attempt at copying; that is flattery indeed. Professor, come and see what you make of these."

The Professor picked up both boxes. "I will take their toys and examine them."

"We will not parley," said Langdon.

"Who said anything about parley? You have nothing to offer. I merely wish to pass a message through you. The government has not listened, not taken me seriously and now it seems as if you are developing a way to thwart me."

"I'm just doing my duty," said Langdon, "to the country, keeping it safe from all those who would destroy it. There is nothing personal, you are a criminal and I will see you brought to justice."

"Fine words," said the Master. "In that case we seem to be at an impasse. You have killed some of my men, but I have plenty more. My demonstrations at the banks have shown my seriousness."

"We foiled your last demonstration. You are no more than a common criminal, taking money with a few thugs. It's hardly the stuff of a 'Master'."

"On the contrary, you have witnessed a small part my power. I was never intending to rob the bank, that was just a test of the Professor's invention. I am not a common criminal."

"You are though, however you dress it up," insisted Langdon, "and as far as we are concerned you will be treated as one."

"Then what do you propose?"

"We thought you might give yourself up. Your scheme is ended, now you see that we can destroy your slaves."

Rodney was unimpressed with the notion. "Hah!" he roared, the mask amplifying the word. "You show me your strength, so that I can devise a counter. We will shortly try your wonderful toy on my men here. I am confident that it will have no effect."

The Professor returned. "I have looked briefly at both boxes, the Sensaurum is the one that was taken from the works, the other is a Wasperton-Byler generator, as I suspected."

"And the purpose of this generator? Is it the thing that's been killing all my slaves?"

"Almost certainly, it produces a field that will destroy the filament, or rather, I should say that it would destroy the first version of the filaments, the one before my latest revision."

"I see, show them what you have achieved, Professor."

Aldithley cranked the Wasperton-Byler generator, with no visible change to the automata surrounding Rodney. Jackson felt a sinking feeling in the pit of his stomach, all that effort for nothing.

"You see," the voice from the mask was triumphant. "We have learned from your success and already gone past that. There is nothing more to be talked about. I expected to hear your surrender today; instead you still believe you can beat me. This is what you will do. The government must resign, immediately. I will be installed, together with my guards, in power. The King will declare me First Minister of State and give me his backing. He will order the cessation of hostilities against me."

The Master put his hand to his mouth and muttered something. Instantly and with a flourish the guards formed up on him. "You can see that I'm not a callous murderer, you may all go to pass my message to those in power. You have two days to comply," he said over his shoulder as they bore him away. "If you do not, my next show of power will dwarf the last. The city, nay the country, will tremble before the Master of Automata."

They were suddenly alone. They got back into their mobile.

"We must continue on our visit to the ministers," said Langdon, "even without the evidence of the boxes."

"Won't Oswald be defeated without them?" asked Jackson.

Langdon stopped the mobile. "Since the Sensaurum was the empty one, I think not. Rodney is aware that we have his man. I have a better idea; you two return to Oswald and update him on events. I will carry on alone; there is little evidence to present now, just my verbal report."

They stepped from the mobile. Before he sped away, Langdon said to Jackson, "Make sure that Oswald knows we have but two days, help him as required. I may be late returning."

Chapter 41

Oswald was not at all dismayed. His first question was, "Did Aldithley look inside the Sensaurum, or just the generator?"

"He had no time to do much," said Jessamine. "He merely reported that the Sensaurum was the one I took from the works.

"Then we are still ahead of where he thinks we are." He smiled. "Neither was that my only Wasperton-Byler generator."

"But it did not work," Jackson explained. "It had no effect on the guards."

Oswald shook his head. "I'm unconvinced. I think it was a game to try and unsettle you. I suspect that the Professor disconnected the mechanism before his demonstration. In short, he lied. As for the Sensaurum, I can understand how it works and can now make a similar machine that will block its signals. The Sensaurum I have will provide a template, the supplies are arriving, all I need is time."

"Then we will not detain you," said Jackson. "The Master said that we have two days. Langdon has gone to see the ministers on his own while you work to ready another box."

"What did the Master mean?" asked Jessamine, when they were alone. "He mentioned a report, something about your parents."

"He was correct; I found another report at the Prosthesium, about the accident that killed my parents. It placed all the blame on my father, but the origin of that blame was the only survivor, Rodney Nethersole."

Jessamine gasped, she held him tight. "You poor thing," she said, "and you've been keeping that inside you all this time."

"I think Langdon knows," he added. "He seemed unsurprised when it came into the conversation."

"He knows most things; maybe that was why you were recruited in the first place, not just for your knowledge of the factory? Langdon would want a lever he could use to make you hate Rodney."

"Well he has succeeded in that. My father would never have been responsible for all that death and destruction. If he had lived, we would have learned the truth. I will not rest till Rodney faces justice for that, as well as his present activities."

"And I will help you do it," she said. "With all that heavy on your mind, you must come to my room tonight. That is if you can bear to be with me."

"We do not talk of those things you do as work," he said. "I pretend they never happened; it does not stop me loving you."

Chapter 42

The next day was spent in preparing for any eventuality. In the morning Langdon told them of his meeting with the ministers.

"Once again I impressed on them the importance of stopping Rodney," he said, with the air of one who had been repeating this message for too long. "In the end, given the fact that we were abducted yesterday, they agreed to mobilise the army, to be ready to contain any mob that might form."

"Well that is a relief," said Fairview, "at last. Did you also ask them to check for soldiers and Watchmen who might have been treated by doctors recently?"

"I did, and it was agreed that would be done. I insisted that the man who was checking should himself be checked."

"What of the demands of Rodney, or should we call him the Master?"

"The threats and demands were dismissed, apparently, His Majesty has been kept up to date with events. His reaction was that the government must stand firm against Rodney, or the Master, whatever he chooses to call himself. He also demanded to be informed of all developments in statics. There was less opposition to my requests this time. It seems to me that Rodney's support among the rich and powerful is melting away."

"Now that they could see we are gaining the knowledge to defeat him."

"Exactly, I told them that my finest agents were performing heroic feats of sacrifice."

Langdon never mentioned Rodney's revelation, or Jackson's knowledge of the accident, instead he exhorted them all to be ready for the threat, wherever it may come from.

"Mr Patching," said Langdon, "have you talked to our captive recently?"

"I have, sir," he replied. "Just this morning, I attempted to obtain information from the captive, again he resisted."

"We have less than one day," Langdon said. "Have my agents in the field reported?"

"Nothing has been heard," replied Fairview. "I'm away to see Clarry after we have finished here. Oswald is working as fast as he can."

"Very well then," said Langdon, "carry on, everyone, and keep me informed." He departed.

Langdon appeared not to have noticed that Jackson and Jessamine had shared the previous night in one room. After an afternoon helping Oswald and emboldened, they did the same on the next night.

At some early hour, they were awoken by the voice of Fairview. He was shouting that there was a huge mob marching into the city from the south. It appeared to be heading towards the buildings of state. Quickly Jackson returned to his room, dressed and prepared himself for whatever the day might bring.

Fairview was with Jessamine when he arrived in the classroom. He had a large map of the city pinned to the chalkboard and was marking on it with a thick red stylus.

"They are coming towards the river, from all parts of the city," he was explaining. "The Watch was sent out to disperse them, but half of them turned on the rest. As we saw at the bank, they were secretly under Rodney's control."

"Then we know not who is untouched and who is controlled."

"Until it is too late," agreed Fairview. "We can trust no-one. Reports indicate that there are many dead, from both sides."

"If the Watch has failed," said Jackson, "what now? Are the army deployed? Will they be sufficient? Are they even uncontrolled?"

"Sir Mortimer is talking with the army commanders as we speak. There are so many more in this throng, ten times or more as many as the mob at the bank. And others are joining all the while. They are approaching up the main road from Hammerham; they are being funnelled towards the Stafford Bridge, where they will arrive in two hours or so. The army is deployed to hold them before they reach the southern end of the bridge. There are several thousand soldiers stationed along their route."

"Will it be enough?" asked Jackson.

"We took the fight to the Western Isles with less," Fairview said, "and there we were against trained warriors, vicious in close combat. These are civilians, men, women and children. Many of these will be unskilled in arms, too young or long past the age of service."

"What of the sheer numbers involved?" wondered Jessamine. "Will our soldiers be able to shoot their own countrymen?"

"What then do you suggest? That we take Oswald's detonator and kill thousands?"

"That is what we must do," said Langdon, striding into the room, "and without delay. Jackson, run down and grab him, tell him we need to go while there is still a chance to avert disaster."

Jackson went to the workroom, Oswald was surrounded by pieces of equipment, wires and switches, the Sensaurum lay open before him, gutted like a fish on a slab. It was clear even to Jackson's untrained eye that it was not ready to work. The man himself was engrossed and oblivious to his arrival.

"Oswald," he said, "Sir Mortimer has sent me, there is a mob approaching the Stafford Bridge. He wonders, do you have the results of your labours?"

"No sir, I do not." Oswald was clearly frustrated. His eyes were red-rimmed form lack of sleep. "Pray tell him that I'm working as fast as I can and would go faster without interruption. I will catch you up, leave me the mobile and Jessamine to operate it. We will come to you as soon as I have completed my work. I know what needs to be done; it's merely a question of doing it. Take the other Wasperton-Byler generator. It may be your only hope."

"We are going to the Stafford Bridge," Jackson told him.

"I will be there as soon as I can," muttered Oswald, already engrossed again in his work.

Jackson picked up the box containing the generator and ran to Langdon.

"Oswald is not ready," he reported. "He has given me this generator and says that he will complete his work as soon as he is able."

Langdon thought for a moment. "We cannot delay, we know what to look for. We will have to separate the pure from the affected, before we can stop the mob. If all else fails, then we must resort to using the generator."

"He asked me to leave him the mobile, and Jessamine. He will follow us as soon as he can. He knows now where we are headed."

"Well, Jackson, now that is organised, we must make haste to the river."

The aerialways were still out of action, the precaution against more derailment was playing into Rodney's plans to disrupt every aspect of modern life, to make him the saviour no doubt, so the group had to take a tram to the bridge. To Jackson, it seemed incongruous that they were travelling thus to save the city. They bumped over the cobbled streets in a form of transport that was obsolete, surrounded by unknowing citizenry. In not much more time than it would have taken them in a mobile, they arrived at the square in front of the government buildings. Ahead was the river with the huge bulk of the Stafford Bridge. The square was cordoned by Watchman, who were laying out barriers as if preparing for an event of state.

"It was all arranged automatically," explained Langdon, "as soon as the mob formed, all government buildings were evacuated and contained. It was done so much quicker after the Master's threats."

A company of soldiers were lined up, with their backs to the structure. The officer in charge greeted Langdon as he showed his identity.

"Well, sir, what have we to expect?" he asked. "I know only that a peril approaches from the south, my men are annoyed that they are held here, they wish to be at the vanguard, not guarding the rear."

"There is a mob forming on the south side," said Fairview. "They intend to cross the bridge and attack these buildings. You are the last line against them if they get over. Do you have scouts in high places?"

"That we do, sir," the officer replied. "Look up there." Atop the statuary of past leaders, were two men, together with a magnifying lens. "What can you see?" shouted the soldier.

"A great press of common folk, sir," came the reply. "They are moving towards the bridge. Barricades have been placed at every intersection; they are stopped, three streets back from the river. They cannot go around it, the ways are blocked by soldiers. There is fighting."

"Then matters seem to be in hand," said Langdon. "Can I ask, have any of your men been ill recently?"

"I don't understand the question, sir."

"Have they visited a doctor for any reason?" Still the officer did not respond. "It will be easier if I show you," said Langdon. "Order your men to form up, facing away from me. I wish to see their necks."

The officer looked puzzled but complied. Langdon and Fairview walked along the line, seeking the tell-tale mark that would reveal one of Rodney's automata. Finding none, Langdon turned back to the officer, who had gone pale.

"And now yours, if you please," he said.

The officer did so; there was the scar that had been seen on so many.

Chapter 43

Langdon turned and called the sergeant-major over. The man arrived and saluted. "Detain this man, take his side-arm," ordered Langdon. "He is an infiltrator."

The officer suddenly changed demeanour. His eyes glazed and his body slumped. He drew his gas-pistol and before anyone could stop him, placed the barrel in his mouth and pulled the trigger. The shot echoed around as the man fell.

As they gazed, shocked at the sight, there was a shout from the men aloft. "The first barricade is breached," they called, "the mob is advancing."

In the distance, there was a sound, like a wave on a pebbled beach. All stopped to listen.

"Sergeant-major, you are in command now; get one of your men up atop the wall over there. Have the rest scour the area."

"Very well, sir. What are we looking for?"

Fairview showed him the Wasperton-Byler generator. "A device like this, it's what caused your officer to do what he did. Look around, there is a man with one of these very close. If you spot him, or her, it's important that you take it from them before they can pull the lever on the side."

The soldier regarded Fairview with disbelief, as if it were impossible, which it must have seemed to him. He gave his orders and the men spread out, searching through the passers-by, and those who were watching the Watchmen secure the square. Suddenly, there was a scuffle; calls for assistance. Jackson glimpsed a wire pointing into the air, jerking around as the soldiers grappled with a man.

"We have him, sir," called a soldier. "We spotted him hanging around, like you said, with a box around his neck." One of the soldiers emerged with a Sensaurum, its strap cut and flapping. "We managed to remove it from him; he was trying to depress the lever. What shall we do with him?"

"Well done, keep him secured and in sight," said Fairview.

He took the Sensaurum and acting as Oswald had shown him, turned its control to the off position. He then opened the box and removed the wires that issued from the lever. "It is safe," he said, replacing the cover.

"Good work, Jackson, now we can proceed," Fairview said, "and have an option for Oswald when he arrives."

Langdon had been quiet, gazing out towards the river. Jackson had been occupied assisting Fairview and had almost forgotten that he was present. He seemed willing to leave all the decisions to Fairview. Now he joined them. "We should ensure that nobody on this side of the river is a threat," he said. "I suggest that we operate the generator, to flush out any more of Rodney's men who may be close."

"Are you sure?" Fairview sounded reluctant.

"I've been pondering it," Langdon replied, "and with a heavy heart, I must say so. Our problem is this; there are only these troops to protect the north shore and these buildings. We cannot let them fall. Oswald is not here, even if he arrives soon, we cannot guarantee to control any automata with certainty. It's a foul choice but one I have to make."

"Very well," said Fairview. With Jackson's help he readied the Wasperton-Byler generator. When they discharged it, the only sign of its effectiveness was a convulsion from the officer's corpse, making him seem alive for a moment.

"Spotters," called Fairview, "is there any change on the mob?"

"Nothing," the men aloft replied. "They have surmounted the second barricade and are now one street back from the bridge."

"The range is still insufficient," muttered Langdon. "At least there were none on this side."

"They need to get closer," said Fairview.

"The third barricade is breached," called out the soldiers and everyone ran to the river's edge for a sight of what was approaching. Now that the mob had broken the last resistance, they moved quickly towards the line of troops guarding the bridge approach. Barely two hundred yards away, the sounds of battle could now be clearly heard. There was shouting and screaming, and the sound of volleys from gas-guns, which slowed the advance. Not because of hesitation, the mob were beyond that, senses numbed by the control they were under. They were slowed by the narrowness of the road and the pile of bodies that the living had to climb, which grew ever higher.

"These are more aggressive than the last," said Jackson.

"It may be a function of the filament," Fairview suggested. "Perhaps the Professor has learned to control emotion as well as action. I'm sure he is not standing still in its development; witness the different state of his private guard, they were invulnerable."

"Unless of course they were loyal to him and not under control by the filament," Langdon said. "He may have just been trying to mislead us. See how that officer was not protected, the signal from the discharge was still enough to destroy his filament."

Ahead of them, the rest of the soldiers formed up to protect the bridge.

"I have an idea," said Jackson. "Now that we have the Sensaurum, Oswald is not needed."

"How so?" asked Langdon. "Quickly now, lad, what are your thoughts?"

"We can start it back up and use it in the same way as Rodney does. If we speak into it, then surely we can control the mob, in the same way as whoever is on the south side. We can say stop and they will."

"But then the man on the south need only say 'start', and we are back where we were."

"Yes, but we have soldiers here. If we can get some of them to the south and remove the man controlling the mob, ours would be the only voice. It's not a perfect solution but it will stop them until Oswald arrives with a better one."

"You are right," Langdon said. "It's a desperate plan but these are desperate times. There is only one way to find out. Reattach the wires and make the Sensaurum ready. Fairview, will you take the soldiers south and seek out the controller?"

"Of course," replied Fairview, without hesitation. "I think it a good plan."

"Things are getting worse on the south side," shouted one of the soldiers. "The soldiers have exhausted their ammunition; they are falling back onto the bridge itself."

The three moved to get a better view. "You will have to go now," said Langdon as they watched the mob overwhelm the remnants. The remaining officer tried to rally his men, but they were engulfed by the throng and ripped limb from limb. Then they stopped, still as statues.

"What are they waiting for?"

Fairview went to the sergeant major. "Pick six men to come with me," he said. The man went off shouting for volunteers, six returned and fell in.

Fairview gave his orders. "We will cross on the next bridge downstream, the Maloney, and get behind the mob. If we are challenged, you must act as if controlled; you have seen the gait of these men. Then we will search for the one wearing that device and remove him permanently. As before, we must not let the lever at the side be pulled." They set off together at a trot.

"We have done all we can," said Langdon. "Now it's either kill everyone or hope that we can somehow remove them from their trance, before they overwhelm us all."

The sound of a mobile approaching at speed, horn blaring, made them turn. Whilst their attention had been fixed on the south shore, the edge of the square and the north bank of the river had been filled by a mass of onlookers, spilling out from the streets that converged on the square. The Watch, a solid black line of men, arms linked, had been effective at holding them clear of their position. They were inquisitive but not threatening. They parted for the mobile which mounted the pavement and halted close to them.

Oswald appeared from it, together with Jessamine. He was clutching the familiar shape of a Sensaurum. "Wait," Oswald called. "We have travelled through streets lined with corpses; you have discharged the generator, have you not?"

"Yes, we have," said Langdon. "But only one man was affected." He pointed to the soldier's body.

"That is because the rest were not yet here," replied the scientist. "They were approaching and had not yet coalesced into a mob. Those on the south were too distant, more's the pity. We do not need to kill them all; I have perfected a lower powered device which should block any signals. It's based on the Sensaurum that you recovered. It uses subtlety, where the generator was brute force."

"They have control on the south, yet they have stopped," Langdon said. "It's difficult to see why, the way across the bridge is clear. Fairview has taken some troops to try and capture the Sensaurum that directs them; perhaps he will stop the advance."

"I suspect that they await the arrival of Rodney," Langdon said, "to witness his triumph, when the mob reach the buildings of state and demand the spoils of his plan. Perhaps they wait for him. Or for reinforcements from the north."

"What of Rodney? We will need to bring him to justice."

"Again, that is secondary to stopping the mob."

The four stood at the north edge of the bridge, armed only with the Wasperton-Byler generator, Oswald's device and the captured Sensaurum. In front of them were the remaining soldiers. At their backs there was the empty square, the crowd held by the Watch. They seemed a puny band, alone and exposed in the face of the throng.

Suddenly there was a growl from the mob; the first of them put their feet on Stafford Bridge. As one they started to march over its roadway. They came perhaps a quarter of the way, their feet stamping out as one. Then they halted again.

There was a volley of shots away in the distance. The mob never faltered.

"Was that from our band of soldiers? Have they succeeded?"

"Who knows? All we can do is stop the mob. It's time to ready the machines."

The leaders of the mob brandished weapons, pitchforks, rusted swords and a few gas-guns among them, they were clearly a disparate band, only held together by the power of the Sensaurum.

Jackson was grateful that they had disabled the Sensaurum that would have roused the north shore to attack. Now they were dead; the remainder just a crowd of sightseers. The question was, which box should they use first to stop their advance? They could operate the generator and kill everyone, or try the other box, but what was the word?

Everyone assumed it needed a second command to stop but what if it was as simple as shouting stop. Could it be? It would buy them time. The leaders of the mob were less than fifty yards from him, funnelled into the bridge, their feet stamping in unison as they crossed the river.

"We have Oswald's blocking generator, we must use it now," said Langdon.

Oswald turned a switch on the machine, spun the handle. He gazed at a small dial.

"Well?" asked Langdon. "It's not working," said Oswald, cranking. "The needle should flicker, I finished it in haste, it cannot be as complete as I thought."

He stopped cranking and opened the front of the box.

"We have no time for this," said Langdon. "Jackson, ready the Wasperton-Byler generator."

"And kill every one of them?" asked Jessamine.

"It's them or us!" said Jackson. "Pardon me if I vote for the greater good."

"Yes," she replied, "but we have a Sensaurum as well as Oswald's new invention."

"Which is not working," Langdon pointed out.

Oswald had his hands inside the box. "I'm going as fast as I can, try the Sensaurum, it has the larger range."

"We discussed this before, Oswald," said Jackson. "If Fairview has not neutralised the device on the south, then our orders will immediately be countermanded."

"It seems that one will merely cancel the other," added Langdon.

"But surely, and no disrespect, once the order has been passed, then blocking the signal will do nothing."

"Except prevent its repetition."

There was a growl from the bridge and a sound of tramping feet, the mob had started moving again.

"No, you miss the point," said Oswald. "The signal would still have to be countermanded, which you cannot do while I am blocking the signal."

The predicament dawned on all present. Oswald continued. "That, I'm afraid is a logical conclusion. However, it is not presently working. First, we need to stop the mob before they take over. Then with the luxury of safety from annihilation, we can experiment."

"This talking in circles is getting us nowhere," said Jessamine desperately. "We need to act." She grasped the Sensaurum, flicked the switch. "Stop!" she shouted. The crowd on the bridge faltered, those at the front stopped but the ones at the rear had been out of range of its signal and were pushing them forward.

Then, they all started moving again.

Chapter 44

Under the rhythmic tramp of so many feet, the bridge started to shake; stones fell from its parapets and balustrades. Langdon shook his head. "They have been reactivated; Fairview must have failed in his quest. We need the generator."

"Is it possible that the bridge will collapse before they get here?" said Oswald.

"How? It's solid stone, it has stood for years."

"The repetition has set up a sympathetic vibration, they need to break step, or reverse their motion, go backwards to safety."

A light glowed in Jackson's head; that was it. "Alyious hadn't finished writing when he died," he shouted excitedly. "It's not rev. Alyious was trying to write reverse, the word to release them is lexis reversed, said backwards."

Huge stones were now falling in the river as its arches split, the footway where it joined the land on the north side cracked, it could not have cracked on the south or so many people would not now be surging across it. A large section of the bridge and many people suddenly fell into the water. There was an enormous noise and sheets of spray, rainbow shot in the sunlight, covered everyone. The unfortunates in the water made no sound as the current dragged them downstream.

The remainder of the marching mob ignored the destruction and came on, more fell as they walked blindly over the edge, yet they did not care, such was the strength of the spell Rodney had them under. Everything shook with the noise. Buildings rattled, glass fell, adding to the chaos. Stones were thrown by the advancing mob, chunks torn from the buildings and the road; railings hurled like spears. They fell among the group. Langdon was hit on the head by a rock and collapsed to the ground. Panic started to spread. The civilians who had come to gawp started to run away. Jessamine knelt to tend to Langdon

Jackson grabbed the Sensaurum. "Stop! Sixel!" he shouted into the trumpet. The wave of humanity broke, just as more toppled into the rushing waters. Released from the spell of the Sensaurum, they milled on the broken bridge, as if unsure of where they were. They then turned and ran back to the south, to safety. They were no longer a coherent phalanx, now just a collection of frightened individuals.

"I have it working!" cried Oswald.

"Then start it now, before they are controlled again," shouted Jackson.

They strained to detect anything as Oswald threw the switch and cranked. Looking at the throng still left on the bridge, there was no visible sign of order among them. "It must be working, they are still aimless and uncontrolled."

"It seems that we have solved the problem. Now we need to find Rodney and the Professor." A Watch officer approached them, he looked dazed by events.

"What in the name of everything was all that about?" he asked.

"We have no time to tell you, the leader of this insurrection is still at large." Oswald had taken command. "We have an injured man as well. We must leave you to disperse the crowds."

The soldiers who had been stood ready by the ruins of the bridge now joined them. "What can we do?" asked one.

"Go south and try to find your comrades," Jackson said, "and the man who led them, tell him we have gone to apprehend the Master. But first, help us get our equipment and Sir Mortimer into the mobile."

"Where are we going, Jackson?" asked Oswald. "Do you have an inkling where this Master might be?"

"We assume that he will be waiting somewhere for news of victory. I think the factory is the logical place to commence our search."

"Do you not consider it more likely that he will be much closer?" asked the scientist.

"He is safe in the factory, protected by his friends, safe from the Watch, he thinks he is safe from us. I imagine that he will come out only when his triumph is reported."

Oswald thought for a moment and looked again at Langdon's

unconscious form in the mobile.

"To the factory then," he said. Carrying the boxes, they jumped into the mobile, Jessamine driving.

"Fairview will have to make his own way," she said, "assuming he has returned from the south side."

"It will take more than a few automata to dispose of our Mr Fairview," Oswald said dryly. "The tribes of the Western Isles tried hard enough and failed every time."

As they left the square, they saw many corpses, the reminder of the effects of a Wasperton-Byler discharge on the neck filament. Jackson realised just how lucky they had been.

They arrived at the factory, the gates were wide open. Inside it was deserted, the machines and even the shaft in the ceiling was idle. Jessamine remained with Langdon. He was breathing rhythmically; a thin trickle of blood ran down his temple. As Jackson and Oswald raced up the stairs to the offices and laboratories, the temperature increased, they found that thick smoke was coming towards them. Dim red shapes danced in the smoke, the building was well alight.

"It's obvious he's not here," said Jackson. "All is being destroyed, all the Professor's work, everything."

Oswald let out a despairing cry, "I need to know his secrets, surely Rodney would not be so foolish, he must have spirited it all away somewhere." He tried to continue into the smoke, Jackson grabbed him and pulled him back. "Oswald you will perish, the materials will be far away, you can be sure of that."

"But his estate in Hammerham was also deserted."

"Then he has a plan, you can be sure of that."

"Where would he be? Where can we search?"

"I don't know," replied Jackson, "but we cannot remain here."

They could feel the heat from the blaze as they hurried down the stairs, chased by smoke and flame, and into the open air. Both were out of breath and coughing as they approached the mobile. Jessamine was stood outside. "Are you alright?" she asked. "I can see the flames in every window on the upper floors."

"We are," answered Jackson, between coughs. "Rodney cannot be here."

"Langdon is stirring," she said. "I don't think he needs to see a doctor, I have dressed the wound on his head. He is awake but confused."

She opened the mobiles door, Langdon was laying on the seat, with a patch of Oswald's healing parchment on his head. His eyes were open. "Where are we?" he whispered.

"We are seeking Rodney; we have come to the factory." Jackson explained, "The offices are well alight, nothing is here."

Langdon struggled upright. "No," he said, shaking his head and wincing with the pain. "You are mistaken. He will not be here. He will be at the place he believes his triumphant coronation will occur. We must go to the House of Speakers."

Jessamine drove with reckless abandon, back to the place they had so recently left. They tore down the road, scattering pedestrians and weaving between vehicles, all the time looking for signs of automata. Oswald had the blocking generator turned onto maximum power, the flickering needle told the group that it was working, masking the commands of any nearby Sensaurum.

The people they saw were dazed by events, aware that great things were occurring but unable to react. The city was covered in dust, blown from the collapsed bridge and wrecked buildings on the south side by a freshening breeze. Save for the corpses and a few Watchmen, the streets were deserted, all the unaffected must have been ordered to return to their homes.

Alighting outside the House, they found a squad of Watchmen. "Ensure that nobody leaves," said Langdon. "Two of you, follow us." Oswald carried the blocking device and Jackson a Sensaurum.

Langdon seemed to have recovered his senses and had resumed command. They ran into the main chamber. Rodney was sat on the First Speaker's chair, without his mask, flanked by a throng of grey-clad people. When he saw them, he stood and bowed. "Welcome, all," he said. "Are you here to witness my coronation?"

"It's over, Rodney," said Langdon. "Your mob are vanquished, released from your control, those that are still alive. You have a lot to answer for, be assured that you will do so in due course. The building is surrounded, there is nowhere to run."

"So, my initial plans have failed," said Rodney, "and now you're here to gloat. Ha! You will never stop me; this is merely a temporary setback. If there is to be no triumph this time, we are leaving." The greys formed a protective circle around him. Winstanley was standing separate.

"Grab that man!" shouted Langdon, the Watchmen held him.

"Stand down! Sixel!" cried Jackson into the Sensaurum but the word was ineffectual on the grey-coated group that surrounded Rodney. He laughed as his group edged towards a side door.

Oswald looked at the dial on the blocking device. "The Sensaurum will not work while the blocking field is being produced," he said.

"Fools," Rodney said. "Do you think I would use the same word or methods for my elite guards? As soon as you stole a Sensaurum, I had the Professor change the way the system works for my closest protectors. Once I have regrouped, I will return, you may be sure of that. You will never stop me."

"We will get the information from Aldithley then," said Oswald.

Rodney laughed again. "You will not find him. All evidence is destroyed; you'll find the Prosthesium ablaze. The Professor awaits me; you will never reach us where we are going."

"I will get the knowledge from you now," said Jackson. "To avenge my parents."

Rodney looked more closely at him. "Ah yes, Jackson. We meet again. I might have guessed that you would be here. I will tell you it all. Your parents were the first casualties of my reign, they learned too much of my plans and were prepared to tell Clynes and others."

"So you killed them?" said Langdon.

Rodney nodded, he had not been cowed by news of his defeat, far from it, he still radiated confidence. "Yes, I did, and I would do it again in a heartbeat. It was worth destroying a room full of people to stop their meddling. Look at what I have created; I have an army to do my bidding."

"Your army has failed," said Langdon. "Come quietly now and you will receive a fair trial. Tell us all your accomplices as well and we will be lenient."

"Ha! Never," he replied. "Look at the boy's face, do you think he will let me live?"

Jackson was shocked by the admission, even though he had suspected. The brazen confidence of Rodney meant that he was sure of his escape. "Then I will avenge them now," he said grabbing a gas-gun from one of the Watchmen. "I will kill you where you stand."

"Jackson, put that pistol down," said Langdon, but Jackson never flinched.

"You see the benefits of my method?" said Rodney. "Unquestioning obedience; isn't that better than your hot-headed band of children."

"Jackson, I order you to drop the pistol."

Before any more could be said, Winstanley chose that moment to break free from the Watchman's grip. He ran towards Rodney's group, between Jackson and his target, just as he fired the gas-gun. The projectile hit him full in the back, sending him tumbling forwards in a burst of red. He fell to the floor and rolled over, twitching and jerking, his boots rattling on the floorboards.

Jackson heard Jessamine scream. Langdon shouted, "Jackson, stand down this instant." He turned his head away. When he looked back, Rodney and his guards had vanished. And so had Jessamine.

Chapter 45

"Where has she gone?" he shouted. They all rushed to the door. It was locked. "They must have her," said Langdon. The Watchmen pounded on the door and forced it open. Reaching the street, they saw a large mobile in the distance, heading towards the Maloney Bridge. "Follow them!" shouted Jackson, desperately. They all got back into Langdon's mobile and gave chase.

"We will discuss your behaviour at length," said Langdon, ominously. "But this is not the time."

"We cannot lose sight of them," said the anguished Jackson. "But we must be careful in our attack; he has Jessamine."

Langdon drove and neither Jackson nor Oswald was brave enough to dissuade him. In any event Rodney's mobile did not race away, rather it led them a dance, as if enticing them onwards. Once they lost sight of the mobile for a moment, then it popped back into view.

The pursuit led them through the city and into winding country lanes. As soon as the last buildings were behind them, Rodney's mobile picked up speed and disappeared from view. Langdon increased his speed, hedges and trees flashed past them but still it did not reappear.

"We have lost them," said Oswald.

"Not so," replied Langdon. "This road only leads to one place."

"Is it Rodney's lair?" asked Jackson. Langdon shook his head.

"Again, no. We are going to a private flying field. Rodney must be escaping by Aero."

As they approached the gate, through the hedge they could see several Aero's and a large flag, indicating the wind direction.

When they pulled into the field, they saw the abandoned mobile and, away to one side, a dark brown Aero, nothing like the one Jackson remembered. It had a military air about it, the engines were set into the wings, not underneath; it looked lethal and menacing.

It was already a hundred yards away, moving further from them, then it swung around to face into the wind. It would take off and it seemed like there was nothing they could do to stop it.

Langdon stopped the mobile, Jackson got out, behind him he heard Oswald, "I'm setting up the Wasperton-Byler generator," he said.

"How will that help us?" asked Jackson.

"That is another function of the field. If I amplify it, the field will be enough to disrupt the controls of the Aero. If an automata is piloting the craft, it will kill him too."

As Jackson watched Oswald work, the mobile raced past them. Langdon was trying to block the Aero's path. Jackson heard its two mighty engines roar and it started to move. It would pass about thirty yards in front of them as it accelerated. Langdon would be too late.

"We must use the generator before it takes off," Jackson said. "Jessamine will surely die if the Aero crashes."

"I'm working as fast as I can," said Oswald.

"If she is not dead already," added Jackson, mournfully. "A life as Rodney's prisoner will be no better than a swift end."

The Aero left the ground, almost scraping the mobile's roof as it passed. "It is ready," said Oswald. "I've amplified the signal as much as possible."

Jackson was overcome with sadness but saw the logic in what he had to do, lose one to gain many.

"I'm sorry," said Oswald, understanding what had to happen.

"I will be the one to do it," said Jackson.

Oswald nodded briefly.

Jackson cranked the handle with a heavy heart, 'goodbye, my love, forgive me', repeating in his mind.

The Aero was no more than fifty feet from the ground as it passed the pair. It carried on climbing for a few seconds, then the engine's note changed. Suddenly it tipped forwards and fell to the ground, sliding along the grass with a terrible sound, as the metal of its skin was crushed and bent by the impact. Jackson started running towards it, followed by Oswald.

There was a moment's silence, birds could be heard singing and Jackson's hopes rose. Then there was a whoosh as the gas tanks exploded. Flames shot high into the air and forced Jackson back, then he was held by Oswald. "Let me go, I have to try and save her." He thrashed but was unable to break the man's grip.

"Jessamine!" he screamed.

Chapter 46

A small voice called from the abandoned mobile. "Is that you, Jackson? I am over here, untie me."

Less than a minute later, they were reunited and oblivious to Oswald's presence, in a tight embrace. "What happened?"

"The greys grabbed me while you were shooting Winstanley, threw me in their mobile. I was tied and surrounded by more of those grey automata. They were so frightening, looking straight ahead and saying nothing. I heard Rodney and the Professor talking. He said that he had enjoyed me so much, he wanted to implant a filament in my neck, to make me his slave. I would do his bidding in all respects whenever he desired me."

She shuddered. "It was a horrible thought. Then when we arrived at the Aero, they lifted me and tried to take me from the mobile. I saw my chance. I thrashed about, distracting them and making it impossible for them to carry me. They must have heard you approaching and left me, getting all the automata into the Aero to make their escape. The rest you know."

Langdon arrived at that moment. He took in the scene, shook Jackson's hand. "Well done, Rodney is defeated. And the best news, that Jessamine was not in the Aero."

He looked at the burning wreck. "There will be little left for Oswald to examine," he said. "Tell me, Jackson, did you know that Jessamine was safe before you set off the generator?"

"I did not," replied Jackson, surprised at how calm he felt. "While I did it, I remembered the words of Alyious. He warned me that I might have to choose between doing what was right and the life of someone that I cared for. I never thought that I would actually have to make the choice. I'm ashamed to say that he was correct, although it hurt me to do it."

"He was right, it was a lesson he learned the hard way too," echoed Langdon, joining in the sentimentality of the moment, while still managing to be the person in charge. "I was sure that I was right about your character from the start, that you would be an asset."

"You knew about the deaths of my parents at Rodney's hand, did you not?" Jackson felt justified to ask. "And you wanted me to stop him. You used me."

"Of course I did," replied Langdon, a puzzled look on his face. "A good leader uses all at his disposal, 'tis a dirty job keeping Norlandia safe. You disappointed me by disobeying my orders and shooting Winstanley. However, you have redeemed yourself. Despite your personal involvement with Jessamine, you were prepared to do what benefited the greater good. Hopefully, you have learned that emotional attachment is not an option; if you wish to be an agent of mine."

He looked at them both. "Don't play the innocents, I know of your relationship," he said and he smiled, the first time Jackson could remember seeing one on his face for some time. "Perhaps, in the case of my best agents, I might be willing to make an exception."

Jessamine and Jackson looked at each other, Langdon's world might just be about to change.

Oswald said nothing. To him the conversation was spoken in an alien tongue. He was far too excited, thinking of all the things he could do with statics.

Chapter 47

Ten days later, Jackson and Jessamine held hands and watched as the land dropped away in the ship's wake. Gulls swooped around them. They were on leave from their duties, a month's break, all paid for by Sir Mortimer, in recognition of services rendered. They had chosen to take a sea voyage, on-board one of the new-fangled ships that were designed to carry passengers on voyages of discovery. Safe from calls to save the world.

"When you said that you chose right over me..." said Jessamine and Jackson tensed. This was the conversation he had been dreading. Was she annoyed that he had chosen her fate, had actually turned the crank on the generator when he knew it would be her death? Could she even consider that he thought so little of her? To his relief, instead of moving away, she spun and looked him in the eye. He saw a tear form. "...I understood exactly," she said, "and I'm proud that you chose correctly. I had to ignore you and your feelings when I went with the Professor, which must have hurt you so much. I miss Alyious, he was wise beyond his years; the greater good must always come first."

"Will we go back and start again?" Jackson asked, eager to change the subject. The past was gone, best to leave the subject until the next time that a madman was trying to kill them all. "There's rebuilding to be done, fresh agents to train, a whole new science to explore. No doubt you can still educate me on the finer points of so many things."

In answer, she wiped her eyes with a lace-gloved hand, then pulled him close. "We've hardly departed, let's not think of returning." She sighed. "I want to enjoy this time, just me and you, and yes, I'm looking forward to continuing your education, just as soon as we have eaten."

She looked again at the ring on her finger, the twin of his. "The best thing is, now we no longer have to pretend to be wed."

The End... for now.

Jackson and Jessamine will return in
The Safety of the Realm.
Read on for a brief look.

Chapter 1
Balawengo, the Spice Islands

The man waiting on the wharf was substantially overdressed for the conditions. Dark patches marked his light brown suit, where perspiration had soaked through. It was early morning; the sun had barely risen yet already it was hot and humid. He was unwilling to remove his jacket, the concealed gas-gun in its leather harness would be revealed and he was unsure of the reaction that might get from the local officialdom. A stranger in a strange land, the weapon was unlicensed, its possession by anyone not in uniform against the laws of this particular state.

The wharf and its sheds were perched on the edge of the jungles that covered the island. A dirt road, little more than a track, led away into the trees.

Months of rain had made the vegetation fecund and helped to grow the valuable seeds and barks that gave the place its name and value. A large settlement was hidden among the trees, yet from a position on the wharf, you would never guess at its presence. That was the advantage the islanders had in times of war. More effort was spent searching for them than in actual engagement. The man knew this from bitter experience, yet now, at least for the present, they were all friends together.

Gazing out towards the ocean, the sweating watcher could see a large metal steamship, its white hull and rows of glass portholes reflecting the low sun as it approached the breakwaters. About time too, he thought. Another day in this place would be too much. He had spent the previous night in an airless room, under a net to deter the insect life. All his meals on shore had been one or another type of Khorri, with no ale to wash it down. It was worse than the last time he had been here, even though then he had been fighting the inhabitants. He scowled; now they were supposed to be his allies, yet too many of his friends had never returned to allow him to think of them as such. Drawing his thoughts back to the ship, and its comforts, he saw that there was a white wave breaking from its bow, showing that it was not reducing speed to engage a harbour pilot.

The ship, the *King Leopold*, was one of the new breed of passenger-carrying vessels. Known as cruisers, they catered for the new middle classes of Norlandia, those who had been elevated in monetary status by the industry of the country. Ships like this departed Norlandian ports regularly, taking the wealthy on excursions to foreign climes such as this place, although the man wondered at the attraction. The purpose of his journey resided on board, they were not expecting him and he wondered at the reception he would receive.

Norlandia was civilised, the climate temperate, apart from the heat and humidity, there was nothing here but dust, flies and an odour that was hard to describe, yet sufficiently obnoxious as to be unpleasant. He had arrived several days before, directly from Metropol City on a trading vessel. It was presently moored in a decrepit harbour on the opposite side of this island, he would be returning to it as soon as his mission was complete. Its purpose was to discharge manufactured goods and load exotic foodstuffs for its return journey.

It had been his intention to remain on board the trader; at least it was civilised. Any hopes of that had been dashed; it had been forced to divert, to allow for the arrival of this vessel. The cruiser had come from another one of the islands, on a more circular route, this was his only chance to catch up with it. There were people on board whose cooperation was required by their masters in Metropol City.

The vessel was less than two hundred yards away now, still coming at speed and showing no sign of altering its course. Its bow would hit the wharf almost directly in front of the man, yet he stood firm. The vessel was close enough that he clearly heard the shout of "hard to starboard, if you please," from the ship's wheelhouse.

Slowly at first, then with increasing speed, the bow started to swing away from the wharf. Surely it was too late to avoid even a glancing blow with solid land. There was the rattle of chains as the offshore anchor was let go, the sound of a bell ringing. Smoke poured from the monster's twin funnels. The ship's stern dropped deeper as its propeller was reversed and bit into the water. Under its influence, and the drag of the anchor, the vessel turned its head away faster, its forward motion faltered.

There was the clanking sound of steam-mobiles from the large wooden shed that framed the rear of the wharf. His attention distracted for a moment, the man watched as two mobiles appeared, one went to each end of the wharf, where large yellow boards were placed, one marked with the word Bow, the other Stern. Several men disembarked and stood, waiting. He could also hear the sound of approaching equines, the jangling of harness and the squeak of poorly greased axles.

No doubt the locals were arriving to tempt the vessel's passengers on excursions through the jungle and settlement in open carriages. And they would be selling trinkets at inflated prices. His foreign appearance had already made him a target of every purveyor of such things that he had met.

When he looked back, he was surprised to see that the ship was stopped in the water, parallel to the wharf and twenty feet away. Its propeller had stilled, and as he watched, light ropes were thrown to shore. As the men heaved on them, heavy mooring lines came with them, to be hooked over bollards. The ship's winches must have been engaged; the hull was pulled sideways and was soon tight alongside. As a gangway was rigged, the man looked up at the crowds lining the decks. Practised eyes spotted the two people he was looking for. At the same time, the female of them opened her mouth in shocked surprise, she waved and he saw her turn to her companion.

The man walked to the bottom of the gangway, where he showed a slip of paper to the crewman. Allowed past, he climbed the steps and repeated the procedure at the top, pushing his way towards his targets. He arrived in front of them. "I'm so pleased to see you both," he said. "It's been quite a journey to find you. Can we go somewhere private, we need to talk urgently."

The male looked him straight in the eye. "Mr Fairview," he said, "according to Langdon, we are supposed to be on a leave of absence, what can be so important?"

"It's not just a leave of absence," the woman added. Dark haired and intense, she fixed the man with a steady gaze. "We are on our nuptials."

"My apologies Jessamine, Jackson," the man replied, unflinching. "The safety of the Realm is at stake. I'm sorry, you are required."

The woman gasped, put one hand to her mouth and grabbed her man's arm with the other. "Not again!" she exclaimed.

I hope that you have enjoyed this story

I hope you've enjoyed reading this story. As an independently published author, I have no huge marketing machine, no bottomless budget. I rely on my readers to help me gain attention for my work. And next to the readers who love my work; reviews, either by word of mouth or online remain one of my most important assets.

Talking about my books, telling your friends and family and reviews on websites help bring them to the attention of other readers. If you've enjoyed reading this book, please would you consider leaving a review, even if it's only a few words, it will be appreciated and might just help someone else discover their next great read!

Find out more about me and my worlds at richarddeescifi.co.uk. where you can pick up a free short story or see details of my other novels.

Why not join my email list for news about me and my worlds. As well as keeping up with what I'm doing, you'll get extra content and early bird offers on new titles. Look out for a FREE Short Story, *The Orbital Livestock Company*, when you confirm. Just follow the link to sign up.

https://richarddeescifi.co.uk/join-the-team/

Thank you very much.

Richard Dee

Printed in Poland
by Amazon Fulfillment
Poland Sp. z o.o., Wrocław

55363369R00179